CLARA
at the
EDGE

a novel

Maryl Jo Fox

She Writes Press, a BookSparks imprint
A Division of SparkPointStudio, LLC.

Copyright © 2017 Maryl Jo Fox

All rights reserved. No part of this publication may be reproduced, distributed, or transmitted in any form or by any means, including photocopying, recording, digital scanning, or other electronic or mechanical methods, without the prior written permission of the publisher, except in the case of brief quotations embodied in critical reviews and certain other noncommercial uses permitted by copyright law. For permission requests, please address She Writes Press.

Published 2017

Printed in the United States of America

ISBN: 978-1-63152-250-5 pbk
ISBN: 978-1-63152-251-2 ebk
Library of Congress Control Number: 2017944691

For information, address:
She Writes Press
1563 Solano Ave #546
Berkeley, CA 94707

She Writes Press is a division of SparkPoint Studio, LLC.

To my family

PART ONE

chapter 1

*C*lara *heard his breathing, smelled his smell of rotten mushrooms and oily sweat. Her father had followed her into the darkest corner of the barn, where she hid. He was going to hurt her, she just knew it. She was twelve. She'd been watching him the last few months. He would give her the look that said she knew the same secret he did—that she was no good and he had to beat it out of her. But she didn't know any secret like that. She was just afraid of him. She'd seen him beat her mother and her twin sister, Lillian, and she knew her turn was coming. Her mother was mild as a moth, always washing doilies and holding them up to the sun to admire their designs. She would keep sweeping the porch until he came and beat on her. And then she just cringed, never fought back. Clara never wanted to be like that.*

When his lantern lit up her face in the barn, wasps came from nowhere and surrounded his head. Wasps! Her heart thudded in her chest. They were furious, in a tight ball, making a sound like a thousand voices. He covered his face with his arms and let out a shuddering scream. She'd never heard him scream before, had never seen wasps like this—an angry swarm with lavender wings and lavender bodies. Her head hurt with how they shimmered and hummed darkly, circling her father's head. Not bothering her, just him.

Suddenly she knew the wasps would always protect her. In the worst moment of her life so far, when she was old enough to know her father could do something far worse than just beat on her, the wasps came to drive him out of there. He dropped the light and ran, crashing into milk pails, never to bother her again. She never knew he was so deathly afraid of wasps. His cries echoed over the flat North Dakota plain.

The next day, she and her twin sister Lillian made a fierce pact. They faced each other in the barn, put their thumbs on each other's foreheads, and vowed to save up money to take the Greyhound to Oregon together after they finished high school in 1946 because Oregon was far from North Dakota and had lots of rain and trees and they had a cousin Loretta there who would never rat on them. The trip took three days—sweltering, cranky, carsick days, but also giggly days. It was worth it. Clara and Lillian went to college in Eugene and never saw their parents again. Never once did their parents try to contact Loretta to see if their children had landed there. Clara and Lillian could have flown to Mars for all their parents knew.

Clara assumed Lillian would always live nearby. But in her junior year, Lillian—such a wonderful artist!—ran off to Europe with her no-good boyfriend and never came back. Clara, heartsick and furious, knew this guy would break her heart, but Lillian wouldn't listen. Clara would make her own home in Eugene and stay there forever. She would find people she could love and who would love her back. She would be safe there. What she wanted most in life was to be safe.

Now in the summer of 2000, Clara screeches the tattered U-Haul to a halt by the side of the two-lane highway. She watches her grown son, Frank, make a wide turn into the big Desert Dan's Casino and Restaurant parking lot in Jackpot, Nevada. Hunching forward, she white-knuckles the steering wheel as she watches. He's shooting for a grand ballet-like turn—if you can describe a fifty-year-old, one-thousand-square-foot house anchored to a twelve-axle flatbed trailer as being at all ballet-like in the way it moves. He's over-shooting the curb, she's sure of it. He's going to hit it! That's how he gets—impatient. This is the end of their journey from Eugene, Oregon, to Jackpot, Nevada. It's June 4, 2000. They've been on the road four days now. They're bushed.

Her heart is pounding. She jumps out of the U-Haul to watch and stands panicked near the wide driveway entrance, clenching her damp hands together. As he rounds his load into the oncoming lane, a car speeds toward him. Frank lays on the horn. The other driver slams to a halt and jumps out of his car, shouting, "What the fuck, man! A *house?* For Christ's sake, what's going on here?"

"Give me a minute here, dude." Frank cranks the trailer cab back out of the oncoming lane with a hard right. The house groans and shifts as it gains the parking lot.

Clara hears something like a muffled crack. She covers her ears, refusing to let it register. But her heart sinks. The house hit the *curb? Cracked?* No, it's just the sighing of old timbers hammered together almost fifty years ago. *Has to be,* she thinks desperately.

The offended motorist careens into the night, blasting his horn for good measure.

Late night gamblers gawk at the highway showdown and the uncommon cargo as it lumbers to the far side of the big casino parking lot, shadowed by the small gray-haired woman running along beside it. Such a drastic step, some might say—uprooting her house to be with her son?

Frank kills the motor and unrolls the window when he sees his mother running alongside the tractor trailer.

"What now?" he barks.

Four months ago, the unthinkable had happened. Bulldozers would soon tear down Clara's house to make way for a new mall. All her efforts had failed—the incessant city council meetings, her outraged speeches, the petition drive she led against the mall with her friend Abigail Morton in front of Safeway—nothing stopped the city. Once she got the eviction notice, she called Frank in a panic. His phone rang and rang. On a layover in Chicago, he finally picked up the phone, sounding sleepy.

She sputtered in a rush, "They're going to tear down the house, Frank. I can't believe it. I thought we could stop them."

Silence. "So what will you do?" he said slowly, mulling on the fact that his mother is seventy-three years old.

"No way will I leave my house to the wrecking ball." Her voice was steely. The line went silent for a minute. "Frank? Frank, are you there?"

"Let me call you back tomorrow," he said morosely.

The next day his voice was barely audible. "Well, there's Jackpot."

"There's Jackpot," she echoed, her voice quavering. She knew he would say this, and she jumped at the chance. Frank is going to Jackpot to see his old friend Scotty who is having back and stomach pain and won't see a doctor. Scotty hates doctors. Frank is going to stay in Jackpot until he gets Scotty to see a doctor.

A small crowd lingers in the parking lot, watching. Clara's voice is tight with panic. "Frank, that sound back there—it sounded like a crack." She's shaking all over. *But he's a good driver*, she thinks in confusion, ashamed of her lack of confidence in him.

"Oh, for God's sake, Mother, that was no crack. The house shifts and settles like that every time I turn or change lanes. A sound like that is old news." Frank looks at her in exasperation, sighs, and jumps out of the trailer cab. His hair is tousled; he could use a shower. "Look, let's walk around the house together. You'll see there's no crack."

"Let me do it. You stay here," she says stoutly, straining to come up to his collarbone.

It's dark, almost ten, on a hot June night. She gestures vaguely for him to stay put by the open door of the trailer cab, a rich sweaty smell coming from inside. He's just glad to be standing up. Glad not to hear her belly-ache at him for two minutes as she disappears behind the house.

She can't *see* any cracks by the light of the neon Desert Dan's sign, but she runs her hands eagerly along the entire perimeter of her beloved house anyway. She can't *feel* any cracks. But a crack might be in a hidden place! She'll look later, when he's not around. Her hands, when she's done, are filthy. She wipes them on her weathered jeans. At least she's had time to gather her wits.

"Remember why you came, stupid woman," she whispers. "To heal things with your son. All those years when you couldn't even talk together." She makes a little gasping sound as her daughter's face flashes before her eyes. "And to save your soul from damnation." She whispers, "And maybe have one last moment of life again?"

She scratches her forehead. Two wasp stings, one above each eyebrow, still itch. Her head aches.

The night before she and Frank left Eugene, Clara was marching around on the driveway, agitated and mumbling about the move. The current purple wasp was flying around Clara's head, trying to see what was going on.

Finally she muttered that she wasn't going to leave Eugene with Frank after all. "Four days creeping along the highway with an old house ready to fall apart? I'm too old. Can't do it. Too much to ask. Too big an undertaking. House will fall apart. Collapse. Might have an accident. Going crazy worrying." Whine, whine.

BAM! Buzzing in a tizzy, the purple wasp stung her forehead twice, one sting above each eyebrow. She shrieked. "Why did you sting me? You've never done that!"

The wasp hummed in the way only Clara could understand. "Think again, Clara. You've dilly-dallied for years about your kids. Thousands of us swore to protect you forever ever since that night in your father's barn. But you won't listen to anything we say about your daughter's death. *Talk,* we say, *just talk. Or you'll die miserable and alone.* But you stay buttoned up. At least on this trip you have a chance to connect with your son, explain how it was all those years." The exasperated purple wasp whirled in dizzy circles. "For heaven's sake, you're an ordinary woman bedeviled by a lion's share of grief and loneliness. Why *wouldn't* you want a chance at peace and reconciliation and truth-telling before you die? Are you crazy? I need to get into your moldy Dream Jars and Brain Rooms to dig out all the muck. But with all your dodging about, I've only got thirty-five days left to do it. Or have you forgotten that wasps only live a hundred and twenty days and you are very late to sign on to this enterprise, missy?"

She wasn't listening. She was a sting virgin, never been stung before. Didn't want any lecturing just now, thank you very much. She gripped the sides of her head to blot out the pain. She ran inside, put an ice pack on the stings, took a Benadryl, and looked at herself in the mirror. The stings had swollen up and looked like two extra eyes on her forehead. She looked like a religious statue with mystical powers.

Clara looked out the window at her winged attacker, still angrily circling the driveway. *This wasp means business.*

But she knew that already. That's why she wanted to back out.

Frank stands by the door of the trailer cab, his muscular arms folded, looking sour and ready to drop. Clara is done looking for cracks.

"Maybe you're right, Frank. Maybe I just heard something shifting around." She wants to make peace with him. He's been on edge the entire trip.

But then so has she. Over four exhausting days, they would pull into rest stops and right away she would jump out of the U-Haul and head for the tethered house. It was empty except for their sleeping bags and a few wardrobe changes. Everything else was in the U-Haul. But she always had to check on the wasps, buzzing furiously in their big beef jerky jars. She kept them in her closet where the two big jars wouldn't roll around.

After she sat down cross-legged on the floor and peered at each of the sixteen wasps, eight in each jar, Frank always knew what was coming next: She would sing to them: "Some Enchanted Evening," "Blue Suede Shoes," "I'll Be With You in Apple Blossom Time"– God knows what other ancient Top 40 songs. Even thinking about this makes him feel like such a fool. What had he gotten himself into? He'd go sit in the trailer cab to escape her singing and have a smoke, his arm dangling out the window, tapping ashes to the ground.

He started smoking again on this trip. Here he is, forty-six and can't say no to his mother. He understood about the house, how important it was to her, that she had to save it. He even understood about the wasps in some dim way he didn't want to admit. But he had just hatched his *own* run to freedom, which he'd have to put on hold now. He had planned to leave the country with his friend Fernando, go to San Miguel de Allende and build houses for gringos. He had enough money now to go anywhere he wanted.

A few months ago, his Aunt Lillian dropped dead from a heart attack outside a London theater as her new lover, Patrick Chalmers, stood shocked beside her. Lillian's will left everything to Frank. She had no children, had never married. So Frank promptly quit his boring job with Union Pacific, for which he had endlessly crisscrossed the country for years. He had quit just as Clara got her eviction notice.

So here they are, mother and son yoked together after all these years of hardly seeing each other. At rest stops, they sat wordless at old picnic tables and avoided each other's eyes. Sometimes they discussed the weather. All along the route, mother and son would ask themselves why they agreed to this hare-brained scheme anyway, tying themselves together like this after years of hardly seeing each other. Tongue-tied, they couldn't talk about it.

Before it's too late, she wants to talk with him, laugh with him, be a mother finally after all these years of halting silence and endless grief. He's her only living family. Her daughter and husband have been dead for years. These deaths, particularly her daughter's, have scalded her soul. She feels responsible for her daughter's death and can't discuss this with anyone. She knows Frank wants to leave the country, but before he does, she wants to reconcile with him, have some loving times with him, heal the painful past they share. She's tired of living as if she were already dead.

Something in her snapped when she heard the house would be demolished. She and her husband Darrell built that house together almost fifty years ago. She will not lose her house, and she will follow her son to Mars if she has to.

◈

Frank sighs and walks into Desert Dan's, where Scotty was supposed to meet them, but he's not there. Scotty owns Desert Dan's. So instead of Scotty's quiet house with three bedrooms, three bathrooms, and beds with sheets, not to mention running water, Frank and his mother have to sleep again in the uprooted house right there in the big parking lot. One bathroom, serviced by a camp toilet and bottled water.

Just as she's falling asleep, someone scratches at her bedroom screen. Frank doesn't hear it. He's already fast asleep on the living room floor in his battered sleeping bag. But she hears it. The scratching stops, and someone snickers and walks away, rattling something, keys or a set of tools. She had slept fitfully, until just now, in the silvery desert morning, when a loud *boom boom boom!* wracks the walls. She listens carefully, not moving. Someone's walking around the perimeter, banging on the house real smarty-pants like. Loud, with a beat: *ta TUM tum, ta TUM tum*. Her house. The house Frank grew up in, the house she's lived in like a nun for almost thirty years, ever since Frank left after high school.

"What's that noise?" Musty with sleep, Frank bolts up from his sleeping bag.

"Nothing. Some kid." She tries to sound brave, but her voice shakes.

"Baloney. Stay here." He does a quick check outside, comes back in. "Nothing. I'll talk to Scotty. We've got to get off this parking lot." He yawns, irritated, and climbs back into his sleeping bag.

She's frightened, wonders if she's dreaming. First the scratching, now the banging. Why would someone do that? On the road those four days, people waved and smiled at their old house rumbling along the highway. Not like this—rude. *Some punk*, she tells herself. Standing up straighter, she marches into the cramped bathroom and stumbles over the camp toilet next to the disconnected toilet. She splashes her face with bottled water at the sink, massages her neck near her strawberry birthmark, and anchors her springy salt-and-pepper bob with barrettes. Back in her bedroom, she straps her Timex with the big numbers to her wrist and dresses in her black sports bra, red knit sweatpants, and blue T-shirt. It's 7:40 in the morning. She's exhausted.

Thin flesh flaps quiver on her upper arms as she stubbornly does hamstring stretches, downward dog, brave warrior. The wasps are buzzing like mad, butting their heads against the two big beef jerky jars in the closet, trying to get out. She pats the well-aerated lids. The wasps clump furiously in each jar, trying to get to where her hand is.

We want our sugar water.

"Settle down. You know I walk first."

What was she thinking, luring them into these jars for the long trip? She's got to let them out, for heaven's sake. She can't asphyxiate them. But what if they escape? She can't be without her wasps. It's as simple as that. She's in a fix, one of many. She'll deal with this one later.

She passes by Frank in his sleeping bag. He stirs, grimacing, his dimples long creases in the brash light, his rumpled sandy hair twisted in crazy curlicues. He waves at her without conviction and mumbles, "I'll be gone when you get back."

"I know." She smiles distractedly and heads for the door.

Wiry, headstrong, Clara will do as she's always done. She will know this place by walking on its dirt.

She hops off the makeshift steps Frank built for the high-riding flatbed and slowly crosses the big parking lot. It's pretty quiet this morning. Even so, stray laughter and slammed car doors are too loud for her sleep-deprived state. But her lungs feel pumped up, as if millions of tiny air sacs have sprung to life. She breathes better in this dry air; that's for sure. In Eugene, her allergies–to ragweed, Douglas fir, molds from the damp climate—were getting to be murder. Her first bout of pneumonia this winter scared her, made her nun-like retreat from life seem suddenly foolish. The sound of bulldozers was the last straw. Everything is conspiring to wake her up, change her life somehow before it's too late. Something is pushing her, some unknown force. Her forehead aches. She itches the stings. She's scared.

She squints into the bleached sun low on the horizon. The intense desert light, even this early, is merciless. There's no shade! Does it even rain here? Signs say, *Wells, 68 miles south; Twin Falls, 48 miles north.* There's a Chevron, a Shell, a video store, drugstore, couple of motels, liquor store, 24-hour market/convenience store, and several blocks of mobile homes and pre-fab houses painted Easter egg colors. They all straggle out on either side of Highway 93 from Desert Dan's, whose parking lot and huge neon sign dominate the landscape. Smaller casinos hover nearby in nestlets of cars:—the Lucky Clover, the Sun, the Straight Flush. Beyond is plain, no-nonsense desert, a vast weedy plate rimmed by distant low mountains. A medium wind never lets up.

She walks out past the mobile homes, the stucco numbers, the short streets named Black Jack, Hi-Lo, Keno, Double Down, Lady Luck, and onto the desert floor—through hunkered-down weeds, gray-green sagebrush mounds, parched gray dirt littered with beer cans, spent bullets, shredded tires, cigarette butts, and old dried condoms. Her heart rattles in her chest. What *is* this place anyway? Frank will be busy with his own life. He won't want to spend much time with her. She knows that. She'll have to catch him on the run. What will she *do* here? Will she even have a friend? With a pang, she thinks of her best friend, Abigail

Morton, moving to Syracuse to be with her children after the petition drive against the mall failed.

Circling back to the parking lot, she stares at her uprooted house. It stands bereft and hallucinatory above all the cars. Its dirty white siding, faded green trim, and hexagon windows shimmer mirage-like in the early morning heat. After all the aluminum trailers and stucco houses she's just seen, *her* house, made entirely of wood, seems freakish out here, unfit for the harsh desert. It looks naked. Termites will eat it. Marauding ants. Unnamed predators, hungry for porous wood. In the parking lot, she squats to tighten a shoelace. She wants to get inside.

Some young guy with long dark hair and cloggy breathing (allergies, she thinks) sticks his head out from behind an SUV. She glances up. Their eyes meet for an instant, hers wide in surprise. He stares hard at her crouched form, daring her somehow, as if he were born to hate the sight of her. Her skin prickles. She stands abruptly and bolts toward her house and the low-hanging sun. He smirks and spits a big brown loogie onto a silver Taurus, then darts back behind the SUV. Her heart races. She will erase this moment.

She climbs the steps to the rickety screen door and peers through the half window. Oh, good. Frank unpacked the kitchen table and chairs from the U-Haul. She can eat at her own table again like a semi-normal person. He's probably off to see Scotty, who said Frank could work the change booth until he heads off to Mexico.

Just as she's ready to go inside, a tall, sharp-eyed woman carrying a leather shoulder bag approaches her. She's dressed in worn tan chinos and a black T-shirt, her long straight hair in a loose bun. She smiles. "This your house?" Her bag is busy with zippers and compartments.

Clara is wary. "Yes. Why?"

"I wonder if I could take a few pictures. I like the way it looks here."

Hungry for breakfast, Clara frowns. "Are you a photographer?"

"Why, yes. I'll give you my card." She zips open a compartment in the leather bag.

"I really need to get inside and eat. Maybe some other time."

With a beseeching look, the woman says, "I'll be quick. I promise." Before Clara can object further, the woman takes a serious-looking camera from her bag and rapidly circles the house and trailer cab, taking quick shots from different angles. Clara is annoyed even as she sees the woman is skilled and fast. "Thanks. I've got a deadline. Don't want to keep you further. Maybe I'll see you around. I come to Jackpot a lot." She waves at Clara and heads toward the casino.

Clara turns on the generator and goes inside, vaguely annoyed by the pushy woman. She's too hungry to face a bottled water shower before she eats. But she can't ignore the wasps. She gets the two beef jerky jars full of frantic wasps and sets them by the sink.

Quit starving us.

"All right, all right. Get a grip."

She takes the Ball Mason jar of sugar water from under the sink and pours some into a cup with a pour spout. Carefully she sprinkles the liquid through the punctured lids. The wasps' steady hum goes up the scale a notch or two as the sweet liquid showers them. They drink or snuffle or whatever it is they do, then clean their wings with their back legs, like flies. Their translucent lavender wings, their slender bodies with purple-and-black banding, their dark heads with microscopic eyes that seem to watch her—she thinks they are beautiful.

CLARA at the EDGE

In Eugene, Clara was Teacher of the Year, Citizen of the Year, Outstanding Volunteer (at the library, women's shelter, hospice, Chamber of Commerce)—but no one really knew her. Not Abigail, her best friend, not even herself. Only the wasps—circling the driveway, buzzing under the eaves—know her. Ever since North Dakota in the barn.

Whenever she had a problem, she would just watch the wasps fly lazily around her on the driveway until she found the solution to whatever was bothering her. If banished memories surfaced, the wasps sensed a disturbance and suspended themselves around her head like hummingbirds, as if they could read her mind. When her friends got old enough to start dying, she had her wasps.

She catches sight of the one that always jumps higher, more excitedly than the others, the one that stung her. A purple iridescence covers its body, especially on its head. Its thorax stripes are purple and lavender, its wings shiny lavender, and its head a knockout purple shimmer.

Back in Eugene, if this purple wasp returned to the colony with news of some discovery, the whole swarm would follow the diva into the sky, depriving Clara of their irritable hum. She listened for their frenzied return after they'd seen whatever the alpha wasp had to show them. She wanted to ask Dennis Stedman, who taught natural science at the high school, about the wasps, but Dennis would say wasps weren't purple and she must be seeing things. So she kept the purple wasps to herself.

Glowing and royal-appearing, they invaded her dreams. Over the years, they spoke to her, sang to her, helped her flounder out of a deep, rancid pool surrounding Samantha's death. *Hold me close,* they sang, whispering in her ear. And she did hold them close and hoped she was saved.

16

This purple wasp is way more intense than the others. This one returns Clara's gaze, slows her frantic business of tumbling and dancing when Clara watches her. This wasp knows something about her, she's sure of it—something about Samantha, on the day she died and even before. Things Clara struggles to keep buried in her deepest mental dungeons.

The purple wasp watches Clara from inside the beef jerky jar. Entirely still, the creature sends up a little *fzz* every so often, as if she's thinking out loud. The other wasps buzz and crawl about in confusion. Transfixed, Clara breathes faster, almost a pant. She fears this wasp yet needs her. She showers the wasp with extra squirts of sugar water. The creature ignores her offering and crawls away to the other side of the jar, aiming her tail disdainfully at Clara. This wasp, so beautiful and piercing and harsh, rouses a buried part of Clara's soul, a part that holds the harrowing truth. Sometimes she feels rising hysteria. Then she chatters, can't think straight, and Frank gets impatient with her. Thank God he's gone right now. She can't stand any more scolding this morning.

Thirty-five days to change her life? What was she thinking?

chapter 2

Last night, Dawson Barth landed in Jackpot too. He slept in a black Camaro he stole in Pocatello, leaving behind a Ford pickup he stole in Cheyenne. He's wandered all his life. Clara's sudden house in the morning sun disturbed him. He didn't want to think about its faded hominess. But he had to get closer, see if the house was even real. He stumbled out of the Camaro and went banging like a brat all the way around the house, hoping to scare anyone inside, just like he'd done last night. The house was real all right, dusty with lumpy siding. Sleepy, hungry, his mind went blank. A few minutes later, he darted behind an SUV as he saw Clara walking briskly toward him in the parking lot.

As she got closer, he heard her deep breathing, saw her perky salt-and-pepper gray hair held behind her ears with two barrettes, her tanned arms, her face a peach blush. He frowned. This woman was good-looking when she was younger. Now she's probably a *grandmother*. He was mortified at the sharp pain this idea caused him—a grandmother *he* sure as hell never had. He was humiliated even to have such a thought, something a six-year-old would think.

Wimp.

She bent down to tighten her shoelace. He heard her tired sigh. She was going toward the old house. On her neck was a strawberry birthmark about half an inch wide. His stomach tightened. His mother had a mark like that by her right ear. He'd forgotten about it. Chomping on a Hostess cupcake from his sack, he pushed spit through the gaps in his teeth to rid them of the pudding-like goo. He spat out a chocolate-brown arc that splatted onto a silver Taurus. Her quick glance made him glower and duck. Then she was up and walking again, faster, toward her house. He raked his hair behind his ears and pulled his Chicago Bulls hat down on his forehead.

Sitting on his mother's lap when he was four or five, Dawson would touch her red birthmark as he nestled against her shoulder. She didn't like him to touch it. She'd slap his hand if he did. She was always getting mad about any little thing like that. He never had a father. When he was six, he remembered she'd been really mad about a phone call she got. Stomach rolls shaking, she marched around the apartment, running her hands through her snarled brown hair. Suddenly she picked up some cups and plates and hurled them against the kitchen wall. The dishes shattered and made a terrible noise that scared him. She'd never done that before. She looked like she was going to cry, so he tried to comfort her. He climbed on her lap and patted her forehead. She slapped his hand hard. She didn't want him touching any part of her face. Crying, he ran and hid in her closet, rich with the smell of her clothes. All that year when he was six, she would get mad every single day and lose her temper with him every minute, and sometimes she would cry and shout about things he couldn't understand.

One day in that awful year, 1980, she dumped him off at a Safeway in Reno. She had a few errands to run, she said. "Wait in front of Safeway until I come back," she said. This was after she made him an early lunch of hot dogs and Kool-Aid. He waited and waited, peed his pants, was getting really hungry in the windy afternoon sun. He wanted to go into Safeway and steal some candy bars, but he was scared he'd miss his mom so he didn't. He sat down cross-legged on the cement and rocked from side to side. People looked at him strangely. A few stopped in their tracks a minute, but no one said anything. When it started to get dark, a nice lady from the police department came and said she was taking him home to her house for the night. For dinner she fed him oatmeal and bacon.

The next day, the lady took him to another place where they asked him a lot of questions he didn't know or wouldn't answer. The rest of his growing up years was all foster parents, some nice but more often mean or crazy, men that stubbed out their cigarettes on his chest or arm to make him tough, women that fed him stale Wonder Bread or spoiled cheese that gave him a belly ache. Those years were all a rubble and he didn't want to think about it. Thinking just got him angry. He's already been in jail four times, prison once, and here he's only twenty-five.

He watched Clara coming in from the desert. "Fuck," he blurted, "must be the old lady from the beat-up house." He didn't know why he tied her to the house. He hadn't seen her come out of it. "Damned old lady gimme a headache," he muttered softly, kicking the pavement. He hitched up his pants, swaggered into the casino, swung back out again, tried to settle himself by shuffling around the parking lot, focusing on late model cars, staring at dashboard designs and buttery-smooth upholstery, swigging root beer and eating Ding Dongs from his brown paper bag. Tall and skinny with blue-white skin, he was hobbled by an elegant facial structure that cut into his tough guy pose: long thin nose, flat cheekbones, long limp hair. Like a stray cat, he rubbed up against the empty cars.

He watched her enter the house, the sun blazing now. He was right. It's her house. Something impossible and longed-for rose in him, something he always squelched, a feeling that could unman him. He looked around. There was no one. He wanted to run his fingers along the siding again, make sure it was real, not a mirage. The old lady wouldn't hear him tromping around. She was probably hard of hearing.

He ran to her house and circled it fast. The house was funky. It almost had a stink to it. It was crumbling, falling apart: gapped eaves, shingles worn thin around the edges, bumpy paint, loose rain gutters full of debris, window frames coming away from the siding. It tore his heart out.

Back among the cars, he mulled. It's her all right, the old lady who lives in a shoe. What the hell is she doing in a place like this? This is no place for her. She belongs behind a white picket fence. He'll show her.

He slid out the screwdriver he always carried in his back Levi's pocket. Pressing hard, he made long scratches on a dirty Chevy Caprice, then on a Honda Accord and a black Lexus with gold spoke hubcaps. On each car he scratched out two letters of a word. The complete word was *wheeee*. He'll be the only one who knows the letters make a word stretched over three cars. The owners will be too stupid to figure it out. He snickered, stuffing the last of the Ding Dong in his mouth, where it bulged and churned.

Later that first day, Dawson watched a sandy-haired man drive the house across the highway. The man parked the house in the far corner of a vacant lot. It was probably her son. Another guy, tall and thin, walked ahead of the load and acted as guide. Dawson watched the two men and the old woman unload the U-Haul. He snickered: The furniture was as ratty looking as the house. But the tall, skinny guy didn't stick it out. He wiped his forehead and slumped back to the casino after about fifteen minutes. So the old lady and her son carried in all the boxes themselves and disappeared inside the house. Later, her son crossed the highway and disappeared into Desert Dan's.

Dawson smiled. *She's alone now, nobody around her.*

The son probably has twenty-five pounds on Dawson, but the son is also older. It would be a good fight if it came to that. A hungry surge of adrenalin pulsed in his veins.

Now it's close to midnight, and Dawson stares at Clara's house in the towering desert night. He's down to his last three bucks; his stomach is painfully empty. He clicks his small yellowed teeth together, shoots saliva around his mouth to knock out the last Ding Dong deposits.

He's sitting in the black Camaro, getting calmer. He scans the horizon, looking for a sign of some kind, the low mountains invisible in the dark. From time to time he pushes his hair away from his face with a sleepy arm movement. The MP3 player he lifted from a Chicago Wal-Mart is secured to an arm band, earphones pulsing. Rap saturates every waking moment these days, an angry male rumble in the summer of 2000. He's just another white guy who secretly likes it. His face grows wistful. He tries to remember a certain song, but he's forgotten it.

He wants to head to Reno, try to scare up his mother after all these years. He's been everywhere else, always with her name, Nancy Jetta Barth, in the back of his mind: San Antonio, Albuquerque, San Bernardino, Casper, Bend, Newark, he forgets how many. Plus a couple of prison stops he doesn't like to think about. His jaw muscles flex.

The light in Clara's house goes out. He dozes off, arms

hugging his thin chest. At two thirty in the morning, he wakes, hungry, and remembers what he's about. He opens the glove compartment, unfolds a paper, and scoots some white powder into a line with his folded map of the Western United States. He leans over and snorts it with his trusty plastic straw that tastes salty because he's stuck it up his nose so many times.

The dingy house is barely visible in the dark, a house with history, a stinking time capsule that doesn't even belong in this tent town. What was she thinking anyway? Random losers come here for jackpots in the sky and blotto, blotto, blotto. She should've stayed where she came from, Mary Poppins land. He gets out of the car, stuffs a flashlight in his back pocket, and strides across the highway.

Hearing a sound, Clara bolts from bed, stands trembling in her nightgown, not knowing if the sound was real or from her inter-rupted dream: a faceless man firing a pistol into a packed concert hall, people stampeding toward the exits.

She crosses her arms, trying to stop shivering, and grasps the sides of her breasts. What's that awful grating noise? Frank must still be in the casino. The house is quiet and he usually snores. So the trip is barely over and now this? In the vacant lot where no one can see or hear her? The area where Scotty said nobody would bother them?

She always stuffs nightmares into her Dream Jar, the ironclad place in her brain, and screws the lid on tight. Her Dream Jar crushes nightmares into cellular waste. Things stay tidy in her head that way. Now the Dream Jar bangs against her forehead, outside her head, making her headache worse.

She hears a knife cutting the screen in the sewing room, across the hall from her bedroom. *Samantha's room!* Sounds of breaking glass, a heavy rock hitting the floor. Weak with terror, she almost crumples, then thinks: *Not me, nightmare man. I will not sink to any floor.*

She creeps into Frank's room next to Samantha's. Barely breathing, she peeks through the curtained window, sees someone's profile in moonlight: someone young, surly, male, plucking glass shards out from the window frame. He's not even trying to be quiet. He's trying to hoist himself through the broken window but keeps slipping back. His jumping makes the house quiver, as if a giant tyrannical parent were shaking her because she'd been bad. *Why are you here, what have I done, is my house against the law here?* Head thrown back, he gulps the last swigs from a can he tosses on the ground. His greasy skin gleams silver in the moonlight; his Adam's apple is huge and moving. He wipes his nose on the back of his hand, lets out an unguarded grunt as he jumps big and the house quivers.

He's in.

Samantha's room.

Crack! That was a cabinet leg! He landed on the sewing machine cabinet directly under the window. Panicked, she almost cries out: the indispensable 1954 Singer, the machine Darrell bought at great financial sacrifice back then, the machine she still keeps faithfully oiled and serviced, the sewing machine she kept in the living room before Samantha died.

Now she's furious. Rage boils in her. She peers down the dark hall, braces herself in the bedroom doorway. He's heading toward the living room and kitchen. He hasn't seen her yet. His flashlight makes a jumpy light show on all her things. He's tossing all her books on the floor from the bookcases Darrell made of oak he scavenged from the old J.C. Penney store in Eugene. He's throwing homemade sofa pillows onto the floor, sweeping magazines off the coffee table. A tinkling crash. *No!*

She'd know that sound anywhere. The robber broke the porcelain ballerina that should be safely hidden in her dresser drawer instead of out here on the coffee table for her to admire because it made the trip safely. She grasps her head. Darrell bought that figurine for her when she was pregnant with Samantha, and by chance the statue foretold the child's talent in ballet. Samantha, now escaped from the memory room in Clara's brain, dances madly in her mother's head. Anger and devastation shake them both.

The robber lifts and slams the small black-and-white TV back onto its TV tray. He shoves the old Emerson radio screeching across the oak end table to crash on the floor. Samantha flees back to her memory room, lit by an eternal bronze-lit light. Even in death, she knows her mother will protect the museum of her childhood home. This is a battle for her mother to fight, not her.

Now he's in the kitchen at the other end of the house, shining his flashlight, sliding out the canisters, sticking his filthy hands into the flour, the sugar, the rice. He sweeps his hands over the kitchen counter, opening drawers, throwing old phone books on the floor, her ancient plastic address file. He finds nothing. She has nothing. He starts back down the hall, heading for the bedrooms, where indeed she has a few things.

She's beyond fear now. She could tear him apart. As he approaches, she steps into the hall, arms tightly folded across her shivering chest.

"There's nothing for you here. Get out of my house. Now."

He's so startled to see her small form in the hallway, speaking so fearlessly to him, that he bolts to the broken sewing room window, leaps onto the steps, and is gone.

Listening hard, hearing no one, Clara throws on her green summer bathrobe and jumps barefoot onto the dirt of the vacant lot with a butcher knife in her hand. Her heart roaring, she carries the wooden steps back to where they belong and stands there, her small arms loose at her sides, hair skewed from sleep. The robber had carried the steps to her window. The air is still. Her ears adjust like a wily animal's to a finer frequency. The desert sky is a stinging background hum. It's the sound of power poles or her rushing blood. Cars pass by on the highway, the ripped air sounding like torn silk. The indifferent hum swallows everything. She feels invisible and savage in the vast starlit night.

Darrell whispers from his eternal bronze-lit room in her brain, the room next to Samantha's. *I would've throttled the guy before he got inside.*

I know, I know. So why did you leave me?

Silently, Darrell fades back into his unchanging museum. For a moment, everything is quiet and her mind goes blank.

Her heart races again. The stranger *knew* he could be brazen, *knew* Frank was in the casino. He had spied on her! Then she thinks: *This is nonsense. I will not play Terrorized Old Person. I will find this young man and talk to him. I will find out what the trouble is.*

Back inside, her impulse is to straighten the house, sleep be damned. She wipes her dirty feet with a wet rag, puts on her slippers, turns on the generator and all the lights, and goes from room to room, putting drawers and cushions and books back where they belong. She sweeps up the broken glass in the sewing room, pushes cardboard from a packing box into the empty window space, draws the curtain over it. He cracked a sewing machine leg. She can fix that. The Lladró figurine has a broken arm and leg. She won't think about it. She leaves it on the coffee table to glue together first thing in the morning. Never in all her life has anyone tried to rob her house. She thought her house was a fortress. She covers her face with her hands.

Welcome to the party, hon, snorts the raucous hum in her brain. *It's a wild world out here. It's about time you leave your prison cell. We've all been waiting, you know.*

Startled, she looks around. A brief shimmer of lavender wings passes before her eyes. The voice is so close, right in her ear.

chapter 3

She hardly sleeps. The smell of someone else is in the house, a stranger's sweat, rancid, unwashed. Where's Frank? Where's someone, anyone—a non-robber—she could talk to? She sets the two wasp jars on the table to distract herself while she eats. The creatures are unusually disoriented this morning. They collide into each other in their cramped quarters, have angry tiffs. Rinsing her dishes, she looks out the window, watches cars come and go from Desert Dan's parking lot. She puts the wasp jars back in her closet. She's got to get her mind off all this.

Well, she always was a movie fan. Set close to the highway, Jackpot Video is maybe 15'x15', packed with velvet pictures of Elvis and dogs; T-shirts, mugs, shot glasses, and coasters, all labeled "Jackpot." Videos line a few shelves: *Star Wars*, *Independence Day*, the blockbusters.

The puffy-looking owner, pale and agreeable-looking, says he just got the new Harry Potter movie.

Clara grins. "How about some Claudette Colbert, Myrna Loy, Bette Davis, Rosalind Russell. How about *His Girl Friday*?"

"Sorry. People around here want Clint Eastwood, Bruce Lee, *The Terminator*."

"That's not surprising," pipes up a voice from the back of the store.

It's the woman who photographed Clara's house yesterday. Clara cringes but at the same time feels friendlier this morning after the break-in. The women smile at each other.

The owner looks at them apologetically. "We've only been open three months. Who knows, maybe I'll get up a classic section. You two like Charlie Chaplin?"

"*Love* Charlie Chaplin," they chorus, then alternate, laughing, as if cheerleading:

"*Modern Times.*"

"*The Gold Rush.*"

"*City Lights.*"

"*The Great Dictator.*"

The owner smiles, encouraging them. "W.C. Fields? Buster Keaton?"

Clara frowns. "Nix. Screwball comedies and selected oldies. I'm actually very fussy."

"I *love* W.C. Fields and Buster Keaton," the woman says, as if she were being personally attacked.

She's not from around here, Clara thinks, intrigued, noticing the woman's expensive-looking slacks and T-shirt, her large horn-rimmed glasses, her caffeinated air of fanatical concentration.

Bemused, the owner looks from one to the other. "Well, ladies, keep coming back. Maybe we can set something up." He gives them each a chartreuse fluorescent key chain that says *Jackpot Videos, Highway 93, Jackpot, Nevada.* They thank him and wander outside together.

The woman turns cautiously to Clara. "Nice talking to you again. But where's your house?" Clara smiles and points to the vacant lot. The woman laughs. "Maybe you should chain it down."

Clara likes hearing the woman laugh, likes being around

someone who's not going to rob her. And the woman isn't pushy this morning. On impulse, she invites her in for coffee. In Eugene, it might take her months to warm up to a new acquaintance.

"I'd like that very much. By the way, my name is Arianna Paul. And you?"

"Clara Breckenridge."

Before they go inside, Arianna runs her hand along the rough siding. "What is this here? All this lumpiness and dried bits of something?"

Clara starts at the woman's bluntness. "Lilacs. Dead lilacs caught in the paint."

"What?"

"The painters were cheap, always in a hurry. They held the branches out with one hand and painted with the other. They let the lilacs slap back onto wet paint." Clara's eyes glisten, much to her dismay. "I was careless for not checking. The bushes were thick around the house. The painters knew I'd probably not check. I had the same painters for years. So on the bottom half of the house, all you see are lumps of paint with bits of brown, beige, and gray sticking out, withered lilac petals in all states of decomposition. My house is a museum for dead lilacs." She clears her throat, looks down at her hands.

The woman gives her a long look. "Would you mind if I took a few more exterior shots? I was in a hurry yesterday."

"It's just an old house. The trip wasn't good for it, see?" Clara pulls on a loose window frame, stares at the eager woman. "Well, if you're quick. I really need that coffee."

"Me too."

Arianna takes out her elaborate camera and shoots more closely the dead lilac petals, the loose window frames with crazed green paint, the bedraggled oak doors that lead to the kitchen and the living room. In the trailer cab, she shoots owner Todd's crucifix and plastic Betty Boop hanging from the rearview mirror, the ripped vinyl upholstery, the fecund trash on the floor. She shoots Clara irritably standing there in her faded jeans and orange T-shirt, her arms folded across her chest, a tendril of wavy hair blowing across her forehead, her brown eyes alert and impatient. The photographer backs off to take quick shots of the casinos, mountains, sky, sagebrush. She studies each shot, adjusts her gauges, then a rapid *click, click, click.* She holds her breath as she shoots, exhales softly or explosively when it's over, like a musician breathes to match the phrasing.

They go inside. Arianna takes in the simple furnishings, the lack of pretense. She watches Clara pour bottled water into a saucepan and turn on the heating plate. "You've really uprooted everything, haven't you?" she says in amazement. She is watching Clara carefully.

"My son and I just got in from Eugene last night," she blurts. "We're going to live here. Maybe."

This is the first time she's spoken to anyone about the move. She feels a little crazy speaking to a stranger. It's as if she can't control herself any more. She shivers. Maybe she's on a thinner edge than she realized. In fact, she doesn't know what she'll do with the house. Will she stay? Go? Everything depends on how things develop with Frank. If he stays, she'll stay. If he goes, she will go. But where? How much more traveling can the house take? Is it still sound? She's got to get running water, for Pete's sake. She had assumed Frank would stay: Frank and Scotty are lifelong friends. She made this move in the heat of passion, and now her thoughts are crashing into a scary reality.

She hears the wasps buzzing loudly in the bedroom. They are trying to tell her something, but they're holed up in the beef jerky jars. She wants them near her. Too much is happening: robbery, harassment, this inquisitive woman.

She tries to still her shaking hands as she and Arianna sit on the couch and sip their coffee in silence. Finally Arianna says, "I've always lived in apartments or lofts, never a house. Your place makes me homesick somehow."

"Me too." Clara smiles.

With quiet resolve, the woman pulls out a plain white business card from her shoulder bag and hands it to Clara: *Arianna Paul, photographer.* Lower Manhattan gallery address and contact information. "Would you mind if I took a few interior shots, Clara? I promise to be quick."

A little dotty from her sleepless night, Clara stares at the woman. "Don't know why you'd want to." She yawns, sets her coffee cup on the coffee table, and massages her temples. The two wasp stings are still sore. Again the wasps buzz loudly from the bedroom, as if they have something to say.

Oh, dear God. How many days are left before my wasp dies? I'm not making any progress, am I? Where's Frank?

Arianna leans toward Clara with sudden urgency. "Right, my dear. You're tired, and I'm on my way to Elko. Look, I'll bring you the prints in a couple of weeks or sooner. Who knows if we'll get another chance?" She pauses, writes a cousin's address and phone number on the back of her card, and hands it back to Clara. "Here's the thing. I've been thinking about this ever since I saw you. I'm going to be in a photography show at the Met opening July first called 'Hidden America: Photography in the New Millennium.' Your house is a perfect fit. I think New Yorkers would really appreciate it. Why not take a chance?"

Clara laughs, pointing to loose plaster fallen in the corner. "You have to be kidding. It's just an old house. Why would New

Yorkers be interested in a small house built in ancient times with no money? Or in an old woman foolish enough to drag her house from near-rainforest to desert? What you've taken pictures of, my dear, is an old house starting to fall apart and an old woman ready for the madhouse." A sudden rush of feeling startles her.

"Now that's nonsense, Clara, and I think you know it." They fall silent again, finishing their coffee.

Clara studies the floor, trying to hold back entirely inappropriate tears. Finally she says, "Oh, all right. But hurry. I've got to get some lunch." She feels worn down and tired. But something about this woman, her steeliness, the light in her eye, intrigues her. Forty years ago, she was like that herself, untouched by tragedy, a fanatical teacher who wanted to change her students' lives.

At Clara's "yes," the wasps go wild in the bedroom. Arianna smiles as if Clara has just given permission to photograph rare jewels before they are snatched away. Camera whirring, she scurries from room to room, starting with the kitchen. A wash of sunlight from the window shines on the chipped porcelain sink, the heavily chromed appliances, green Formica table and chairs, cream tile countertops, scuffed linoleum floor. Motley canisters line the counter. Crocheted hot pads hang from magnet hooks on the oven door. In the living room, the twelve-inch TV sits on an old metal TV tray, a VCR under it on the floor. A shapeless sofa in worn navy velvet occupies the opposite wall. The plain oak coffee table is thick with magazines. An adjoining wall has a matching easy chair and two oak bookcases stuffed with dog-eared books. Opposite is a plain oak rocker and oak end table with the old Emerson radio on it. Darrell made all the furniture. Somehow she's irritated that Arianna's looking at it.

Click! Clara freezes. The broken ballerina—*I should have put it away!* she thinks in dismay. It's as if Arianna had X-rayed the special room in Clara's brain where her daughter lives and handed the X-ray over to the *National Enquirer*. Arianna senses that she has blundered onto something she must not inquire about.

Clara turns her head away and speaks gently to her daughter, who has begun to walk the corridors of her brain. *Not now,* she whispers, determined not to weep in front of this visitor. The lost daughter looks at her mother with sorrow and retreats to her Brain Room.

Collecting herself, Clara is bewildered, then annoyed. Her furnishings are just utilitarian. No outsider could ever understand how this simple house, unchanged for almost fifty years, has shielded her, cocooned her, let her just live despite the horrors of 1963. It has kept her safe. Without the physical comfort of the familiar, she would die. She's sure of that. Bursting with these thoughts, she tries to calm down, desperately wanting to end this encounter.

They walk down the short hall to the two dingy off-white bedrooms. Worn oak floors are strewn with multi-colored rag rugs Clara made. Samantha's old room now holds only the Singer sewing machine in its maple cabinet, a floor lamp, and a cabinet for sewing supplies. The broken window is hidden by curtains. Cases of bottled water cover the floor.

In Frank's old room, a single bed is covered with an army blanket. A stained suitcase is open on the floor; another one is closed. Clara hasn't seen Frank since they unloaded the furniture. In the bathroom, there's the tiled peach floor with avocado trim Darrell installed the year before he died, and the camp toilet, plastic basins, and bottled water that will barely do until plumbing is restored.

In Clara's bedroom, Arianna shoots the '50s blond dresser

covered with old squeeze-spray crystal perfume bottles, a framed picture of Clara and Darrell on their wedding day, a photo of Frank and Samantha when they were three and five, a back-yard snapshot of the whole family picnicking among the lilacs, a mirrored tray with a silver-plated brush and comb from Darrell. Scattered on the dresser are more family pictures that Clara took from a big manila envelope last night to soothe herself after the attempted robbery. Flanking the bed are blond nightstands with table lamps. All lamps in the house have the same white satin lampshade in different sizes she ordered from the Sears catalogue years ago. In the doorway is a small Turkish rug Darrell gave her on their fifth wedding anniversary.

Arianna pauses, transfixed. Two small paintings hang on the wall facing the bed. Vibrant colors surge in abstract waves. These paintings belong in a different house. "Did you do these, Clara?"

"My sister Lillian painted them." Her face closes.

"Talented woman." Arianna moves right on, points to the bed. "Did you make the quilt?" Clara nods, her face expressionless. Arianna gushes, "You've put the pieces together so inventively, according to what adjacent squares suggest in pattern and color. Artistic talent runs in the family. Do you pursue it?"

"Not really," she says lightly. This woman wants to know *everything*. Clara will never talk about her own acrylics of landscapes and people, done in her own colors, not true to life. These are private, stowed in boxes.

Clara excuses herself to use the bathroom. Returning, she sees Arianna crouched near the loudly humming beef jerky jars in the closet.

"These wasps—you brought them with you?" She laughs in delight. "I had ant farms as a kid."

Furious, Clara folds her arms across her chest. "You go too far, Miss Paul. Did you photograph these wasps? "

Abashed, she nods.

Clara glances at the agitated creatures. "This is very private to me. I'm afraid we need to end our little tour now, Arianna. I'm really quite tired." She is formal, cold.

Coloring, Arianna abruptly stands. "I'm really sorry, Clara. But please know I can't use pictures or interview material unless you give me the rights." She swallows hard. "I didn't mean to offend you. That's the last thing I wanted to do."

At the door, she says, "I can't thank you enough for letting me photograph your home. It's truly American. No sham, nothing flashy. Your house is what houses are for: to give shelter, fill basic needs. People forget that these days."

Vaguely, Clara nods. She's flattered and offended by Arianna's interest. Secretly she admires the woman's wily way of getting what she wants, even if it's a form of invasion. She smiles to herself. *That woman could find a way to photograph powerful people using the toilet.*

Arianna walks slowly down the wooden steps. Shielding her eyes from the bright afternoon sun, she turns toward Clara. "Thank you for the coffee. I'll bring you the shots next week if I can. I'm going to approach the curator of the show I mentioned. Your house is perfect for it. "

In a low voice, Clara says, "I'm not promising anything."

Undaunted, Arianna holds up one hand with crossed fingers and strides toward the casino.

Clara locks the kitchen door and flops down on her bed. The visit started so well. Why did it end so badly? "You'd think taking pictures was the only thing in the world. That woman needs more balance in her life."

She frowns. Everyone wants her to *do* something—the wasps, Arianna, even the video store owner. She's overwhelmed. "Why can't people just leave me alone? We just got here! Where's Frank?" Instead, the scent of another female is in the house, something citrus and sharp mixed with the burglar's stink.

Lying with her hands behind her head, she thinks how Samantha would have been forty-nine now. Arianna looks about the same age, give or take. Would her daughter have been canny, driven, ambitious, like Arianna? When Samantha was nine and ten, she was already bookish, retiring, reading precociously about foreign countries. Samantha would never barge into someone's house like that. Even when she was eleven, she had better manners than that. Frank too. Frank is a gentleman.

Without warning, she bursts into tears.

Things are falling apart and they just got here. She gets out the Lysol to get rid of the smells, but the Lysol smells bad too. She opens the kitchen door to air out the house, but now flies come in through the broken screen. In confusion, she closes the door and sits at the table, fly swatter in hand. She pours herself a cup of cold coffee and sits back down, losing interest in the flies to watch the unruly wasps in their beef jerky jars that she just put on the table to distract herself.

They are particularly frantic this morning. She needs to feed them again. She gets the sugar water for the wasps, a peanut butter sandwich for herself. Holding the measuring cup, she's suddenly weeping over Darrell, something she hasn't done for a long time. He could help her now. They could be a team. She looks at the wasps, flailing about in the jars.

After Darrell died, she became a health food nut, probably because his death scared her. She didn't want to die so young like that. He was only thirty-five, dead of a massive heart attack on this very kitchen floor. So she turned to megavitamins, herbal teas, Ayurveda, homeopathy. Vegetarianism for herself, while Frank remained a stubborn carnivore. Prevention, prevention, prevention to this very day—everything to stay safe and alive. Staring now at the disheveled wasps, it seems her whole life has become one long attempt to hold off the inevitable march of worms through her skull.

Sitting at the table, something comes over her—a loosening, a desire to shout to the sky in the hot Nevada sun. She's tired—bone tired—of being prudent and sensible and gray, of holding back, holding in, guarding against God knows what. For heaven's sake, hasn't she done enough guarding all these years? What good has it done? An irresistible whisper rumples the air.

Roll the dice, kid. It's time to wake up. You've got nothing to lose.

Slowly she unscrews the lids of both beef jerky jars and lays them on the table. The wasps burst deliriously from their prisons and swarm the kitchen, tapping against cabinets, careening through the air, buzzing against the sunlit window over the sink. They spread through the house, exploring every nook in wild ellipses. Walking around with them, she concentrates on their joyous latticed hum.

Gradually she swallows the lump in her throat and wipes her eyes. A little smile lights her face. Will they like their new home? But the desert air will be a drying oven for them. Well then, she'll buy a humidifier, create Eugene air in here. They will be humidified house wasps. She smiles.

She sits down at the table and pours herself another cup of cold coffee in her old Greenpeace mug. A special wasp contingent gathers around her on the table, puffing their tails up and down, cleaning their wings with their legs. One by one, they tap against her face and hair and arms, one by one settle there, ruffling their wings and crawling gently on her orange T-shirt. Before long, all the wasps are perched on her. The design they make on her vaguely suggests a biomorphic space helmet with upper body armor. She laughs. A picture of her now would make the evening news, but she would keep that same picture in her dresser drawer, quiet and private. She closes her eyes, feels the wasps' feet gentle as elfin slippers padding over her. She almost dozes off under their delicate tapping. They are giving her a little massage, knocking on the doors of her skin, the drapery of her T-shirt.

Hello! they say. *We've come to pay a visit. What's new? We're fine. Thank you!*

They are little healers. They brush her and snaggle her and hum. They want her in their hive. They snuffle her smell into their smell memories so thoroughly that they'd know it anywhere, even in a crowd of ten million people. She smells like Jergens lotion, Prell shampoo, Secret deodorant, and Ivory soap. She can't smell any wasp smell. *Her* nose is too primitive. But she *hears* them—their rufflings, their languorous tizzies like grease spurts on a fire.

The wasps still cover her. She slowly gets up from the kitchen table, feeling much better. She sets out jar lids full of sugar water in each room—the three small bedrooms, living room, bathroom, kitchen. The wasps stay perched on her until they understand about the sugar lids being in every room. They leave her one by one to lazily take their fill of sugar water, then doze like overstuffed piglets on top of the refrigerator.

chapter 9

Frank appears for lunch looking haggard. He hasn't slept at the house for three days. He's probably been out gambling and partying with Scotty. No telling where he's been, and it's none of her business. He's a grown man. But she feels stiff around him, on guard. She holds herself tall.

He and his mother don't say much. Frank makes himself peanut butter and jelly, this time with two Dr. Peppers, so Clara knows he's really tired. She has her usual apple and cottage cheese with fresh black coffee in her old Greenpeace mug. Both have been too preoccupied to think of groceries. Silence reigns, broken only by the slick pages of *Time* magazine turning and the chewing of food.

She wants to tell Frank about Scotty's brief visit an hour ago. He had stopped by the house to offer her a part-time job greeting gamblers who come down on buses from southern Idaho twice a week. Amazed and amused, she accepted his offer. Maybe she'll meet someone, make some friends. She wonders what Frank would think.

Frank passes her the magazine. Not interested, she passes it back. Should she tell him about the break-in? What good would it do? He'd just worry and get in a worse mood than he's already in. She doesn't want him to say, "I told you so." He's frowning at the magazine. For about twenty-five years, wandering on Union Pacific, the whole country was his home, not this house. Even so, she's surprised to feel shy, even uncomfortable, now that they're actually here together. She wonders how he feels about *her* in such close proximity. She's afraid to ask.

"So Frank, what do you think?"

"About what?" He looks up.

"Jackpot. This place."

He looks back down at the magazine. "I might like it if I could get some sleep. Scotty knows how to get a little party going."

"How is he anyway?"

Frank looks at her without expression. "He doesn't look good. His third wife left him."

"Marcy? Oh, the poor man. Well, I didn't like her much."

"Keep it to yourself. He doesn't want it known yet."

"He's such a nice man. Why would anyone want to leave him?"

"Well, Mother"—his voice is sarcastic—"it's clear we don't know what goes on with Scotty and his wives."

His barbed tone unnerves her. She wants to connect with him so badly that she lacks good judgment when he gets like this. She plunges on, trying to keep a conversation going. "Scotty dropped by this morning. He asked me to be a greeter a couple days a week. Can you imagine?" Frank looks up, one eyebrow raised. She plunges on. "He was telling me about this waitress who's crazy about theater. Sometimes he lets her do these little performances in the casino. Short: three minutes max. She has a following. Have you seen her? I'd like to see one of her pieces." She's rattling on.

Frank is silent. He wishes she'd stop talking. He's got a bad hangover. "You know, Mother, it's really none of your business if I've met some waitress or not. But I'll tell you anyway. No. I haven't."

Clara is stricken. Of *course* she can't ask her grown son anything about a woman. But usually he's more accommodating toward her. "Sorry, Frank. I'm just intrigued that someone wants to do theater in this god-forsaken place."

"Yeah? Well, I wouldn't know—or care. Why don't you ask her yourself? And who says this place is god-forsaken? I like it here. No one puts on airs, the air is clean, the land is wide open. Lots of possibilities. People leave you alone." He glares into the magazine.

Meekly, she replies, "You're right—it's too early to make judgments. Sorry, Frank. Sorry." *You are a stupid woman, Clara Breckenridge. Why don't you just keep your mouth shut?*

Clenching his jaw, he puts his dishes on the sideboard and grimly returns to the magazine. They sit in silence. He can't ignore her presence, though he'd like to.

She's drinking her coffee, trying hard not to slurp. He hates slurping.

He jiggles his leg under the table. She's driving him crazy. Being around her and the old house for a week has made him remember things he usually keeps in deep freeze.

"So." He clears his throat, wanting to talk about *something*. "That was some trip we had."

She looks at him. He can see the hope in her eyes. "Yes, indeed," she says.

Long silence.

He decides to just say it. "On the road, I wondered why we never talked about Dad and Samantha all those years."

She puts her fork down, her face going white.

He won't stop. "You always changed the subject. I never

understood it. All those years, it was a taboo subject. Like when Bobby Kennedy got shot, I heard his family never talked about it." He stops, taking a deep breath.

She stammers. "What? Bobby Kennedy was five years later." She looks in her lap. "What do you mean we haven't talked about it? Haven't we talked about it?"

"No, Mother, we haven't. Not really. You always change the subject." He feels angry for some reason.

She looks down at her plate. "What's there to talk about? I don't know what to say." She blinks at him as if he were a strange new creature. "Why bring this up now?"

"I don't know, I've just been thinking about them. They weren't bad, you know. They were good. Good sister. Good dad. Things like that. Don'tcha think?" He's sarcastic now.

She feels a hammer strike her heart. "I know. Believe me, I know." Her eyes falter and drop.

A long silence opens between them. She does not want to pursue this topic. All these years, Samantha and Darrell stayed in her Brain Rooms as much as possible. She never wanted them tromping around in daylight. Especially if someone *else* invited them out.

He gets some water, sits down at the table, thumbs through a *USA Today,* skips an article on Armageddon cults. His mother is confusing him. Why *shouldn't* he talk about his own father and his own sister after all these years? His throat tightens. He studies a Smirnoff ad. Maybe it's really too late. Maybe he should just seal up his memories in a concrete box like she apparently does and throw it in the ocean. He's a fool to talk to her like this.

Nervously, she gets up to clear the dishes and swab the counters, thinking. *He bought it up with no warning. I never talked to a single person about Darrell and Samantha, only the wasps.* She almost pants with anguish as she wipes the counter, whispering to herself, her defenses thin and falling. *All these years, Clara, you've been so wrapped up with your own sorrow and guilt that you never even thought of healing your son's pain, your son's pain, your son's pain.* She wipes her eyes with her arm. *Selfish! You're so selfish, Clara!*

As her dishcloth slaps to and fro, she unintentionally rouses the wasps from their back counter perches, where they drowse after another mid-afternoon sugar run to the lids. Despite their glutted ease, the wasps have watched Frank ever since he came inside. Their quivering wings alert each other that Frank is in the house.

Frank and the wasps have a long history together. Swarming along the driveway, the wasps ignored him unless he got too close, which he did just to taunt them. Then they'd sting him on the neck—always just the neck. He would laugh. He wasn't allergic, so the stings quickly faded. But Clara always got very upset. She said the wasps wouldn't bother *him* if he wouldn't bother *them.* She said just ignore the wasps. But he didn't, couldn't. He had some vendetta against them. A testosterone challenge, she thought. He hated these corseted-looking creatures. To him, wasps performed no useful function. They just buzzed and caused trouble. Not like bees, who made honey and fertilized fruits, vegetables, and flowers.

And the wasps remember his smell—a mixture of almonds, honey, cinnamon, sometimes tobacco—and they remember the bitter smell of his hatred. The smells mean one thing: attack.

Two mini-swarms rise in the air, as if guided by a unified intelligence. They line up in small battalions on the old Kenmore range behind Frank's chair. He and Clara sit in a mild food stupor, both wanting to keep the peace but not knowing how. In a lazy dive-bomb maneuver, two wasps go for the back of Frank's neck and form a buzzing clump below his hairline. He feels a sour welt of pain and slaps at them as the first duo exits and the next duo tries to land but can't. Clara bolts up, flails her arms at them. Frank lunges from his chair, briefly mesmerized with pain, swatting at the insects, his sleepy gray eyes flashing with anger.

"You let wasps out *in the house?* Are you *crazy?* What's the matter with you?"

"You just have to shield your neck, Frank. They always go for your neck. You know as well as I do they leave you alone if you don't nosy in on them."

"Did I bother them? Did I *bother* them?" Frank shouts from his bedroom, where she hears him unzipping a suitcase.

She's ruined everything. Full of anguish, she goes to the sink and blindly washes all the silverware with trembling hands, forgetting that she washed it yesterday. She glares at a tatty beige motel visible from the kitchen window. "They could at least *paint* it," she snaps. Drying her hands, she swats at the wasps, still flying around in agitated swarms. "Get away!" she shouts. They form a menacing halo around *her* head.

She flops down at the table and roars, "Get away! Now!" The wasps retreat to the top of the refrigerator. A drab-colored peacekeeper lands on her arm, fanning its wings to calm her. She brushes it away, glares at all of them. "You have to learn house rules! You can't act crazy like this!"

In the kitchen doorway, Frank laughs bitterly. "That's just fine then, Mother. You and your wasp pals can chat all day long. I'm outta here. You knew I wouldn't be living with you anyway, and I'll be damned if I'm living with wasps."

He throws his belongings into two suitcases, slams out the door, and guns the trailer cab over to Scotty's. He's furiously chewing three sticks of Juicy Fruit. "She's going off the deep end," he mumbles. "I should have known."

He shakes his head, remembering the trip. "Talking to them every night at rest stops. Brushing her hair and *singing* to them, for Christ's sake–'Stranger in Paradise,' for the love of God. Swearing she even had a purple wasp to protect her."

"You're an intelligent woman, Mother," he had snapped. "Gimme a break. You know wasps aren't purple." She had clammed up then and wouldn't talk to him for two hundred miles. At rest stops, she sat at a different picnic table and walked in different parts of the lawn than he did.

Gingerly, he touches the stings on the back of his neck and screeches to a halt in front of Scotty's house. "Driving with her all that way was bad enough," he mumbles darkly. "I need the company of a clear-headed man."

But Scotty isn't home, and Frank doesn't have a key. He slumps inside the trailer cab. He could go over to Desert Dan's but he doesn't feel like it. On the other hand, maybe he does.

The purple wasp has twenty-nine days left.

chapter 5

Frank was just going to have a drink or two and then try to find Scotty. Scotty's one slippery guy these days, always going off somewhere, having a meeting, looking exhausted, avoiding his old friend, it seems. You need an appointment book to see Scotty. It's all very mysterious.

But the woman at the bar is alone and has just signaled the bartender for a second Cosmo. She's dressed too nicely for Desert Dan's—beige linen suit, white silk blouse, nails manicured in a neutral shade, plus Frank knows an expensive haircut when he sees it—blunt cut, layered in some way he knows is current. He absorbs her beautiful sad blue eyes and trim figure. What makes him approach her is the proverbial deer in the headlights look she gives the bartender when she orders the second drink.

He knows then she probably needs the alcohol for some sad, urgent reason. So Frank, Mr. Fix-it Man in Levi's and a T-shirt, goes over and sits next to her on the bar stool and orders a whiskey straight up. At first neither speaks. She stirs her drink with the little swizzle stick. He reaches for the bowl of peanuts, swings it over toward her.

"Care for some?" he asks softly.

"No, thanks," she says. She says "thanks" like "tanks," the ending *ks* hitting hard. This interests him. She wasn't born here.

She has a thin, hard air about her, hunched over her drink, trying to relax, drinking the second Cosmo faster than if she were already relaxed. She starts to take off her jacket. Their eyes meet. He holds the jacket as she takes it off. His hand brushes against the soft pale skin of her arms. A shiver runs up his spine. "Tanks," she says again in that interesting way. She lays the jacket across her lap. They are quiet. Then she says, "Please don't ask where I'm from. Yes, I have an accent, and yes, I'm from Germany"—she says "Chermany"—"and yes, I'm leaving tomorrow. Just passing through." She clams up. He looks at her in the mirror. She looks defiantly back at him.

He lowers his gaze, finishes his whiskey, orders another, and finally says, "I'm not here for long either." They sit in silence. It's comfortable sitting here with this enigmatic woman, as alluring to him as an endangered butterfly. "So, what's your name, beautiful woman?"

Her face softening, she looks back at him in the mirror, and he knows he's in. Her eyes flicker; her blue eyes are luminous. "Gretchen." She looks away.

"Frank," he says a beat later.

He leans back on the bar stool, his pulse rising. He smiles at her, dimples creasing his cheeks. Her smile is reluctant. She has small, even, very white teeth. Her blouse is short-sleeved. He wants to touch her arm again, so he moves his arm over a little, reaching for the peanuts, and feels the electric charge of early contact. She looks a little startled but doesn't move her arm away. He's moving into his second whiskey, and she's ready for her third Cosmo.

"So, Mr. American Man, Mr. Frank, how do you spend your days?"

He takes his time answering. "I've done lots of things, been lots of places. I'm with Union Pacific at the moment." He watches her. "Good way to see the country, meet interesting people. Like now." He lets the compliment sink in.

Her face changes subtly. She smiles. "That's why I left Chermany. To see the States. The world. Go all over. Not call any place home." She stops, swallows hard. The corners of her mouth quiver.

They sit in silence. Something is really bothering her. He moves his hand closer to hers. She doesn't move it away. He takes her hand. Their hands are warm together. After a moment that somehow contains solace, she says she has to drive to Boise in the morning, that she's tired. He gives her a questioning look; she nods.

They leave the bar together. Everything now has an air of inevitability. Up in her room, she's done considerable laying-in of booze. Johnny Walker Black, Jack Daniels on the dresser. He gets the ice bucket filled. She pours them both whiskeys, hers with ice. They sit on the small couch, arms touching, talking about nothing, the weather, different parts of the country, traveling. Behind it all is rising tension. He puts his arm around her, feels her relax.

He's getting excited, knows to calm himself. She smells of something floral and expensive. Their kisses are a little shaky, intense. In due time they move to the bed. Talking brokenly now and crying, she buries her face in his neck. She had fallen for her boss, a partner in the San Francisco law firm where she worked. Married. Not willing to divorce. The guy had just dumped her a few days ago as the office closed for the day. "I really loved him," she says, near to sobbing. He tries to soothe her. "Don't worry. You'll find someone much better, someone who will treat you right."

She looks at him. They are ready. And it's good. Very good.

But afterward, he feels the familiar emptiness. He looks over at her. She has the same sad face he saw at the bar. He'll never see her again, but it upsets him to see her looking sad like that. He looks away. They grip each other's hands.

For years he's been this wanderer, this sex machine. He had to have sex every day or he couldn't sleep. Got irritable, jumpy. It was an itch, an addiction. To get it, he was skilled, calculating, sensitive. Underneath, he felt a certain anger, impatience, or worse, a sadness that bubbled up just as he finished with the Woman of the Day.

He doesn't know what's happening to him. For the last few years, he's felt empty and depressed most of the time. The sex wasn't helping as much. Even more confusing is when—like now—he sees the same sad look on the woman's face. They're looking for the same thing he is. It's all a muddle and a mystery.

When he was a kid, maybe eight, he heard low music coming from the living room late one night. He crept outside his room, down the hall, to see. His parents were dancing to music from the portable phonograph. They were kissing, their mouths moving together as if they were chewing on something. It scared him a little, they were so intent. Later, they crept outside to sit in the lawn swing and smoke their cigarettes, punctuating their quiet talk with the hands holding the cigarettes. His parents' moving hands, outlined by flame, made a magic circle. The child watched and felt with a stab of his heart that he would never be allowed inside that magic circle with them. And it was true.

He had felt that exclusion his whole life. While his father still lived, Frank watched his parents every day as they made little jokes he didn't understand, as they touched each other's hair or hands or face to emphasize something they were talking about, as they whispered to each other or quietly laughed. It jars him to remember this now, in his forties. Gretchen is looking for her own magic circle. Until she finds it, she's just another passing soul, sad like him.

She has already passed out. In despair and relief, he turns over and falls asleep. A little before three, he wakes up, dresses, and lets himself out the door.

He wakes in his own bed when it's already hot. Clara is out somewhere; the wasps are nowhere in sight. Cranky and tired, he turns on the fan and fixes himself a mug of strong black coffee and puts a couple of Entenmann's donuts on a plate. At the table he's cursing himself. He didn't come to Jackpot to service a bunch of sad women. Been there, done that. What did he come here for then? Scotty? Himself? Pause. Someone else?

Later that morning, he sees Gretchen get into a black Mercedes and head north, screeching her tires for effect.

chapter 6

After Frank got stung and stormed out, Clara sat unmoving at the kitchen table, trying to put her thoughts in order.

1. She had just refused her son's desire to talk about something important. But she *came* to this god-forsaken place to talk about important things with him before she dies.

2. She needs the wasps around her, but they are driving her son away.

3. She shouldn't have let the wasps out, but they can't stay in the jars forever.

4. She won't abandon the wasps to the howling winds, but she didn't plan what to do with them once she got to Jackpot.

5. Why did they have to sting him? He wasn't *doing* anything! She's got to do something about them—she's got to see her son!

6. What's happening to her orderly life? She didn't come to Jackpot to have her life fall apart. Is this what the desert does to a person?

Groaning, she lies down on her bed.

Each thing Clara experiences builds its own little room in her brain and wires itself to memory, the central screening room. Some rooms are more walled off than others. A few are fortresses. The day of Samantha's death, for instance, is so upsetting that she can't fully revisit it. It's locked up tight, and that's her problem. It's getting moldy and infected.

Brain Rooms contain the whole of her life. Sometimes these rooms have thin walls that flap and break and spill into the room next door. Then these adjacent memories get all jumbled up, sending out their incendiary contents to jam up transmission lines between other Brain Rooms. Sometimes these flapping walls feel like herds of wild broncos tearing up the shrubbery. She's got headaches nearly all the time now. Isn't sleeping. Has to take little naps just to get through the day.

And those wasp stings on her forehead are still bothering her. The unhealed stings seem to be getting bigger. It feels like something is working on her, burrowing. This has to be her imagination.

After Frank stormed out, the Demon Death door in her brain flew open and stays open. *Let it bang and carry on,* she thinks, staring at the ceiling from her bed.

The day Samantha died, Clara found Frank in the hall full of swarming kids at the end of the school day. He was only nine. Her hands shook, her face was streaked with tears. His eyes got wide, seeing his mother like that.

"Samantha has been in an accident," she said quietly. "I'm going to the hospital, and Abigail will come to pick you up. You must wait in the principal's office until Abigail gets here."

Staring at her, he whimpered, "But I want to go with *youuu.*"

"Not now, sweetheart," she said firmly. "I'll pick you up as soon as I can."

He was so scared. His father had died just four months earlier. He could hardly comprehend that something terrible had happened to his sister too. But he obediently played Legos at Abigail's until his mother came back, pale and distraught.

At the funeral, the dirt hole for the casket was covered with fake grass. Clara welcomed this subterfuge, but the fluorescent grass was scary to Frank. "What's all that shiny plastic for the grass? Where's the real grass? Why is the lid closed? Samantha can't breathe in there."

Numb, Clara looked at him. "It has to be closed. It's better that way." She couldn't face the details of death with him, at least not then.

He started to cry. He let her put her arms around him just that once. Back home, he ran to his room and slammed the door.

Every night, Frank hid in his room and Clara sat like a statue in the living room. Some Demon that steals *only those we love most* had a special hankering for her family's blood—that seemed clear. This idea was the only way Clara could endure her double loss, Samantha at eleven, Darrell at thirty-five. To fool the Demon, Clara had to mount a special disguise to keep Demon Death from taking *Frank too*. So she made his favorites: meat loaf, fried chicken, chocolate chip cookies. She kept a clean house and his clothes mended, helped him too much with homework, and later refused to let him try out for football. She wanted to corral him somehow, wrap him up in cellophane—keep him from the terrors of the living world.

But she never really *talked* to him, never *explained* what she was doing. Outwardly she was a caring Betty Crocker mom, but emotionally she was stiff as a fence post around him. She wouldn't let herself kiss or hug him for fear Demon Death would see how much she loved him and take him away. She practiced all this restraint so the Demon would get bored and *flee* her cursed house!—go steal spouses and babies from *other* people who foolishly had their hearts throbbing right there on their sleeves where everyone could see. Everyone knows that too much public display of feeling invites the Evil Eye—better known as Demon Death Red Alert Attack Mode.

It was no use. She couldn't keep the world away. Instead of cellophane, Frank chose raw contact. After the double deaths, he morphed from a quiet, industrious little kid into a wild boy. In fourth and fifth grades, he stole bikes and threw them in dumpsters, took a paint scraper to car exteriors, broke store windows and stole merchandise from the exposed window displays. The police talked to Frank and his mother, getting more stern each time. They knew he'd lost a dad and a sister, but the boy just had to buck up. They found stolen merchandise in the garage. His grades fell. There was some question of whether he would pass fifth grade.

Distraught, Clara went to his teacher, Mrs. Beaumont, a placid woman whose mouth receded into her several chins. "He'll be all right," said Mrs. Beaumont in a honeyed voice. "He's just got to work it out."

Clara swallowed hard, gunned her car home, and rocked all evening in her rocker. How could Mrs. Beaumont be so calm, like a Buddhist nun floating above the world? Did she have any children herself? Every night, Clara sat in the living room, needing to feel her beating heart as proof she was still alive instead of burning in a fiery pit.

Losing half her family made her mute, maybe nuts. She withdrew from Frank so much it was cruel. All those years. She didn't realize. They couldn't talk. How could she be so stupid? Frank didn't know why she didn't talk to him, why they never had any fun together.

Frank's wildness continued into high school. He always liked girls, had constant girlfriends. Girls were more important than grades. *That* upset her. But nothing upset her more than the affair he had with the pretty new chemistry teacher, Alice Martin, when he was three months shy of graduation in 1972. Frank! Her son! With a teacher! When Clara herself was a teacher! She heard it through the grapevine.

Frank got expelled, and Alice Martin got fired. This was her third teaching job, and here she was only twenty-six—that was the scuttlebutt. Alice's specialty was sex with her students. Clara stayed home from school three days from the shock of it. Frank stayed with Scotty for two weeks after he saw Clara weeping in her rocker. The Big Silence returned when he came back home from Scotty's. The principal wouldn't let Frank be in graduation; he got his diploma in the mail. Among his friends, of course, he was deemed a master stud. Clara heard them laughing about it outside the house one day and she covered her ears. All these years, Frank and his mother never once spoke of this affair, like they didn't speak of so many things. Love and fear made her tongue-tied. Frank just wanted to get away.

But she had a living son. He was still alive. No matter what, the need to fool Demon Death was always on her mind. Each day she had to make the Demon think her love for Frank was garden variety, not volcanic and total. Then the Demon would lose interest in Frank and she could keep one quarter of her family. Was that too much to ask?

The purple wasps thought she'd made a devil's bargain with her silences. But Clara wouldn't listen.

Frank, of course, didn't understand the tangled subtleties of mother love. Missing something essential from his mother, something he couldn't put into words, he always felt angry and disappointed around her but didn't know why. The upshot was he left her through his wanderings, almost as surely as Darrell and Samantha left her through death.

He hitchhiked away from his mother's sad home in 1972, knowing his high draft number would keep him out of Vietnam. His goal was Montana, because he'd never been there. A trucker's tip landed him in Idaho instead, wrangling horses and branding sheep at a family-owned guest ranch in the Sawtooth Mountains. Whispers spread of the fringe benefits he offered female guests whose husbands were conveniently away on long pack trips in the Sawtooth wilderness. The wives settled for short pack trips and the Saturday night dance at the Stanley Rod and Gun Club. In the winter, he taught skiing at Sun Valley. After fourteen years of this, he got a job on Union Pacific and worked his way up to chief engineer. Like his restless mentor Alice Martin, he got to see the country.

Now in his forties, every route seemed the same—same cities, same meals, same restaurants, same lines used on any number of women, their bodies the same shapely walls of flesh—scented, lightly furred, skilled, even athletic in the sex act, an exertion that never opened the door to the secret place he unknowingly sought for years.

He's wasting his life. He wants to find something for himself that has nothing to do with a woman. With his aunt's lucky inheritance, he fled to his old friend Scotty, who's like a brother to him. But he sees now that Scotty's just as lost as he is—and sick.

28 days left.

After Gretchen screeches up the highway, Frank drives the trailer cab down to Salmon Falls Creek, a little turnoff on the highway.

It's deserted, just as he thought it would be. Just the sound of water from an itty-bitty creek. He gets the gnarled burl from his glove compartment. He found it in the front yard the morning he and Clara set out for Jackpot. For years he's made small sculptures from wood scraps he'd find at lumber yards—oak, cedar, walnut—hunks of wood a portable six or eight inches, a size suitable for his roving way of life. His women friends seemed to like what he made. Working with wood always helps him think.

He gets his leather case of carving tools from under the seat—chisel, carving knife, spoon gouger, wood veiner. Most days (or nights) since they got here, Frank sculpts things at Salmon Falls Creek. He sits in the passenger seat wearing his headlamp, the cutting board on his lap as he carves and chisels, trying to get a shape that interests him, but the burl remains an ugly lump. Frustrated, he slams out of the trailer cab and walks around the creek area, smoking a cigarette.

Things are at a standstill. He and his mother have been in Jackpot six days now, and he's only spent two nights at her house. He's bunking at Scotty's because of the wasp stings, but Scotty's never there. He wants to get Scotty to a doctor, but Scotty's apparently in hiding. He wants to get Clara settled, but they just sit around in painful silence or talk about the weather.

Clara is drinking coffee at the kitchen table. The wasps keep landing on her head, buzzing angrily. "Leave me alone," she says, batting them away. "I set you free and you just bother me."

The purple wasp is losing patience. "Look, you've got twenty-eight days left to get some kind of deliverance from the things that have haunted you. I die in twenty-eight days, whether you like it or not. That's the end of my life cycle. It could be the start of a whole new cycle in *your* life. Or you can keep stalling like you've done for almost forty years. So, what'll it be?"

She explodes. "Believe me, I *know* time's passing. I'm *already* tired of the camp toilet and the bottled water showers. But nothing's settled with Frank. How can I buy a lot for my house and connect the utilities when he might vanish tomorrow? I can't find him. I can't talk to him. He's always gone."

She gets up from the kitchen table and flops onto her worn couch, her arms folded, holding back tears. She yearns for her son. Maybe she'll go looking for him. She keeps hoping he'll come through the door. Surely this stalemate can't last. She didn't come here for all this nonsense. The purple wasp is the only creature who still talks to her. Even the nosy photographer has vanished.

Refreshed after a short walk near Salmon Falls Creek, Frank climbs back into the trailer cab. He sets the cutting board back on his lap and puts the burl on the cutting board. He sits there and looks at it. And looks at it. Applies chisel here, veiner there. He's never worked on a burl before. Curdled deformed wood. Finally a rough form emerges—a gnarled pair of eyes, branching heavy eyebrows—something like the top half of a bulging skull. He sits back and opens the window. "OK, a partial skull. I can work with that." His mind goes pleasantly blank.

Frank catches Scotty just as he's ducking into his office. "Where in hell have you been, big guy? You've been playing hide and seek ever since I got here."

They slap each other on the back, and Scotty motions Frank into his office with its big desk and leather chairs. As they settle themselves, Frank takes a good look at his old friend.

He's only seen Scotty for a few nights of serious drinking after he told Frank his third wife just left him. He helped Frank unpack the U-Haul that first morning when they drove the house across the highway to the vacant lot. But Scotty was panting and sweating before they finished unloading, so Frank and Clara finished the job by themselves.

Seeing Scotty labor like that made it painfully obvious to Frank that something was not right with his friend. In the quiet of the office, he finally lets himself see that Scotty has lost a lot of weight. His trousers hang on him, the skin around his neck is sagging, he has bags under his eyes. Back in Eugene, he was chubby and strong.

With false cheer, Frank says, "So, what's up, my man? How the hell are you?"

Scotty leans back in his chair, his legs crossed on the desk. "Well, I'll tell you, Frank. It's one damned thing after another. I'm always running around. It never stops." Sighing, he swings his chair around, reaches into a cabinet behind him, and brings out a bottle of Jack Daniels. "Have a nip?"

"Ah sure, Scotty."

Scotty rises laboriously from his chair and makes two whiskeys on the rocks. After a silence broken only by the clink of ice, he continues. "I thought this would be the capper, you know—this business. It's a good business, I can't deny that. Maybe I'm just getting old. But I'd like to enjoy myself a little before I turn in the key for good. Is that so bad? I've been working straight through since high school." He takes a healthy swallow. "So, the big secret is I'm thinking Colorado or New Mexico. Buy me a multiplex or a chain of Laundromats. That wouldn't be so bad, now would it?" He waves his glass at Frank. "Want to come along?"

Frank looks at him in surprise. "You've got the biggest casino outside Reno, right? Why would you want to give up a sure moneymaker?"

Scotty shrugs and looks tiredly at him. "You want to buy it, Frank?"

chapter 7

The busload of gamblers pulls into Desert Dan's parking lot around three o'clock. Still jarred by this rainless, sun-drenched place, Clara watches the passengers disembark. Mostly pudgy and white, a few Latinos and Chinese, they look disoriented, some clutching small paper bags full of change. Kind-faced women wear Bermuda shorts, their thigh skin accordion-pleated around their knees. Still grumpy about Frank's wasp stings and their inability to talk, Clara forces a smile and greets these people in her red Desert Dan's sun visor and T-shirt and her old Levi's. She's never worn a sun visor before. Words written on clothing make her feel like a billboard. This is her first day as a greeter for visitors who come by bus twice a week from southern Idaho— Jerome, Hazelton, Burley, Twin Falls. Clara's supposed to make sure they don't wander off to Scotty's competitors.

She decides to get into the spirit of the thing. She pumps her arms with crossing guard gestures toward the casino, saying firmly, "Welcome to Desert Dan's." But the passengers mill about, some heading off to Rodman's Hide-Away and the Lucky Clover across the highway. Scotty has coached her. "Free dinner pass after four games of keno," she shouts. "Half-price late owl lunch going on right now!"

The people head back in the right direction—all except for

two people in their early twenties arguing near the bus. "Look Edie, I told you, it's not Vegas. It's just this stupid pit stop, OK?" The rubbery young guy, some part of him always in motion, has a video camera slung over his shoulder.

The tall, striking girl leers down at him with a cross-eyed pout. "Just be quiet, OK, Neil? For one fucking second in your life, can you just shut up?"

An older man, sunburned except for his white forehead, hovers nearby with a resigned air and watches the young people tangle.

The girl has a scar extending the length of her right forearm. The scar is tattooed with black roses. The scar is ragged and lumpy, as if done by a quack. The forearm is unnaturally narrow; a bone is missing. She has the barest, whitest midriff Clara has ever seen. A diamond-studded gold bar is anchored to one side of her spectacular, saucer-like navel. Fake diamond studs dot her tongue, nose, and ears, and two gold rings pierce her left eyebrow. Her bleached white hair with black roots is short like a boy's. Her shapely figure, encased in tight black capris and a black halter top, is alarmingly on display. Clara feels instantly protective, wants to put a poncho over the girl's head.

The girl strides impatiently toward the casino. Neil and the older man doggedly follow. Clara catches up, positions herself between the girl and the two men. "Hi there, I'm Clara Breckenridge. Welcome to Desert Dan's."

The girl stops and snorts, her yellow-green cat eyes fixed on Clara as if she were an oddly disturbing anthropological specimen. Her brother, in a constant jitter, looks past Clara—scouting footage shots, she guesses. The older man, his sunburned cheeks raw, accepts Clara like rain, his face relaxing into a smile.

"Hi there," he says with a little salute. "Jim Porter here." He points to the young people rapidly moving away from them. "That's my niece Edie and my nephew Neil. They're visiting from Los Angeles. Neil's studying movies someplace in Hollywood. Edie's studying art," he adds in bewilderment.

Clara sees Edie's capris are cut so low that anyone can get a hint of what lies south. "Oh, honey," she calls out impulsively, "watch out for those cowboys."

Edie stops, comes back, looks coolly down at Clara, who is only five foot two, and says in measured tones, "Grandma, I don't need any help. *At* all." She snorts again and turns away. Neil is filming this exchange. Edie grabs the lens end, violently jerking it away. "Wouldja just cut it out, motherfucker?"

Neil smirks at Clara. "See what we have to put up with? My sister's a bitch every day of her life just because we're *poor orphans*," he says in falsetto tones, as if he's used to trading on this fact.

Jim Porter says, "I wish you two would mind your manners. This woman has done nothing to you. Why don't you apologize for being so rude?"

Edie resumes her fast walk toward the casino lobby. Neil mumbles "sorry" and follows behind his sister. They disappear into the casino.

Clara clasps her hands together in confusion. It's true, no one has been so rude to her in a long time. Helplessly, she asks herself what if Samantha had turned out like Edie, insulting Frank, disrespecting Clara, getting herself pierced and decked out like that. But that's how they dress these days, she corrects herself. It's the *attitude* that upsets her. Edie's probably in her early twenties. Samantha would've been forty-nine, old enough to be Edie's mother. She begins to tremble—she can't keep comparing every young woman to Samantha or she'll end up insane.

Jim Porter is saying, "Sorry my niece and nephew are so rude. Edie's a firecracker. No telling what she might do. I worry about them."

Without warning, he takes a tumble on the blacktop, badly scraping his elbows and hands. Embarrassed, he pulls himself up. Clara settles him on a bench inside, gets a security person to clean and bandage Porter's scrapes, gives him water. Shaken, Porter leans toward her, as if his fall has purchased sudden intimacy.

"Those kids act like spoiled brats—but they've had a hard time. They *are* orphans, just like Neil said." He has her attention now. "My brother always had a vicious temper. He and the kids' mom were drinkers. One night on a two-day bender, he took out his .45 and shot her. The kids were standing right there—teenagers! My brother disappeared—left the country is my guess—so my sister down there in Long Beach finished raising them, but she had her own problems and nothing good came of it. They're both just lost kids trying to act tough. I send them money now that they're on their own. At least they're both in some kind of school." Sighing, he leans against the wall. "Sorry, Clara, I get a little dustup and you can't shut me up."

She pats his arm. "Don't worry, Jim. It's all right."

He leans back on the bench and closes his eyes, so Clara gets up to pace the slot machine aisles, looking for Edie. Despite Jim's story, she's still not sure if she feels protective or wary after the girl's rudeness. She finds Edie in front of the giant progressive Wheel of Fortune machine, quickly stuffing in silver dollar tokens, walking away bored and sullen-looking when her money runs out. Men of all ages pause from gambling to stare—some with more subtlety than others—at her deformed arm and white skin and firm, round breasts. She gambles and languidly strolls the slot machine aisles. A security guard cards her.

"I'm twenty-one," she snarls, dragging a driver's license from her beaded chartreuse drawstring shoulder purse. She folds her mismatched arms across her chest and looks away from the hapless enforcer. He stares at her and hands it back. Scowling, she resumes her bored saunter, her eyes blank and mean. Under the casino lighting, her bone-white skin absorbs thick powdery light. She looks like an alien or someone with a terminal illness. "Fuck off, cowboy," and "Get lost, grandpa," pepper the air around her. She barely glances at Clara.

Nothing and no one interests her.

Until she gets to the blackjack table.

Edie stops to watch this man crouched at the table with his chips. His eyelashes are long and curled like a girl's, his nose thin like a weasel's or a French aristocrat's. Something catches in her throat. Coughing, Edie covers her mouth and can't stop staring. This tall, gaunt man with the big Adam's apple, long black hair, skin pocked with acne scars—this man rattles her breath. Edie's eyes widen; the pupils dilate. She's mesmerized, Clara can tell. The man gestures the dealer like he's swimming underwater. His eyes flash and flare like little spy cameras as he watches people slap their cards on the table. Edie licks her lips. To her he looks delicious, a bad boy through and through.

Clara's staring too. That crouch, that posture, that hanging hair (needs washing!), that man pushing thirty who lives on Ding Dongs and root beer (he left trash)—Clara would know him anywhere. It's the guy who broke into her house.

She's found him.

He didn't make himself very scarce.

◈

Turns out the surveillance booth is watching the skinny guy too. He's got a sleepy-looking partner with a fat face. In the short time they've been working the table together, security has noticed gestures between them that could be suspicious. His partner has won a disproportionate amount. Maybe accidental, probably not.

The skinny guy orders a whiskey neat from the waitress. She cards him. Security sees this, contacts the waitress, asks his name. "Dawson Barth," she says quietly. Security runs a quick check. He's got several aliases and a record, but nothing current on him. Security decides to just keep watch for now.

Dawson only wants a couple hundred bucks. He's not stupid. After cleaning out his partner, whom he met in the parking lot, he'll do a last-ditch hunt for his vanished mother in Reno where she left him, and then he will disappear forever into the sprawling limbo of Los Angeles.

Turns out his partner doesn't want to share. After twenty-five minutes and six hundred dollars to the good, the partner mumbles he's got to piss and slips his chips quick as a gazelle into a drawstring bag.

Helplessly, so as not to create a scene, Dawson watches the guy cash in his chips at the cage and almost run to the parking lot. Dawson tries to keep his face a mask, but his stomach clenches as he grips the cards. He's got to bet everything now. He found a twenty in the glove compartment. It's all he has.

Edie's eyes are locked on this tall guy and his pale skin. She sucks in her stomach. Her breasts seem to swell beneath her black halter top, her nipples perk up, her lips flush. Her body moves like water toward Dawson, but Edie's not aware of what her body is doing, only of heat. Clara sees these signs, remembers them from long ago—does anyone ever forget? In some dreaming, underwater way, Edie looks like she's been waiting for Dawson Barth all her twenty-one years. She's shaking.

So is Clara, knowing she can't protect this young woman. Some residual image of Samantha flashes before her eyes until it fades into darkness. *My baby.*

Dawson feels someone's eyes on him, looks beyond the cards and flinches, seeing Clara. Standing five feet away, Clara stares right through him with those endless brown eyes of hers. Spit flows to his mouth. He wants to spit. It's the old lady with the strawberry mole and the haunted house. He looks down at the green felt table, remembering. He knows the bumpy feel of the pockmarked siding. He remembers the rock smashing her window, the rickety sewing cabinet quivering after he hoisted himself through the window, the *clink* of a flimsy doodad he broke on the coffee table, the kitchen drawers full of dish towels but no cash, not even a penny in the kitchen canisters. He didn't take anything. He's done nothing wrong. Nobody here can say he's a robber.

He's terrified and furious at the way Clara's looking at him. Her eyes are alert, without malice. She's a ghost from a world whose doors have closed to him.

Clara sees him swipe at his nose with a Kleenex. His nose is red. He's either got a cold or allergies. *Allerest,* she thinks helplessly. *He needs Allerest.* She sees his terrified look, how he suddenly looks twelve, like he needs his mother. *Don't fold now, old girl.*

She comes right up to him at the table, breathes into his ear. "I want to talk to you. About what you did the other night." He could be one of her students, now grown up and turning bad. Her voice is firm.

He shrinks from her. His skin gets goose bumps. "Get away,

old lady. You bother the air here." He speaks low, his voice adenoidal. The sudden shine in his eyes embarrasses him.

She's mystified, touched. *What's he doing here in the casino? Is that tears? He's lost.*

"Hey Dawson, stay mellow, buddy," says the guy who heard the waitress give his name to security.

Furious, Dawson tells himself to stay cool. *It's not worth it.* He and the others lower their eyes.

For a while, he only sees the game. Win. Lose. Draw. *Just concentrate.*

Clara steps into the background. She can wait. So, his name is Dawson. Why does her heart go out to this man who insults her and then gets tears in his eyes?

Finally composed, Dawson looks up and sees Edie staring at him with a little smile. Edie, waiting so patiently. Hands on hips, her damaged arm breaks the symmetry of her pose. Her eyes burn a laser hole right through his brain. Clara sees his stunned look. Edie sighs. At last she can enter the tide that draws her so strongly.

He salivates, swallows, hypnotized by her surly, chemical blondness, her raised nipples, her expanse of skin, her cat green eyes that don't even blink, her freaky arm with black rose tattoos, her sunless arched body.

The air between them trembles. Anyone can see it.

His concentration lost forever from the game, forgetting Clara, forgetting his stupid partner's betrayal (who could possibly be bothered by these trivial things?), he jerks his head slightly up, signaling Edie to step closer. Hips swaying, Edie weaves toward him. Her eyes glisten.

"Hello," she says through the smoky haze at the table.

"Sit down, beautiful," Dawson says, yielding his chair.

chapter 8

Sitting at the kitchen table again, Clara rifles her hair with strong fingers until it snarls. She counts on her fingers: "I have my son, my house, my breathing, my wasps. I have everything that's important. I can't get involved with these people. Dawson and Edie are trouble."

Silence, more coffee.

She exclaims, "Edie could end up just like Samantha, dead on some road. She has no mother or father." Straining, she relocks Samantha's central dungeon in the back of her head. The key turns hard, like a cramping blood vessel.

The trouble is Nevada, she decides. In Eugene, her life was starched, thin, regulated. Nothing crazy. After all the dying and Frank leaving home, she knew how every minute of every day would unfold. She had her teaching until 1993. She had Frank's occasional visits with their awkward silences and self-conscious warmth, an ocean of withheld feeling between them. Those visits were all she really had. Oh, she had her magnificent lilacs—and the wasps carrying on every day. And her volunteering—at the library stacking books; at a hospice, where she sang old songs and got patients to talk if they could; at city hall where she redirected lost visitors; at a shelter for abused women where she got them jobs and housing. On the streets, she ran into her ex-students who seemed happy to see her. Sometimes she and Abigail went to Ashland to see summer Shakespeare. She had regular bridge games with Abigail and Abigail's sister Susannah, weekly lunches at the River Road Coffee Shop (where she got the beef jerky jars), petition drives with Abigail at Safeway, where they set up a card table for any number of causes over the years: reduced class sizes, Oregon forest restoration, voter registration, objection to the inevitable shopping mall. It wasn't as if she had nothing to do.

She gets up to wipe off the counter.

But those things just filled time.

She could have been a marionette.

Something was always missing. She gave up real life—heart-pounding, hands-sweating life—in 1963. She always knew this.

Well, she wants it back, the chaos and glory of life, if only for a week or a day. With Frank.

So DO something, Clara. You've got to get him in the door again. God, you are slow-witted. How did you ever get through college?

A cloud of wasps circles her head like a ceiling fan. They understand the same thing she does: Her son must feel safe in this house before anything else can happen.

But the wasps always want to sting him. On the neck.

She runs into her bedroom and snatches her old Willamette Elementary School Crossing Guard T-shirt from the drawer. It's faded yellow with black letters. She sits on the bed and cuts five inches off the bottom with her pinking shears. She puts it over her head and looks in the mirror. The rest of it drapes over her shoulders. It's her only souvenir from the adult crossing guard program she started after Samantha died. This butchered relic will protect Frank's neck when he finally comes to see her again. The wasps always go for his neck.

Feeling energetic, she Windexes the beveled mirror over her dresser, dusts the framed family pictures, takes the ratty lambswool rug out for a shake, puts it back beside her bed. She sits in the oak rocker and finishes a puzzle in the *New York Times* crossword puzzle book, listening to music from the '40s and '50s on the scratchy radio (it survived Dawson's manhandling).

She gets up to fill her mug with Sparkletts water, looking trancelike out the window as she drinks.

Dawson and Edie emerge from room eight of the rundown Sagebrush Motel.

"Oh, dear God."

Vampire pale, they move slowly, hands low on each other's buttocks, their sinewy bodies sheathed in black. Edie's cropped hair is askew, Dawson's long hair in tangles. Clara stands transfixed. Trading sloppy kisses, they feed coins into a vending machine and glide back to room eight with several cans of soda and a cardboard bucket of ice.

She feels a mixture of fear and fascination. She knows what's going on in that room. They are having so much sex they're probably dizzy and exhausted, and for heavens' sake, she doesn't even want to think about it. She thumps her Teacher of the Year mug down on the kitchen counter. Her Dream Jar isn't working! She had already stuffed Dawson into it—but the jar jumped out of its cubicle and shattered on her forehead. Now Dawson's on the loose. With Edie!

The purple wasp flies in circles and makes passes at her forehead. *Now you're in for it, baby. Your lollygagging days are over.*

She gives the wasp a dull look of recognition. She's afraid Dawson and Edie are going to come over here and get her because the skin on her hands is mottled and her bones are lighter than theirs and sex is not on the agenda for her, not like it is for them, and their hidden skin is smooth like a baby's and they don't even realize how beautiful their unmarked skin is, but one day their skin will be just like hers and when they look at her they just want to smash her because she is old and curdled in their eyes and she doesn't even belong here, not in the same tribe at all.

Desperately, she watches the wasps circling her head.

They can't help her now.

They're buzzing and darting about in lopsided circles as if they don't have a care in the world—now when she really needs them. All except the purple wasp, her steadfast friend, who lands on top of her head and won't leave it.

She never felt frightened about her age in Eugene. Oh, there was the time she was walking by a hardware store and she stopped at the display of teapots and gladioli in the window. A stooped man with filthy hair passed her with a bitter laugh, spitting so close that the wiggly yellow blob just missed her tan walking shoes. "Old hag," he rasped. She was so shocked she immediately walked into the hardware store and bought a teapot she never used.

She's got to put Edie and Dawson out of her mind. But she's got to talk to this Dawson character. She's done tough stuff before. She raised Frank alone. And the adult crossing guard program was her baby. No student fatalities or injuries since 1963. In 1964, she testified before the Oregon state legislature, speaking in favor of phonics-based reading instruction over "picture book guess and shuffle." The state went her way. She turned a few heads, didn't she, as she sailed into the Salem legislative chamber. Her black cloche hat, a crimson feather curving dramatically under her chin, matched the crimson buttons on her black suit. This outfit is still encased in plastic somewhere in her closet. She grasps her firm thighs, touches her still resilient breasts, looks at herself in the small mirror by the table. *For heaven's sake, I'm not an old hag. Not yet anyway.*

The purple wasp is fanning Clara's face as she paces from room to room. Suddenly she sees that the wasp's head is freakishly larger than before. It's swollen like a bruise or a turban, especially where the two curled antennas protrude above its eyes. Alarmed, she sits back down at the table. The wasp's head is almost at the breaking point.

Ever since her father almost trapped her in the barn, the wasps have watched her carefully—listening and recording her thoughts and experiences, passing on their knowledge of her from generation to generation of wasps, living out their 120-day life cycles as dutiful scribes. When Samantha died, they redoubled their efforts because Clara was so broken up about it. Their job is to get as many secret memories as they can: unadulterated thoughts, withheld emotions—to arrive at clarity, the only thing that will redeem the tortured woman and set her free. Clarity: She's got to come clean about the days leading up to her daughter's death, simply acknowledge what happened. Otherwise, the wasp's head will burst—hers too?—and she will die miserable and alone.

She returns to her rocker, finishes one crossword puzzle, begins another. Outside, nothing stirs. She listens to her Emerson radio, hears of a sharp decline in the stock market, a prison break somewhere, an earthquake in Japan. Later she fixes a simple dinner and prepares herself for bed, thinking despite herself of Edie and Dawson. Not until she's in her nightgown and starts brushing her hair does the purple wasp leave the top of her head and fly to the nightstand, where the creature watches Clara all night long in her restless sleep.

In her dream, two Oregon pigeons (surprise visitors, bobbing and ducking) escape from a cage on her dresser, warbling and moaning in excitement until they fly to the other nightstand. Clara opens her eyes. Two pairs of red eyes peer back. Their rich calls are baroque. Girlish trilling and chest-deep moans eddy around the bedroom in a private pigeon serenade. She feels warm and young. It's thrilling.

Aren't you pretty, says one pigeon.

"Don't be silly," she says, her cheeks glowing. She has always loved the throaty moans of pigeons.

Both pigeons chorus: *Once we had babies, but all our eggs smashed on the ground and now we have you. We will take care of you.*

"No need," she says, still in her dream.

Don't you know, Clara? You need so much caring, they whisper in her ear. *You need a home.*

The wasps swarm in from the kitchen and dive-bomb the pigeons. *We have more manpower. We can take better care of her.*

Her voice is drowsy. "I will not have fighting in my house. I love my son, and I love all of you."

The purple wasp sidles up to her ear. *Take what you can get, sweetheart. Notice anyone else out here trying to help you?*

The purple wasp always sets her straight. She *will* fix things with Frank. She *will*.

All night the wasps tap their silky wings against the bedroom walls. Their wings sound like tiny brushes tapping off-rhythms on a papery drumhead, accompanied by the pigeons, who sing soulful contralto. She burrows into her bed, draws the sheet around her, dreams she's on a jungle cruise. Dew spangles her face, the humidity she so misses. In the canopy of the rain forest, the macaws and orangutans and leopards are cawing and screeching and growling at each other. Nuts and ripe fruit fall to the ground and are eaten by lizards and flamboyantly colored parrots. Rubbery damp leaves brush against her hands. Flying insects bump against her shoulders, get into major tizzies over her head. She is in a seething mass of life all night long.

chapter 9

Frank slides into a booth at the casino, orders a meatball sandwich, and absently looks around the restaurant. He's tired and hungry, doesn't want to think about anything right now. He'll think about Scotty later. He rubs his temples and shuts his eyes. Finally the meatball sandwich comes.

As he's tucking into it, he notices a woman with her back to him up near the cash register. She's listening to an old man and a young woman in tense disagreement about something. The way she leans toward the old man, to listen more closely, makes Frank catch his breath. She's focused, still, coiled to attention. She wears a maroon blouse and black skirt, hasn't bound up her hair yet, or maybe she's just unbound it. A hairnet dangles from one fist, a pencil in the other, knuckles jammed onto her hips, hair shining in loose auburn waves around her shoulders. Her body is not a workout addict's body, toned to infernal perfection. It has some heft to it, pure strength. She has the body of someone who could accomplish enormous amounts of work—hard, sweaty work, the work required to keep the species alive. The unhurried way she turns her head from one disputant to the other makes Frank sure she will solve whatever problem is going down. He's amazed he can keep staring at her back and not immediately want to see her face, her breasts, the frontal curve of her hips. It's like the breath has been knocked out of him.

The old bearded man wears a white skullcap and a white tunic. The young dark-haired woman slouches in jeans and a tank top. The man, likely the girl's father, stands straight as a general. They're an odd couple, attracting stares. The man has an aristocratic bearing somehow. This is no dirt farmer. The man talks with a hushed urgency that makes the girl and the waitress lean toward him. The young woman has removed her earphones. Her face shows great consternation. The man's face is stoic as he pays the bill and turns away from her. Suddenly he makes an angry gesture toward her attire with both hands, palms up. The girl flinches. The man looks scornfully at the waitress, says angry words to both of them and stalks off through the casino, heading to the parking lot. Head down, the girl meekly follows him.

Looking upset, the waitress stands there a minute before speaking briefly with the cashier, a plump woman in the same maroon-and-black uniform. The waitress disappears into a side room. A few minutes later (it seems like hours to Frank) she reappears with a coil of nylon rope draped over her shoulder and walks briskly into the casino. Frank looks down at his half-eaten meatball sandwich and Dr. Pepper. He chomps a few more bites and hurriedly pays the check. He's got to keep the rope-carrying waitress in sight.

The casino at noon is noisy. Women with helmet hairdos, men with white foreheads and red cheeks feed coins from paper cups into clanging machines. Bulging midriffs and turkey jaws shudder when levers are pulled. Pictures of cherries and black bars spin under small plastic windows. Churning sounds of country music, jackpot buzzers, and coins smacking metal suddenly overpower him. He's still hungry, but where is she? There.

Tall and definitive, she cruises the aisles, moves to some inner rhythm as she chats with patrons. There's a power about her, something irresistible. Her eyes are brown pools shining with amusement, her skin sunlit, her figure something to drown in. He can't believe its dips and valleys. He can't see her name tag yet. He takes a deep breath and slowly exhales.

Still bantering with customers, she hasn't seen him yet. She's checking up on spouses and surgeries while she parses out the coiled rope to maybe one-third its length, ties it around her waist, and lets both ends fall to the floor at uneven lengths. Then she just stands there. Some ignore her and keep gambling. Some smile as if they know her tricks. Others frown as if she's batty.

She attaches a mouth mike to her ear. The cashier, her shift over, takes the longer length, goes to the next aisle and ties the rope around her waist, leaving a lot of rope still free. She stands there too. Eventually a sunburned cowboy, who just won a jackpot on the dollar slots, approaches the cashier. He takes the long rope end across another aisle and ties it around his waist. Then a Chinese grandmother, a young Latino with long sideburns, and several others rope themselves together at the waist.

Some just clown around, shimmy their hips. Others are silent, as if it's a serious responsibility to tie a rope around one's waist. Disgruntled bystanders ask what's going on. The ones who know say, just watch, it won't take long. The last people to tie on—a young guy in camouflage gear and a matronly woman in a yellow pantsuit—circle back near the waitress's start point. The short end of the rope still dangles from the waitress's waist. She raises her hand and speaks softly into her mike. Most people in the small area stop gambling and listen.

"So folks, imagine we're all tied together here and all over the world." A short pause, then she pulls on the rope, causing the cashier and others to lose their balance. "Whoa!" they cry. She continues. "One group thinks their way of thinking is the only right way and everyone else is dead wrong."

Others pull back, testy-playful, trying to unbalance others down the line. "Watch it!" cries a frowning man.

"See?" She's animated now. "*Kaput!* We're out of balance. If we were serious, we could make the other side crash and fall on the floor. We could start a war!" Her voice goes low and hypnotic. "Just saying: Watch out for my-way-or-the-highway folks."

A heckler calls out, "All tied together, huh? Sounds like lefty propaganda to me."

A smattering of laughter and boos. Someone says, "Let her be. Stella's a good egg." General cheers. One by one, the participants untie themselves in reverse order and return the rope to her. The performance took three minutes.

The waitress looks surprised as Frank slowly walks up to her. "You're late, mister. The rope trick is over." Her name tag says *Stella*.

"It is, huh." He speaks as if to contradict her. Long-legged in Levi's and a faded green T-shirt, hair askew, his eyes are locked on hers. Heart racing, he draws the unused end of the rope out from her waist, backs up maybe four feet, and ties it around his waist.

She's looking at him. Nervous, she looks away.

His smoky eyes are fixed on her. "I saw you trying to keep the peace in the restaurant just now. Looked like you were trying your best, but the guy wasn't buying it." He just wants to talk, have her talk back, not disappear.

Looking confused, she meets his gaze again. "Mr. Hamdi, yes. He's about to give up on us Americans. His daughter is so Westernized, he thinks she's going to hell. Thinks we are too.

Americans. Going to hell." Flustered, she recovers herself. "He's going back to Saudi Arabia, taking Aisha with him. It's a pity. Aisha's just been admitted to pre-med at Boston University. They're both lovely people." She stops, still nervous. "They've been here before. Always just to eat. No gambling, not even a nickel. I have my spies." Her hypnotic brown eyes pierce him. "And you? Where are *you* going?" Her eyes turn humorous.

He's silent a moment. "Well, I'm not going to Saudi Arabia any time soon, I can tell you that."

She laughs.

"No pre-med plans that I know of."

Her laughter is uproarious, wonderful. "Where *are* you going then?"

He looks at her. "I'm not going anywhere."

Her voice drops to a lower register, almost a whisper. "And if not pre-med, what?"

Confidence surges in him; he can't say why. "Horse wrangler. Cowboy. Ski instructor. Railroad man." If she wants some twit, then *hasta la vista,* baby.

Her eyes glisten. She leans toward him, takes a small step forward. "You here for any length of time, Mr. horse wrangler, cowboy, ski instructor, railroad man?"

He lets her approach. He can just about smell her perfume, something musky that could drive him wild. "I just drove my mother's house here on a flatbed truck. You might've noticed it."

She raises her hands in mock surprise, all the while looking at his chest and tousled hair. "It's the floating house that came down from the sky. Everybody's talking about it." She studies his dimples. "So, *you're* the driver. Now isn't that interesting." She folds her arms, as if intrigued by a sudden thought. "Ever been in theater, Mr. Adventure Man?"

"*Theater?* No way," he blurts. He'd never prance around some stage. Wait—she wants a gofer—someone to open her shows with a juggling act? He gives her a fleeting glance. She's serene, utterly compelling; she's got something behind the eyeballs, something complex. But . . . theater?

It's her turn to look confident. "Maybe I can persuade you otherwise."

"Maybe. Maybe not. What have you got in mind?"

She smiles, looks down. "Mr. Hamdi and his daughter have given me an idea, but I have to work on it a little."

He begins to untie the rope around his waist. "Well, I'll be around." As if by way of explanation, he adds, "Scotty and I are old friends."

"You're kidding. Ever since you walked up, I wondered if you were the famous Frank Breckenridge Scotty's told me about." She smiles tauntingly. "So you *are* the one."

"The one what?"

"I'll never tell."

"Maybe I need to shine up my reputation a little."

"I like your reputation just the way it is."

"Do you now?" He folds his arms across his chest.

"Yes, I do." She's sputtering again.

"Now look, I haven't proposed yet." He's deadpan.

She looks puzzled, then laughs that full-throated laugh again. "I like a man with a sense of humor. You and I will get along just fine, Frank Breckenridge."

"I'd bet my life on it." He checks her name tag again.

She flushes the most appealing peach pink and extends her hand. "Stella Shapiro." He takes her hand, lingers with it.

He needs to get hold of himself. "See you around, Stella." His voice is low, almost a whisper. He hands her the rope, steps close enough to smell her musky fragrance again. He gets serious. "Why does Scotty let you perform in his casino?"

"He played the Stage Manager in *Our Town* in high school. Never got over it. I keep it real short and don't do it often. I don't cut into his profits."

He nods, backs away, looking briefly into her eyes, and turns to leave. Glancing back, he sees her staring at him.

After sleeping at Scotty's, Frank fritters away the next morning. He takes a long, hot shower, goes to the mini-mart for orange juice, whole wheat bread, a pack of cigarettes, and a dozen eggs, stowing them at the uprooted house. Clara's working her shift at Desert Dan's. He thought he'd surprise her with the food. He's feeling more sympathetic toward her this morning, and the wasps are nowhere in sight.

Still restless, he brings out a sponge and bucket of water to wash dead bugs off the trailer cab—crusty corpses spattered on the windshield. His whole life he's been spectacularly inattentive to such matters, and here he is washing off a vehicle and laying in stores of food. He's filled the morning only to delay the moment of seeking out Stella again.

He puts the pail and sponge back under the sink and washes up. He'll just walk the itty-bitty streets full of trailers and pastel apartments until he finds her.

When he said he was a horse wrangler, et cetera, she ran her fingers through one side of her hair, smiling like the sun just came out after a hard rain. It was the most welcoming smile he'd ever seen. But he can't imagine she'd want anything to do with some rough rider who never even went to college. He liked her rope trick, liked what she said, but he wonders if she, or anyone these days, still believes we're all linked. Then too, she can't be more than thirty-five. He's forty-six. But he's not totally hopeless. He's been a closet reader all these years. Times when his social life stalled, he'd pick up paperbacks here and there, mostly from friends: *The Guns of August, Working, All the Pretty Horses, Catcher in the Rye, A Farewell to Arms, Roughing It, Life on the Mississippi.*

All morning, his mind's been nattering on like this. "Just shut up, fool," he says, kicking gravel, burrowing his fingers deep in his Levi's pockets.

Now he's on Royal Drive. Window signs say, "Don't tread on me," "Warning: In case of the Rapture, this car will have no driver." He loves these signs; they make him laugh. A mother with her baby wrapped in a rebozo comes out of a trailer, a low-lying ponytail hanging down her back. The woman smiles at Frank; he smiles back. Down the block, Stella comes out of a small gray trailer, carrying a plastic bag full of something. She doesn't see him. She has a distant look, like she's thinking about something.

He hates it that he's nervous. But how can he *not* be, when her auburn hair swings loose around her shoulders and her swaying hips and air of composure make her look like a goddess. He watches from a distance, hidden beside a toolshed. She's walking quickly. He follows her, mumbling, "OK folks, here we have Frank, the teenage stalker." She enters Jackpot Video.

On dull nights with Union Pacific, he would find a video store in some town and browse the aisles, checking out the latest release playing on the big overhead screen. Always he would look for some woman to pick up. Sometimes he found one. If not, he would drift back to his motel room to read or watch TV, ending up with an ashtray full of cigarette butts when he couldn't resist the pull of nicotine.

He looks through the store window, doesn't see her, steps

inside. The video is at medium volume in the small store—gunshots, screeching brakes. She's talking intently to the owner, back by the tiny office. Neither looks up.

He walks out, having just missed looking like a fool. He crosses the highway, looks at the quiet hills in the distance, wondering what to do. Minutes later, she emerges, carrying an even larger bag of videos. She sees him and calls his name.

"Hello!" he says in mock surprise.

She smiles, stops. "It's the man with the flying house!"

Buoyed, he crosses the highway again and walks toward her with quick, sure strides, trying to tame a wave of desire. She's wearing yellow capris, a white T-shirt, and sandals, her hair in loose waves around her face before it cascades in back.

"Did anyone ever tell you that you look damnably healthy?" He reaches to take her bag of videos.

She pulls the bag away. "Did anyone ever tell you that women carry their own bags these days?"

His confidence is returning. He just needed to see her, talk to her. *This is crazy,* he thinks. He taps her bag. "So, you like movies and theater."

"The only games in town." She points to the bag. "Like here's *Being There*, with Peter Sellers. Seems like a good time to see it again. I love its politics." She pauses. "Or have I offended you?"

He laughs. "I generally stay away from politics. They all seem like a bunch of nitwits to me."

She nods. "It's really bad."

"What else you got in there? I missed *Being There*. Missed a lot of movies. Too busy being the Marlboro Man." He mimes lighting a cigarette with his Bic, mimes a languorous draw, tips an imaginary cowboy hat.

She laughs. "I have to say, you look very sexy when you

do that, even though, for God's sake, that's supposed to be the wrong thing to say these days." She's looking at his lips.

He takes a deep breath. "Lots of things are supposed to be the wrong thing to say these days. Like 'Baby, you're so sexy I can hardly stand it, and you are not even smoking.'" The words tumble out of him.

Laughing, she flicks her hair back in a gesture of pure animal health. "Let's stick to the movies right now. So tell me. What's your favorite movie?"

A little smile curls his mouth. "Sure. Easy. *The Deer Hunter*. I still watch it every chance I get. Too bad Cimino's out in the wilderness somewhere. I actually tried to find out about him. I think I saw him up in Sun Valley once. A damned genius. Looked like hell."

She nods. "I loved that movie too, except the wife kept sending her husband socks after his leg was blown off." She rolls her eyes. "Cimino must think women are ditzy."

"Right. She wasn't getting with the program. I never thought about that before." They walk in silence. "OK, your turn." He looks at her humorously, as if to say, *Don't worry, I'll play this little game with you.*

"Too many, too many," she laughs. "*Blade Runner, Stage Coach, High Noon, The Last Metro, Singin' in the Rain, All That Jazz, The Sorrow and the Pity, Dog Day Afternoon.* This conversation could go on for hours. I'm all over the place with movies."

"How about *High Noon?* A classic."

She takes a mock-heroic pose. "Honor. Courage. Grace Kelly shoots a bad guy to defend her man after she's denounced violence." He raises his hand to see if she'll give him a high five. She does, laughing. "Oh my god, where did my feminist credentials just go?"

"Your feminist credentials are just fine."

They walk slowly in the tattered matte desert, share a speaking silence as they approach her trailer. "Are you hungry?" she says tentatively. "I mean, it's lunchtime. Are you free, Frank?" She stops, as if surprised at herself, then plunges on. "I've got a mean taco casserole in the fridge."

"I'm free. I'm hungry. Been a few days since I had a home-cooked meal."

"Thought so." That welcoming smile again. "Let's talk about you and theater. You did a theatrical thing just then, lighting your cigarette like the Marlboro Man, tipping a cowboy hat. Mostly your expression. You're a natural."

"Now look, everybody knows about the Marlboro Man. That doesn't count." He wants to touch her hair, but it's too soon.

She leans close. Her breath smells like peppermint. "Maybe we can work on something more original then."

She's playing with him, but he falls for it, gets weak at the knees. He tries for a sober tone. "Scotty says you want to put a big theater tent in the vacant lot."

She looks at him. "Scotty told you that?"

"But the house is in the way." His look is serious.

She stops. "It's *not* in the way. It's the house that fell from the sky. We could build an interesting theater piece around that house." Her step is buoyant as they reach her trailer. "These days, a movable house is a good thing to have in case of trouble. See? Ta-daaa!" Flinging out her arms, she heralds her small, dented aluminum trailer. He loves her high spirits, but he also liked her seriousness with the Saudi father and daughter.

Inside, she sets her bag down, turns on a fan, goes into the kitchen. "Make yourself at home, Frank. You like margaritas? I'll fix us some margaritas."

"Always ready for a margarita."

He looks around. The place is tiny. He's six feet. The ceiling is a bit of a squeeze. If he stamped good and hard, the whole shebang would rattle. The living area has two hot pink velvet armchairs and a purple chenille loveseat. The colors make him smile. The coffee table is piled high with magazines and newspapers, mostly *The Salt Lake Tribune* and the *New Yorker*. Two crammed bookcases line the walls, bed and bath down the hall.

He walks around with a silly grin on his face. The walls are plastered with movie posters, theater posters, enlarged glossies. You can't even see the fake knotty pine paneling under all the posters: Gloria Swanson in *Sunset Boulevard*, Gary Cooper in *High Noon*, Marlene Dietrich in *The Blue Angel*, Harrison Ford in *Blade Runner*, Charlie Chaplin in *The Gold Rush* and *Modern Times*, Gene Kelly in *Singin' in the Rain*, Fred Astaire and Ginger Rogers in *Shall We Dance*—Fred in a tux, elegant, tails flying; Ginger in a spangled gown.

He whirls around from the posters. "You like dancing?" In high school, his dancing was legendary. Stella's loading a tray with margaritas, chips, and salsa.

"Do I like dancing?" She sets the tray down, waltzes toward him. He takes her hand in the small, rattling space between the breakfast counter and the purple chenille loveseat. As if they've done this for years, they twirl, come together, separate, hum in unison "Dancing in the Dark," "Sophisticated Lady," "September Song," "Dancing Cheek to Cheek." The words to the old standards just roll out of them, Frank's baritone to Stella's contralto. He forgot he knew these tunes, his parents' favorites, played plenty at the house. Normally he's a Jim Morrison man.

He's also forgotten about dancing like this. This is pure play. Before, he used his dancing prowess strictly to seduce. But now, almost forehead to forehead with him, Stella moves like she's on an electric sidewalk, smooth as a Black Russian, like she can match any move and it's all a wonderful joke. He continuously tests her. They can't help laughing. He slides into slo-mo rumbas, sambas, a waltz, a he-doesn't-know-what, and she follows like she's joined at the hip. Taking Astaire and Rogers' lead, he throws in little teasers—heel-toe-tap, heel-toe tap. They're flushed, exhilarated, a light sheen of sweat on their faces by the time they stop, the finish marked by a long pause held in regular dance position for who knows how many beats, their bodies close until he leans her backward and she holds on tight and their arms slide around each other and they kiss as easy as breathing, then laugh and kiss some more, and it's wonderful—hot and sexy and good. He brings her upright and they laugh, keeping it light in all their surprise.

"I love to dance," she says.

"No kidding."

"Never found a partner before."

"Now you have."

"It's been kind of lonesome out here in the desert."

"Me too. Back there. Everywhere."

The moment extends, too delicate for words or anything else. They're both a little scared.

He says, "How'd you land here, stay here? You could go anywhere you want."

"Nevada's a blank slate. Full of possibilities."

"Possibilities," he says. "Yes."

Her eyes flicker up at him. "How about those drinks? They're going to get sloppy." She moves into the kitchen.

He sits on the purple loveseat, watching her. Something about the way she moves, sensitive like she's got antennae, but also a little resistant, like she's saying "convince me," and then these showgirl colors, hot pink armchairs and purple loveseat along with a couple of lime-green pillows bordered with sequins. *Sequins,* for God's sake. Her furnishings belong in a Broadway dressing room. Everything combines in his head to make him so ready for her that he has to take deep breaths and pick up the black eight ball on her coffee table to distract himself. He's afraid to ask it a question, but the eight ball answers anyway when he turns it over: "Try again another time." That's a good answer, an answer he needs right now. He feels calmer by the time she joins him with the margaritas, salsa, and chips. The taco casserole in her microwave is beginning to smell like heaven.

Two days later, Stella says she'll drive Frank to Twin Falls on her day off. He wants to buy Clara a used Honda Civic like the one she had to sell in order to drive the U-Haul from Eugene. Plus she needs a new cell phone. Dropped her old one in dishwater right before they left Eugene. Normally Clara would get her own car and cell phone, but she's been sitting around shell-shocked since the move and can't seem to get anything done yet. She will pay him back quickly, he knows. She hates debt. She just needs to get reconnected, he thinks. Maybe then she'll forget about the cursed wasps and let them go. He doesn't want to dwell on the wasp episode or her refusal to talk about their family.

He walks over to Stella's early from Scotty's and finds her crouched on the kitchen floor in old jeans and a T-shirt, repairing the faucet under the sink. "Leak and a jammed pipe. Driving me crazy. Almost done." He's transfixed. Her strong haunches, bare arms radiant with electric little hairs in a delicate wash of freckles—he's never seen a woman repairing a sink. The sight arouses him. She's focused and quick, removes the leaky pipe with strong twists of a pipe wrench, shortens the new piping with tubing cutters, tightens both ends with new gaskets, tests the water flow again. "Done," she says without fanfare. "I'll go change." They kiss lightly.

He sits at the small kitchen table, trying to recover from the sight of her working this way. He hears the shower going, tries not to think of her beautiful body with water running down it. On the table is a sketch of some structure, a building with pillars and a huge rounded skylight. It looks like a church or a civic building.

She comes out from her bedroom in a blue sundress that gives him pause. *Go slow,* he tells himself. They pile into her red Mustang. Gently he touches her damp tousled hair as she pulls onto 93 North. He likes her strong square hands on the wheel. She's a confident driver. He's comfortable with her in some fundamental way and they've hardly met.

He asks how she landed in Jackpot. She smiles. Well, she jumped in her Grandpa's car after his estate was settled, headed out from San Francisco to try her hand at theater in New York or film in L.A. She'd decide which city and vocation after she got on the road. But she got waylaid taking routes she'd never been on, plus she had car trouble in Jackpot and heard Scotty needed a waitress. That was a year ago.

Grinning, Frank says he's wandered around himself, always looking for something he couldn't quite put his finger on. Now he has the money to think about it a little, and his old friend Scotty said he could work the change booth if he wanted to.

And the posters? Her dad was a Hollywood stuntman and her mother did makeup. He left her for a gorgeous young girl and got killed in a motorcycle accident when Stella was seventeen. She and her mother fled to San Francisco to live with the grandparents. Her mother ran off with a potter from Bainbridge Island, so Stella stayed with her grandparents through college and joined the San Francisco Mime Troupe.

"Street improvs fit me to a T. I like to raise hell. The little piece you saw was just a warm-up."

He looks at her. "I've done my share of hell-raising."

She has a slow grin. "Why am I not surprised? So why the house?"

"That's all she has."

He thinks about this a minute, then tells her the sad tale of 1963, hints at his womanizing as he looked for something that made him feel . . . alive.

She looks at him. "Someone who made you realize you were just sleepwalking before."

Slowly he takes her hand, kisses her open palm. "That's it."

Her eyes water with surprise. She has decelerated from eighty to fifty, her knuckles pale on the steering wheel.

He says, "Let's change the subject or we'll get in an accident."

"So what are we doing, Frank? This is crazy." She glances at him. "I've been watching you. You take things in and have a calm head. You don't bullshit. I feel I can trust you. Help me out here. Everything is going way too fast."

"Baby, I'm as lost as you are. We got to take it easy."

They drive in silence. He says, "What was that drawing on your kitchen table?"

"My theater. If I ever get one."

His voice is serious. "Maybe I can build it for you."

Her face is solemn. "Maybe you can."

"Just don't ask me to act in it."

She grins.

In Rogerson, population about twenty, they pull up to a small bar and restaurant with an unpainted wooden front. Before they go in, he draws her to him with a sigh. Slowly they kiss each other's face, mouth, eyes, forehead. He inhales her hair, the scent of something fresh and clean. He wants to wake up with her smell on him, on the sheets, everywhere. He never wants her out of his life.

They stop, look at each other. They go inside.

Pie is clearly the main attraction. Chocolate cream, coconut cream, strawberry, apple, boysenberry, cherry, lemon meringue, pumpkin, pecan, banana cream, blueberry, butterscotch. She orders lemon meringue, the meringue four times higher than the lemon filling. He gets pecan. The coffee is amazingly good. The pie is spectacular.

In Twin Falls, he buys his mother a cell phone and a used Saturn. No Civics are available just now. He'll pick up the Saturn next week. Back at Stella's, they circle away from each other, delaying. They sit at her table and eat a scant dinner, food they will not remember. He can hardly swallow. She is quaking, still. They watch each other in the lamp light.

They move toward the purple couch, stop midway. "How do you want to live?" she says quietly, as if everything is already settled.

His voice is low. "I want to build houses, buildings, sculptures, your theater. Whatever it takes. I want to build a life with you."

"If we haven't lost our minds," she says. They laugh, grow silent. She says, "I want to make people feel safe enough to have new thoughts. I'd like to teach somewhere, do performance. I've always wanted to shake things up." She takes a step toward him. "I want you, Frank."

He can stand it no longer. This is so crazy. All he knows is Stella is the woman who holds his body and soul in her arms. With her he feels safe and whole after all these senseless years. He moves toward her, takes her trembling hand, puts it inside his T-shirt to feel his thundering heart.

"Now?"

She nods.

He strokes her hair, kisses the pounding in her neck. She draws up his T-shirt and tastes his light brown nipples. "You taste like cinnamon," she murmurs. Slowly he lowers the straps on her blue sundress and touches her lovely breasts. Without even knowing how they got there, they are naked on her bed, bobbing like seahorses in the foaming sea, first he on top, then she, one creature with two heads, all the night long, both alight in the magic circle he has waited his whole life to enter.

chapter 10

The next day, Frank hands his mother a new cell phone. "Couldn't find a Civic. They sell fast, so I got you a used Saturn. Needs some work. I'll pick it up next week."

"Thank you, Frank, for doing all this." She's delighted to see him, but nonplussed he bought these things without telling her first. She has paid her own way ever since Darrell died and takes great pride in her independence. Careful to disguise her irritation, she writes him a check that covers half the balance, even though he tells her she can wait until the car is ready. She starts charging the phone on the counter, scribbles the number on a 3x5 index card and tapes it by the phone. She's got to memorize it. "Hungry? I've got some cold spaghetti. It's really good."

"No, thanks. I've eaten."

Neither mention his angry exit from the wasps a week or so ago. She looks at him and smiles. A weight feels lifted from her. He looks like an aging rocker in his black jeans and black T-shirt. She comments on his freshly barbered hair.

"Stella cut it." His smile is sheepish. She smiles.

Clara had seen them out walking together. They had their arms around each other's waists and were deep in conversation about something. She was so pleased to see him looking happy.

"I've seen her in the casino. She seems like a terrific girl. I'll have to meet her properly one of these days."

He wants to change the subject. "Wasps still out?" He's tired of the stinging game. In response, she picks up the faded yellow Willamette Elementary School Crossing Guard T-shirt. Now it just says *Willamette Elementary School*.

He is shocked and moved. *She would never have cut up that T-shirt before. Samantha died at that school.*

"This one had the biggest neck," she says crisply. "To frame your face. I just trimmed it so they can't get your neck." Her hands are shaking. Her voice catches. "I just want you to be safe, Frank. That's all I ever wanted." He studies her face, smiles.

The purple wasp spins in delirious circles around the kitchen sink.

Clara pulls the T-shirt over his head so that his neck is well covered. "Good fit," she says.

With his face peeping out from the T-shirt opening, he can't help saying, "This is ridiculous and you know it, Mother." But he's got no fight in him this afternoon. He's too crazy in love. He'll wear it just this once if it will make his mother happy. She's got that air about her now that he remembers: pursed lips, neck tendons sticking out. He smiles to himself. *What is it with all these hell-bent women?* She's like Stella when she gets on a movie rampage, like she did this morning with *Thelma and Louise*.

Gingerly, he starts in on a Dr. Pepper with his face sticking out of a cut-up T-shirt. If Scotty could see him now.

She smiles. "You look charming." She's having her regular lunch of black coffee, cottage cheese, and an apple. They sit quietly chewing, leafing through Scotty's *USA Today* and *Time* magazine.

The wasps are gathering on the counter from hidden places.

They buzz and wing-tap each other. Suddenly two wasps fly out from the insect wad and go for Frank's bare cheeks.

Bingo.

He bolts from the table, tears the T-shirt off. "You're making it fucking impossible for me, Mother—what's *wrong* with you? Are you trying to drive me away?" He heads for the door.

Abruptly she stands, her voice almost a whisper. "For God's sake, Frank, how can you even *think* such a thing?" Sternly she goes to the sink. "Come here. Let me put something on those bites." Quickly she stirs up a thick paste of baking soda and bottled water. "Always they went for your neck, *never* anywhere else, and only when you teased them. Now it's your cheeks! And you weren't even bothering them, just like the other day!"

She pauses, looking thoughtful. "It's like they're getting senile. All those years of flying in and out of my life, they never challenged me like this."

He frowns and pushes the paste away. Making a scornful sound, he opens the kitchen door to leave.

She can't bear it. Softly she says, "I don't know what to do about anything anymore." She looks down at the floor. "I know I let you down all those years, Frank. Can we talk? Can we ever talk? I love you so much."

Surprised by these words, he's still too mad to stop moving. He slams the kitchen door, and the door frame quivers. The wasps too are surprised by her honest words. They circle her head in a brief celebratory cloud. Frank roars off in Scotty's car.

She stands there a minute, wanting desperately to fix the situation. The kitchen is quiet. Slowly she looks around for the wasps. Always buzzing, they are silent. She walks through the house. She doesn't see them. Or hear them. Where are they?

Then she sees them huddling together in a corner by the

stove. They are silent, unmoving. They seem to be looking at her, waiting for something to happen. This is odd. Maybe it's just her imagination.

Something murderous grows in her. She looks at the silent wasps, then walks slowly to the outside door and opens it wide. "Freedom? You want freedom, there it is." She points to the open air. The wasps stay huddled. She waits, goes again to the door, and looks back at them.

"Go." She points to the sky. But the wasps do not move from their sheltered place. She raises her voice. "Just get out," she says, feeling these strange words on her lips. "All of you. I'm tired of the trouble you bring." Still the wasps don't move. After a while, she closes the kitchen door and plops down tiredly at the kitchen table. She sits there with her head in her hands.

She is shaking. *Can't I do anything right?* Now the wasps are flying around in confusion. They seem to sense that the moment of danger has passed. They could not survive in the desert.

Frantic to resolve *something* in this god-forsaken place, she struggles to collect herself. She will get something out of this day. Yes. She strides over to the casino, looking for Dawson. A new window. Yes. She can't get along without a new window.

After all, he broke it.

For once she's lucky and sees Dawson in the bar, alone in a dimly lit booth. In his limp gray T-shirt, he looks like a cobweb. His head sags onto the back of the booth; his pasty skin gleams with grease. She slides in opposite him.

Nursing a double whiskey neat, he stares as if she were an apparition escaped from his head, but he knows exactly who she is. He's been inside her house, knows its smell. She laces her blue-veined hands together on the table. In his drunken state, he mimics her gesture. "Aim to do some praying over me, lady?

Want me to kneel down, say God almighty, I'm sorry for the trouble I caused this woman?" He sounds adenoidal.

She fixes him with a level gaze. "I didn't come here for any praying, young man. I came to ask for the twenty dollars minimum it'll take to replace my screen and window." She is dry and clear. Couldn't be calmer.

"What screen? What window?" he asks dully, his nose needing to be blown. "I don't have any twenty dollars, lady. If I did, I'd be outta here. Gimme a break."

She sees his discomfort, doesn't take her eyes from his face. "Well, we could talk, couldn't we, like two human beings?"

"What the fuck," he mumbles, rubbing his face as if trying to wake up.

"Tough times, Dawson?"

He sets the whiskey down in slow motion, as if trying to contain himself. His voice is quiet. "Lady, you are some nosy bitch. How do you know my name? Why don't you mind your own business?"

Her voice is equally low. "Someone said your name at the blackjack table, don't you remember? You could mind *your* own business too. I don't even know you, but I'll tell you my name: Clara Breckenridge. So why did you break my window and trash my house? Do I look like a rich person? *Do* I?"

His eyes flicker. She isn't going to take no for an answer. Usually people like her just want to give him a religious pamphlet or make him stop eating red meat. Usually he can make them go away. "Fuck. I don't have any money for no fucking window. I'm waiting for my girlfriend, OK? We're clearing out of this shitty two-bit dump."

She's undeterred. "You can go all over the world and still be miserable, don't you know that? A different town isn't the

CLARA at the EDGE

answer. Trouble starts *here.*" She accidentally taps one of her unhealed wasp stings and visibly flinches. "I haven't had an easy life either"—she's acting on a hunch—"but I haven't gone around doing the things you have." She looks at his bony neck, almost thinks of giving *him* money. But she would never. His Adam's apple is going up and down; his face is flushed.

It's not just the alcohol, she thinks. He's not used to hard motherly talk like this. Her voice is suddenly husky with feeling. "I have allergies too. Chlor-Trimeton is good. You should try it."

He laughs incredulously. "Now you're giving me *allergy* tips?" He rolls his eyes, his voice rising. "I don't even *know* you, lady. You're not my grandmother. And you sure as hell ain't my mother." A vein in his forehead throbs. "Stick with the blue hairs, lady. I don't need any advice from *you.*" Hands trembling, he picks up his drink with a sour laugh. "So you had a hard life too. Your mom go down by the lake to screw some guy while she left you at the gas station and you heard them wailing away on each other? Foster dad make you sleep in the garage when it was ten below? Foster mom make you clean the whole house before you got your slice of Velveeta and a graham cracker? Make you do the floor twice because you missed some spots because you hadn't eaten for three days and she kept you locked up in the house?" He gulps more whiskey.

Her eyes flicker at these grim details. Nobody has valued him. But *she* can. *She* can get him back in school, find him a job! With him, she starts clean. No failures, a clean slate. She's almost giddy. She can turn his life around! It's much harder with Frank: too many mistakes and missed opportunities over too many years.

Dawson sits there massaging his temples, his eyes closed.

She leans forward. "Look, I'm not playing games about who

had the worst life. I'm just saying you can stop the path you're on. You could be headed for real trouble. Think of what can happen. No girlfriends, only boyfriends: prison."

He laughs, surprised she knows these things, surprised she knows anything at all. "I don't need any stinking advice. You don't know anything about me, lady. Don't you have somebody else to talk to? Like who's that guy at your house—your son? Why don't you talk to your son? Give *him* advice. Why fuck around with *me?* Christ, no window screen is worth *this*."

She knows he really means the opposite—he *needs* her advice but can't admit he needs an older woman like her.

For an instant their eyes lock.

He gulps the rest of his whiskey, shoves the glass hard across the table at her, and lunges out of the booth. The glass hits her in the chest, splashing the last drops of liquor onto her Eugene Public Library T-shirt before it bounces to her lap.

She looks up. He's gone. The whiskey smell goes deep into her lungs. The pungency of the fumes tells her how much he hates her, fears her, needs her.

He crashes out the back exit, urinates in a molten stream beside the dumpster. As he pees, he swallows a sob and knuckles his head hard with his free hand. This Clara-Whoever-The-Fuck-She-Is makes him sweat. *Ghost who abandoned him.* The words come from a secret spot at the base of his stomach. It's intolerable to be reminded. Roughly he arranges himself and zips his fly. Back inside, he sags into the same booth. She's gone. Dully, he stares at where she sat.

Back at her kitchen table, she thinks, *Maybe I'm just fooling myself. Maybe he doesn't need me at all. Maybe I'm just a useless failure.*

22 days left.

◆

At the casino, Edie finally glides toward Dawson, her breasts hammocked in a makeshift red bandana tied with string around her neck and back, her black capris in need of a wash, her cropped white-blonde hair stiff with spray net she stole from the mini-mart. She's got no changes of clothes, thinking she was only on a day trip to Jackpot.

His drunken smile is wide. She's beautiful. She slides into the booth, is warm in his arms. In a few minutes, they go back to the motel.

chapter 11

*lara sits at the kitchen table drinking cold coffee. She frowns at a lone wasp that lands next to her cup offering companionship. Dawson is sadder, more damaged than she'd imagined. No problem kids in school ever assaulted her or invaded her property. He's out of her league. She needs to talk to Frank, but he would just say, *Mother, get real. You can't help this guy.*

The purple wasp sidles up to her ear. *It's easier to deal with a stranger than with your own blood—right, hon?* She looks at the wasp. More than anything, she yearns for her son. Just this one time she'd like the comfort of his arms around her, to celebrate their safe landing here, celebrate that he even puts up with her at all. With this latest sting, she wonders if he'll ever come back.

She puts away the crossing guard T-shirt he threw on the floor, stands there thinking a minute. Then she carries the three-step kitchen stool into the bedroom and sets it in front of her closet. On the top shelf are several hatboxes from the fifties and sixties. She puts them all on the bed. The hat she's looking for lies protected in the biggest hatbox, somewhere in the back. The wasps circle above the bed like a giant lacy ceiling fan. She opens a smaller hatbox out of curiosity. "Look at these silly pillbox hats," she exclaims. The net is too coarse for her purposes.

It's no wonder she doesn't like pillboxes. The sixties for her were gray and flat. After Kennedy's assassination and her own losses in 1963, the rest of the sixties and early seventies were a time of upheaval: Vietnam, the civil rights struggles, assassinations, riots, the burning cities—all these events hardly registered with her, yet they paralleled her personal ruin. With her young husband and daughter unbelievably dead, she hovered like a statue over Frank, training adult crossing guards, going to school board meetings and city hall to urge higher wages for crossing guards who could well save a child's life.

People in town whispered about her unending grief, her monomania about the crossing guards (though they admired her cause), her odd jokes. Once at a city hall meeting, she cracked, "Just think. With well trained crossing guards, you don't have any further responsibility." There was an awkward silence before a few people laughed. Some thought she'd gone mad with grief. Clara sensed these currents around her and just kept busy.

She lifts the lavender garden party hat out of its box, an extravagant swath of net swirled around the starched organdy crown and wide brim, the lavender net cascading in back all the way to her waist. Looking at herself in the mirror, she dons this fairy tale creation. The hat looks ridiculous with her Eugene Public Library T-shirt, but she doesn't notice. She wore this hat and matching dress on May 11, 1949, at her sister Lillian's engagement party, where she met Darrell, the love of her life. And married him on June 15, 1950. Thirteen years of marriage, that's what she had.

Darrell and their short years together flee the special room in her brain and fill the bedroom. Their honeymoon in Yosemite, where they were so tender and fierce and barely left their cabin, sleeping and eating whenever the mood struck. Moving into this very house he built on weekends, she helping with the sanding, varnishing, and painting (until she got too pregnant), laughing and eating hot dogs late at night, Darrell making most of the furniture himself. Samantha's birth, then Frank's: Samantha thin and fussy, Frank fat and robust. And always Fourth of July picnics in the backyard among the lilacs, the wasps circling lazily above—fried chicken, watermelon, corn on the cob, her simple chocolate sheet cake with powdered sugar frosting. Sitting on the porch swing with Darrell for hours after the kids were asleep, the smell of lilacs in the air. Dancing in the living room to big bands, ballads from the forties and fifties on 78s and LPs on their portable RCA record player: Harry James, Glenn Miller, Ella Fitzgerald, Louis Armstrong, Nat King Cole.

She runs her fingers over the hat's wide, sweeping brim swathed in layers of lavender net, sheer as spun glass, the brim dipping and peaking at rakish angles. It was Lillian's hat. So was the matching dress in lavender chiffon with an empire waist, the hemline dipping long in back, a lovely dress of World War I vintage. Lillian let Clara keep the dress and hat because she met Darrell in it. There's the dress at the end of her closet, covered in plastic. Clara, her eyes stormed with tears, can hardly see the dress.

In 1946, after their bold Greyhound escape from North Dakota, Clara and Lillian got full scholarships at the University of Oregon: Lillian in art, Clara in English and education. Their easy-going cousin Loretta gave them a deal on a low-rent apartment and often had them over for dinner. Clara worked part-time at the university library, Lillian at a vintage clothing store. They got by.

In her junior year, Lillian met Jan van Beek, an extravagant Dutch exchange student, who convinced her he would be the next international art star, so Lillian abandoned everything to go back to Amsterdam with him. It was a fiery romance.

Clara was furious. She couldn't believe her twin sister would sacrifice her own considerable talent to serve a really disagreeable man. She and Lillian had huge fights about it. Clara said van Beek was a soul-sapping egotist who would suck Lillian dry and leave her with nothing. Lillian said he was going to introduce her to major galleries in Amsterdam. But Clara was right. Van Beek proved to be an abuser and a lazy liar with a succession of mistresses. Lillian was unable to break away. She squandered her own talents to promote his.

Eventually van Beek did become a minor success with a series of art exhibits in Europe before he drowned in a boating accident in 1995 on Lake Como, along with his latest mistress. Then in early 2000, Lillian had a heart attack outside a West End theater in London as her new lover Patrick Chalmers looked on aghast, a man who was everything van Beek was not—considerate, supportive, gentle. Chalmers shipped most of Lillian's oil paintings to Clara. They're packed away in her closets.

Lillian had extraordinary talent, and nothing came of it. Clara blames van Beek to this day. From the first, Clara disliked his preening ways, his way of captivating a room, rendering Lillian colorless and silent, muzzling her wry humor so he could pontificate at will. Lillian never wanted to return to the U.S. She felt European, loved its old buildings, gray streets, superb food and wine, outdoor cafés, her friends who loved to discuss philosophy and art. America was too real for her, too brusque and unresolved. It reminded her of their painful childhood, years both sisters wanted to bury.

Despite their huge fights over van Beek, Clara and Lillian came together as dedicated sisters for Lillian's engagement party. At the last minute, Clara suddenly realized she had nothing appropriate to wear.

"I have just the outfit for you," Lillian said with a smile. Clara was too practical to own a romantic outfit like this. It was Lillian's style—dazzling, not of this world, the dipping hemline, the glass beads on the bodice and the wafting sleeves. Clara felt like an imposter queen trailing around their cousin Loretta's wonderful rose garden on River Road, not far from the small apartment they rented from her.

And then a tall man named Darrell walked up to Clara, where she stood next to the Charlotte Armstrong rose bushes. The top of her head reached his armpits. After pleasantries, he looked around awkwardly and began to speak gravely of Roosevelt and Truman. She couldn't stifle a laugh at his serious topic.

"Sorry!" she blurted. "I've never met anyone who started talking about Roosevelt and Truman the moment I met him."

He blushed and laughed too. "Sorry. I'm not good at small talk. Maybe you can teach me." Then he asked if she liked to dance. She laughed and they danced right there on the grass by the roses. He was a wonderful dancer, and he hummed the tune of "Mona Lisa," saying he didn't know the words. Afterward, he plucked a rose petal, yellow and fragrant, and gave it to her. Smiling, she tucked it into her small purse. After the party they walked the streets of Eugene, talking, talking, still in their finery, until they arrived at Clara and Lillian's apartment and Clara fed him cold roast chicken and sliced tomatoes. She still has the shriveled yellow rose petal in her jewelry box. She remembers his lopsided smile, his hair standing straight up in cowlicks on the right side of his head, one shoulder riding higher than the other, his tie on crooked. He hated appearance-mongering and folderol of all kinds. His gray eyes clear and straightforward, his absolute integrity: How could there ever be anyone else? She sits on the bed, tears welling.

They had one of those intense love affairs that exclude

everyone else. To Frank, his parents lived inside a magic circle. Samantha at an early age retreated to books and ballet lessons, while Frank ran after girls. Clara knew something had changed with Frank when he was almost nine, but she wasn't sure what or why. Had he caught his parents in a private moment? He watched the way she and Darrell lightly touched each other while talking, the way their eyes sought each other in a silent language. The boy seemed lonely, despite all his girlfriends and many friends. Clara watched him, and he watched her back.

In the evenings, Clara played the piano. It helped her relax. Darrell was refreshed by Clara, her piano playing, and his two children. Growing up in the Great Depression, too young to serve in World War II, he was grateful to have a steady job as a linotype operator at the Eugene *Register-Guard*. He had only two years of college. The incessant roar of the linotypes (like giant typewriters) and printing presses, the repetitive selection of iron letters from long trays, loading them onto the linotype, carefully cleaning each letter—all this wore him down. But he had the woman he wanted, and they had a family to raise. He would never disrupt the steady money. So he stayed at the *Register-Guard*, his supply of Tums and Phillips' Milk of Magnesia never enough to quiet his fiery belly full of ulcers they didn't discover until the year before he died.

Every weekday afternoon, Frank and Samantha listened for his key in the door at four fifteen. He was the first parent home, fresh from riding his bike to and from work. Clara drove the Chevy. She stayed at school correcting papers until five thirty while Darrell made dinner. Once home, she marched around telling detailed stories about her students. After dinner, she did the dishes and played Schubert and Bach on the piano for a half hour before the children finished their homework.

This was the time of day when Frank and Samantha gained admission to the exclusive world of their parents, a world in which Clara was the star and no one talked. At least they all belonged together then.

The Parenting Room in her head creaks open as she sits on the bed with the hats. *I paid more attention to my students than to my own kids.* Her heart constricts at the welter of memory and insight coming at her: She was too strict, too indulgent, too self-absorbed, too complacent. Millions of examples come alive in her head. A parent's regret lacerates to the death.

She can't go on nattering this way. She can't hallow the past anymore. She has to deal with the present, and that's that. She gets out her scissors and makes a decisive cut through the layers of net on the lavender garden hat. She must have a way to protect Frank in an emergency. She's got to train the wasps. She wants no more stinging in her house. So she cuts a lavender net circle to protect the neck opening. She sticks the circle to the neck opening with Velcro, so the opening can be free or closed, depending on the threat level of the wasps. She cuts up a few more of her T-shirts and makes a net face mask for each one, in case her social calendar fills up. She tries on one of the altered T-shirts and laughs with delight. She looks like a veiled woman from the Middle East. Nobody will get stung now, especially not Frank. Relieved, she keeps working. The wasps, bunched together on top of her head, see she's happier. They set to bickering and jostling among themselves like playful puppies. The purple wasp cartwheels around her as she works.

In the morning, Clara's out walking. She likes the plain desert, the absence of shadow, the early silver light. Missing Frank, she lopes onto the short streets just to be around people. To see others going about their business, watering a potted plant or walking hand in hand, gives her hope that maybe she too might live a normal life around normal people before she dies, that she and Frank might finally talk about painful matters.

On Royal, a younger woman exits her ramshackle trailer, talking to herself. Twice she trips as the curb ends at a cross street and as she blindly steps on a Raggedy Ann doll lying on the sidewalk. Recovering her balance, the woman takes in great whiffs of caffeinated steam rising from her travel mug. A hot pink shoulder purse slaps her thigh. Absently she smooths her Desert Dan's uniform with her free hand, still talking to herself.

Clara grins. She used to start her teaching days like this, talking to herself in the car, inventing teaching tricks as she drove to school. She knows this is Stella from seeing her with Frank, just as Stella knows this is Frank's mother.

"Hi there." Clara catches up to her.

Startled from thought, Stella spills coffee on her skirt. "Oh!" she cries.

"Sorry! I thought you heard me coming."

Stella's laugh is easy. "I'm in a deeper trance than usual this morning."

They introduce themselves. "Scotty told me about your shows," says Clara. "I've been hoping to meet you." They're heading toward Desert Dan's.

Stella's tone is conspiratorial. "You like political theater? Performance art?"

"I'm interested that you're trying to do something different in this god-forsaken place."

Stella laughs. "It's not so god-forsaken after you get used to it. I'm a city girl– L.A. and San Francisco. I like it here. No one puts on airs; people have a lot of heart. I like that."

You haven't met Dawson, Clara thinks morosely.

Stella blows on her coffee. "I'm trying to come up with a new performance idea. It's got to be short. Scotty sticks to the bottom line. Three minutes max."

"So, what's your project?"

Stella tells her about Mr. Hamdi's hatred of Western ways, his anger at his Westernized daughter, his intent to take Aisha back to Saudi Arabia to make her a proper Muslim woman, Aisha's acceptance into pre-med at Boston University that she'll have to abandon.

Clara nods. "You see that a lot, young immigrants clashing with their parents over American ways. When I taught high school, I had several bright Latinos give up on college plans because their parents wanted them to go to work right away."

"Well, Aisha's father thinks Western ways will make her a prostitute. Wearing jeans and a tank top means she's already lost her way. Culture shock is part of it, of course, but I'm blown away by the man's complete distrust of his daughter. She was accepted to a top pre-med program, for Pete's sake."

Clara frowns. "Well, but in our own culture wars, we sometimes *kill* people– homosexuals, abortion doctors."

"True, we go tribal. So, what do you think–would people side with Mr. Hamdi or his daughter? Jackpot's pretty conservative, you know–mostly redneck, but a surprising number of liberals, more than you might think."

"Might be a hung jury."

"Might be interesting. The traditional patriarch versus the rebellious daughter. Some kind of moral tradition that must not be breached. Trouble is, my kind of theater has a lot of improvisation. Things can go off the rails. My players involve the locals, and the locals often don't know it's a performance. They think it's real. Might cause trouble."

"I can see you're a born troublemaker."

Stella winks. "That's my job."

chapter 12

Dawson and Edie laugh and grapple and shed their clothes inside the door of the motel room and collapse onto the bed. It was supposed to be a quickie, but it turns into another marathon. Edie's mock-pouting because Dawson's got to work the swing shift at his new temporary job, washing dishes at Sam's Steakhouse, another grab at small change before they hit the road. Laughing, they roll over and over, almost fall off the bed. She's biting his cheek, neck, arms. For the first tireless days, they would have sex and eat and sleep and have sex and eat and sleep. They've had sex on the bed, in the shower, on the floor, on the dresser (they almost broke it), in various inventive positions. They have sex, they eat Ding Dongs and Fig Newtons and beef jerky and Hershey's with Almonds and they drink Snapple and Coke. Dawson has an old padded vest from army surplus, convenient for shoplifting at the mini-mart.

She could drain a man, he thinks, though he loves her wildness. She's a lot younger and nicer than Beth, his last girlfriend. He broke up with Beth in Cheyenne three weeks ago and vowed never again to hook up with an older woman (Beth was thirty-six to his twenty-seven). Beth kept tabs on where he went, how he spent his money, the kind of shaving cream he bought, even the state of his digestion, which could be better. He finally nixed

Beth after he saw her at a sports bar flirting with a guy who had enormous pecs and biceps and a muscle T-shirt that said *WHITE POWER* on front and back. Dawson didn't want to mess with any of that, so he just stole a car and ended up in Jackpot.

Edie's not like Beth, thank God. She's only twenty-one, and all she wants is sex. He certainly doesn't mind that. In the last week he's sleeping better than he's slept in months. But Edie's a strange one, mysterious. Whenever he tries to turn the talking to a personal vein, she clams up. Usually *he* clams up when a *woman* asks personal questions.

He dozes off for a minute, then wakes with a start. She's lying there naked, smoking and watching him in his postcoital nap. "What the fuck time is it," he mumbles, turning onto his stomach again.

"Four thirty." She draws deep on her cigarette and grinds it out in the clear glass ashtray on the nightstand.

"Christ, I was supposed to be at work a half hour ago. Why didn't you wake me up?"

She climbs on top of him, blowing smoke in his face. "Let's do it again before you go," she says with a sleepy smile. For a minute he weakens, then stops himself.

"Doll, we got no money. I don't wanna get fired on my fourth night. We got fifteen bucks between us. Lemme go." He gets the clothes they dropped by the door. He's hungry. Even the Ding Dongs are gone. He'll snag something at the restaurant.

He had to get a job after Aw Shucks ran off with their gambling money. He's still pissed about that. Edie's tired of hearing about it. The kitchen at Sam's Steakhouse, not far from Desert Dan's, is steamy and loud with rattling dishes. He likes it that way, to be surrounded by a cloud of steam. Nobody sees him. He's just a pair of wrinkled white hands at the sink because the rubber gloves he has to wear have holes in them. He rinses crud off plates, plops the dishes into the big dishwasher, runs it, empties it, the cycle begins again, over and over, for eight hours, four p.m. to midnight. It's disgusting to see plates of half-eaten food—fat from bloody steaks, half-gnawed bones, wilted lettuce, curdled sauce, lipstick stains on cups and glasses, imagining people's spit on the silverware. He's only working there a week or two, just to get exit money to L.A., after wasting time in Reno to look for his mom.

Edie lies on the bed watching him shimmy into his smelly clothes. Every night when he comes back to the motel, he smells of detergent, bleach, and sweat. In the steamy restaurant kitchen, his clothes stick to him. They need to find a Laundromat pronto. She's had to wear Dawson's clothes: boxers, T-shirts, a couple of bandanas she found in his old duffel bag, not knowing she'd be staying in Jackpot.

"I got a job at the drugstore," she lied to Neil and her Uncle Jim the other day when she saw them waiting to board the bus heading back to Twin Falls. "I'm staying awhile." She was surly, as if fixing for a fight, but her uncle just looked down at the ground.

"I was afraid of that," he said softly.

Neil fiddled with his camera.

"No pictures, dammit," she said, embarrassed by the feelings rising in her. Ignoring her, Neil corralled a passing woman to take the picture as he and their uncle quickly gathered around Edie. They scurried into the bus as she walked away, her head held high. She took a deep breath. Her life was really starting now. She might be famous someday. She sees her flushed face in somebody's big truck mirror.

Now, in the motel room, she looks up at the rust-stained

ceiling, wishes she'd brought some colored pencils and a drawing pad with her. At least then she could get some decent sketches of this god-awful place. As it is, all she does is watch TV while Dawson's at work, because let's hear it again, they have no money, not even for a little gambling. Cranky, she clicks onto a rerun of *Gidget.*

"How long we gonna stay here?" she calls out. He's trying to untangle his long black hair at the bathroom mirror with a half-toothless pink comb he snagged from her little green purse. Edie barely looks at him when he comes into the room. She's involved in the movie.

"Well, we can leave any time, doll, long as we get some money. They'll pay me tonight. But a hundred bucks ain't going very far." She doesn't say anything. He gives her a quick glance. "Don't go gambling tonight."

"Jesus Christ, I know that." Her eyes are glued to the small screen.

He winks at her as he waltzes out the door. "Maybe we can get some money fast, doll."

"I'm all ears."

The door clicks shut. Alone now and sullen, she lights another cigarette. As soon as *Gidget* is over, she's going over to Desert Dan's. Maybe she'll win big.

When the movie ends, Edie gets out her black nail polish with silver sparkles and gives herself a manicure and a pedicure. Holding out her thin arms, she splays her fingers out and winks at herself in the crazed dresser mirror. Her wrists are unnaturally limber. She can bend her hands way back, especially the arm with the deformed forearm bone they had to take out. Dawson says she's made of rubber. She stands on tiptoe to adjust her skimpy attire in the mirror—the black bandana (Dawson's) that she made into a halter top secured with string, his red boxer shorts rolled dangerously low, her shorn bleached hair, her hairless legs, face and navel piercings glittering on her corpselike skin, the black roses tattooed on her forearm, her four-inch silver platform sandals. Running out of spray net, she spits on her fingers, twists shoots of her spiky hair. She sticks a ten-dollar bill Dawson forgot on the dresser into her little green shoulder purse and sashays on over to Desert Dan's. On the way over, her stomach constantly growls. She needs to win.

Inside the casino, she changes the ten for a cup of nickels at the change booth and makes her way to the nickel slots. People stare at her, like always. Tonight she ignores them. She's so hungry she's a little nauseated. Cruising the nickel aisle, looking for a good machine (one or two cherries or black bars on the screen), she settles on two cherries already in the window. Pumping, pumping, she wins five, then ten, then fifty nickels. She loves to hear the coins clanging out. She's got nothing but men in her aisle. Their eyes linger on her body, their faces masklike. It's so stupid and annoying. She's taken, man. They have no idea.

Soon a tall man moving slowly down the next aisle gets her attention. He's talking urgently about something, drawing a little crowd. He's wearing a beige tunic, beige pants, and a little beige hat like a bowl. Some kind of uniform. She wonders if he's one of those people that used to hang around airports dressed like doctors or nurses, wanting money for something or other. He's probably in some group all right, but she doesn't know what. He has a slight accent she can't place. He looks nondenominational with his sandy hair and dimples, but the close-fitting uniform must mean something. The guy looks nervous that people are actually paying attention to him. He looks trapped, like he'd rather be somewhere else.

Surrounding him are men with red faces and receding hair-lines, women with frazzled hair and pinched, tired faces. They look worn out—the gumption knocked out of them somehow. Edie ignores them, keeps feeding in her nickels, keeps win-ning. After a while, she counts her coins. She can at least buy a drink now. She flags a cocktail waitress and orders a bourbon and Coke. She's actually more interested in the Coke than the bourbon and imagines the sweet bite of the carbonated beverage sliding down her throat, settling her stomach.

Pretty soon the guy and his fans enter *her* aisle. He's still riled, she can hear now—about *gambling*? "Gambling leads to loose morals and greed," he says. "If we're really serious about improving this country, we should outlaw gambling for starters and shut this casino *down*," he intones, as if he's finally found his punch line.

"Right!" exclaim a few followers, who then look around in surprise, as if wondering what to do next.

Edie snorts. How did this guy get in here? He can't be a Hare Krishna, because those guys are way mellower than this guy. And Hare Krishnas don't wear beige. Or maybe they do, she can't remember. The five or six people around him lean for-ward to catch his words. "We need rules of behavior. Things are too confused in this country. If we had more rules and everyone knew the rules, there'd be less violence. *Uncertainty* is what causes trouble." Their faces light up. Finally someone is speaking of things they secretly believe but have kept to themselves before. They gather closer to the man in beige, who still looks surprised all this is happening, as if he really wishes they'd go away. He's a puzzle to Edie. He looks nice enough.

The group stops about ten feet from her, a couple of them

murmuring and looking hard at *her,* others just looking around dazed and tired at no one in particular.

A bodybuilder type with a shaved head latches onto the group. He's got biceps bigger than grapefruits, a creased forehead, and a gold stud in one ear. He's wearing one of those wife-beater T-shirts with no sleeves, the low-cut neck and back displaying his ripped pecs and delts. His eyes light on Edie, and right away his face starts to glow.

Oh, for Christ's sake, she thinks, disgusted at herself for even looking at him. She hates it that her heart is beating hard. Viciously, she pulls the lever and gets twenty-five nickels. The rattle of the coins distracts her for a few seconds.

The bodybuilder starts moving toward her. The others follow, but the man in beige looks alarmed. With a feeling of dread, Edie coldly turns her back on the intruder and faces her slot machine once more. Her thin shoulder blades are hunched up and stick out like baby bird wings. The bumps show on her spine, and the dimples further down.

Watching her, the bodybuilder hitches up his belt and speaks softly. "Looky here, folks. This young woman is living proof of what the man says here. Who's looking after her? She needs guidance, not all this freedom." He gestures at her outfit. The small crowd is electrified by the man's daring. Their faces freeze.

Edie's skin crawls. He's going to make a dirty remark or a Jesus pitch, she just knows it. Tears well in fear and outrage, tears she viciously wills away. Arms crossed, she whirls around to face him. "Who asked you anyway? Mind your own business, asshole."

Voices ring out in the next aisle. "Atta girl." "Give 'em hell." "This is a free country." "We came here to have fun, not get preached at." "Where's Scotty anyway?" "He'll kick these assholes out."

Encouraged, Edie defiantly glares at the man in beige's fans, though they've said nothing to her. Surprised at her hostility, they take a step back. *What kind of person is she anyway?* their shared glances say. An air of muffled outrage infects them. The bodybuilder steps closer. Her hands tremble. She just wants to get away. She scoops her winnings into her cup and holds it close to her chest. The bodybuilder is going to touch her, give her a blessing, or do something worse, something that will make her puke—she sees it in his eyes. The man in beige gives Edie a sympathetic look. Seeing this, her face softens a little. Maybe the man in beige didn't mean for this harassment to happen. After all, he was only talking about gambling, not wardrobe choices.

Glancing around to plot her escape, Edie notices a familiar gray-haired woman standing around watching this scene. Edie grimaces. It's the old lady she met when she and her brother Neil just got off the bus. Now the old lady is waving her arms hard at the man in beige, as if she knows him well and wants him to stop what he's doing. The old lady acts like she's trying to control the action, like she's the director. She looks silly, waving her arms around like that. Edie's mystified.

Standing beside the old lady, a beautiful redhead is just taking in the scene. Edie's seen her before too. She's a waitress, but tonight she's in Levi's. Edie wishes they'd all just go away and leave her alone. She just wants to eat. Maybe she can duck into the restaurant and grab some fries.

A commotion breaks out at the end of the aisle. Scotty, looking exhausted, is followed by four angry-looking men. Scotty elbows his way past Clara and Stella and halts in front of the man in beige. Scotty stares hard at the man, as if sending him an urgent message of some kind. "I can't have you bothering my customers, sir. Gambling is legal in Nevada, and I intend to keep my business open." The man in beige looks surprised. Cheers from the next aisle.

Suddenly the bodybuilder grabs Scotty around the neck and puts him in a hammer lock. Scotty coughs, turning red in the face. "You should listen to this man," the bodybuilder growls, pointing to the man in beige. "He's trying to make us better Americans. Not like you with your gambling den!"

Suppressing a grin, the man in beige tries to pull the body-builder off Scotty. This confuses the onlookers. The man in beige opposes gambling, yet he's protecting the owner, who will keep the casino open! This doesn't make sense to the onlookers.

The four angry men tackle the bodybuilder and knock him down. Women scream, including Edie, who's trying hard not to look scared. She's always so good at acting tough. In fact, she's frightened to death of these crazy people who want to tell every-one how to live.

Forget the bourbon and Coke. She doesn't want to die right here in this hellish place, ambushed by a muscled madman and four pissed-off guys. Her glittery green purse slides off her pale shoulder as she elbows through the crowd, heads for the exit, and vanishes into the night.

The confrontation ends almost as soon as it began. Scotty tiredly tells the bodybuilder and the four angry men that the whole episode was a little bit of theater. Something about try-ing to understand other people's viewpoints without resorting to violence. His look is sardonic. "It didn't quite work out that way, did it?"

"Whoa!" exclaims the bodybuilder. "I had no idea. Sorry

man, you had *me* fooled."

Frank, who is the man in beige, just wants to get rid of this guy. "It's OK, man, no harm done."

"Shit, why didn't you tell us?" an angry man says to Scotty. "We just want to gamble in peace. No preaching."

"Things were getting messy, so I had to stand as the man in charge." Scotty is breathing hard. He's beginning to think he better rein in Stella on her little performance pieces. Things could get dangerous.

The bodybuilder gives a little salute and threads his way through the casino to rising cheers. People don't know why they're cheering him, only that they'd heard a scuffle there in the corner, and this strong-looking man striding toward the exit looks like he could settle a fight in twenty seconds flat. The four angry men fade back into the crowd.

In Scotty's office, Frank starts in. "Why'd you horn in on our show? I wasn't happy about the bodybuilder hijacking my theme and bothering the girl. I'm sorry he tackled you, but he was just following my cue. He had no idea what was going on. I could have brought him around. You should have trusted me."

"Listen, Frank, a couple of those pissed-off guys had guns. I saw the bulge under their belts. Did you? They just wanted to gamble, not debate moral values. I wasn't going to have a body count because of our little experiment in cultural understanding."

The two old friends exchange hard glances and a long silence. Frank finally says, "We should get over to Stella's. They'll wonder what's keeping us."

They're silent on the way over. Frank would like to find the young girl and apologize. He vows he'll never be shanghaied into one of Stella's nutty theater pieces again. He's upset Clara didn't get to be the mother who calms her immigrant son because she understands his culture shock. *She* was supposed to be the hero of the piece, for Christ's sake.

That morning, Clara had gone over to Stella's so they could work out Stella's last-minute idea of Clara as hero. When Clara walked in the door, she and her son silently embraced, holding it long. Stella busied herself in the kitchen.

"I'll come over tomorrow," he said quietly to his mother.

"That would be wonderful," she said.

Then the three of them worked on the Clara-as-hero twist.

As Frank and Scotty shuffle over to Stella's for the post-performance wrap-up, Frank fumes. "It all went haywire. The girl and the pissed-off men came out of nowhere."

Stella had warned Frank that unexpected things might happen and he had to just deal with it. *So this is what she likes,* he thinks bitterly—*actors in the soup with chaos.* He rattles someone's chain link fence hard enough to make Scotty give him a quietly watchful look.

Stella opens the door to their unhappy faces and exclaims, "It took a wild turn, didn't it?"

Frank is immediately sorry he came. He's already talked way too much tonight. He's in no mood to see Stella or anyone else right now. What he'd really like is to drive somewhere in the trailer cab and work on the fucking burl. He sits down on the purple loveseat beside Clara, but he doesn't want to talk to her either. Seeing his mother just gets him pissed off about the wasps again. He takes a deep breath and tries to relax.

Scotty has collapsed into an armchair. "I'd sure like a cold beer."

"Copy that," Frank says.

Stella hustles two Budweisers from the fridge. Scotty and Frank down hearty swigs in silence, digging into a big bowl of tortilla chips and salsa on the coffee table. The women watch the men stuff themselves.

"So. What do you think?" Stella's cheery tone fools no one.

Scotty tells the women that four guys had guns and threatened to use them if the anti-gambling crap didn't stop.

Stella looks chastened. "Wow. That's street theater for you. But nothing happened, thanks to you and Frank."

Clara studies her fingernails. "I was concerned about the girl. I know a little bit about her."

Frank flares. "I *bet* you do. Is she your latest charity case? Watch the line form in the morning, folks." As soon as he says this, he regrets it. "Sorry, I didn't mean that, Mother."

Clara blanches, then gets angry. "I can't believe you liked to see the biker spotlighting the way the girl was dressed. Are we advocating wardrobe police now?"

"Hold on, Mother. I wasn't happy the biker drew the girl into our scenario either. She looked pretty scared."

Awkward silence.

Stella's voice is husky. "The last thing I want is to abuse my friends or a young girl."

Scotty tips his beer to her. "You didn't abuse us, Stella, and the girl will recover. We all had an idea this thing might get a little wild. The good thing from my point of view is it didn't involve the whole casino, just the one section back by the restaurant. And it was short." He gives Stella a meaningful look. "People seem kind of touchy these days. We might want to cut back on polarizing topics."

Stella swallows, nods. "The country's a tinderbox. I should

have realized."

Scotty sets his empty beer can on the coffee table. "Tell you what. I'm really not in the mood for a grisly postmortem. I'm calling it a night."

Clara gets up, her eyes snapping. "Me too. I'm tired." She's tired of always feeling like a beggar around Frank. He knows how to make her feel guilty—this time by bringing up her big focus on troubled students when she was teaching.

Stella hugs Clara and Scotty. "I'm sorry we didn't have time to turn it around to Clara Triumphant."

Frank stands expressionless at the door beside Stella. He leans toward Clara and says quietly, "See you tomorrow."

She nods. "Yes. Good."

Stella clears away beer cans and snacks onto a tray. Frank watches her a minute, decides to make this quick. "OK, look, Stella, here's the deal. I need some time to myself right now. All this was a bit much for me."

She looks up from the counter where she just put the full tray. She looks like someone has punched her in the stomach.

"This kind of acting, maybe any kind of acting, it's just not in the cards for me, babe. I need to think a little bit. And so do you."

Her face collapses in surprise, her eyes wide brown pools. But she wants to accommodate him. "OK, sure." She stands there, arms hanging limply at her sides. "I'm so sorry, Frank."

He moves toward her and kisses her on the forehead. "Nothing's wrong, Stella. I just need a little time."

She kisses his chin. "I understand. It's OK." She looks at him. "When will I see you?"

"Tomorrow. Don't worry. I'll see you tomorrow."

"OK then."

He lets himself out the door.

Stella stands by the loveseat, hears him gun the motor and drive away. Her spare neighborhood is silent once more in the night. Her trailer creaks like it often does, as if the earth were restless. Tonight the sound seems amplified. Absently she finishes the cleanup and drapes the damp dishrag over the faucet. The pipe under the sink makes a thumping sound. Not again! Exasperated, she goes back to the loveseat and flops down, too frazzled to check the faucet tonight. She kicks off her sandals and puts her shapely feet up on the coffee table.

He had resisted this role all along, felt deeply uncomfortable with it. She had pushed him. He only did it to please her. She feels ashamed. She thought it would be a great thing if he discovered he could perform, respond to unexpected moments. For her, performing is the answer to every problem known to man. The stage is a holy place, she likes to say, and the stage can be anywhere. The stage was where we faced human problems way before the early Greeks.

She leans her head back onto the loveseat and closes her eyes. She could control every other man she ever knew, outsmart them, end up getting her way. And all these men bored her to death. She didn't respect them. Frank, she sees more clearly now, is like her father. Stubborn. Headstrong. Intelligence steaming under the surface.

"You can't control this man. Don't even try." Her voice is anguished. "This is the man you want. Just let him be. Don't drive him away, for God's sake. Think you can manage that?"

She picks up her sandals and pads to her bedroom, where she angrily strips off her clothes and falls naked onto the bed. She keeps listening for the guttural sound of the trailer cab. The night is still.

Clara sits at the kitchen table. Agitated wasps circle her head. She watches them, not really seeing them. She's been getting pressure headaches ever since the purple wasp stung her forehead twice right before the trip. The stings haven't healed. And lately she's had intermittent pain in her chest—not a hard pain, just a kind of off and on electrical charge radiating willy-nilly around her chest, like it's doing now. Just when she thinks she should tell Frank, the pains go away. On this unsettled night, her thoughts turn dour.

It's just a wobbly time, nothing more, she decides: the move, Dawson, Frank, the invasive photographer (*where is she anyway?*), the determined purple wasp pushing her toward something she signed on for but still resists with all her might. But she's not going to be a mother who plays the health-slash-age card. Restlessly she walks through the living room, down the hall into her bedroom. She touches the satiny oak door frames along the way, inhaling the scent of lemon oil. She sees the timeworn objects that fill her house, all of which she would trade for no other. From her bottom drawer, she takes out the big manila envelope full of family pictures and spreads them on the dresser to examine. She often does this when she can't sleep. After hours of disquiet, she finally sleeps. The wasps are restless until dawn.

Perching on Clara's night table, the purple wasp casts a cold eye on her as she sleeps. The wasp, her swollen head aching, knows Clara is stalling like mad—so hung up about Frank that she can't even approach the cesspool surrounding Samantha's death. Clara has to come to peace with *both* her kids before she dies—has she forgotten? And what about a chance at personal happiness?

Would that be so awful? The wasp's job is to heal Clara, but Clara has to be an active partner. The purple wasp has to act fast.

20 days left.

After leaving Stella's, Frank drives the trailer cab a few miles down the highway to the Salmon Falls Creek picnic area. It's deserted and unlit this time of night—a few picnic tables on concrete slabs, trash cans chained to the cement, rest rooms portable. High grasses grow beside the lazy stream. Tonight a cigarette doesn't even sound good. He gets out of the cab, goes around to the passenger side, gets in, slams the door hard, locks both doors, and gets out the adjustable headlamp he always carries in case of car trouble. He places it around his head and turns it on. He gets the wooden slab he uses as a work surface from behind the passenger seat and puts it on his lap. He puts his tool case and the half-finished burl on the work surface.

He picks up the burl. In the headlamp's glare, the half head looks eerie, crazed, like some totem from a savage society. He readies his tools and digs viciously into the unfinished places around the eyes, nose, and mouth. In a previous session, he gave it a mouth because he couldn't stand that it lacked one. Now he wishes he'd left it mouthless. The features are cramped and distorted, dwarfed by the oversized forehead. The expression on the face is one of torture or terror, as if the enlarged brain causes the personage great agony. He makes the mouth an empty tunnel going all the way through to the back. He digs at the eyes, making a deep hole for the retinas. One eye is squinting, the other one swollen. The brows are beetled, hanging with a few straggly roots that had taken hold in the crevices.

He works for almost an hour, scarcely aware of time. Finally he runs out of things to do to it. He lifts it up and examines it in the glow of the headlamp, sets it down again, rolls down the window. It's gotten stuffy in the cab. He lights a cigarette, takes a deep drag, lets his arm hang out the window, tapping ashes off, realizes he doesn't want it. When the flame is nearly down to his fingers, he stubs out the cigarette in the crammed ashtray on the dash. Outside it's quiet, nothing but a lone cricket and the sound of nearby sluggish water. He scoots down in the seat, leans his head back. He's tired to the bone. At least Scotty gave him a key. He looks at the completed head again, once more shines the headlamp on it.

It looks like trash. It looks like nothing he would want. He digs a hammer from under the seat, gets out of the cab, sets the work surface with the burl head on the ground, and brings the hammer down hard on the head. It cracks in two. He bashes and bashes until it's in small pieces. He feels better. He picks up the work surface and slides the shattered burl pieces onto the ground. The pieces hitting the ground sound dry and rustling, like tinder. He walks around to the driver's side, gets in, slams the door, puts his tools back in the leather case, puts the case and the work surface under the passenger seat. He revs the engine and heads over to Scotty's.

chapter 13

Sprawled on the motel bed, Edie pulls on her zirconium navel ring as she stares at the cottage cheese ceiling and the rusty water stains above the dresser. She's just wolfed down a Hi-C, some Corn Nuts, and a Baby Ruth from the vending machines near their room and feels a little better, but not much. She pours the rest of her nickels into the little green purse, now bulging with them, and throws the plastic coin cup away. She doesn't want to think about anything until Dawson gets back from work. Hands resting on her flat belly, she dozes off a few minutes, wakes, and stares again at the ceiling. Listlessly she hums a song from "*Grease*". She parks an ankle onto the opposite knee and rocks back and forth, wishing she knew the rest of it. But she can hum it, and repeats it over and over, until she almost dozes off again.

Like everyone else, she'd laughed at the words from *Grease* over the years. Now, having seen where the words come from, she knows it would be fatal to tell anyone she secretly envies Gidget. Gidget had all those people protecting her–parents, the surfer guys, everyone bending themselves into pretzels to keep her safe, the innocent virgin. The thought of all this is too painful for Edie. Lighting a cigarette, she thinks, *Don't be stupid, bozo.* Gidget's dead; Gidget never was. Good riddance to fairy tales.

She massages her stomach and examines her glittering fingernails. It's too quiet. A car door slams somewhere. It's 11:25 on Saturday night. Everyone is still out.

She stares at the generic motel room painting that hangs opposite the bed–a horse-drawn covered wagon commandeered by a bedraggled man under a pale desert sky. Two skinny kids and a bonneted mother peer from the wagon opening. Edie has no idea how these people could stand to come all this way west, but then again, history was never her strong suit. She yawns, turns on the late local news, finds it boring, and promptly falls asleep.

When Dawson gets back at 12:20, she's limp and twitching in her sleep. Disappointed, he takes off his clothes and flops down beside her. Soon he's snoring. In the morning around ten, he slowly opens his eyes and looks over at her, the dry roar of the air conditioning already numbing his mind.

She's facing him, chewing viciously on a piece of beef jerky he brought back. She starts right in. "This place is such a sorry ass dump, Dawson. I mean it. Let's get out of here. I can't stand it another minute."

He gets a cigarette from the bed table, lazily lights it, and flops back down, staring first at the stained ceiling and then at her. "What're you so steamed about, baby?"

"Me? Nothing a little food wouldn't help," she fumes, her lips tight.

"Come on now, you know we'll eat." He looks at her. "I know something's bothering you."

She burrows on top of him and mumbles into his neck. "These stupid guys at Desert Dan's were carrying on last night about how gambling is a sin and we need rules instead of freedom and I need guidance. Can you beat that? One guy had a little hat and this beige outfit, a tunic. He looked like a Hare Krishna. The other guy was this ripped bodybuilder. He was the worst. He thought I was dressed like a slut and all."

"What? What guys? You dress beautiful, baby, you know that. Those guys are asshole losers." He tries to lift her chin to look at him. "What were you doing at Desert Dan's anyway? I told you we don't have any money."

She keeps mumbling into his neck. "Keep your shirt on. I didn't gamble. Those guys were so obnoxious, Dawson. Preaching like they knew better than anybody else. The guy in the tunic said we should shut down the casino, only he didn't really mean it. It was so stupid." She rolls off him, lights a cigarette, inhales deeply, faces him again. "So the bodybuilder gets the owner in a hammerlock, other guys pile on, and it starts to look bad."

"*Serious?* Come on now, don't fool with me, baby. Where was security?" His cigarette ash is almost ready to fall onto the bed. She offers her ashtray; he taps it in. She snuggles against him.

"Good question. I left. It was too crazy for me." She buries her face on his chest.

He slowly counts all the rust stains on the ceiling: five. "Baby, don't ever listen to guys like that. They don't know nothing. How beautiful you are. How smart." He squeezes her hand. She turns onto her back. Lazily he blows a perfect smoke ring. They both watch it float higher and higher, until it expands and disappears. The air conditioner roars. He turns his head and speaks softly in her ear.

"Smoke rings are one of the prettiest things in the world, don't you think, baby?" He blows in her ear. She giggles and rubs her ear. "Smoke rings don't hurt anyone; they don't ask you to do anything or be anything. They just float and get all cloudy and soft and then they disappear, but not really. You know the smoke's still around somewhere, but you can't see it, and it's fine not to see it. First it's in your lungs and you blow it out, and it gets all invisible and nice in the air. And if you open the door, all this invisible stuff that was in your lungs goes up into the sky. So part of yourself ends up in the sky, and you didn't even know it. Ain't that nice?" He doesn't say anything for a minute. He nibbles soft kisses around her eyes and forehead until he's surprised to see tears running down the side of her face into her black roots and hacked-off blonde hair. "What's wrong, baby?"

She turns and buries her face in his shoulder. "I never felt as close to anyone as you, Dawson. You're like a miracle to me. I always feel better when I'm with you."

"Aw, baby." He wraps his body around her.

She's full-on crying now, but trying not to. "The only way to be in life is mean. Even when you don't feel mean. I know that as much as you do. I'm no fool. Everybody's out to get you one way or another. But I get tired of it all, good and tired."

"You gotta be mean, baby. It's curtains if they get you."

She looks at him for a long minute, tears glistening. A cloud passes over her face. "Just don't leave me, Dawson. At least not for a while. I'll look back and remember you, every minute of it, and be happy." She cries some more.

"Aw, baby, I'll never leave you, you should know that. You and me, we make a team. I never had a team before." Choking up himself, he holds her and lets her cry. He swallows hard, trying to control himself, clear his mind so he can figure out what to do. He needs a plan.

They lay there entwined as her tears subside. He thinks he loves her, but the idea of it frightens him. Love rips you up. He knows that for a fact. His stomach still tightens when he thinks of his mother leaving him at the Safeway in Reno. Finally he musters himself, as if waking from a dream. "You're right, baby, we need to clear out. Time's up for this dump."

She knew he'd buck her up. He always does. He's the idea man. He already showed her how to shoplift at the mini-mart. And how to meditate, sitting on the stained motel carpet with his legs crossed, palms up on his knees, making her chant "Om" one night when she was bummed because she thought she'd never see her brother Neil or her uncle Jim ever again. It wasn't that she got along so well with Neil and her uncle. On the contrary, she and her brother were always fighting. And Uncle Jim, the Idaho farmer with his sugar beets and tractors and his white forehead, was really boring. But she sensed her life with Dawson would take dramatic turns she couldn't quite make out yet, and there would be no going back to studying art in L.A. or seeing what was left of her family.

Dawson said she could see her relatives any time she wanted. He wouldn't stop her; he'd go with her and she could introduce him to the family. "Family. That might be interesting." His voice was harsh. A few nights later, he told her how his mother dumped him at Safeway. He said he wanted to see his mother just one more time and that would be enough. After all, he's been without her for twenty-one years. Edie had looked at him gravely, her eyes blazing, and said he should do it, go look for his mom. He said he had an aunt in Reno and maybe they could start there.

Her tears over, they lie on their backs and stare at the ceiling. "Let's do it," she says firmly. "Let's go find your mom." They solemnly shake hands. Dawson feels exalted. He's got a real partner now for the first time in his life.

In Edie's mind, she's already gone from this place. She sees herself sitting beside him pushing ninety in the stolen black

Camaro, windows rolled down, the straight ribbon of highway like a ruler on the desert floor, hurtling toward Reno. She's already got her homemade souvenirs from this motel—their first motel—stuffed in her little chartreuse shoulder purse. Dawson copped a pencil from Sam's Steakhouse the other day, so she used the three measly sheets of Sagebrush Motel stationary to draw three pictures: of him, her self-portrait, and a sketch of their room.

The drawing of Dawson shows him sleeping on his back with his mouth open, thin patrician nose, drool creeping tenderly across his cheek, black stringy hair in his eyes, arms folded across his skinny chest. He looks eighteen, new to the world, unmarked by pain or sadness. Her self-portrait is half her face looking in the mirror. She looks suspicious and sad. Facial hardware pierces her eyebrow, nose, and tongue; her mascara is smeared, an angry zit on her left cheek, her butch haircut sticking up every which way, puffy lips a sensual smirk. Her expression surprised her, because when she drew it she was really happy. She and Dawson had just made love and she felt like a female lion protecting her pride as he lay there making small snoring sounds like little hiccups and gasps and his breath hit his teeth and made a little whistle. Sometimes his teeth would click together as if he were snapping at something. She always likes it when he dreams and snores and has all these contortions.

Now he's wide awake staring at the ceiling. His eyes move back and forth as if he's reading, but she knows his eyes being jittery like that means he's thinking.

He's thinking he never got through all the rooms in the old lady's house, just the kitchen and living room and then she appeared like a ghost at the end of the hallway. The way she looked scared him off. He thought she'd be cowering in her bed, but no, she told him to clear out in this strong voice. He gets mad all over again thinking how he got scared off. He should've tied her up, kept looking for the money. He won't let that happen again. Adrenalin surges in him. He'll show Edie how he operates. She'll be impressed. He turns to face her.

"Those guys telling you how to dress, baby; everybody's on your case, right? I got people on my case too. Must be something in the air here. Remember that old lady you told me about when you first got off the bus? Well, she plopped herself down in the booth where I was waiting for you the other day. She wanted to know all my business. Acted like she had some rights over me, like she was going to set me straight. She wanted me to pay for some window that got broken, but she can't prove I broke it. She even had the gall to give me advice about my *allergies*." He snorts. "Bunch of nosy people around here, doll. Old lady's been on my case ever since I landed here, sticking her nose in where it don't belong. What I'm telling you, baby, is you're not the only one with people butting in your business. I got the old lady telling me how to clear up my snotty nose and you got assholes telling you how to dress."

Edie's been listening intently. "Yeah, now I remember. That old lady was in the casino last night. She was listening to the bodybuilder and the tunic man preaching about rules and regulations. She looked all stern, waving her hands at them to stop bugging me. That's what it was. The bodybuilder was mouthing off at what I was wearing and the old lady was waving her hands at the bodybuilder so the beige guy would lay off of me—like I couldn't take care of myself—like I'm a *baby*."

Helplessly, she flashes on Gidget's parents squirming because those horny beach boys might take advantage of their untouched daughter. Her laugh is bitter. Dawson looks quizzically at her.

She never had any parents saying who she could see or how she should act. No, what she had was a front row seat to her mom getting killed, and then she and Neil had their junkie aunt Betty to take care of them. Well, she won't fall for that Gidget crap and get her feelings all hurt because she never had any parents like Gidget's. Parents aren't like that anyway. It's all in the movies. No old lady's gonna step in and help her now. Besides, she never tells *anybody* what happened to her real mom. Nobody.

They trade glances, checking to see if the other one is only pretending to be brave. Edie's probably a robbery virgin, he thinks, but she won't chicken out with him around. And Edie knows Dawson's a pro. Falling silent at last, they furiously smoke and watch militant smoke rings fill the room.

"What the fuck," he says, sitting up. "An old lady like that probably has a lot of money socked away. Her whole life, she's got nothing to do but hide her money. I bet it's all in jars lined up in the back of her closet. Or where she keeps her towels." Energized by this fantasy, he says, "Let's see what she's got. Let's go right now." He gets a wide, leering grin on his face. "Nobody can tell *us* what to do. We set our own rules. Right, baby?"

"Fuck yeah." She's barely blinking. She likes this idea, likes all his ideas. The other day over at Rodman's Hide-Away he picked a lady's purse. The lady was busy gabbing with her friend, and he sidled up to her purse next to the slot machine and aced out a twenty from it. His eyes just glowed right before he did it, like they're glowing now. She stubs out her cigarette. The hairs on her arms stand up. "Now you're talking, dude. I like your style." She's never done a robbery before. She's scared and wants to hide her fear. She rips out a yell, sounds like a banshee.

He has a quarter bottle of Jack Daniels he copped from a liquor store in Cheyenne. While getting dressed, they trade chug-a-lugs and throw the empty bottle in the waste basket. She's wearing Dawson's navy-blue boxer shorts and his black T-shirt, which she cut up with her nail scissors, giving herself a bare midriff and a hint of the bottom part of her breasts if she stands up straight.

Dawson grins. "Here we go, baby. It's Reno or nothing." Witchy drunk, they're ready to light out for the territory, as they say. He tosses the paper sack with his toiletries, underwear, and an extra T-shirt into the back seat of the Camaro. Edie dabs on dark purple lipstick from her little shoulder purse that bulges with nickels. Her stomach is tense.

They burn down the highway a little ways to warm up the Camaro before doubling back and crunching into the huge vacant lot. This has got to be quick. Unfortunately, it's daylight. Slowing down to avoid undue attention, they pull up to the shabby little white house perched on the flatbed trailer. Dawson's mind is teeming. Stupid woman bothering him, bothering his girlfriend, setting him on edge, her life savings in a shoe, that's where it is. He'll teach her all right. Not even her son cares about her. He's always gone, leaves his mother wide open.

19 days left.

chapter 19

Anxiously looking at herself in the mirror, Clara seals the lavender net all around the neck opening again. She's a veiled woman. Wasps can't get in there. He'll be safe. Her unease about the abortive show last night has been replaced with giddiness. She's been dithering all morning in anticipation of her son's promised visit.

Suddenly sober, she looks in the mirror again and realizes he might not *want* to wear this contraption. Even if it keeps him safe.

And she might not blame him.

It *does* look kind of silly—a T-shirt like a shroud, a face obscured by net.

But she's got to make her son safe.

Surely he can understand that. Safe with whatever she has at hand.

Someone knocks.

Frank, at last.

Peering through the netting, Clara opens the door, smiling triumphantly.

It's Dawson and Edie, drunk, stunned, hooting at Clara and her headpiece. "Edie, will ya get a load of this? *Crazy* old lady! What the *fuck*." Transfixed, Dawson starts feinting blows right and left, as if to box with her. "Whadaya think—she wanna play hide-and-seek in that getup?"

Astonished, frightened, Clara leaps backward to dodge his blows. Her breath catches; she can hardly breathe. He swaggers into her kitchen, leaving Edie at the door.

Edie stares blankly at Clara. "She's playing hide-and-seek all right. But I can see that face, yes I can-n-n." She chants in a singsong voice, pushing Clara aside as she too marches into the kitchen. "First thing on our playdate here is *food*." She opens the refrigerator, her deformed arm ablaze with black tattooed roses. She guzzles from Clara's bottle of Cran-Apple juice, leaving purple lipstick marks all over the lip. She finishes it off, tosses the plastic bottle into the sink. Then she starts in on the cottage cheese, dipping out great mouthfuls with her fingers. She hates cottage cheese, but she's so hungry she'll eat anything.

She remains stone-faced, as if she thinks all old people wear strange T-shirts over their heads when they're home alone. At the same time, Clara's fright and obvious confusion almost makes Edie lose her resolve. The young woman glances at Dawson, who looks hard, without pity. OK then, she's got to stay strong too, and bring this thing off. They need money all right. She stares at Clara's headpiece as if she's hallucinating.

Clara stands paralyzed by this turn of events. Her mind has gone blank.

One by one, the wasps gather on the counter. Soon the wasps circle in a wild blur above everyone's head.

Edie looks up, frightened. "Jesus Christ, Dawson, she's got *wasps* in here!"

Dawson ignores Edie as he rifles through the kitchen drawers, trying to find money, trying to recover from the shock of Clara's getup. Seeing her look so ridiculous, so vulnerable, so grandmotherly, opens, against all reason, the unquenchable loneliness he has run from his whole life. "I won't abandon you." *Who said that? Did she say that? What's the matter with me? This friggin' woman is a nutcase, for Christ's sake.* He's embarrassed, furious. The way she makes him feel is intolerable. Why did he even *talk* to her that day in the restaurant?

Clara just stares, unable to believe Dawson and Edie are inside her house. *Where are the wasps?* she thinks dully, looking around. The wasps have formed a tightly packed circle over her head, flying so close together, making such a racket that it's as if they're shouting, planning something. The purple wasp leaves the circle and individually taps each wasp's wing, as if to enforce the importance of following some special instructions. Clara is bewildered. *What are they waiting for?*

Suddenly Dawson picks her up, all one hundred pounds of her, and sets her roughly onto a kitchen chair. Her involuntary shuddering angers him more. Roughly he ties Clara's wrists to the chair with clothesline from the Camaro. Dawson's ripe liquored breath surrounds her.

Licking the last of the cottage cheese off her fingers, Edie nods at Dawson—no words, just a nod of approval at him. Her little smile makes him swell with nervous pride. He can deal with this nosy old woman. He can tie her up. He's in charge here.

Dawson snatches the index card with Clara's new cell phone number from the wall and stuffs it in his pocket, a smile spreading on his face. If it's her number, he'll call her in the middle of the night. She'll wish she never laid eyes on him. But where's the cell phone? He looks around, sees only the charger.

Clara sits in terror, her eyes tightly shut as Dawson and Edie slam through the house, yanking out drawers, rifling her purse, cupboards, closets. Everything is happening so fast it can't be real. She's bound to wake up soon. She tries to free her hands. A hot bud of anger grows in her.

Finally the wasps—filled with fury to see their fragile mistress tied up, taunted, bullied, slammed onto a chair—go after the invaders, arcing wildly around Dawson and Edie's heads. The wasps dive-bomb their necks, arms, faces, Edie's bare stomach. She screams, tries to swat them away, but the wasps keep coming. The purple wasp and a squadron of supporters lead the fray, urging the others to greater ferocity as Dawson and Edie yell and curse. Usually the regular wasps do all the stinging. Purple wasps sting only in extreme circumstances, like when Clara threatened to chicken out of this whole trip. The stings above her eyebrows throb badly right now, as if she just got stung, or as if her stings are in touch with the chaos around her. She can't understand it.

Dawson swats at the creatures with a fly swatter, which angers the wounded insects in their death throes. Still the robbers stay focused on unearthing her meager treasures. The kitchen door is wide open. The wasps fly outside, circling furiously around the door. Dawson mutters, "She doesn't even have much cash." He's found sixty-five dollars.

The escaped wasps again gather forces and sizzle back inside in a dark cloud. Clara has never heard them buzzing so loud. The wasps sting the invaders on every bare skin surface, which on Edie is significant. Her corpselike white skin is blemished with welts. The young people scream anew; the purple wasp is busy indeed.

"Go get 'em!" Clara cries, unable to resist her fury. "Get 'em good!"

The robbers doggedly find Clara's few pieces of jewelry, including her wedding pearls, Frank's extensive coin collection,

$110 in cash. They dump everything into two paper shopping bags from under the sink.

The wasps are still on the attack, but some find the allure of the open air too much to resist. Despite the purple wasp's frantic corralling buzz, maybe a third of the wasps rise in a small cloud and disappear into a pale sky.

"Stay! My babies!" Clara yells in despair. She's beside herself that she's tied up and can't close the door.

Stunned, Dawson and Edie both think she means for *them* to stay. Edie is instantly close to tears. For a moment, she stops pillaging to stare at Clara. An impossible vision of Gidget's parents embracing her—she claps her hand to her mouth, remembering the fragrant rhubarb pie her Aunt Donna in Idaho took from the oven the last time Edie and Neil visited.

At the same moment, Dawson stops rummaging through bookcases for hidden money and involuntarily approaches the bound woman in the kitchen. Again Clara cries, "My babies! Don't leave!" He's mortally embarrassed to see her addressing a bunch of wasps that have landed on the kitchen table.

Clara stares at the young people, suddenly understanding what they thought. She's shocked, moved by their rank neediness, their rich body odors, their unhealthy pale skins. They need a mother, a father, a family, her. Nothing makes any sense at all.

Dawson shakes his head, cursing his own weakness. No *way* would she want them to stay. Still dancing from the painful stings, he jumps off the flatbed, followed by Edie, who swallows her tears, swats the furious creatures away from her ashen belly, and runs toward the car.

With a mighty tug, Clara at last unties her wrists and rips the netted T-shirt from her head. She's free. Dawson had tied her up carelessly, no doubt thinking she was too old and feeble to get loose. Blinking in confusion, she hears liquid spattering outside. She's got to get the wasps back! Panicked, furious, she marches down the steps, stops in disbelief.

Dawson is splashing gasoline from a five-gallon can high onto the siding and eaves, all around her house. Clara stares at him, then at the wasps. The purple wasp is flying around Dawson's head but isn't stinging him! The other wasps aren't either! How can this be?

She tries to wrench the gas can from his grip. "I've lived in this house for forty-nine years—do you hear me, Dawson? Forty-nine years!" Enraged, she wrestles him. "Give me that can! I won't have it!" He's a good nine inches taller. She's no match for his taut string-bean muscles. Suddenly she releases him. "You do these things, and you'll get thrown in jail, and you know it, Dawson. Call it off right now and just straighten up. Get yourself a decent life." Eyes brimming, she pelts him in a fury of blows. "For God's sake, just settle down. Your mother abandoned you, but I won't, even after this. Stop wrecking your life, do you hear me?"

He laughs, stunned. *She's crazy; I'm crazy. "I won't abandon you." I knew it before she said it!* His brain, her brain are mirror-image motherboards, united by a cable that flashes the same teeming signals to each brain. He hates her, loves her, wants her to care for him as if he were still that abandoned boy so long ago. But he can't tolerate such a thought: He'd be pudding. Coughing from the gas fumes, he realizes the only way to save his manhood is to burn down the house, burn her.

Furious, he splashes gasoline on *her*—on the back of her gray hair, on her Levi's, her long-sleeved blue blouse, her faded red Keds. As he's splashing, he roughly embraces her to make sure he gets gas on her back. He's nauseated, near to sobbing. She's wreathed in stink.

He's out of his mind. He pours this noxious liquid on her, yet he dares to embrace her? "No!" she shouts, slapping his face hard. Her brown eyes water with fury.

He throws down the can. Again, she's stopped him cold. He's truly on the verge of tears now. Clara sees this and her own eyes fill. "My boy," she says quietly. "For God's sake, what are you doing?"

Edie, watching this exchange, can't believe her eyes. He's chickening out! Shaken, she tosses some matches from the glove compartment toward him, shouting, "Just do it, Dawson! She's caused us enough trouble!" Swept up in pure action, Edie wants some grand finale, some way to just get out of here. On a sudden impulse, she opens the trunk and gets out a second five-gallon can of gasoline and runs inside Clara's house. Clara and Dawson barely notice her, so engrossed are they in their own drama.

He can't fail now. Clara stands still as if to dare him. He opens his flimsy match folder with the Firestone Tires sign on the front, lights a match, and throws the match at the gas-soaked siding. It flames up with a roar, spreads quickly.

Clara gasps. Still the wasps do nothing. They're just flying around Dawson's head. He lights another match, this one for Clara. He steps back, pauses before her. Time slows. His throat gorges. His eyes water with rage and some uncontrollable inhibition. He cannot this moment harm her further. He hates himself, hates her.

For a moment, he thinks to light himself afire. Why not finish the job? His life has been nothing but torment. He is filled with fury and sadness. He had no way planned a fire, only a robbery, and then he just grabbed the gas can. Now flames lick all around the little house in a fast swoosh, rising higher and higher on hungry siding that bubbles and blackens. The match burns down to his thumb and forefinger. Dazed, he drops the match and the pack of matches on the ground. Clara stands blankly looking at him, her arms useless at her sides. She glances at the burning house and quickly looks away. She can't move, can't look, can't absorb what he's doing to her house. In a mighty show of strength for his girlfriend, Dawson calls Clara one final name and runs to the waiting car.

But Edie's not there. She has run down the hall to Clara's bedroom. Once there, she stops, transfixed by the scattered family photos blanketing the dresser, some still inside a manila envelope. Riotous, joyful, playful pictures—the family on a wild coast, running into the waves, a father carrying his kids piggyback separately, the family playing badminton, singing, laughing at a birthday party, everyone wreathed in crowns of lilacs. Underneath this profusion are the framed pictures, hovering together like a shrine. A much younger Clara in a wedding dress standing close to her husband, two young children smiling and happy, the whole family picnicking among big lilac bushes on a summer day.

Edie's passion explodes on these pictures meant for Clara's eyes alone. In great swoops of the gas can, she defaces the whole dresser top with gas, then sprays the bed, throws a lighted match onto the dresser, and runs back down the hall, sloshing gas in every room as fast as she can, running hard to outrace the flames that try to catch her before she runs out of gas in the kitchen. Dawson looks on in astonishment as Edie bursts from the house. He's already in the car. She barely escapes the flaming house. She throws the empty can into the trunk, bolts to the passenger side. They take off in a cloud of exhaust as Edie weeps.

The old lady is Gidget grown up.

❖

Reeking of gas, Clara sits cross-legged on the bare dirt. Flames lick the dry siding and rise toward the overhanging roof. She can't look. The rumpled traces of lilacs in the paint are surely gone now, their delicate tracery, her soul's imprint, replaced by charcoal smears and singe. Flames, wild in the desert heat, threaten the rafters. She covers her eyes.

She'll get up in a minute. She has forty gallons of bottled water in Samantha's room. She will put the fire out; yes, she will. But right now, she moves like molasses. Sitting on the ground, she watches a chain of ants busily carrying particles of sand, touching each other as they go.

Maybe the house *should* burn down. All that pain and history, why not just let it go? She finds the abandoned pack of matches, rips out a match, savagely lights it, and throws it toward the house before realizing she risks an explosion with her own gas-wet clothes. She runs a hundred feet away. Looking back, she sees the match has fallen short and sputtered out. She sits back down on the ground and covers her face with her hands.

PART TWO

Clara pours warm water over herself in the bathtub as she sits in waist-high water. Watery tendrils drip down her upper body, her pores soften as if she were thirty years younger. Her silky chin-length gray hair is brown again, long; her lungs are supple balloons. A pot of ivy raises its leaves in the humid air. The steamy bathroom air hangs like suspended net, blurring everything into mist. It's as if she's near-sighted, but she is not.

She rises, towels herself off, walks outside into the evening rain that feels like a baby's breath. Next to the huge lilac bush blooming in the backyard, her husband Darrell stands waiting for her—young like he was before he died, a cowlick on his forehead. Beside him are their two children—Samantha, before she died, and Frank, still with her. The children are eleven and nine. She crosses the yard toward them in an uptake of breath. Arms around each other at last, they embrace in a close circle.

They are naked and homesick.

They are homesick, yet they are home.

The door is open, but they cannot go inside.

chapter 15

Clara sits in shock on the ground, staring dully at a broken fingernail. Frank, Stella, and Scotty come running across the highway. Grimly silent, they spray their fire extinguishers along the siding until the propellant runs out. The fire got a deadly head start before someone at Desert Dan's saw the burning house in the empty vacant lot. Scotty calls the Jackpot Fire Department on his cell phone. Frank tries to check inside the smoke-filled house, but flame and smoke drive him out. Coughing, he grabs Clara's purse and her Greenpeace mug, parked on the kitchen counter. The purse is unzipped, no doubt rifled. Dazed and furious, he runs back outside. All three bedrooms, the hall, and the living room are crackling. He can't believe it—the house she fought to bring here! His heart pounds. Why would anyone do this? She's a harmless seventy-three-year-old woman.

Frank, Stella, and Scotty mill around, unable to sit or be still, waiting for the fire truck. Their movements gradually penetrate Clara's stupor. "The wasps!" she cries. They stare at her. Frank runs back inside, runs out again. He sees the wasps swirling crazily in the sky. He forgets about the wasps, becomes dimly aware that the kitchen was spared. Badly shaken, he just wants his mother to be safe, wants to know what happened.

The fire truck whines in the distance. He promises himself

he won't fight her any more if she can just recover from this. At the same time, he hasn't talked with Stella since the post-performance party. Things are unsettled between them. He and his lover exchange pained looks. Their discussion will have to wait.

Scotty is winded and sweaty. "What happened, Clara?" His voice is weak. He looks down at her as she sits on the ground.

Slowly she answers. "Robbery. Young people."

"Which way did they go?" Frank asks.

Her voice is labored. "North. Not sure. Maybe south. Black Camaro. I didn't get the license number." Arms wrapped around her knees, she lapses into silence, too tired to say another word. She sits facing away from the house. She doesn't want to see it.

"Better than nothing," Scotty mutters. He takes out his cell phone to call the sheriff before he realizes he needs more information. He puts it away.

Frank is angry. "They weren't very smart. It's broad daylight. Who were they, anyway?"

"A guy, a girl," Clara is weary. "Two lost kids who needed money. Dawson somebody, Edie Porter."

Scotty looks hard at her. "Describe them." She gives him the basics. He stares. "Good God! I've seen them in the casino. Just the other day, security pointed out a guy named Dawson who had a little con going at the blackjack table, but it fizzled. Dawson Barth—that's it." He claps his hand to his forehead. "I should've run them both out of town!"

"I'll be fine. Everything will be fine." Clara's voice is hollow.

The fire truck shrieks as it comes closer.

Frank is suddenly still. "The girl sounds like the one who got drawn into our skit last night. Bleached hair, body hardware, minimum clothes . . ." He pales.

"That's her."

An awkward silence falls over the group. Dimly Clara stares at Frank, who stares at Stella, who stares at Scotty. Stella slowly sets her fire extinguisher on the ground and brings her hands to her head, as if warding off a blow, as if finally her form of theater has yielded a result she would never have asked for.

Frank stares at his mother. "For Christ's sake, I can't believe it."

A motley group arrives pell-mell from Desert Dan's, having seen the fleeing car. Some guy says, "Wyoming plates, license 1-36-542-J. Heading south. Need any help?"

"No thanks, we can manage," Frank thanks them profusely The strangers head back to Desert Dan's. Scotty writes down the license number.

Clara lifts her head. "Wyoming plates. Yes."

Now Scotty can call the sheriff. Still unnerved, Frank glances helplessly from his mother to Stella to Scotty.

Stella is moved by Clara's silent confusion, sitting there on the ground, looking blankly out at the highway. The fire truck arrives. Firemen easily kill the lingering flames and smoke. The embers sizzle. Quietly, Stella asks one of the two firemen if he could look in Clara's closet for any usable clothes.

Clara adds in a small voice, "Other closets too."

The burly fireman soon comes out with a second pair of sneakers and a few changes of stinky, smoky clothes. "You're lucky," he says. Stella gratefully accepts the bundle. She will take it to the Laundromat. As they are leaving, the fireman says, "Looks like the arsonists ran out of fuel. You've still got your kitchen." Clara looks at him, not comprehending.

Frank takes Scotty aside, then squats beside his mother. "OK Mom, you're welcome to stay at Scotty's for as long as you want. He's got lots of room."

Scotty says, "Sure thing, Clara."

Clara, frightened by this new development, looks uncertainly at her son.

"It's OK, Mother. You'll be comfortable there. I'll be there as much as I can. Scotty too, he'll be there."

She nods, dazed.

"We'll take care of you, sweetheart." Stella helps Clara stand, keeps her arm around her.

The sheriff arrives. He talks quietly, first to Frank, then to Clara. She looks frightened of the sheriff, watches him carefully and, when it's her turn, whispers something to him that makes the man look sharply at her. "Don't worry, ma'am. We'll do our best." He drives off. They watch him go.

After an awkward silence, everyone slowly shuffles away from the devastation, staying close together. Clara is the last to turn away, grasping her purse and her Greenpeace mug. She buries her face against Frank's shoulder, refusing to look back at the ruins as they walk to his trailer cab parked in the Desert Dan's parking lot. Frank drives his mother the short distance to Scotty's. Stella and Scotty follow in Scotty's car.

Once they're all inside, Stella says, "Let's get that awful gas smell off you, dear." Her voice is quiet. She leads Clara down the hall to one of Scotty's bathrooms.

Clara is momentarily stunned. The plumbing works! Hot water comes from the tap! No bottled water. Two washbowls. No camp toilet. Room to move around.

Stella will take Clara's canvas shoes and her gas-marred clothes to the Laundromat near her mobile home. Gently she helps Clara undress. Her movements are capable and unobtrusive. Clara is grateful, as she's unsteady now, the shock of events finally hitting her.

"Are you sure you'll be OK?" Stella asks, unsure whether to leave her alone in the bathroom.

"I'm fine. Don't worry." Clara tries to sound brusque. In truth, she wants some time alone to absorb what's happened. Soon after Stella closes the bathroom door, she is overcome with quiet sobs.

Stella has lingered outside the door to hear just such sounds. She knows Clara needs her privacy now. To Frank's and Scotty's concerned expressions as they sit in Scotty's barren living room, she mouths, "It's OK."

Weeping, naked, Clara stands shivering in the shower, though the water is warm, almost hot. She scrubs hard with Scotty's Dial soap and Head & Shoulders shampoo, inhaling the smell of these unfamiliar products deep in her lungs. *The wasps!* she thinks, panicked. *They won't get near me with these foreign smells. Where's the Ivory soap and Prell?* She feels powerless and confused. *Where are my wasps? Where's the purple wasp?*

Frank joins Scotty, who sits motionless on the couch. Stella puts Clara's smelly clothes outside in a shopping bag, ready for the Laundromat, along with the other clothes the firemen saved. The open door allows two escaped wasps to come back in, buzzing loudly above the armchair, where Clara, now deodorized and squeaky clean but still shivering, has planted herself, wrapped in a light blanket. She's wearing a pajama top of Scotty's that hangs to her knees. *At least two came back,* she whispers to herself. Scotty and Frank are too distracted at first to notice the wasps, and when they do, just look blankly at each other and say nothing. The four wasps that stayed during the melee buzz around her head like a wobbly fan. None come close. *They hate Dial and Head & Shoulders. Stinky stinky.* She looks around. *Six out of sixteen. They've all flown away, my wasps and my house. The purple wasp vanished too. She didn't defend the house. She just flew away.*

She's on the verge of tears. *The purple wasp tapped on everyone's wings separately, like Morse code. I saw her. And the wasps did nothing. They let those kids burn down my house.* She pauses. *Did the purple wasp tell the wasps to let the house go?* Startled by this thought, blood rushes to her head and her face grows hot. She bursts into tears and is immediately embarrassed. Frank, Scotty, and Stella look at each other, then at her.

Tonelessly, she says, "Frank, could you please bait the beef jerky jars with sugar water and set them outside? I've got to get the wasps back—if I can." Her voice trails off. She hasn't yet grasped that the jars would have exploded in the heat of the fire.

"We've got you covered, sweetheart," Stella says, nodding to Frank. He heads over to Desert Dan's for some jars.

Sweaty and pale, Scotty is stricken by his failure to run Dawson out of town. All he can do is putter around and smooth couch pillows. He asks if Stella needs help in the kitchen. She is focused and intent and doesn't need any help, thank you very much. Scotty falls in a heap on the couch.

Frank returns with two big olive jars, sets them up with sugar water, and puts the jars out in Scotty's backyard. Grimacing at this unaccustomed sight on his tidy lawn, Scotty needs to retreat to his office to calm himself, rest in quiet. Gallantly he kisses Clara's hand. "Make yourself at home, Clara," he says. "Anything you want." She thanks him, her eyes filling again as he shuts the door.

"Such a sweet man," she says to no one in particular.

Frank knows that Scotty is not well, but this is no time to talk to his mother about it. He can barely face it himself. Scotty still won't see a doctor. Frank sits with Clara in the living room while

Stella heats canned soup and makes grilled cheese sandwiches. Still stunned by the destruction, he studies his boots. "I wonder what they took," he says.

Her eyes are blank. "I don't know."

"We'll have to wait a day or so before we can go through the ashes."

She looks dully at him. An awkward silence follows, and then she decides to tell him about the earlier screen-slashing incident.

He listens somberly, leaning forward, elbows on his thighs. "Why didn't you tell me about this, Mother?"

"I thought I could handle it. I didn't want to bother you. Besides, he didn't hurt me. He ran away when I told him to get out."

"That's crazy talk, and you know it. He invaded your house and might have hurt you. For God's sake, Mother, *any* harassment of a woman your age calls for strong action. Do you think you're some kind of superwoman? Why open yourself to a random screwball? And this is the same guy who just burned down your house?" He shakes his head in dismay. He should have been with her! He should have been protecting his mother!

She flares. "But he's throwing his life away. He has no family. And his girlfriend is just as bad off. Her father killed her mother and ran off when she was just a kid. Her uncle told me about it. Both those kids are going to the trash heap if nobody steps in."

Stella stays in the kitchen, clattering dishes around.

Frank speaks quietly. "This guy's got to change his *own* life, Mother. The girlfriend too. You can't do it for them. No one can change another person's life. We have to do it by ourselves." He sighs. "They sound like the students you used to take on. All those parent conferences, phone calls, weekend visits with them.

Sometimes I thought you cared more about them than us." He bites his lip. Bad timing.

Her mind careens away from his words. "That's utter nonsense," she snaps. "This young man never even *had* a mother. She abandoned him and dreadful things happened to him."

He's exasperated. "So, you think you can sweep into his life when he's what—thirty?—and be his mom? His grandmother? For the young woman too? Really, Mother, you should think about that."

Clara's exhausted. She's in no mood to continue this talk. Warmed by the blanket, she leans back in the armchair and closes her eyes, effectively ending the discussion. From the kitchen, Stella senses a truce, or stalemate, and quietly sets out steaming bowls of Campbell's tomato soup and grilled cheese sandwiches on TV trays. They sit huddled together in the living room. Conversation lags.

Stella quietly washes the dishes, comes back to the living room, drying her hands with the dishtowel. "I've got to go," she says to Frank. "My shift is starting. Your mother needs some rest." She leans down to hug Clara, who hasn't moved from Scotty's armchair.

Clara fondly touches Stella's cheek. "Thanks for all your help."

Frank and Stella step outside for a minute. They at least need to touch base, after last night's painful postmortem. She stands looking at the ground. He studies the ants still scurrying in circles. Silently, he bends down to kiss her cheek. She lifts her eyes to his. "So, where do we stand?"

"This is a weird time to talk, but I'll just tell you. I'm not cut out to be a leading man for you, babe. That's the long and short of it. For your plays, you need to count me out."

She flushes, looking down. "What about otherwise?" she says in a thickened voice.

"Otherwise, I'm your man. If you want me."

She throws her arms around him. "Is that all? Oh, I'm so relieved. I thought . . . I thought . . ."

"You thought wrong."

They fiercely embrace, trying to be quiet. When he returns, his hair is tousled, lipstick smudges his mouth.

Clara smiles up at him. "She's a lovely girl."

Frank and his mother sit together on the couch, not needing to talk. They listen to scratchy Puccini on the Salt Lake station she finds on Scotty's radio. Soon she closes her eyes and says she's tired. He leads her to the guest bedroom, finds a light blanket for her. Later he stretches out on the couch.

Her sleep is addled with dreams.

In a tight black cloud, the lost wasps surge through the broken window and land on her head, full of surly threats. "What do you want?" she cries.

"Open your eyes, or we will sting your eyeballs," they say. "Open your mouth, or we will enter that long canal that begins in your throat and ends at your anus. Quit your stupid delays, or we will crawl inside your nose."

"I won't let you do any of these things," she cries. "What do you want from me?"

"Stop your sniveling and turn to your son. Open the Heartbreak Room in your head that contains Samantha and your son, and just deal with it. These things are why you came to the desert, foolish woman. We don't have forever."

In terror, she wakes. "Frank!" she yells. Stumbling over his boots, he comes running from the living room. She stands trembling by the bed, batting away nonexistent wasps. He puts his arms around her, his strong heart pounding against her ear. She embraces him with her small, thin arms. They stand like that for some time in the dark, saying nothing. He feels her frail bones, her fluttering heart. She feels his reassuring bulk. How long has it been since anyone has embraced her like this, since she has embraced her own son? *Forever.*

"Oh, Frank, I've missed you so."

"I've missed you too, Mother."

The next morning, Frank is up before she is. Scotty did not come home. Stella has put Clara's sack of clean laundry on the back porch. Frank has made coffee, toasted an English muffin for her, lathered it with peach jam, bought her a new Cran-Apple juice and cottage cheese for lunch. He's got his hard-boiled eggs and toast. A halo of the six loyal wasps circles her head as she leaves the bathroom. He smiles. She looks like a tottering queen with the agitated creatures wobbling around her.

"What are you grinning about?"

"Nothing. The wasps around your head like that."

Too tired to question him further, she finds a cereal bowl in the cabinet and pours a little sugar water into it. The wasps leave her to feed from the cereal bowl. They've had no interest in Frank since the robbery, nor he in them. She opens the refrigerator and sees with pleasure the new cottage cheese Frank bought. But she has no appetite for it, not since she saw Edie plunge her small square hand with black fingernail polish into the carton and shovel great mouthfuls of the white curd into her purple-lipsticked mouth. Same for the Cran-Apple juice. She shudders despite her pity for the girl. Tomorrow will be time enough for cottage cheese and Cran-Apple juice.

Spread with peach jam, the hot English muffin is delicious. She even wants another one. Frank has poured her a cup of strong coffee. They eat, saying little. She is grateful for his kind gestures. "Thank you for shopping," she says. He nods.

After they eat, he silently goes outside for about a half hour. She sees him sitting in the trailer cab, smoking his cigarette, the windows unrolled, his left arm hanging out the window, flicking the ashes. He sits motionless, staring at the horizon. It calms her to see him sit there, silently smoking. After a while, he douses the butt in the ashtray and flicks his Bic lighter open and shut for several minutes, his arm still hanging out the window.

She recalls the rough ride down from Eugene, her satisfaction that she'd preserved a bubble of continuity by bringing the house and saving it from the demolition crew. Nothing would change, she had thought, except the outward circumstances of Jackpot. She would still have her cocoon. Bitterly she conjures up the smell of scorched wood and coughs.

Restless, she turns on the portable radio by Scotty's refrigerator and comes upon a talk show about Bush and Gore, interspersed with audio clips. Bush still can't manage a clear sentence, while Gore pontificates. Jolted by the outside world, her temper flares. In the dead of summer, June 2000, the news seems brainlessly placid, as if the whole world is tired of itself and can't keep anything straight anymore. She doesn't want to think about this nonsense and turns the radio off.

Moving back to the armchair, she's still stumped by the last clues to the *New York Times* crossword puzzle that she found stuffed in her purse. She'd been working on it all week. Usually she's a crossword whiz. This one she can't finish to save her soul. Morosely, she wonders if she's heading for a stroke. She's had headaches all summer, ever since the purple wasp stung her forehead twice and dizzy spells that almost made her lose her balance. She's made no progress in confronting Samantha's death. Frank, too, is still on hold. Will she die miserable and alone, as she fears?

18 days left.

She checks her purse. Her wallet is empty. Edie and Dawson took her cash but left her single credit card alone. Smart move– they can't be traced. Shivering, she looks out the window and sees Frank still sitting in the trailer cab. It seems rude to watch him like that, so she pours a second cup of coffee from Scotty's fancy coffee maker and walks aimlessly through the big, empty house with its featureless woodwork and cottage cheese ceilings. His house looks unlived-in.

The purple wasp sits unseen on a bookcase shelf in the living room, registering everything that has gone on since the robbery and fire. The wasp never did abandon her. Whether the creature betrayed her is another matter.

Frank finally comes in and sits on the couch, leafing through a *Salt Lake Tribune* on the coffee table as Clara glances through a *Newsweek*. Three more escaped wasps collide against a window, setting up a furious hum. Frank rouses himself and goes outside to sprinkle sugar water in a trail from the house to the olive jars. Clara's right behind him.

He never would have helped her before. Pleased, she shyly looks at him. He looks away with an embarrassed smile. They sit together on the back porch steps, waiting to see if the wasps will come to the new jars. And they do, circling lower and lower, as if sensing the sugar water inside the jars.

"Come along now," she says, watching the creatures hover over the mouths of the jars, as if smelling one jar, then the other.

And they're in, buzzing.

For the first time, Frank smiles to see the disgusting creatures back where they belong. Clara sees his smile and can't help smiling too. They both look away again.

"Well trained," he says, deadpan. "They know their mama."

Grasping her knees, she rocks back and forth on the steps. "I have magic skills, my boy. Your mother is not of this world."

"So I've noticed. Maybe that's one of our problems. Now me, I'm just an earthly guy. No surprises." His smile is ironic.

"I've never believed that, Frank." She smiles indulgently.

He sprawls on the porch, gnawing on a twig. For once, she's right. New ideas and rebellions are alive in him these days. Stella is waking him up. He wants to build things, make things with wood, metal, stone, whatever he can get his hands on. Plus there are compromises he won't make, things he won't do—for Stella, his mother, or anyone else. He's done with sleepwalking. He's been sleepwalking his whole life.

Clara stares at Scotty's parched grass. She and Frank have never talked easily together. Yet the dream last night said to stop all her diversions and turn to him. *If I'm so good at diversions, why are all the important things so hard?*

"Are you hungry, Frank?"

"We just ate. Why don't we go for a walk?"

Her face brightens. "I'd like that."

They drive out to Salmon Falls Creek. The picnic area is deserted and the creek is low, but the sound of any moving water at all soothes them both right now. And she can't smell any smoke out here. Silently they walk along the creek, parting the tall leathery grasses that feel like sandpaper against their hands as they grip clumps of it.

"Weren't you afraid of the guy? He tied you up, threw you onto the chair."

"I had no time to be afraid. I was mad. He was messing

with my house, disrespecting me." She's lying. She won't admit her fear to Frank. "Look, he's almost a foot taller than I am. He could have really hurt me, but he didn't." She's silent a minute. "Let me tell you something. Right before he threw gas on me, he got tears in his eyes and put his arms around me. Then *I* teared up, and he threw gas on me. I pushed him away hard. I think I slapped him. At some point, I slapped him. It was crazy."

"You're imagining things, Mother. A guy like that would never show tears around you."

She looks at him. "It happened."

Tired of coddling her fantasies, he pulls out a folded paper from his Levi's. "Just read this. You'll see what this so-called Dawson Barth is really like. Scotty had an updated FBI check done on him yesterday. Security got his name from a waitress who carded him. Scotty dropped the report over this morning before you were up. Now he feels even worse that he didn't check when security said Barth was a troublemaker. Scotty could have gotten the authorities on him, and none of this would have happened."

She reads the sheet of paper.

"Dawson Barth, a.k.a. Steve Waddell, Roger Blake, Gus Krebs, Trevor Hanson, 6'2", 165, DOB 11/16/74. Blue eyes, blond hair usually dyed black, thin nose, sometimes shaved head and eyebrows. Known places of residence: Reno, Dallas, Houston, Albuquerque, San Bernardino, Casper, Bend, Butte, Fargo, Newark, Chattanooga, Orlando, Gulfport. Served time for forcible entry and robbery, San Antonio Correctional facility, 1996–1998. Grand theft auto, assault with a deadly weapon, Rahway State Prison, New Jersey, 1998–1999. Outstanding warrant in 2000 for breaking and entering in Fargo. Father unknown, abandoned by mother at age six in Reno, placed in foster care, multiple states, a runaway before age of consent. GED, 1999, San Bernardino, CA."

"Oh, dear," she finally says. "He really *is* in trouble." She walks quickly now, unaware of the creek.

"Scotty says the cops in Reno have drawn a blank so far. He and the girl have disappeared."

She stares at the water. "I can't believe it."

"Well, believe it." His voice is harsh. "If I'd gotten a gander at this Barth character, I'd have made mincemeat of him."

She looks steadily at him, thinking, *No, you wouldn't, dear boy. You're a defender, not a fighter. I made sure of that.* Feeling faint, she crouches on a log as her Brain Rooms again refuse to stay shut. She sees Lillian hiding in the barn, huddled against the mare, the cold North Dakota wind whistling outside, their mother knocked out on the kitchen floor, a bruise on her face, the front door open, her father vomiting in the snow. Clara was hiding behind the barn door clutching a shovel over her head, ready to hit him with it if he came in. He didn't.

Then she sees her mother dithering about, straightening a placemat as her father falls into a rage and strikes her again and again, her eyes flinching. It was a terrible thing for a child to see—his advancing fist, her mother's drowsy smile as if luring him on.

Clara had resolved early on never to be undefended or weak, never without a profession, never to marry a mean man or let any son of hers be mean and domineering. And Frank and Darrell were none of those things. At least she'd done *those* things right. She was always on watch when her father was around. She never knew when he might come from behind and haul her off somewhere. The threat hung in the air like a distant wildfire.

Lillian as a child escaped into fantasy. All she needed was

a big tablet with blank pages. She drew houses with dozens of rooms and secret passageways, whole villages connected by underground tunnels for escape. There was always a way out of a bad situation for Lillian.

As for Clara, thinking about the past like this as she sits by the creek just makes her Samantha Room door fly open. Her mutinous brain flashes a screen of Samantha lying sprawled beside the tractor trailer, her young face startled, pale, unmoving, dead. As she crouches screaming next to her daughter, someone else—someone unbearable—stands beside her and says, "Hush. Hush now, Clara."

She cannot allow this visitation. Will not.

Pressing her hands against her temples, the screen miraculously fades to black. She looks at her cloudy reflection in the creek water. Her head aches. All these years, she's made a fortress of herself. Kept everyone away. Buried her deepest secrets about Samantha's death—in order to live, not die, in order not to lose her mind. She is the calm statue, the ice queen—tottering, if you look closely enough. For it is *her fault* Samantha died. *Don't tell me it wasn't!*

Abruptly, she brings herself back to the treasure she still has, the stalwart son who has put up with her all these years. He's peering into the grasses. She calls out. "What's going on?"

"Lizards. Whole family of lizards—little ones, big ones. Come see!" He looks delighted.

Her deathly anguish fades to something bearable. She takes a deep breath, walks over to her son, absorbs his calm movements, his confident stance, the jittery lizards darting and stopping, darting and stopping like a silent movie. She murmurs, "Do you know how good you are, Frank, how fine it is you haven't disowned me after all these years?" He looks at her. This time, neither looks away. Till the day she dies, she will remember his surprised look, shot through with affection, the sun behind him lighting his sandy hair. Oh, she loves this man.

She throws a pebble into the stream.

Then he does.

They laugh and make a contest of who can throw pebbles farther. Finally, the sun is really too hot. It's time to find shelter in a dear person's empty beige house with a dusty beige interior, no personal touches of any kind to identify the owner.

Drawing her arm through his in a rare gesture as they walk, she feels the strong pulse that will outlast hers. She's sorry for all the years they couldn't talk, their years apart. Still mystified as to why she couldn't be a better mother, she has an idea the reason might be her will to survive horrors. She can only focus on one important thing at a time: one death, one child, one father, one mother, one student—and now, one fire.

I'm a little retarded, she thinks helplessly. She looks at him. *We're still not talking about the past.*

But for her, starved as she is for companionship, just to be together with her son like this is wordless talking of a high order. To share the sun, the grasses, the lizards with him, to see the manner of each other's walk, the tilt of the head, the shape of the hand. It's all a prelude to talking. They will both talk when they are ready, she is sure of it.

He helps her hoist up into the cab. He looks peaceful, his tanned face gleaming in the sun. Smiling, she looks at him, her heart full of so much love—and sorrow for all the wasted years.

He says, "It was good to come here, spend some time together, Mother."

"Yes, it was." For some reason, she laughs in pure exultation.

He laughs too, for just a moment.

They drive in silence back to Scotty's house. He touches her hand. She feels the sting of happiness. It makes her cry.

Stella sits waiting on the back porch. She stands and waves, looking radiantly alive in a yellow sundress, her healthy frame seeming to vibrate. Frank lifts her into the air. They laugh.

"Take good care of him, Stella, do you hear?"

"I hear."

chapter 16

At first, Edie encouraged Dawson—she grew up without a mother too. But it's nuts to look for his mother now when the cops are on them. He won't listen. He'll risk cops; he'll risk anything. He's wild to find her for the last time maybe ever because he's leaving the country. He's sick of always wondering, never knowing if she's even alive. He and Edie have had huge fights about it ever since they left Clara's burning house.

They changed cars in Wells, Winnemucca, Lovelock, and Elko, stealing Cheetos, beef jerky, and Hershey's almond bars from gas station mini-marts. They just snagged a Chevy in Reno after some old guy limped into a liquor store without locking his car. Aimlessly driving, they turn off onto a side street.

He doesn't remember exactly where his Aunt Sylvia lived, just the general area. It was a small house set back from the street in a lot of trees. Pine trees. You could hardly see the house. That's all he remembers. Syl is the only one who might know where his mother is. The houses are scattered now, rundown; nothing looks familiar. Hungry and tired, they share a package of Cheetos and a Mountain Dew, smacking their lips, salty with the cheesy coating that permeates the little turdlike pellets.

The shopping bag with Clara's wedding pearls and opal ring and Frank's coin collection rests between Edie's knees on the floor of the passenger side, where she's meticulously licking her salty fingers. *The old woman's a whack job*, she tells herself. She'll never miss the stuff, and neither will her son. She and Dawson are going to Mexico to just disappear—end of story. He has this dream of living in some out-of-the-way fishing village, living on fish, bananas, and tequila, spending the rest of his life with Edie, maybe working in a restaurant where he'll get free meals and bring food home to her. She wants to bring in some money too, keep on drawing. She can make her own charcoal, her own paints from plants and alcohol. She can sew old clothes into arty numbers for herself, mend Dawson's clothes, sell her drawings to tourists. They can stretch out Clara's bounty a long time. And then something will come along. They'll think of something.

They hatched this idea in between fights on the drive from Jackpot. This fantasy helped them make up. Now that their future is perfectly imagined—the glistening fish, the fruit-heavy banana trees, the tequila carefully rationed—Edie takes Dawson's free hand to her lips and kisses it. She puts his arm around her neck; he fondles her breast. He gets an erection, and she reaches over to touch him.

Suddenly he slows the car, looking intently at a dingy little house, set way back from the road, surrounded by spindly pines looking slack in a season of drought. His erection wilted, he brings the car to a halt. "I think this is it." His voice is tense. She watches him. "I remember something about a yellow front door with a big cast iron knocker." He squints, staring. The door is faded—dirty yellow or beige, hard to see from this distance. Where a knocker might be is a blank space of bare wood. He looks at Edie. "You game?"

"Yup." She looks around for a cop car, but the street is empty and her heart is loud. Trying for bravado, she rummages in her chartreuse purse, streaks a fresh coat of purple lipstick on her pale lips, pinches her bleached short hair to stand up in peaks again, looks in the rearview mirror. She straightens her wrinkled black halter and pulls up Dawson's gray boxers to cover the diamond-studded bar anchored to her belly button.

His mouth has gone way dry. He's licking his already chapped lips. "Desperado," an old tattoo on his forearm, pulsates as he clenches his fists and opens the car door.

They walk down the long dirt entrance road lined with frail pines, tightly grasping hands all the way, like children lost in the woods. His hands are icy. Wanting to ease the moment, Edie picks up a fist-sized stone and bangs it on a pine tree. *Dum de da dum dah.* The hollow sound startles her. She giggles nervously. If he'd even *smile,* she'd get some riff going, contort herself into silly poses, use the dead trees for drums.

But no. He flares at her darkly, "Don't mess around, Edie." He keeps looking straight ahead, never taking his eyes off the house, as if his steady gaze will prevent it from disappearing. Sullenly she returns to his side, feeling unappreciated.

He stops. "We shoulda brought her something. The coins. We shoulda brought one of those cardboard things full of dimes or something. Let's go back to the car."

She folds her arms over her chest. "Your mom wouldn't want something like *that.* She'd want the pearls or the ring."

He swallows hard, his Adam's apple painfully prominent. "I'm not giving *that* stuff up."

"Well, it's too late to go back to the car. We're almost there." Her tone is peremptory. *Someone* has to take charge. Before her very eyes he's folding. His mouth is slack, his pupils dilated. She stands up straighter, pulls her shoulders back.

They reach the door, dusty with peeling yellow paint, no

doorbell, no knocker. He raps loudly with his fist, pushes his dark hair behind his ears. Lifts his chin, trying to look like a big shot. His aquiline nose and long, curly eyelashes would make him look refined if it weren't for his unkempt hair and pasty face scarred with acne. They wait, holding hands. Long moments pass. No sound, no movement from within. He knocks again.

Boots clomp on a bare floor, chain lock and dead bolt unlock. The door opens and a pinched white face peers out to reveal an underfed woman in her sixties, maybe six feet tall, a little shorter than Dawson. Her thin gray hair is balding on top; she's wearing sagging corduroy pants, an oversized men's work shirt, dusty work boots.

"What do you want?" She's irritable.

"Sylvia? Aunt Syl? It's me, Dawson. Nancy's son. Do you know where she is?" His voice is low, almost a whisper. He recognized her at once, even though the shock of her aging—sagging skin, sparse hair, plain boniness—makes his heart contract with dread. He lets go of Edie's hand and looks Aunt Syl in the eye. His mother might be dead. Or living in Canada or South America with another man. Or back with his unknown father, reunited and happy. He just wants the truth. His hands are sweaty.

After a quick look of recognition, Sylvia studies the cement porch. "What do you want with your mother after all these years? Hasn't she given you enough grief?" She tugs at her shirt. "You wouldn't want to see her, Dawson, even if I *did* know where she was."

He regards her with steely eyes. "You *do* know where she is, don't you?" Quickly he steps inside, catching her off-guard. "Let me see her." Edie scrunches herself tightly behind him before Syl can slam the door. A smell of sour milk, rancid cheese, and dirty clothes fills the room.

Sylvia is angry now. "Same old Dawson, barge right in. Nancy always told me how stubborn you were, how you never did what she said. This is not a wise move, Dawson." With her arms folded across her chest, Syl's eyes travel quickly over Edie's pale frame. "And who is this person?"

"The most wonderful girl in the world, that's who it is. Her name is Edie. Edie Porter." He puts his arm around Edie, who shrinks next to him. "I want to see my mother, Aunt Syl. Where is she?" He's moving into the dusty, littered room, filled with faded furniture, stacks of the *Enquirer* and *Star*. The smell of animal droppings overlays the other rancid odors.

Aunt Syl has changed. Her house was always clean. She never used to be grouchy. One Christmas, she gave Dawson a whole box of Hershey's chocolate bars with almonds. He never had such a wonderful present. He rationed himself to one Hershey bar a day. At age six, that's about all he could handle. He would close his eyes as the creamy chocolate melted in his mouth. It tasted like heaven. One morning, he darted over to his dresser to pick which candy bar to have after lunch. The box was empty! The whole last layer of chocolate bars in their rich brown wrappings with the gray block letters had vanished. He always thought his mother took them but never found out for sure. That was when she was getting all the phone calls that made her cry and throw dishes around, right before she dumped him off at Safeway.

He wonders why Syl is so cranky now. She's like a different person. It's been over twenty years since he saw Aunt Sylvia. She stands there frowning, her arms crossed over her rib cage. Suddenly, her arms drop to her side. "Oh, come along then. She always thought you might track her down." Her voice sounds tired. She leads them down a long, dark hall that smells of filthy laundry and rotten cheese. The smell is familiar to him. His throat gorges; he suppresses a wave of nausea. He grips Edie's hand.

"Wait here," says Syl as they approach a closed door at the end of the hall. She goes inside. They hear Syl whispering urgently, hear a loud "Ahhhh!" in response, as if the responder had been stuck with an arrow. After a short while, the door opens and Aunt Syl beckons them in. Dawson can't remember how he got inside the room.

In a king-size bed lies a woman fat enough to have two or three other people zipped inside her. The pale, swollen woman, her skin bloodless as bleached jelly, draws a food-stained blanket up to her neck, then throws it to her waist, as if she's having a hot flash. She breathes heavily under a no-color nightgown, apparently frightened to death of what she sees.

Dawson is speechless. He hardly recognizes her. Her hazel eyes are nearly obscured by pouches of fat hanging from her cheeks. Only the strawberry birthmark by her right ear proves this is his mother. Her stringy hair is snarled dishwater blonde streaked with gray. Her hands are swollen, her breasts half-deflated dirigibles. Empty cartons of chocolate milk litter the nightstand.

His impulse is to run. But now that she sees him, her eyes take on a greedy light. "Dowser! After all these years. I see you've found yourself a woman. I knew you'd be better off without me." She leers at Edie, devouring her scant outfit and pale skin. "Well, hello there, young lady. Is he treating you well? I *bet* he is." She lets out a braying, sensual laugh. Shocked and embarrassed, Dawson and Edie tightly hold hands. Then Edie's hand goes limp.

Aunt Syl steps toward the bed. "Nancy, you've not seen Dawson for twenty-one years. Show some manners toward your son." Sylvia's look is grim, as if she knew very well the turn this conversation would take.

His mother takes on a pleading tone. Her swollen hands restlessly travel the blanket. "Dowser, my boy. Put some meat on those bones. Way too skinny. The girl too." She wrinkles her nose. Awkward silence fills the room. As if remembering something, her eyes light up. "Did you bring your mother a present, Dowser? After all these years? Some chocolate maybe?"

He looks into his mother's nearly obscured eyes, his voice faltering. "I didn't bring a gift, no, sorry." He turns toward the door, then turns back to face his mother once more. He blurts, "You ate the last row of my almond Hershey's that time."

She laughs loudly. "They were mine, Dowser. You stole them from me. You stole my whole house from me. Gary left because of you." Her smile shows big teeth. "Your girlfriend has nice little titties, Dowser."

Bewildered and shocked by her words, Dawson can only mumble, "Uh, Edie and I have to get going now—long way to go before dark. Um, take care."

"Too bad you can't stay. We're having dinner soon, aren't we, Sylvia?"

He doesn't hear his aunt's reply. He's had enough. The ripe hallway has a suction power, as if it could vacuum them back into his mother's room if he'd let it. In fact, he and Edie briskly approach the front door. Aunt Syl trails behind.

At the door, she says, "Sorry, Dawson. At least you know now. She doesn't talk sensibly any more. All she does is eat and laugh to herself. It's been like this about four years. It's hard for me to control her in any way."

"I'm glad you're with her, Aunt Syl." He extends a trembling hand. She clasps it in both of hers.

Edie just wants to get out of there. She nods at Aunt Syl.

Somehow they make their way to the car and wordlessly drive off. Before they reach Highway 395 that will take them to California and points south, Dawson pulls off at a rest stop. "Just for a minute," he says, not looking at her.

"Sure thing."

She goes to the restroom, spruces up her spiky hair again, buys an Orange Crush from the vending machine. Sitting at an empty picnic table, she shuts her eyes, trying to calm herself, open her mind to the hum of empty sky. In the grassy area, parents sit exhausted at picnic tables. Dogs frolic; kids chase each other.

At the far edge of the grass, Dawson sits on his haunches, flicking ashes from a cigarette, not taking it to his mouth. He's looking out toward the highway. He stubs out the cigarette in the grass. Edie sits at the picnic table watching Dawson and the cloudless sky. She takes out a nail file and carves their initials as best as she can into the dried wood: EP ♥ DB

The sun is hot overhead. The sky is an empty bowl.

chapter 11

Clara wakes early. A silvery hush floats over the desert. She huddles into a blanket and sits outside on Scotty's steps, sipping steaming black coffee from her old Greenpeace mug. Silence and coffee and the comforting blanket fortify her for what she must do: take a good look at her house. She can avoid it no longer. Her time with Frank yesterday has given her strength. She sets the empty mug down on the porch and slowly walks up Black Jack Drive toward the highway and crosses it, hugging the light blanket around her. She keeps her eyes down until the house is at hand. Then she can't help gasping.

Blackened two-by-fours that framed the rooms are exposed willy-nilly to the air. Most of the siding is gone, all of it charred. Flames shot up to the eaves in several places and burned clear through the insulation and rafters. The ceiling is gone and over half the siding. It looks as though someone has set the house over a gas flame and let the flame blacken much of the pot. The smell of ash and charcoal fills the air. She sneezes. Her eyes water and sting. Numb to her presence, two lone wasps circle the wreckage.

But the kitchen! Only it has survived. In part. It's covered with ash as if there's been a volcanic explosion nearby. She jumps onto the flatbed and wipes the muck off the counter with a dishtowel. And there are her canisters, cupboards, and drawers, the

177

green linoleum floor—all undamaged—and the oddest sight of all, her green Formica table and chairs, the same as they were, one chair still toppled from when she finally broke free of Dawson's flimsy knots and ran outside to confront him. The kitchen is a bizarre monument of a ruined place. She can't bear to look.

She jumps to the ground and makes herself touch what's left of the siding. She rubs the gritty charcoal ash between her fingers. The ghostly lilac smears, the shriveled brown petals sealed for years in lumpy paint, are burned to bubbled muck.

She has to face it. Her house is gone.

The only thing to do is jog. Anger and grief war in her as she dashes back to Scotty's, throws on jogging clothes, does hasty stretches. Bolting out the door, she sets up a stubborn pace after a walking start. *Thock crunch, thock crunch*—she pounds the desert floor. Soon sagebrush does its medicinal work on her burning lungs. As she works up a running high, she circles back around—past Royal, where Frank's weathered trailer cab sits in front of Stella's place. Down to a walk again, she circles the streets in a daze, pauses at Jackpot Video, where the same cluttered window display holds Elvis pictures, plastic dolls, and empty VHS jackets.

No terminators, androids, or days of the jackal for her, thank you very much. Only the Little Tramp could cheer her now, but she suspects he's still nowhere to be found here. It's nine o'clock in the morning. The store is still closed. She's vaguely disappointed. She would love to see the friendly proprietor and engage in banter about what's a good movie to see.

Immersed in gloomy thoughts, she begins to cross the highway, heading back unthinkingly to her old house. Realizing her error, she throws up her arms in despair, stopping dead on the highway as a truck barrels straight toward her. At the last minute, she registers the onrushing vehicle and sprints to the side of the road. The driver takes his hands off the wheel in a gesture of hopeless anger as he passes her.

Something comes untethered in her. She wants to follow right after that trucker, give him a run for his money. She strides back to Scotty's. The open road lures her like the waters at Lourdes. She's got to get out of Jackpot. Silence, stillness, smallness can't contain her right now. "Burning Down the House," the Talking Heads song, roils her brain. Her high school juniors always gave her tapes. They liked her and wanted to educate her. Frank always laughed when she gyrated around the house to songs like that. He never understood how she identified with rebellious teenagers, but her students knew her as a kindred spirit. Fists clenched, singing at the top of her lungs, she stares irresistibly back at the tarnished spectacle of her house.

A feeling of hysteria overtakes her. Everything is gone. Even the wasps. The family pictures she spread out on the dresser the night before are burned to ashes. And they must have taken the pearl necklace that Darrell gave her, plus the opal ring he gave her for their first wedding anniversary. Frank's old coin collection was worth quite a lot, and she had some money lying around. She thinks she's so tough, but maybe it's all killing her—the lost possessions, the burnt lilac traces, the gutted house, her lost husband and daughter, her son virtually abandoned all these years, wholly beyond her intentions. She sits on Scotty's steps and covers her face with her hands, trying to calm herself. A single wasp circles above her.

Her extreme response frightens her. The only thing that could comfort her now, she realizes, are the actual lilacs that surrounded her house, the great bushes pregnant with flowers, the laden branches bobbing in a light wind, their scent invading her dreams, her thought always that the lilacs were alive with spiritual presence. Those fat, unpruned bushes were a sanctuary. She always wandered among them to forget whatever trouble made her seek them. Now these lilacs exist nowhere in the world except in her soon-to-be-crumbling memory. Developers have made sure of that.

Suddenly it occurs to her: Arianna Paul! That busybody photographer is the only person in the world who has photos of everything important—family pictures and close-ups of wilted lilac petals entombed in the siding, the backyard lilac jungle where her family spent long summer afternoons picnicking and listening to crickets as daylight darkened and fell, the wasps always circling above them.

She's got to get those pictures! It's been almost two weeks. Maybe Arianna ran off with them or threw them away. She's that nervy all right—sneaking a wasp shot while Clara was peeing.

Rushing inside, she rifles through her purse and digs out Arianna's card. Two wasps land on the card, as if encouraging her. Her mood lightens. She'll find that woman. She'll drive to Elko this very day. She must have an intact record of her life—her most private delights and healing spaces. How else can she know she even existed in the world?

Pacing in Scotty's kitchen, she suddenly doubts Arianna's whole premise. Why would anyone in Manhattan want to see her little homemade house? "Just imagine," Arianna would chuckle to her friends, "this strange woman made her son drag that ramshackle house to this backwater, and there it sits, rotting in the sun." The thin ladies in summer linen would shake their heads and smile.

Enough nonsense, Clara thinks. She doesn't need fantasies like this. All that's important are Arianna's pictures and the peaceful time she had with Frank yesterday at the creek. Something like a blessing has occurred between them, something necessary and long sought. Fresh trouble made them finally reach out to each other. Among other emotions, joy creeps into the mix.

Many would say that of course a son would be kind to his mother if she'd just been assaulted and robbed and her house burned down. But Clara is not like other mothers. She takes nothing for granted just because she gave birth. Any kindness toward her she meets with amazement and denial. His kindness must have been an accident, a momentary lapse. It probably wouldn't happen again. This is how she's survived, given the secrets of her upbringing, secrets locked in her innermost Brain Room. A little like a cactus, she protects her vital center.

Nervously, she calls the number on the back of Arianna's business card. To her surprise, Arianna answers, hears her out, and readily proposes lunch at the Rancher's Hotel at twelve thirty in Elko, adding that her uncle, visiting from New York, might join them.

A giddy feeling overtakes her, a feeling of release. She's itching to get on the road, cast herself into the unknown, escape her demons for a day. The nine wasps in Scotty's kitchen are flying around in erratic circles. "Now don't make a production of this," she says crisply, laying out honey water as a special treat. "I won't be gone long. Someone will take care of you." She throws a change of clothes into an overnight bag of Scotty's (she's sure he won't mind), a couple of *New Yorkers*, and her crossword puzzle book in case she wants to stay overnight in Elko before coming back. It's 130 miles each way. She might be tired.

17 days left.

◈

She rushes outside only to find the usual car space empty. She forgot. She has no car! The car Frank bought her is at the garage for the second time in less than two weeks. That buggy's a lemon.

This is no time to stand on ceremony. Walking quickly, she waves at the owner of Jackpot Video, who saunters on Double Down, having a smoke. His genial face lights up. "Hey now, you're the one who likes Charlie Chaplin and Rosalind Russell. Drop in sometime. I got some new classics."

"I'll do that. Right now, I'm in a hurry."

"I can see that." He smiles. "Don't wear yourself out now."

"No chance of that," she shouts over her shoulder.

At Stella's, Clara sticks a hasty note under Frank's windshield wiper. Back at Scotty's, she sticks a similar note under the wipers of his blue Ford pickup. Gamely she smiles at his white Mustang. She had chided Scotty for leaving keys in both ignitions. "I'm forgetful," he said with his easy grin. "This way I never have to look for my keys. Besides, nothing ever happens in Jackpot."

Hunched behind the wheel, she turns Scotty's white Mustang smoothly away from the curb and quickly adjusts to its ways. With a rush of wildness, she takes it up to eighty on the empty highway south of Jackpot. The car runs like an oiled panther.

"Son of a gun," she whoops, "what've I been missing all my life?" But she's no fool and isn't about to get in a wreck. Reluctantly, she takes it back to sixty-five and keeps it there. She misses her old Honda Civic. It was as reliable as the legs she walks on. But the Honda never made her feel like an exhaust-chuffing cowgirl. Smiling, she checks her teeth in the rearview mirror.

She's not alone in the car. The purple wasp made her surprise appearance from behind Scotty's coffee maker this morning, holding fast to Clara's hair as she sat down to her banana and Bran Flakes. After Clara phoned Arianna, the wasp danced around on the counter, as if she too liked the idea of Clara taking off like this. But now the creature is staggering around on the dashboard, toppling over from time to time.

"What's the matter with you?" Clara cries. "You're acting drunk." She looks more closely. "What on earth did you do to your head?" She slows down, trying to get a better look. The wasp's head is freakishly swollen, worse than she's ever seen it.

The creature waves her antennae around. "I'm going to be a taxidermy specimen before long, my friend, at the rate you're going. You say you want peace with your kids and a taste of life before you die? Got to step it up a notch then. You've got a start with Frank, but zilch with Samantha and the life bit."

"My stars, you're trying my patience," Clara says heatedly. "All you do is lecture. If you're here to help, why did you let that arsonist burn down my house? I couldn't believe my eyes. You flew above his head as if you just *loved* to see him dump gas all over me and my siding–as if you didn't want me to keep my house! Whose side are you on, anyway?"

The creature smirks. "That's for you to figure out, my dear."

Driving Scotty's Mustang puts her in a strange state. Her heart feels transparent, warms her chest with white light. Something's opening in her that has long been closed. Attacked by messed-up young people, she's on her feet and moving. Rigid brain battlements have lowered a tad: The wide unknown seems less threatening. Adventure! Conquest! That's what she wants. She'll get her pictures and her past back. She'll find out if Arianna Paul is a crook.

The purple wasp staggers around to some inner beat on the dashboard. Her wings are wrapped around her swollen head like transparent earmuffs—as if she's planning something and wants no distractions.

Clara leans back and turns on the radio, finds only Christian or country music—not the classical station out of Salt Lake City she's looking for. Maybe Scotty's radio's on the blink. She misses NPR. Closer to Elko she might get it. Well, she likes Johnny Cash anyway, and what do you know, here he is, singing "I Walk the Line".

She sings along, tapping the steering wheel. Come to think of it, she also likes Tammy Wynette, Waylon Jennings, Dolly Parton. But Dolly looks like a cartoon woman. Maybe that's the point. Dolly's no fool.

At heart though, she's a Johnny Cash kind of girl—a one-man woman. Darrell was her soul mate, their passion as pure as bed sheets dried by the sun. He rode an old bike to work at the *Register-Guard*, made his lunch every morning—sandwich, apple, cookies, thermos of coffee packed in a metal lunch box he hung from the handlebars. Weekends, he read *Colliers* and *Time* while eating slow lunches at the kitchen table—sardines with mustard on toast or creamed tuna on toast, along with a glass of Ovaltine. His life was a kind of poetry to her. No false moves, no showy gestures, just the thing itself.

She purses her lips. *OK, give it up, Clara. You know he wasn't a saint.*

All right, all right: She knew he had an affair with Jessica Wagner down the street, a pretty divorcée who brought them blueberry pie until she stopped bringing blueberry pie. That was after Clara saw Darrell leaving Jessica's house one afternoon as she was coming back from Safeway. Saw him and her heart dropped to the floor. That night in bed, his musky smell was lay-ered with something like sweet peas, the barest hint, even though he had uncharacteristically showered before dinner. She hugged her side of the bed for weeks. One day, she needed her prun-ing shears and went out to the shed where Darrell and Frank did their woodworking projects. Darrell was standing at the tool table, hastily wiping tears off his face. They never talked about it, and life went on.

Their sex life suffered for months. If he had kept seeing her, she would have left him. Even with the kids, she would have left him.

She sewed shirts for Frank, dresses for Samantha. She made a navy-blue terrycloth bathrobe for Darrell in their first year of marriage. He never wanted a new one, even when the blue-and-white sailcloth lining frayed and separated from the terrycloth. She still wears that bathrobe when she's sick. Darrell was six foot one, so it trails on the floor, but she would never think to shorten it.

"Oh my god," she exclaims. It's "Lady in Red" on an easy-listening station. Memories cascade from the '80s. She was on a Greenpeace kick back then after Darrell died, went to local meetings, almost went with Greenpeace to save whales in the Antarctic but couldn't bring herself to do it. Even now, she blushes to remember Charley Fender, a wild-eyed man at those meetings. She hasn't thought of him in years, made herself not. Madly male and sexy, he was an adventurer—clean-limbed, roguish, maybe a little dangerous (a hired mercenary in a couple of third-world conflicts, it was rumored). He served in Korea, traveled the world, saw enough bad behavior to make him favor the animal world. "Animals kill because they have to, not out of meanness," he said.

Sitting in her rocker at night, she used to imagine raw-boned adventures with Charley—traveling the Middle East, Asia, Africa, everywhere—with only their backpacks, a change of clothes, and lots of cheap local food. But he was married. Clara wasn't going to fool with that. Once at a New Year's Eve party at his house, Charley sidled up to her, held his arms out to dance to "Lady in Red." When the music ended, he held her close and said, "I'd like to see you really happy, Clara." Startled, she just looked at him. He walked away, his wife calling from the kitchen.

Her bottled water in the holder shimmers from the motor's hum. She takes a swig; its coolness pools in her stomach. She nods at herself in the rearview mirror. Though she hardly knew Charley, she liked his style—nothing fancy. His living room had handmade furniture. He was like Darrell that way.

The lightness in her chest makes her feel like flying.

She'll catch that Paul woman, get her pictures back. She can rent an apartment and live near Frank and Stella. She's tired to death of worrying about blackened siding and messed-up young people. She'll tune it all out, tune in something better.

Does she have time? There's the familiar pain in her heart again—off-on, off-on. She's been having these spells enough to concern her lately, but she's trying to ignore them. And why aren't those two wasp stings on her forehead healing, for Pete's sake? Maybe she's just addled by all that's happened, especially the lovely moments with her son. Whatever the case, all her regrets, grief, and lonely years are in some transformative yeast within her, changing to a lighter element that frees her from care.

The purple wasp must not like her taste in music. She's hiding under the passenger seat.

Well, all right, she'll turn the darn thing off.

Silence.

The engine's purr/whine.

Idly she taps on the steering wheel as she holds the Mustang at sixty-five.

Out of nowhere, an image of light blue panties lays crumpled on the floor.

"No!" She slams on the brakes, tries to steady the fishtailing car. It rocks dangerously. She will die right here, on Highway 93 between Jackpot and Wells. No one will find her after the car rolls over and over on the blank dirt and sagebrush. The smoking wreck will be mistaken for a wildfire. Fire trucks will arrive too late.

Finally, the car steadies. She pulls over, kills the motor, cradles her head on the steering wheel, and weeps. Almost in a swoon, she pushes her hair back from her face in soothing strokes.

Got to take it easy, just take it easy. The purple wasp is worming herself into my brain, going to tear it wide open. I can feel it.

Grimly she wipes her eyes and resumes driving. Elevator music on the radio is suddenly a balm out here in the dry, unbearable country, the landscape of hell. For a while she drives without incident.

From the corner of her eye, she senses a disturbance in the air, feels sudden pressure in her chest, worse than before. Is this an actual heart attack? Too jittery to take her eyes off the road, she does anyway. "My stars, what have we here!" she blurts as the car swerves.

A small person maybe four inches tall bobs and weaves on the dashboard, mumbling about plots to silence her, people wishing her ill for what she knows. She pales, pulls over again.

This impossible vision is decked out in jeans, boots, and a cowgirl shirt with sequins around the yoke. Her hair is a casual updo;

her eyes are brown and friendly. Actually, her eyes are hypnotic. A person could stare into those eyes and tell the creature anything in the world and the creature would just stay calm. Clara looks more closely. The tip of a lavender wing hangs from the creature's shirt cuff. In wonder, she stares at this shimmering membrane. A death and rebirth has occurred right here, right now.

Panicked, she rubs her eyes. "Where's my wasp, my purple wasp?" She looks under the seat and in the glove compartment. No purple wasp. "She's disappeared! What did you do with her?"

"I can take you further," the creature whispers seductively. "Much further than the purple wasp can."

"What?"

"You're a tough case, Clara. Sealed tight. It's clear we need stronger measures if you really want to break open your cocoon and join the world. You're doing better with Frank, but Samantha is still trapped in your moldy Brain Room. You've put this whole undertaking in serious jeopardy with all your stalling. I only have seventeen days left out of a hundred and twenty. My job is to give you clarity. And joy. We all vowed to help you that night in your father's barn, never knowing how hard it would be. I may not look like a wasp, but in my heart I'm certainly half wasp and half human. You've got maximum intervention right here." The creature taps herself on her chest.

Clara's hyperventilating. "What if I don't *want* to go further?" She tries to catch her breath. "I just want my wasp back—the one I already know."

"You're going to stonewall yourself to death if you aren't careful, kid. Either you'll continue with Frank and open up about Samantha's death, or you're going to die miserable and alone. So what will it be?"

Clara considers. With Frank, an easy yes; with Samantha, not possible.

She concludes that this hallucination waltzing on her dashboard is what people see right before they die—a cowgirl angel of death. That's it—she's got minutes left on this earth.

Or her mind has collapsed on this empty highway and she will crash and die.

Or she just has a tumor on her retina.

So now this sudden new person goes into a soft-shoe routine on the dashboard—pratfalls, leaps, distorted postures so rag-doll and exaggerated that Clara can't help but laugh. At first, she thought the creature was sent to scare her about dying. But now it looks like she's an entertainer. She's even got a pair of dime-sized castanets clacking away.

What in God's name is happening? Thank heavens she pulled over, or she might be in a wreck by now. She looks longingly out the window. That sea of sagebrush out there isn't trying to take her any further. It's just sitting there, minding its own business. A couple of escaped sagebrush balls blow calmly across the highway. She waves at them.

Come to think of it, she could sure use some entertainment right now. If this is a hallucination, she'll take it. At least she's not alone anymore—she's been alone for thirty years. That's quite enough. She snatches another look at the writhing person-ette two-stepping above the glove compartment now. Clara is *glad* this hybrid midget has appeared. She wishes the other wasps were here too. *They* could help calm her down. (*Is this all happening because I stole Scotty's car?*)

Why didn't I trap all the wasps in the jars again and bring them with me? Where are they, anyway? Vanished in the sky? Hanging around the cinders? If they all turned into human-looking thingies like this one, I'd have a regular battalion to entertain me. Fanfares from the glove compartment. Spirited marches across the dashboard. Chorus lines circling the drink holders. She laughs, her mind whirling in a panic of invention.

But she can't have fantastical beings prancing around in Scotty's Mustang. She'll have an accident for sure—she hasn't lost *all* her marbles. She massages her temples, fiercely ignoring the apparition circling the dashboard.

Until she sneaks another look at this cowgirl invader.

The creature pierces Clara with a powerful look that scares the bejesus out of her. As if her little eyes shot out electricity. Burned her face. Were Samantha's eyes.

She shuts her own fevered eyes, keeps massaging her temples. The creature's *not* some sweet thing—she just pretends to be. This creature's going to push her further on the Samantha issue than the purple wasp ever could. Just like she said.

This creature is real, powerful, and she's going to hound Clara to death.

Oh my.

Luckily the cell phone is turned off, charging from the cigarette lighter. She can't handle any frantic calls from Frank or Scotty just now.

Has she toppled into insanity?

But the small person is *right here.* Clara sees her leap onto the camel-colored leather passenger seat and reach down to wipe invisible dust off her comfy-looking boots with a perfect white handkerchief the size of Clara's thumbnail.

Clara takes a deep breath, tries to relax the small of her back. A nice cold beer is what she'd like right now. But it's only eleven thirty. She's got to free her mind, just focus on the road. In a few minutes, she'll see if the creature is still there.

She starts the engine, grateful the car still runs.

The landscape is surprisingly beautiful, a sagebrush plain with lavender mountains that seem suspended in air.

Will Arianna have her pictures?

The question drums in her head. Now that she's closer to Elko, she's getting nervous.

Maybe she just *imagined* the creature gave her a dirty look about Samantha a minute ago. That's it—she's just imagining things. She tries to smile. She *welcomes* the idea of someone else in the car. A companion is exactly what she needs: She must stay sane in order to get her photos back. The creature doesn't *seem* threatening. Maybe she should withhold judgment—after all, the thing's just been born. (Unless it's really a hallucination, and Clara's going to die right now from a brain aneurysm.)

Then there's the forbidden issue—the creature popped up right after those light blue panties escaped from her quarantined Brain Room. Or was it from her Dream Jar? Or did the blue panties just fly in the window? Flying blue panties? She fixates on the double yellow line bisecting the highway. She won't think about it. Or talk about it.

The person-ette isn't talking either. She's moving around, lifting her legs and arms up and down, adjusting to her new shape. Willing away her sudden dark mood, Clara tries to sound cheerful. "As long as you're my roadie, young lady, I might as well know your name. Or am I *your* roadie?"

"Who can say?" the creature says, winking at Clara. "I'm Lenore Cooper, your guide." She pauses. "We don't have much time, you know. You've been fooling around for a long time."

Clara extends her hand in wary greeting. "Pleased to meet you, Lenore. Clara Breckenridge here," she murmurs, wanting to keep the peace on this necessary journey in this shanghaied car.

"Oh, I know who you are," Lenore smiles. "I've known who you are for a very long time."

Flying without visible wings, she leaps up to meet Clara's hand.

On her open palm, Clara feels the delicate brush of a wasp's wing.

chapter 18

The big Rancher's Hotel is an old Western hotel at least seventy years old, Scotty once told her. An enormous "RANCHER'S" marquee on the roof is lit by hundreds of small bulbs. She pulls into the parking lot and pours sugar water from a jam jar into a Gatorade lid for Lenore.

"Don't worry, I can eat human food," the creature says gently. Clara is relieved. "That will simplify things." With her cuticle scissors, she cuts air holes in the cloth bag she brought for Arianna's photos. Needing no explanation, Lenore climbs right into the bag. Clara is amazed how easy it is to adjust to this creature.

In the cool blast of the hotel, she lines up with the noon crush—clamp-jawed men, plump women, bored kids shredding paper napkins, families in stupor or quiet talk. On every available wall, murals of horses, cowboys, a cattle roundup, and stylized bull faces etched on glass booth enclosures.

But no Arianna, no uncle. It's twelve twenty. Arianna said noon. Finally, a waitress seats her at a corner table with water, iced tea, and menus. The cold water tastes like heaven.

The fabric bag jiggles in her lap. "Quiet!" she whispers, nervously stashing the bag on the floor. It's twelve forty-five. If they don't show up, she'll camp out in front of the cousin's house until they do.

Grimly she orders a hamburger, tells the waitress to hold a chef's salad. When the hamburger comes, she cuts up half of it, wraps the two halves in separate napkins and stuffs it all in the shoulder bag.

"Don't smack," she murmurs to Lenore.

"You think I don't have manners?"

"Just shush." Stomach growling, Clara irritably works on her crossword puzzle. Thirty-five across: "extreme discouragement."

Finally, Arianna slumps onto the adjacent chair. "So sorry, Clara. We had a flat tire." Winded and contrite, she shoves her horn-rimmed glasses higher on her nose and flicks hair away from her eyes. "Thanks for waiting. Haskell's washing up." She places a large leather bag against her chair leg and signals the waitress for two waters and two iced teas.

Clara regards her tardy companion. "Do you have the pictures?"

Lenore echoes in falsetto: "Do you have the pictures?" She's apparently thinks Clara is jumping the gun. Clara nudges the bag. *She* is in charge of this meeting, not some freaky midget, thank you very much.

Arianna looks around, bewildered. "Let's eat first, do you mind? I'm ravenous. How about you?"

"I've already ordered and . . ."

Shambling toward them with a crooked smile is a lean, loose-limbed, golden-skinned man with a slight limp. He startles Clara from her absorption in Arianna's disheveled state. As he lowers himself into the chair, he trips on the table leg and rapidly sneezes twice.

"Allergies?" she blurts with a frown, thinking of Dawson.

"No allergies," the man says with a surprised smile, quickly downing some water.

Reluctantly, she takes in his weathered state—his flushed face, newly dampened golden-gray hair curling around his ears, wilted tan shirt, a wicked scar cutting into his left eyebrow. In her focus on the photos, she hadn't given Arianna's uncle a second thought. Now his hazel eyes unsettle her. *This is supposed to be a business transaction. That's the focus here.*

"Clara Breckenridge, Haskell Roberts," Arianna says, smiling.

"Hi, Clara."

Avoiding his eyes, she glances at the sweat rings around his underarms. Embarrassed, she examines her silverware before looking up again. "Nice meeting you," she says.

"Likewise," comes from the floor. Clara nudges the cloth bag again.

Momentarily puzzled, Haskell takes in her fluster, her small, toned form. "You and your house have made quite an impression on my niece, Clara." His voice snags across sandpaper as it sails out of his throat. "The owner of that house would have to be as reliable as daybreak. No folderol of any kind." He sees her irritation. "We had to get a new tire. Sorry we're late."

She nods, examines her fingernails. His steady gaze disturbs her. *What's this man doing here? He's disruptive.*

"Shall we order?" Arianna is back to the menu.

"Let's," he says.

They exchange pleasantries about the atmospheric hotel, how nice it is to come off the long desert highway into occasional towns. Clara struggles to keep her mind on the conversation instead of his world-weary eyes with their fleeting sadness. His age is hard to pin down, maybe sixties? His eyes glint with humor as she nervously runs her fingers through her hair, restrained with barrettes near her ears. He surveys the large room, gives her a questioning look. Again she looks away.

The food is tasty and conversation is easy. Arianna and Haskell just got back from Burns, Oregon, where she finished a commission. Next they're off to San Francisco. He hasn't been there for five years, and a gallery wants to see her work. Then on to Santa Monica, where she soon has an opening at Bergamot Station.

Smiling, he looks around the room. "My niece is a hot ticket. Commissions and invitations for shows are coming in right and left these days." Arianna smiles and looks down at her plate.

Haskell's a photographer too. He's on a cross-country trip in an RV. "Never could have told me I would do such a thing." His face dissolves in self-mockery. "In New York, no one drives, as I'm sure you know. I had to take lessons." He leans back, looking at her. His leathery voice rises from winey depths. *Bedroom-sounding.* She frowns, studies her hands. *Emphysema more likely,* she thinks tartly. Lenore tries to climb her leg, but Clara swats her away. *Why is Lenore being such a brat? I can handle my own business.*

He leans back in his chair. "And what a country I've discovered. Should've done this years ago. Did the trick too. Got my mind off myself." Sadness brushes his face like a fast-moving cloud. He glances at Arianna, who gives him an encouraging nod.

He has absorbed Clara's reluctant smile, her flushed cheeks, brown eyes warm as molasses, her snug jeans and simple blouse. She looks at least ten years younger than she is, seems pert as sunlight, and has barely said a word. Drawn by her reticence and understated appearance, he thinks, *She doesn't need to impress anyone.*

She fumbles for words. "You're traveling by yourself?"

He smiles. "Friends from all over the country are hitching rides with me. I had to get out of New York awhile." Abruptly, he says, "Enough about me. What about you, Clara? What brought you and your house to Jackpot?"

They've finished eating, and his direct question unnerves her. "That's a long story. But I can tell you why I came to Elko." She turns to Arianna. "I'd like to have the photos. I need them. Especially now." Her throat constricts with anxiety. She eyes Arianna's leather bag on the floor. Lenore rubs against Clara's ankle, trying to get her to relax.

Arianna clears her throat. "Let me explain, Clara. I sent the photos to the curator like I said I would. He's still got them."

"Still got them?" Furious, she knows she must contain herself. "Then why did you have me come here?" No one speaks for a minute. "What if the curator loses them? Who's responsible? Those pictures are my only record." She clasps her hands tightly together on the table.

Lenore skitters across the restaurant floor. Clara grabs Lenore's cloth bag and takes after her. She snatches Lenore just as she starts running up a cowboy's boot, dusty and smelling of manure. "Don't you *ever* go running off like that again," she hisses. Looking bewildered, the cowboy reaches down to check his boots. Clara stuffs Lenore back in her bag and sits down again. Arianna and Haskell share a glance that says ignore whatever just happened.

"Ben won't lose the pictures, Clara." Arianna leans confidentially toward her. "He wants them for 'Hidden America,' a photography show that opens July first at the Met. He wants to catch an invisible America just as the new century's getting under way. Your house, your journey are just what he's looking for." She drains her iced tea. "He called last night, wants the negatives ASAP. There's been a last-minute cancellation, so he can get you in. He's very excited about it."

Clara relaxes. "So you have the negatives?"

Arianna takes out a binder of negatives from her leather bag. "Look at them in your lap. The table will shade them."

She examines the negatives carefully, focusing only on the family pictures on her dresser and the lilac traces on the siding. And there they are—a dozen negatives from every angle. Her eyes glisten. Arianna got some great shots. How amazing they were preserved in celluloid just days before Edie and Dawson destroyed her house. Relieved, she returns the negatives to Arianna. Haskell has been watching this whole exchange. Even Lenore has been quiet for once.

She's confused. "But when will I get the pictures back?"

"After the show closes on August tenth. No problem." Coolly efficient, Arianna takes a manila envelope from her bag. "Here's the release that lets the Met use your pictures. Don't worry about the photos. The Met treats its properties with great care. When you sign, I'll FedEx the release and negatives to Ben. He's got some great ideas for their display." She takes out a ballpoint pen. "So, are you ready to sign?"

Clara's in a panic. Too many things are happening. Lenore is jumping up and down in the bag, and this man is staring at her.

She just wants her pictures back. Wants to find a place to live in Jackpot so she can sit at the kitchen table in the morning and calmly drink her coffee. She wants to listen to cars shrieking by on the highway, listen to NPR if she can find it. Have Frank and Stella over for good dinners and rum drinks. She wants to get a little tipsy. She wants to read the latest books Abigail recommends from a list she'll send from Syracuse—a biography of Benjamin Franklin or Matisse, a novel by Haruki Murakami or Wallace Stegner, stories by Alice Munro. She'll chat with the owner of Jackpot Video about his classics section, herd people into Desert Dan's for Scotty. She'll do crossword puzzles, volunteer at the little library she discovered the day before her house burned down. There's got to be a school nearby. She can substitute teach.

Right now these scenarios don't really comfort her, though reading Murakami would help her feel better about Lenore and this quietly unnerving man sitting across from her.

"If I refuse to sign, I could get the negatives right now, couldn't I?"

Arianna is dumbfounded. "Not sign? For the Met? But this is a wonderful chance to see the Big Apple. You can stay at my apartment, see the sights, go to the opening, have the town at your feet."

"But I hadn't planned on going to New York." In confusion, she looks from Arianna to Haskell. They stare quizzically back at her. The cloth bag is quivering against her foot really hard. After a long silence she says, "OK, I can't deny it: I'd like to see what the Met will do with my pictures. I can't imagine it." Dazed, she looks at both of them. "This is completely new territory for me. I might need some help."

The bag is dancing. Haskell leans back in his chair and smiles. Arianna laughs. "Of *course* you'll go to New York, and of course we'll help you. You'll be the talk of the town. The pictures will be a smash."

Clara looks sharply at Arianna. "But I don't *want* to be the talk of the town. I just want my pictures back when it's all over. All of them. Undamaged."

Slowly Arianna says, "I'm beginning to understand—better than I did in Jackpot. Your house is central to your life, almost like a diary, right?" Her voice has softened. She looks at her uncle, as if to draw him in.

Clara nods. "A visual diary, yes." She thinks to herself, *So why should I let strangers look at my visual diary? And how do I tell* THESE *strangers my house has just burned down and I've lost everything–when I can hardly speak the words to myself?*

Haskell watches her closely. "You can't understand why you should let strangers look at something as private as the house your husband built for you. He did build it, didn't he? This looks like a house made with a lot of love." He puts a tentative hand on hers.

She quickly takes her hand away. "Mr. Roberts–*Haskell*, you don't know anything about me or my life. So don't make a lot of hypothetical statements just because you want your niece to get a credit at the Met. I'm no fool. I know some things."

It's his turn to look dumbfounded. Before he can reply, the cheerful waitress reappears and sets a pitcher of iced tea on the table, her pencil poised above their ticket. "You folks ready for some dessert today? We have pie–coconut cream, lemon meringue, apple. Cake–we have carrot cake and chocolate. Ice cream–chocolate, vanilla, strawberry." They shake their heads; the waitress bustles off.

Dead silence at the table. Haskell looks chastened; Arianna looks worried. Clara sits with no expression.

"All right," Clara finally says in a soft voice. "I guess so. I'll sign." *Not a word,* she murmurs to the quiet bundle at her feet.

Watching her closely, Arianna slides the paper slowly toward her. "You're sure? I want you to be sure, Clara. Please read it first."

She reads it, not really understanding it after this amazing day, needing now to simply trust.

She signs.

All business now, Arianna puts the document in the leather bag. "If you don't mind, I'd like to FedEx the negatives and the release right now from the hotel. Ben was really very insistent last night. I can't thank you enough, Clara. I don't think you'll regret this."

"I hope not," she says weakly.

"Back in a few."

They watch Arianna disappear. Both start talking at once. Lenore is dancing in the bag again.

"I didn't mean to assume anything," he says.

"I shouldn't have spoken so sharply," she says.

He laughs; she frowns. "I don't know you, Haskell. I haven't set eyes on you before this day."

"I understand." He fingers his silverware.

She's trying to get a fix on this man. He plays with his water glass, takes deep breaths. An air of stillness, complete receptivity lies beneath his words and gestures. He takes his time asking and answering. Sometimes he seems puzzled, but his knowing look suggests he wouldn't be startled by whatever came his way—that naivety is a planet he left long ago—that he'd be calm even if she sprouted an extra head. She's never met a man like this. She remembers how he sneezed and nearly fell into his chair when he first sat down. She smiles to herself. *He's not perfectly varnished.*

If she'd admit to it—which she certainly will not—she wonders what it would be like to touch that scar above his left eyebrow, his honey-colored hair, those somewhat crepey eyelids. *My stars, it's been decades.* Could she really curl up beside this man, his barnacled voice going on about this or that? Her beleaguered brain notes that her solar plexus has released tension she didn't know was there. This will never do. *Get a grip, girl.*

She squares her shoulders and lifts her chin, as if preparing an interview for national media. "Just what kind of photography do you do?" she asks primly.

He turns weary. "Catalogue shoots. That's what I do. I spend too much time setting up shots of some gizmo that no one needs. I know all the bells and whistles—the lighting, the filters, the product enhancers—tricks to make the gizmo look better than it really is. It's just a job, but it pays well if people know your name. My work is nothing like Arianna's. She's an artist. My job just pays the bills."

"So people 'know your name.'" She's checking to see if he's vain.

He shrugs, then smiles. "I've built up a clientele. I know how to butter people up."

She's disarmed by his honesty. Maybe he's buttering *her* up. In a way she doesn't mind. It's been a long time since anyone tried to butter her up. She can handle it. She studies her hands folded neatly in her lap.

Arianna rejoins them. "Well, that was easy. The negatives will arrive tomorrow morning." Her gaze is relieved, birdlike. "So, what's on the agenda, folks?"

He grins. "How about if I order some champagne to toast the soon-to-be star of 'Hidden America: Photography in the New Millennium' at the Metropolitan Museum of Art?"

"Champagne? I'd fall right asleep," Clara says briskly. "I'd prefer a walk."

A little smile curls Arianna's mouth. "I agree with Clara. Let's sit awhile and get our check."

He turns to Clara, speaking intently. "You focused on the siding and some pictures on a dresser. Any particular reason for that? Tell me if I'm being nosy."

She sees he's trying to be sensitive and respectful. Her hands are damp as she realizes she'll have to tell them about Dawson and Edie. Somehow her encounters with these young people are personal. She wanted to guide them and look what it got her.

She leans back in her chair. The crushing reasons to come to Nevada return—the needed reconciliation with Frank, her quest for redemption with Samantha (from which she's running like hell), and her desire to just change her life, turn a corner somehow. *This man better git while he can. I can never have a plain, normal life.*

She lays her hands flat on the table. "You *are* being nosy," she smiles, "but I'll tell you anyway." She tells them how, over the years, house painters didn't truss up her lilacs properly, so the bushes would flip back onto the wet paint, trapping petals in the paint. "I didn't really notice this until my son got my house jacked up on the flatbed to come here. Lilacs are in my past, shall we say. Any souvenir of how I used to live interests me very much."

She takes a deep breath. "As for damage, a young man in Jackpot slashed my window screen and climbed into my house with the intent of robbing me. I scared him off, but he came back later with his girlfriend and tied me up. They robbed me and pretty much burned down the house and tried to set *me* on fire, then took off with my valuables, such as they are, in a stolen car. This happened a few days ago. His girlfriend destroyed my family pictures. I don't know why."

Haskell scrapes his chair back. "Are you serious?"

Arianna leans forward. "Assaulted you? In Jackpot? Burned down your wonderful house? My god, Clara."

"Black. Any remaining siding is singed black." She takes in their startled looks. "My house was untouched for almost fifty years. They went south, but the police haven't found them. They've disappeared." She examines her napkin with lowered eyes. "This young man has a prison record, grew up in foster care. He's twenty-seven. I feel sorry for him, even though his actions are inexcusable." Haskell and Arianna stare raptly at her. "I guess they'll be robbing mini-marts and gas stations to get wherever they're going. His girlfriend is a tough case too—she saw her father kill her mother. I hate what they did to me, but somebody's got to reach out to them—if we want to call ourselves civilized." She studies her hands still spread out on the table.

Haskell leans forward. "Did you get the license number?" She nods. Quietly he asks, "What did they take, Clara?"

She looks at him. "Some cash, my son's coin collection, my wedding ring, a pearl necklace and the opal ring my husband gave me."

Speaking softly, Arianna catches Haskell's eye. "The police no doubt have an all-points bulletin out on them."

"I'm sure of it." His eyes are gentle. It occurs to him that Clara didn't have much to take. Those people probably took all she had of value in the world. He's somewhat awed by this idea, a little envious.

He himself feels throttled by possessions. So many things tie him down, things like expensive Manhattan real estate, beautiful carpets made overseas by small children, heavy silver and copper pieces bought in seething Middle Eastern countries, furniture handmade from rare woods, covered with special hides. Things he himself was indifferent to but his wife hotly wanted. She bought all these things. Stuff was her drug. He feels laden, won't feel free until the entire loft is bare and he has left it.

He looks at this trim, clear-eyed woman with her plain green blouse, worn Levi's, no jewelry, and hardly any makeup. He feels lighter just by looking at her.

He flashes on his small study back at the flat, furnished simply with a secondhand desk, faded couch, two lamps, some books. His wife never touched that room. "The Salvation Army special," she called it. But the simple room always calmed him. What would Clara think of it?

She blurts, "I don't want these kids in a shootout or something crazy. They just need to stop this nonsense."

"Where's your son, Clara?" Arianna asks gently.

"Frank would just deck the boy. He's mightily upset with Dawson. As you would suspect."

Almost to himself, Haskell says, "Amazing. They do these things to you, and still you want them to survive well." He pauses. "You're not *looking* for these kids, are you?"

"Certainly not." She gives him an impatient look, not used to being challenged by anyone except Frank.

Arianna is puzzled by Clara's interest in these losers. The hard-luck cases just get you off track. She worships light, form, and composition, at almost any cost. She relishes the fact that she's just sent off necessary documents to get her photos shown at the Met. *Another notch. Things are picking up at last.* She's been in anonymous hell for twenty years. Triumphantly, she pushes her glasses up on her nose.

Clara glares at the fabric bag. Every time Haskell opens his mouth, the bag quivers, as if Lenore is beside herself that a man has entered the scene. She will give Lenore a good talking to back in the car. The creature should stick to entertainment. She said she'd guide Clara. *So guide.* She clenches her hands under the table, feeling thoroughly lost.

The talk turns to other matters. As they wait for the check, Clara excuses herself to call Scotty from the lobby, taking Lenore in the bag with her. He answers, sounding beleaguered. "Clara! We've been worried sick! Where are you? Hold on– Frank, here."

"Mother! How could you disappear like this? And with Scotty's car? I thought you were kidnapped! Unbelievable. What's going on?" He is clipped and hyper.

"Didn't you read my note? I'm in Elko having lunch at the Rancher's Hotel. I told you everything." She turns toward the window, as if facing an invisible judge. She agrees it was irresponsible to take Scotty's car, but she had no choice. "I had to get down here, Frank, before Arianna disappeared on me again. The house pictures will be at the Metropolitan Museum of Art in New York in July, in a photography show. Can you imagine that?"

Long silence. "So when are you coming back? We had a nice time together the last few days—a really nice time. After all these years. I think you would agree."

She flinches, surprised at his bitter tone. "Don't, Frank," she says in a whisper. "It *was* a wonderful time. More wonderful than you could ever know." *He's right. What was I thinking?* She frowns. *But he's a grown man. Doesn't he realize I have other issues to settle too?*

He barrels on. "Sometimes I don't understand you at all. I really don't. Sometimes you don't seem . . . sensible." His voice trails off in exasperation.

"The damage to the house made me crazy, Frank. It's been my cocoon. The pictures Arianna took are the only record of my life. I would have crawled on my hands and knees to get those pictures. Of course I'm coming back. Give me a day or two. "

Scotty grabs the phone. "Now don't worry, Clara. You'll be safe driving that car. Just keep in touch, OK?" His tone brightens. "Maybe it's good to get out of Jackpot for a few days, after what you've been through. Is that the idea here?"

"I don't know, Scotty. The only thing I thought about was getting the pictures."

He's reassuring again. "Just check in every once in a while so we won't worry, OK? And don't worry about Frank. I'll settle him down. The wasps are fine. We checked on them right after we got your note."

Somewhat pale, she sits down at the table again. The waitress has brought two checks. Haskell picks up hers. "Here, let me take care of that. Are you all right, Clara?"

She slaps her credit card on the table. "I'll take care of my check, thank you."

"Is everything all right?" Arianna asks.

"Everything's fine. My son is very upset that I took Scotty's car."

Arianna and Haskell raise their eyebrows, say nothing.

Clara sees their look. *They think I'm nuts. Fine. Let them think that.* Now she's on the verge of tears and struggles mightily to control herself. Quickly she tells them about moving down from Oregon and needing a car to get to Elko. As they listen intently, Lenore in her bag is warm against Clara's ankle.

Abruptly she stands, hefts her purse and the cloth bag over her shoulder. "Scotty knows I'll take care of his car. He trusts me, even though nobody else seems to. And now that you think I'm insane, I need to get going. Thank you very much for your company." She grabs her check and heads for the cash register.

Again Haskell looks dumbstruck.

Arianna calls out. "Wait, Clara—I'm paying. This was a business lunch."

She refuses Arianna's offer to pay, takes the credit card, and pays the cashier in cash. She's tired of everyone questioning her sanity. She wants to get out of there. Haskell and Arianna are right behind her, also paying in cash. He takes Clara gently by the arm before she exits to the parking lot. Arianna discretely heads to the ladies' room.

He looks into her angry eyes. "Can't you stay a little longer? We could walk around this afternoon. There's a good city park, or we could drive to the mountains for a little hike." He points to his RV, a late-model maroon Winnebago. "Arianna wants to see her cousin here before we leave for San Francisco. Or she could hike with us. Whichever you prefer." His manner is courtly. She feels a little dizzy.

It's that armchair feeling again. She could lean right up against him as if he were an old leather armchair. What's the matter with her anyway? She doesn't have a Brain Room for this kind of thing. She just needs a friend. She takes a deep breath as tears well, falling down her cheeks. Astonished, she tries to wipe them away. He takes a fresh handkerchief from his shirt pocket and offers it to her. She dabs at her eyes. He puts his arm around her, which only makes her tears flow more freely. It's mortifying. She doesn't know why she's crying. All those years. He smells like candy corn and sage. It's the most delicious smell.

"I like his smell too, especially the sage," Lenore whispers from her bag.

His voice is low. "I know it's hard. You've been alone for a long time, doing everything alone." His words only make her weep more, though she's desperately trying to stop. "It's hard to rely on your grown child. He needs to have his own life, am I right?" Silently, she nods.

He speaks slowly. "I'm alone too. My wife died last year. I've been pretty much a basket case." He has unobtrusively steered her outside the hotel for more privacy. Now he stares into the distance. "Her passing was hard. We were very close. We had no children together." He clears his throat. "I finally had to shake myself out of the doldrums. That's why I'm on this cross-country trip. Arianna's been very understanding, a godsend."

Clara looks at him. He's trying to smile. A little unsteady on her feet, she tips toward him for just a moment before catching herself and wiping her eyes for the last time.

"I see," she says.

chapter 19

o here she is, sitting in an RV with someone she just met. Arianna has disappeared into her cousin's house on Pine Street. The reasonable part of Clara's brain says she's just overwhelmed by this turn of events. But she's nervous. The cloth bag quivers in her lap. Curious, she brings it to her face.

"Big ol' puppy needs no harpy."

Slowly, she lowers the bag to her lap. *Now you're giving me behavior lessons? What foolishness is this?*

Haskell heard something like static coming from the bag—a voice? a recording? Looking bemused, he watches as Clara restlessly jumps up and explores the vehicle, running distracted fingers over the granite countertops, clear maple cabinets, leather couch, a very involved-looking stereo system.

She purses her lips. Her friend Abigail Morton just had one of those small camper shells you attach to a pickup. The two of them fit just fine in a bunk bed during Shakespearean summers in Ashland. And Abigail's camper was agile on the road. This thing would be a monstrosity to drive.

She folds her arms. "Well, you're hardly living from hand to mouth here."

He lets out a delighted laugh. "Actually, you're right. It's a bit much."

She leafs through a rack of reading material by the couch: *New York Times, Art in America, Wired, Sports Illustrated, Cowboys and Indians.* Glances into the bedroom–queen-size bed, coffee-colored duvet, gleaming ebony nightstands. She feels like a prairie dog let into the castle. *If he has a Rolex watch, I'm out of here.* She's trying to find every excuse. She's being idiotic and knows it.

He gestures at his living quarters. "You like?"

"Can't say as I do." She fixes him with a level gaze.

He roars with laugher.

She's undeterred. "Your camper is very nice, but something smaller would get you better gas mileage."

Her plain speaking delights him, as does her smooth peach skin, her shiny hair springy with life. She seems fresh and untouched, absolutely straight arrow. Something about her makes him feel free and clear. He needs this feeling right now. But she's carrying a burden of some kind too, something deep and unresolved. A minute ago, she picked up that bag with a staticky voice coming from it. *A radio?* he wondered, confused. She closed her eyes and shook her head at the bag. He was startled and moved by the gesture.

"I'll let you in on a secret, Clara. My sister insisted I get this rig. It's a birthday gift from her, a rental. She wanted to do this big thing. She thought I'd mooned around long enough after Sandra's death. I wouldn't have picked this RV myself." He nods. "It does *not* get good gas mileage." This time they both laugh.

She steals a glance at his watch–a Timex with plain large numbers and a black leather band. She lets out her breath, didn't know she was holding it.

Two days ago, she was calmly feeding her wasps in Jackpot. Tomorrow she expects to return to Jackpot, round up the few remaining wasps, and try again to salvage her life. *For heaven's sake, Clara, just settle down.*

Haskell could stand a good stiff Scotch right now, but he puts *that* thought out of his mind. A good walk would do. This unpredictable woman is intriguing. He wasn't planning anything except to get out of New York for a while.

Lenore needs some air, Clara decides, so she lays the cloth bag open on the floor. Lenore scampers back to the living area, joyfully leaps on the glass liquor cabinet, the leather couch, the media cabinet. It's clear what *she* thinks of the RV. The creature touches a button on the media cabinet. The doors retract, and the TV goes through a dizzying channel shuffle.

"Stop that!" Clara says.

Haskell looks up from a map he's reading. "What's the matter?"

"The TV. It's malfunctioning. Don't you see?" She points. The cabinet is closed.

He had felt a sudden gust of air through the window, nothing more. He looks at her carefully. "You've been through a lot, Clara. What would you think of staying in Elko a few days just to take it easy? We don't need to be in San Francisco right away."

Long pause. "You might have a point there." *What if he discovers Lenore? Would he think I'm crazy? That he's crazy? Am I just imagining Lenore?*

He pulls up to a city park. "Join me if you want, after your nap. I'll just be walking around out here."

Hearing his footsteps fade, she falls into a deep sleep on the couch. An hour later, she jolts awake. Lenore is twitching on the kitchen counter, asleep in her bag.

Clara frowns, deep in thought. This unruly ultra-midget is

pushing her in some way that makes her doubt her own sanity. She knew Lenore was trouble the minute she heard the "push you further" poppycock. *Further into the unholy mess of Samantha's death.* She cringes, knowing she left Eugene to excavate that very thing.

What a coward I am, she thinks as she puts on her lipstick in the bathroom mirror.

Relieved to leave Lenore asleep in the RV, she joins Haskell in the park. Trying to act "normal," she checks if he's looking at her funny–he's not. Gradually she feels more relaxed, more forgetful of the mysterious Lenore. She's grateful for the dry, clear air, the shouts of children, for this unexpected man who acts so considerately.

"Was the Winnebago comfortable? Is the weather too hot for you?"

"Everything," she says, "is fine."

She doesn't believe it for a minute. *What's he hiding? He's too perfect.*

They approach a play area softly floored with wood chips. Sharp cries ring out as children commandeer the swings, the climbing bars, and big pipe tunnels. At the swings, a tall boy in scuffed clothes and dusty hair, maybe ten, crowds in line where three younger boys, about six or seven, wait their turn. Clara looks around, sees nobody who might be in charge of the interloper. She steps forward, makes eye contact with the boy, speaks firmly. "You need to wait your turn, young man. I think you know that." He looks defiantly at her, gauges her look, swaggers to the back of the line. The younger children give her grateful looks.

"You're a pro," Haskell says as the shrieking children race to swing highest.

"I was a teacher. Grammar school, high school, briefly a principal." She watches his reaction. After the Rolex test, will he fail the one about wanting trophy women?

"Christ, Clara, my grammar school teachers were like angels to me." He's ready to tell a story, but she pulls away, her eyes darkening.

"If you're looking for angels, don't count on me. I just like kids. That's all. Do you have children?" she asks, forgetting he said he didn't.

His swift look is veiled. "No. No kids." He looks away.

She sees his pained expression. *Maybe there's more to him than I thought. Maybe I've been the superficial one.*

He glances sideways at her. *So she's not an angel. Maybe we're more alike than I thought.*

After fetching Arianna, they buy groceries and drive to Lamoille Canyon, twenty miles southeast of Elko. Miles of massive cliffs and forest line the road into Humboldt-Toiyabe National Forest, the second biggest national forest in the country. Clara and Haskell have never heard of this place. Arianna says it's usually deserted; she comes here whenever she can. The clean, dry air always clears her mind.

They park on an overlook and start hiking down a nature trail that circles down to Lamoille Creek, then up again. As Clara inhales the smell of pine and the sound of water, her Oregon Brain Room flies open. It's like coming home.

Arianna happily points out a yellow-bellied marmot scurrying around. Clara sees a mule deer unmoving in the distance. Haskell finds a stand of elderberries and eagerly picks some to share.

"New Yorker turns nature boy." Arianna chuckles and goes ahead on the trail, taking pictures, disappearing from view.

Clara and Haskell walk on in silence broken only by aspen leaves clicking in a pristine chorus. "Listen," she says. They stop walking. "I could stay here forever."

Thumbs in his belt, he gives her a lazy smile and leans back on his heels. "Not New York City, right?"

Shading her eyes, she looks at him. "Wouldn't know. Never been there."

"Oh, baby, are you in for somethin'."

Suddenly she's besieged by the memory of Dawson tying her roughly to the kitchen chair, Edie slurping Cran-Apple juice from the bottle, their wide-eyed stare when she cried, "Stay! My babies!" at the wasps' delirious escape to the sky. Then the stink of gas on her clothes, the whoosh of fire shooting to the eaves, Dawson with tears in his eyes, angrily hugging her before he threw gas on her.

By her held breath, he knows she's experiencing something. "What?" He leans toward her.

"Oh, those kids and what they did."

He touches her shoulder. "I wish I could've been there to protect you."

She lowers her eyes, not having heard such words in years.

At dusk, the three of them are chatting amiably, stocking feet up on the coffee table, drinking purified water at Arianna's insistence, Haskell knows, to delay the start of booze. Lenore is hiding under Haskell's bed, listening. The vehicle is fragrant with mountain mahogany and bristlecone pine branches they brought in from the trail and draped on cabinets. In the fading daylight and beautiful setting, Clara resolves to put trauma to rest and just enjoy the evening.

Revived and hungry, they set up a production line for a cold chicken salad. Haskell and Clara are tearing apart a precooked whole chicken they got at Albertson's. Arianna slices four oranges, a handful of Kalamata olives, a red onion, and diced fresh rosemary. She flings each heap into a big yellow ceramic bowl already full of the shredded chicken and torn Romaine lettuce.

Clara's hands glisten with meaty juices. She watches him gnaw the gristle from a thigh bone, his chin glistening with grease. "You do that? Me too!" she exclaims, laughing. She gnaws on the other thigh bone. They laugh, watching each other tear at bones for a moment until Clara turns away, uncomfortable. *Slow this down. This is not like you.*

Arianna makes a dressing of olive oil and lemon juice, throws in some sliced almonds, and mixes everything up. Haskell readies some sourdough rolls for the toaster oven. As the women watch, he pours a good white wine and cues up mellow jazz: Dexter Gordon, the Modern Jazz Quartet, Stan Getz, Ella Fitzgerald, Peggy Lee, all the oldies— "You Go to My Head," "Black Coffee," "September Song," "Out of Nowhere."

The jazz sends shivers up Clara's spine. With jazz, she's stepping into a foreign but infinitely inviting territory. Darrell mostly liked big bands—Tommy Dorsey, Glenn Miller, The Andrews Sisters—"I'll Get By," "We'll Meet Again,"—music evoking Pearl Harbor, ballrooms, large crowds, courage, winning, the country making sacrifices together. Darrell loved the era, though he was too young to serve.

Jazz like Haskell's calls up a completely different sensibility— intimate smoke-filled rooms, easy laughter, sensuality, a worldly music of loss and heartbreak, the listener finding solace in hard liquor and slow cocktails. Clara gets it right away. *My stars,* she wishes she'd known about jazz all these years.

Talk is easy and slow, making no particular sense, and no one seems to mind. Haskell, his scarred face gleaming in candle-light, watches her as she slowly sips wine. He easily downs half a bottle of Chardonnay and opens another. Arianna gives him a look. He doesn't seem to notice.

Music, talk, and wine swirl together. Clara runs her fingers over the arms of the butter-smooth, cognac leather armchair. It's like well-cared-for skin. So different from her plain rocker at home—burned up!—sliced from an oak tree, soothing only when rocked.

He wonders what she's thinking, stroking the armchair like that. So does Lenore, watching from the corner. The sun is down now.

Arianna folds her legs onto the leather couch and firmly pushes up her horn-rimmed glasses. Wine glass in one hand, she relaxes her other arm on the back of the couch. "Nevada's supposed to be an empty state," she says lazily. "But it's a mad-house out there: lizards, eagles, beavers, geese, snakes, mule deer, mountain goats, rats, spiders, hawks, jack rabbits—critter holes crumbling and springing up everywhere. It's a predator's feast." She smiles.

A little tipsy on her second glass, Clara nods to Arianna. "Drama on the ground, in our heads, the sky. Drama every-where." She scratches the unhealed wasp stings on her forehead. The itching is getting worse instead of better. Her forehead pulses. Maybe she should see a doctor.

"Forget teeming nature," Haskell says a little belligerently, plunking his empty glass down on the coffee table. "Nothing's emptier than a room full of people you don't care about. I've been to plenty of cocktail parties just to hustle a photo shoot. It's a pretty lonesome business."

Arianna sips her wine. "When I was a teenager, I went around snapping photos of all our relatives when we got together. I didn't like them very much. They were nosy and self-important. But in the photos they often looked lonely and insecure in a way I couldn't see in real time. That fascinated me."

Haskell and Arianna get refills; Clara demurs. She's not much of a drinker. She can't even remember the last time she was with worldly adults, conversation ricocheting here and there. She's like a starving person stumbling onto a well-stocked pantry. Her life for the last thirty years is beginning to look like a sensory deprivation chamber.

They sit down to eat. The salad is delicious. They eat it all, along with sourdough rolls, the best they could find in Elko, Sara Lee's Heat and Serve. Haskell lights more candles. The RV in evening light is an intimate mountain retreat, sealed off from the world. More talk, more jazz to captivate Clara—Paul Desmond, Dave Brubeck, John McLaughlin, Gerry Mulligan, Carmen McRae.

Arianna says, "I keep thinking about your house, Clara. It captures something about this country that people forget these days. Like let's get back to basics, folks."

Clara makes a wry face. "Somehow I can't see a nationwide stampede to own one-thousand-square-foot houses . . ."

Arianna stares into her wine glass. "The country just seems lost somehow. People maxing out their credit cards, owning a hundred pairs of shoes, having weddings or bar mitzvahs or sixteenth birthdays that cost one hundred thousand dollars. It's all getting crazy."

Clara warms to the subject. "With taxes squeezed, I think the president wants to put us back in the nineteenth century when we had little government to speak of. No paved roads, no national parks, no environmental protection, no Social Security or Medicare . . . just defense." She's silent a moment. "God help us if anything really bad happens. I don't know if competent people are valued in government anymore. People come to Washington to line their pockets. No checks, no balances, no follow through." She snorts. "Let's hope the Middle East doesn't blow up again."

Haskell rouses himself. "The Middle East is *always* going to blow up. Now and forevermore."

"I think you got that one right," Clara says.

"Let's toast to the Middle East blowing up." He has a gleam in his eye.

Clara glances at him. "Well, I don't want to tempt fate."

He's adamant. "I don't believe in fate. I believe in action and the consequences of action."

She's unconvinced. "What actions? What consequences? Do you know something we don't?" *Is this a new side I'm seeing?*

He shrugs.

"Haskell is talking rubbish, Clara. Too much wine. He gets this way."

"I'm fine." He tips his empty glass to his niece.

Rattled, Clara turns to Arianna. "So where do you call home, with all your traveling?"

She shrugs. "My gallery is home. Museums. Photography shows anywhere."

"No settled place? You don't mind?"

"The idea of an actual home bores me. A house and a picket fence sounds like prison. My home is work. It consumes me."

Haskell rummages unsuccessfully in his pockets for a cigarette. "I'm trying to quit smoking again." His tone is rueful. "As for me, I've lived my whole life in New York. I don't know if I could ever leave it. I'm like Woody Allen, wedded to the place. Isn't that right, Arianna?"

She smiles. "You're nothing like Woody Allen."

Clara is quiet. This talk of home highlights something that's been roiling in her head longer than she might care to admit. "Sometimes I wonder if the whole idea of home is overrated. I've staked my whole life on it. Maybe I've been a fool." She gets up and begins to stack the dishes.

After considerable discussion, Haskell sleeps outside on a cot with an air mattress and the women sleep in the RV, Clara on the couch, Arianna in the bed. Clara had wanted to get a room at the Rancher's Hotel, but they convinced her that was unnecessary and it was too late to drive these mountain roads anyway.

In the morning, Haskell whips up wickedly good scrambled eggs, and finally they're ready for another hike. As they pull up to a promising trailhead, Clara's cell phone rings. Frank, she thinks, opening it to much static.

"Hey, Clara. Me and Edie made it. Cops can't get us now."

The familiar adenoidal voice makes her stomach clench in anger and shock. "Dawson! Where are you?" She covers her eyes with her free hand, as if fending off a blow.

"Guess. Fresh fish, good tequila, cheap living."

She swallows. "For heaven's sake. Are you in Mexico?"

"Bingo. Eight cars later."

Haskell grimly studies her face. Arianna touches her shoulder. Clara gestures for them to leave her in privacy. They get out and stand beside the vehicle, looking at Clara hunched over her cell phone in the passenger seat.

Hearing Dawson's voice fills her with rage at the damage they did, the things they took, the irreplaceable photos burned.

Her tone is sharp. "I'm surprised you called, after what you two did."

He takes his time answering. "Sixty-four-thousand-dollar question, why'd I call." He clears his throat. "Only thing I can think of is, you do a crazy thing, I do a crazy thing. The world is crazy."

"For God's sake, Dawson, talk sense. What crazy thing?"

"You stuck your nose in. Nobody else did. Ever." He clears his throat, tries to joke. "You're a nosy broad, you know that?"

Anger mixes with wonder. She can't imagine what he's encountered to make him call like this. Her voice softens. "So maybe it's not so bad to be a nosy broad. Because then *you* do a crazy thing, and call." Bounding into her mind's eye, Edie, wild Edie, against all reason, is now a full-grown Samantha.

My wayward babies, she thinks in despair.

Silence, then his final rush of words. "Look, this is a bad connection. We're sorry we took your stuff, Clara. We had to. And we didn't mean to light up your house. I don't know what made us do it. It was a rotten thing. There, I've said it. *Hasta la vista,* baby. Gotta go."

As the line goes dead, she looks at the phone in wonder before snapping it shut. "He said my name," she whispers. "He said they were sorry. I can't believe it." She bounds from the vehicle to join Haskell and Arianna. They are full of questions. She tells them everything Dawson said.

Arianna says, "Who knows, maybe they'll forget the rough stuff now."

"I wouldn't count on it." Clara's look is sober.

"I agree. Let's not be foolish here," Haskell says grimly. "They didn't *have* to take your stuff. Or manhandle you. Or wreck your house."

Clara meets his gaze. "True. He apologized, though. He apologized." Her eyes are bright.

Haskell considers this. "Yes, he did."

She persists. "He has some good in him, or he wouldn't have called, and he wouldn't have apologized."

He frowns. "Forget the Misunderstood-Kid-Turning-Over-a-New-Leaf thing, Clara. This guy's been around. He might be setting you up for something else."

"Maybe." She looks away. Suddenly light at heart, she says, "Can such a thing as grace exist in the world?"

He looks at her, his voice neutral. "It would be nice."

"OK, boys and girls, let's hike." Arianna has started down the trailhead. Clara sprints after her; Haskell follows right behind.

Lenore, snug in her bag on Clara's shoulder, murmurs, "Careful, this guy is complicated."

"So am I," Clara whispers, smiling.

"I know," Lenore says, falling silent.

Arianna's camera whirs and clicks as she disappears down the trail. Clara and Haskell walk more slowly on the irregular rises and dips. Clara is silently reliving the attack on her house again and doesn't see the scenery. After a while, she sighs: It's just too amazing that Dawson called.

In the dense growth, they take in the sounds of distant water, snakes and gophers rustling in dry undergrowth, aspen leaves clattering in a slight wind, the cawing of hawks cutting the sky like a knife, bighorn sheep motionless on the canyon rim.

By now they've absorbed each other's distinctive gait—Clara's upright posture and brisk stride with little wasted motion, honed from many jogging years; Haskell's sturdy gait (except for a slight limp—bad motorcycle accident in his twenties, he said). He holds his arms slightly away from his body as if claiming territory or preparing to defend against lurking enemies, a posture that makes Clara smile. Her faded red Keds aren't adequate for this terrain, but of course she had no idea her quest for the photos would lead to a hike in Lamoille Canyon with unexpected companions. His firm hiking boots are more appropriate. On an uneven surface, she stumbles.

"Oh!"

"Gotcha!" He catches her before she can fall. With his arm around her, he looks at her wide forehead, her warm coffee eyes, her face glowing in early light. She absorbs his skin crisscrossed with not-unattractive lines and scars, his knowing hazel eyes. She looks away.

Haskell has met many women since his wife died a year ago. None made him feel as he does just now—shy.

They find a boulder to sit on. "I won't let you down," he blunders out.

Amused, she looks at him in surprise. "But I'm not expecting anything."

He grins. "Then I take it back."

She laughs. "So you *will* let me down?"

"Don't try to confuse me."

Laughing, they hear Arianna coming back. "Great shots, the trail is beautiful," she exclaims. She is loose, happy, doing what she loves most in the world. Seeing their moment, she circles them, camera clicking, as they sit on the rock. They barely notice. She wanders off again.

Deep in thought, Clara wonders if she's been making her aloneness into a shrine all these years. *Our lady of sorrows, is that it?*

Then this man comes along, distracting her with the ragged scar above his left eyebrow. *I just need a friend,* she thinks once more, trying to calm her nervousness. *A real friend.*

As for him, none of his encounters with women this past year had lessened his loneliness and grief until he saw this pint-sized woman sitting quietly at the Rancher's Hotel, drinking iced tea. She calms him in some profound way.

They sit on the rock, thinking fleeting confused thoughts. This is just a brief adventure, she thinks. Or not even that. This man is simply a respite from talking wasps and her burning house. Maybe the natural setting makes her sentimental. Trees always were her soft spot.

For him, this cross-country trip after a year of mind-boggling grief has opened his mind to the possibility of a new turn to his life. His whole life has been chaotic. Surely this calm woman sitting beside him on this rock doesn't trade in chaos.

For both, the thought of dying makes them momentarily headlong on this beautiful summer day. He grips her hand. She pulls away. "We're acting like teenagers!" she exclaims.

"More power to us!" He plants a single kiss on her hand just as Arianna reappears. Her busy clicking makes them laugh uproariously. It's a cosmic joke of some kind.

The next day, Arianna diplomatically gets a plane ticket to Los Angeles to confer with her gallery at Bergamot Station in Santa Monica. They stand inside the entrance to the small Elko airport. Arianna is beaming. "The curator called last night. He's going to feature your photos, Clara. So what do you think of that?" The three of them exchange high fives.

Lenore twitches in her bag so much that Haskell wonders if Clara's having a bad shoulder spasm. "Are you all right?" he asks.

She smiles ironically. "I'm just ducky."

Arianna's all business, looks at both of them. "So call me when you get to New York. End of June. OK?"

They watch her walk to check-in.

15 days left.

chapter 20

rank has worked in the change booth at Desert Dan's ever since he and his mother came to Jackpot. It's boring to just sit around and exchange lunch sacks full of coins and bills for chips. But it's only for a few hours each day in the late afternoon, and he has to earn something. The money from Aunt Lillian isn't quite enough, and Scotty offered him the job. He sees Stella in all their off hours. They talk about moving in together. Their lives are wonderfully full, except for their gnawing worries about Scotty's health. He still won't see a doctor.

Scotty has introduced Frank to a retired sculptor from the University of Nevada in Reno who said Frank could have the alabaster, limestone, and marble that he wouldn't be using any more. Frank couldn't believe his good fortune. Immediately he set to work on a translucent piece of alabaster. The color, light orange, is like a living person, the mineral veins like human veins coursing through it.

At first, he carved in Scotty's fenced backyard because Stella's property is open to anyone who wants to walk off with the stones. Since the fire, he does his carving on Clara's Formica table in the burned-out house. He couldn't have explained why—some protective instinct maybe. Keeping watch over her damaged property until she returns. He stores the unused stones in Scotty's shed. Each morning he gets in the trailer cab and brings the alabaster, his tools, and the dust mask over to Clara's burned-out house. When he's done sculpting for the day, he takes his materials back to Scotty's shed. For his open-air work place, he made a sandbag by tying off an old sheet of Stella's and filling it with sand. The sandbag protects Clara's kitchen table when he bangs the alabaster with his chisel and mallet to rough out the shape he wants.

He loves this primitive setup, the silence of the burned-out house, the mild wind, the dry air all around him. The four Formica chairs are still there. One chair remains toppled where Clara lunged from it after she got free of Dawson's rope and ran outside to confront him. For some reason, Frank doesn't want to move this chair. He moves another chair aside when he works at the table.

He brings a lantern for the few times he works in the dark. Sometimes at night he thinks he hears rustling sounds coming closer from the direction of the Sage Motel. Then the sound stops. He doesn't bother about it, and the sound goes away. He occasionally carves at night for this very reason—to show mischief-makers they might face some consequences if they mess around this place. He's got a pipe wrench on the counter.

Now he chisels with panache into the alabaster. The work goes quickly. Even the rough outline conveys passion and speed and delight. Gone are the tortured burls of screaming human heads. He made a second burl head soon after he smashed the first one. He smashed that one too. He's done with burls.

Working with real stone is a revelation for him. He shows his first effort—the light-orange beautifully veined piece—to Scotty. It's a languidly sprawling male nude lying on its side, ready to leap up and—what?—claim the world. He laughs. Scotty, on his way to Salt Lake City, says he's crazy about the piece and will try to sell it for him. Scotty shows it to a friend, who promptly offers a thousand bucks for it. Scotty counters with fifteen hundred. Sold at twelve fifty. Ecstatic, Frank insists on giving Scotty a good commission before Scotty mysteriously flies off to Salt Lake in his private plane.

Frank calls his mother to share the good news. The connection is staticky. They usually can't get through to each other at all–the mountains, they both assume. But they both keep trying. His call comes in when Clara and Haskell are leaving the Elko airport and are heading back to Lamoille Canyon.

"Frank, how wonderfu!–your first sale! All those wood carvings you made with your father in the back shed–I always *knew* you could be a sculptor. Do you have a picture of it? And I have a new friend to introduce you to: Haskell Roberts. We'll be seeing you soon. I'm so happy for you, Frank."

"Terrific. That's great news, Mom–about your friend."

To celebrate the sale and his mother's "new friend," Frank and Stella drive to Twin Falls to feast on fresh Idaho trout and a primo bottle of white wine at a good restaurant Scotty recommended. They put the rest of the money in savings, and Frank sets off on another piece of alabaster. Every day he carves for several hours, cleans up meticulously, stows everything back in Scotty's shed, does his stint at the change booth and goes back to Stella, who is usually done with her shift by then. Frank has never been happier.

The fire totally destroyed Clara's house except for two adjoining walls still standing in the kitchen. One wall was all cabinets and counter. The other wall had the sink and more cabinets. A few days ago, the wall with the sink burned down and the sink vanished, leaving only the wall with cabinets and counter. So now the gutted house looks even more bizarre and precarious.

Just once, Frank wishes he could get his hands on the bastards who burn down houses just for kicks. He can't get the city to remove the whole sorry mess until Clara comes back. Who knows if she'll even give permission?

The house has other visitors too. Late at night after most of Jackpot is asleep, three or four people wearing dark hoodies come sauntering down to the flatbed from the Sage Motel. They sit on the ground near tires not visible from the highway and take out their drug paraphernalia. They talk briefly and then light up, shoot up, or snort, leaning against the tires or lying on the ground, shielding themselves as much as possible from prying eyes. They usually come around two in the morning and leave by four, before the wasps come to drive them away. They snicker and curse the stupid wasps when they hear them coming.

One night, soon after Frank sold his first sculpture, a group of six or eight people follows Stella across the highway to the vacant lot and the burned-out house. It's eleven o'clock. They've brought blankets and/or pillows. They sit on the ground near the house and get themselves comfortable. They sit in silence, not knowing what to expect. "What are you aware of in this unusual setting?" Stella asks. "The smell of burned wood," says one. "The hum of passing cars," says another. An occasional distant shout. A tireless cricket. Sounds of shifting bodies looking for a comfortable position. A thermos being opened. Sounds of swallowing, throats clearing. Sighs. Breathing. A few coughs. The thermos being screwed shut again.

They focus on the toppled chair after their eyes adjust to the dark. Someone asks, "Why hasn't anyone picked up that chair?" No one answers. Long silence.

A low-pitched hum gets louder and louder above them, filling the night sky with fury. Several people stand up, ready to move fast. The angry hum creates a torrent of air around the pilgrims. They realize—or recall from childhood—that the humming dark ache of the sound is a cloud of wasps invisible in the dark, circling dizzy and angry overhead, grazing people's heads as the visitors shout at them.

Grimly, the people run from the battered house and jog to the safety of Desert Dan's in tight silence. The wasps stop hounding them only at the boundary of the highway, refusing to cross it, then fly back to the gutted house, where they buzz darkly on the lone kitchen counter, according to someone who used night goggles. *Don't screw with the house or us,* the wasps seem to say. The expelled humans huddle outside Desert Dan's before going to their respective rooms for the night.

chapter 21

Looking out the window of the RV, Clara falls silent as Haskell drives further from the airport and gets closer to the canyon. Finally she says, "So we're just getting acquainted here, right?" She looks at him, this unpredictable stranger from Mars. She wishes Arianna were still with them.

He glances at her, sees her somber face.

Nervously she fiddles with Scotty's keychain. "The idea of a friendship. Is that what we're working on here?"

Mildly surprised, he glances at her again and tries to get into the spirit of the thing. "Well, we could go to San Francisco before I take the Winnebago back to my sister. How about that?"

She nods quickly. "We can try a cooking schedule. I'll take Monday, Wednesday, and Friday. You could take Tuesday, Thursday, and Sunday. Saturdays we'll drive to Elko and eat at a restaurant. We'll sleep separately," she says with studied casualness.

He looks at her, nods. "Sure. You take the bed; I'll take the couch. It's a comfortable bed, a comfortable couch."

"I might like the couch instead," she says mildly, then continues, "You're a better cook than I am. But we both like poached salmon, turkey meatballs, sliced avocados with lemon juice, and dark chocolate anything."

"For starters," he says, smiling.

"We'll stay in the canyon only as long as we're enjoying ourselves." Of this she is positive.

He nods easily. "We need to be in New York in ten days at the latest."

He can see she's all wound up. She's probably been alone for years. He reaches over and squeezes her shoulder. "Don't worry," he says. "Everything will be fine."

She stares straight ahead. She's got a splitting headache.

They are camping in the canyon beside a stream. The hot day has cooled, they bought groceries in Elko, Lenore has fled to the comfort of the bushes. After some good white wine, it's easy to change the plan a little.

"Make dinner together?" She smiles. "Just this once?"

"Why not?" he says with a wink.

He makes poached salmon, and she makes a salad. They sit outside in the two reclining chairs, talking quietly as they eat, drinking their wine. Other campers are already inside their vehicles. When he asks about her life, her rusty 1963 Brain Room door unaccountably creaks open a little. Her heart pounds. Before she can stop herself, she tells him briefly about her marriage—that Darrell and Samantha both died in 1963, that Frank has wandered the country since 1972, when he graduated from high school.

"You've been alone since then?"

"Yes."

He doesn't push her to say more, and she is grateful. That she can say anything at all about these things is amazing. Scary. She just met this man. For whatever reason, she finds herself adding to the story, talking fast as if needing to beat the clock—her solitary life after the deaths, raising Frank alone, her failure to understand his needs, her refusal to teach after the accident, instead becoming a crossing guard to prevent other deaths, then teaching again, this time high school, working long hours. She says nothing about who is at fault for the accident that killed Samantha. He listens carefully. Her hands are sweaty. All this talking. Will she pay for this? How can she even do this? Something is changing in her head. Is Lenore doing something?

Terrified, she stops talking. The wasp stings above her eyebrows just won't go away. Her head throbs. Sometimes she thinks there's something growing in her head—that these wasp stings are controlling her somehow. Making her Brain Rooms fall apart. Is that what's happening?

They sit, listening to the water. She tries to catch her breath.

"You put a lot on yourself, Clara," he says soberly.

She looks at him.

He takes the plates inside.

Lenore is still in the bushes, listening to everything. Now the creature half walks, half flies over to Clara's reclining chair and begins to bite her—little rodent-like bites on the back of Clara's neck.

Clara squirms. "Why torment me now? I'm *talking*. That's what you want, isn't it? In your hundred twenty days, have you ever seen me exchange more than five words with a man? It's been decades. Ask your siblings. So what's your problem, Lenore? At the restaurant, you were all excited, jumping around in your bag when Haskell sat down. Now you want to put *me* in a bag." Clara pushes her away to stop the needlelike torture of the bites.

"I'm worried you'll get totally immersed in this guy and forget about the kids when we hardly have any time left."

Clara flares. "But my kids aren't *here*, are they? Do you *see* them? Am I supposed to go dig up Samantha's grave and haul Frank away from his lover so I can talk to them? You're making me sick."

Her whole body is a phantom itch. She scratches her arm until she can't stand it. She tries to leave her arm alone but finally surrenders to the delicious intensity of scratching until she draws blood.

Finally Lenore's sharp teeth, smaller than a rat's, stop their torment, and she runs to the bushes. "Pay attention to me, Clara!" Her cry echoes in the night.

Haskell comes back outside. Seeing Clara trying to compose herself, he decides to say what's on his mind. "But those deaths were so long ago." His words frame an unasked question.

"Better to turn inward, concentrate on my teaching. Easier that way." She's breathless.

"Easier than finding a partner?"

"So much easier."

Puzzled, he looks at her.

"Rule out rather than rule in. That's how I operate. Always cautious, always looking for safety." *Except tonight*, she thinks. *Tonight I'm going to die if I can't stop talking, if I can't get Lenore to shut up.*

He slouches in the chair, looking at the stars. "Wow. I had the opposite problem. I was a glutton for almost everything. Safety never occurred to me."

"You're a man," she says.

He ignores her. He's intent on what he wants to tell her. "These stars remind me of something. Promise you won't laugh?"

"Shoot." In her mind she shoots him. Now that he's changed

the subject, she feels all closed up. Oh gosh, she can't be playing these sudden crazy games with herself. Games are coming out of her head with no warning.

He continues. "When I was maybe ten, I was shivering in my backyard in Saginaw, Michigan, hugging my skinny knees and watching the stars strewn across the sky. The stars just knocked me out—the random scattering, the sense of beauty without end. I wanted to make something just like those stars, that design—something excessive and arresting. I was *jealous* of the stars." He snorts, refilling his wine glass. "Talk about ego. I've done nothing of the kind. My life has been one long soap opera."

They look at the clear Nevada sky. Dryly she says, "Well, no one could accuse you of lacking ambition."

"You said you wouldn't laugh."

"I'm not laughing. I'm impressed."

But she does laugh, and he's glad. He had wanted to cheer her up.

"OK, so you want to hear my soap opera?"

"I can hardly wait," she says, smiling. She can see he's nervous.

"I was doing bad pop art in the sixties and getting nowhere in the Village. The coffee houses were full, underground art and theater were everywhere, and there was always a party. The artists shared whatever they had—cigarettes, beer, a pot of spaghetti, a sack of oranges. Everyone stuck together; nobody starved. Sandra was starting out as a clothing designer. She was ambitious and focused. I don't know why she chose a guy like me. I had no focus then. She moved into my loft. It was a very romantic time." He clears his throat. She looks at him.

"Even then, things got a little complicated. It took me a long time to realize I'd never make it as an artist. Meanwhile, Sandra's clothing business took off like gangbusters. She worked night and day, and that was fine—she was happy. I cooked dinner and sat around trying to get gallery shows, but really just showed my stuff in friends' lofts. By the time we got around to having a kid, which both of us really wanted, nothing happened." His laugh is bitter. "This got her really low, so she decided I couldn't support her in the style she wanted. She started complaining about money when there was no need to. Bottom line, she left me for a sculptor, some hotshot up and comer. Left me for four years. Had a child with him, a boy. I was devastated." His voice is husky, brusque. "That was a long time ago." She touches his arm. He struggles for composure.

"I remember her moving out of the loft as if it was yesterday. Movers had just boxed up her favorite things—Turkish copper trays, Italian pottery, Egyptian rugs. She'd cut off all her hair, and it fell in little waves around her face. She was wearing jeans and a gorgeous shawl from Oaxaca, but it didn't hide the fact she was pregnant. She looked beautiful. Our good-byes were formal, very restrained. I knew she was upset.

"Those four years, I went out with a lot of women." She looks at him. He does not elaborate. "Finally, we got back together. Her sculptor friend had some paternity suits pending. It was Sandra's turn to be devastated. But I still loved her, and I loved her son—Victor Scalpino. You might have heard of him. He's a very successful sculptor now, like his dad, lives in Rome. I see him every couple of years. We're on good terms. I raised him from the time he was four. His real father never had time for him. I know what that's like. I never had a father either."

He drinks his wine. "When Sandra and I separated, the good thing was I finally found something I could do, which was photography, like Arianna, only commercial. I peddled my photography to whoever would take it—catalogues, private commissions, some gigs with *Time* and *Newsweek*. It's a funny life, commercial photography. Everything depends on lighting, angles, surface. You spend half the day lining everything up to shoot an Italian ceramic bowl full of oranges or a diamond hair-clip on a gorgeous model or some necktie for Christmas. It's a hothouse life. Your focus gets very narrow."

He looks again at the sky. "I always wondered if she took me back because I was finally hauling in a lot of cash. Every few years she had to redo the kitchen, the bathroom, the bedroom. She would fly to Istanbul or Marrakech or Paris and bring back these rugs and vases and tables and paintings, beautiful stuff. She was successful, I was successful; the more she spent, the more I had to earn. She had to have these things because I loved her. I had no interest in these things. We tried to have a kid again, but it was no go. Luckily, we had Victor and lavished attention on him. Weekends were special. We took him to museums, special classes, on New England jaunts. I did a photo book of him when he was growing up. I have to say it turned out well. I'll show you when we get to New York."

Abruptly he says, "This trip has convinced me I should've been a nature photographer. My life would have been a lot calmer."

He looks at her. The light is almost gone. He can hardly see her features.

She's absorbed by the moving water in the stream. "I'm sure you have the eye for it. You certainly have the contacts. Do you have any pictures with you?"

He gestures inside. "Lots."

"Let's see them." She's glad to focus on something concrete. She's overwhelmed by all his talking. Her ears ring. For thirty years she took a vow of silence, and now Haskell has blasted it all to hell.

He's frazzled from his story too. "Let's sleep on it. Show you in the morning."

They rise to go in. "Go ahead," she says. "I'll be just a second."

He disappears inside.

She hurries over to the small stand of aspen where Lenore lurks. The creature stands up at Clara's approach. Now she's six inches tall and all lavender except for some wild purple hair. Clara takes a step back. "Leave me alone," she says, frightened by Lenore's sudden growth and color changes. "Just leave me alone. What's the rush, anyway? I'm tired of living in a box. For once I'm just trying to live my life. For heaven's sake, let me do one thing at a time. My children are way harder to deal with than this man."

"But your children are the crux. And time is short." Lenore is implacable. "In ten days, we have to be in New York. A few days after that, my hundred twenty days are up, and I'll be dead. If you haven't faced your kids, the rest of your days will be hellish."

Clara looks at her. "You're joking."

"You already knew this. I'm not joking. Don't let this man distract you from settling your scores with Frank and Samantha. It's nice to fall in love but even better to find redemption. Isn't it? Think, Clara. You were so stuck to your house that you had to drag it with you, cracks and all. It took a messed-up kid to finally burn it down for you. And now you're free. You've been wasting a lot of time. Years and years."

"In love? Who says I'm falling in love? We're just getting acquainted."

Completely exasperated, Lenore again grows before Clara's very eyes—to eight inches—no, ten!

Astonished, Clara realizes Lenore gets bigger when she's mad. The creature is starting to look like a real person, an extreme midget.

"How much bigger are you going to get, for heaven's sake?"

Lenore disappears into the bushes, mumbling to herself. "So much effort to bring peace to this crazy woman. Why do we bother? What do we get out of it? *She* will get the joy of clarity and honest description, of speaking, understanding and connecting instead of hiding and retreat . We are not meant to be blind and alone on this earth . . ." Her voice fades as Clara strains to hear more.

She flees inside and collapses next to Haskell on the couch.

"For God's sake, Clara, what happened out there? You look like you just saw a ghost."

"I wouldn't rule it out."

In the morning, he lays out his photos on the breakfast table. Endless shots of graffiti-ridden dead trees felled by insects and drought, bullet-riddled trail markers, overflowing trash cans, trails blocked by avalanche, streams clogged with TV dinner trays and shampoo bottles, oil derricks doing clear-cutting that leaves ugly gashes among the diseased trees. The shots are from all over—the Kansas plains, the Appalachians, Mount Rainier in Washington, Arapaho National Forest in Colorado, the Rocky Mountains.

He wants to arrange the photos across long walls in Hockney-like collages, the photos printed in different colorations according to time of day and mood, but mostly in this old-looking sepia, the color of tea, some in mauve or muted grey, as if beautiful scenes are fading to memory alone. He would place the human intrusion shots sparingly, so the main feeling is elegiac, for a beautiful land sullied.

She looks at him. "These are terrific shots. Maybe Arianna can get you a showing."

"I need more experience first."

"I think you've already got a good show. As your first fan, I say go for it."

He laughs. "But I'm *your* fan. Clara Breckenridge, the woman who takes on robbers and old widowed men."

She laughs. "Don't press your luck."

He scoops her up in his arms and sets her beside him on the couch. They play and carry on. And she laughs, listening to his barnacled voice that lifts her spirits.

Later that afternoon, she leaves him nursing a beer at a sports bar in an Elko strip mall as she ambles into a clothing store to buy some necessities—robe, slacks, a jacket. Then she sees this dress, too dressy really, but she keeps looking at it: drapey soft green jersey, three-quarter sleeves, skirt that swishes as she walks in her bare feet. Then she finds these strappy gold sandals with one-and-a-half-inch heels, a freshwater pearl necklace, apricot lipstick, and soft brown eye shadow. *Stop,* she tells herself, delighted and surprised at herself. She hasn't done anything like this for over thirty years.

She changes back to her plain blouse and Levi's.

After dinner at a good Italian restaurant with some excellent pinot noir, they return to the canyon, lazy and relaxed. They chat and sit on the couch and she gathers up her nerve. She has him cover his eyes until she comes back to the living area, twirling and sashaying about in her new green dress. The girlishness never leaves, she thinks, starting to tremble. It just goes into hiding. Can she trust him to do this? He rises from his chair and kisses her several times before they walk laughing into the bedroom.

Quite soon she realizes she can't do this. Why did she let him think she could do this? Despite his patience and all her efforts to relax, she can't go through with it. She's terrified. *Maybe I can never do this again in my life. I should have realized, should have known, should have stayed away from this.* She hides her face against his chest. He feels his chest getting wet. His eyes fill too.

Both know her problem lies elsewhere.

9 days left.

In the morning, he tells her about Sandra as they sit on the couch after breakfast. Nine months ago, she got pancreatic cancer. It started with back pain. She'd been working out a lot, so they thought it was nothing. But she lost her appetite and was dragging around really bad. By the time they got to the doctor, it had spread. At the end, she was in terrible pain and just wanted to listen to Indian ragas. All they could do was sedate her. In two months, she was dead.

"So I hit the parties and bars." He looks at her, then looks away. "I can tell you one thing: It was exhausting." She laughs, a little uncertain.

"Go on."

"I had regulars, very nice women—one on, say, Saturday afternoons, another on Tuesday evenings. I fixed their toasters and TVs, we talked, we ate. We each got what we needed. It was a mutual rescue squad."

He looks over at her. "How are we doing? Less description?"

"Well, it looks like we're not in Kansas anymore, Toto."

He laughs.

She murmurs, "I'm sorry about your wife."

"In about three months, I was calming down, didn't go out

so much. I took long walks in Central Park. One day, everything just got quiet, as if a buzz saw had stopped." He takes a deep breath. "I started selling our things on eBay like a madman, try-ing to empty the loft. I didn't want all those things around me anymore. I buried myself in work again, but the whole New York scene just seemed pointless. I needed to get away. So my sister rented the Winnebago, and here I am."

"Here we are," she murmurs, "the nun and the sex maniac." They laugh.

She is quiet for a long time. "You and I reacted so differently. I became a recluse after my husband died."

"I'm not surprised."

A slippery thought escapes a crypt. For the first time, she realizes she's nothing but a common liar. Quickly, she shoves this thought back in her head. She grips his hand. "You have a big soul, Haskell—taking your wife back, raising her son like you did." She's thinking, *Is your soul big enough for me?* Her hands are trembling.

He sees she's upset. "At the hotel, I suspected that I'd never get bored with you, Clara, that I could rely on your judgment." He pauses, groping for words. "You make me feel lighter, like nothing needs to weigh me down, that I don't have to earn the gross national product of a small Caribbean island. I can live and explore on my own. And so can you. I think we're onto something good here."

Struggling to control herself, she looks out the window.

He watches her somber profile. They are silent. Whatever has wounded her enters his heart too, like a grave drum roll.

◈

The sun is stronger now. He makes coffee, brings two steaming mugs to the coffee table.

"I want to show you the city before the show opens. We need to go east pretty soon." He blows on his coffee. "We can drop off the Winnebago in Boise and fly from there."

"I was wondering about that." Her voice grows stronger. "Haskell, I need to see my son before we go to New York. I need to talk to him. Who knows when I'll see him again?" She has a feeling of foreboding.

"Now, that's nonsense. We'll come out. We'll certainly see him at the Met. His girlfriend too, I bet." He touches her cheek. "So first we go to Jackpot. Is that what you're telling me?"

She gives him a watery smile. "Yes."

"Don't worry. We've got plenty of time."

"No we don't, Haskell. We don't have much time at all."

Puzzled, he looks at her.

8 days left.

chapter 22

When Clara went chasing after the photos, the wasps guarded the burned house, especially the dishtowel drawer, where faded smells of Prell, Ivory, Secret, and Jergens were strongest. Frank, Stella, and Scotty knew nothing about these Clara smells, but they saw the wasps' interest in that drawer. So they poured sugar water into lids and placed the lids in the open drawer, attracting three more wasps, making twelve total.

In such cramped quarters, turf wars erupted over square inches, resulting in lost legs and torn wings. Losers massed on the counter and hissed. Winners strutted in little circles on the rice canister. Four of the most antic wasps became official mood lifters. They did lopsided dances on the counter and sudden plunges to the floor, but nothing cheered up the other wasps. The trouble was their new caretakers. Their smells were *terrible*—Frank's Old Spice, Scotty's Bay Rum, Stella's Obsession. They just wanted Clara's smells—Jergens lotion, Secret deodorant, Ivory soap, and Prell shampoo. Where *was* she anyway?

One June morning when Frank was watching them snuffle up their sugar water, all twelve wasps suddenly rose in the air—*zzzzz* w*hoosh!*—and vanished into the sky.

"Come back!" he yelled, ripping Clara's altered T-shirt off

his head as he looked skyward. "Come back!"

The creatures rose high in the sky, circling round and round as if to dive-bomb him any minute. He flailed beneath them, waving the T-shirt in the universal signal of distress. Heading north, the wasps disappeared without a backward glance.

Frank was horrified. He hated the creatures, but he wanted them here for Clara. Every day he looked south on the highway, hoping to see Scotty's white Mustang barreling up the road from Elko with Clara sitting beside her new friend. She'd never done anything as radical as steal a car or pluck a "friend" from a restaurant. He hoped this meant romance at last for his solitary mother. Or maybe her long-denied need for a boyfriend had addled her brain.

He had no idea that the purple wasp had become a powerful hybrid that could blast open Clara's entombed anxieties better than any simple wasp could.

Scotty stumbled on a news story on the Internet saying that a huge swarm of wasps had arrived from the south to hover over Twin Falls, Idaho; no one knew why. Hundreds of other wasps had joined them, coming from everywhere and nowhere, it seemed. To the subtle observer, the swarm seemed guided by a unified intelligence. The wasps came by day to Jackpot, hovering along the highway as if waiting for someone. By night they returned to Twin Falls, forty-eight miles away, where they massed on flowered lawns and fed voraciously.

Wherever they flew, the skies were full of tumult and confusion, heard as a terrible low hum. Startled homeowners thought the noise might be spy planes from a hostile country. Distracted farm workers, feeling something unusual in the air, picked fewer potatoes, threatening local profits. These odd reports briefly raised Scotty from his persistent torpor. He did computer searches for hours.

Frank felt this unease too, so he took to reading Stella's *New Yorker* to see if he could find the source of it for himself. In summer 2000, Kyoto seemed dead, suicide bombings were up, Arafat and Sharon remained deadlocked, the Americans could do nothing. The whole world seemed stalled, off-kilter. To Frank it was no wonder we had twelve wasps fighting turf wars in a burned-out house in Nevada.

Even Frank the wasp-hater could see that the straggler wasps missed Clara. Why else would they hang around fighting over the dishtowel drawer? After all, his mother sang "Some Enchanted Evening" to them on the trip. She chatted with them every night as she brushed her hair. She treated them like *people,* he thought, embarrassed. Everyone else had swatted at them in their short desperate lives, tried to spray poisons on them, battered down their nests, and sent them homeless into the sky. *Let's face it. My mother is a nut case, and I'm getting there too.*

Over the years he's seen her talk to a balky fire hydrant, a doorknob that wouldn't unlock, plus the more standard leaves, moths, birds. He's seen her kiss apple cores goodbye. With all this communion between animate and inanimate, he wonders if the grateful wasps sense trouble is coming and want desperately to keep her safe.

6 days left.

chapter 23

Every morning for a week now in the canyon, Clara wakes up feeling like a vise has clamped her head. In her dream, she walks into the kitchen and the linoleum floor opens like a zipper. She peers down into a dark hole and sees Samantha's head floating on an ocean of mud. Horrified, she seizes the head and wraps it in a towel. She takes it into the bathroom and washes the head lovingly with a warm soapy washcloth, carefully rinsing off the filth. She dries it and wraps a towel all around it. The head is silent, hasn't said anything. She cradles the head while sitting in her rocker, rocking back and forth. She will do nothing in her life but cradle this head. "Thank you, head, for letting me do this," she murmurs. Suddenly the head moves. She feels it moving. Trembling, she unwraps the head. The eyes are open, staring at her. "No!" she screams. Haskell comes running.

With time running short, Lenore is desperately shaking up Clara's brain at night, trying to dislodge scary dreams and moldy memories stuck for years in her Dream Jar. If she's lucky, Lenore can screw the lid off and capture a dream like the abandoned head dream. The dream flies out in a little packet. Lenore grabs it and plays it over and over for Clara by tossing the packet from one hand to the other. Electric sparks fly from the packet and invade Clara's head, lighting up the hideous dream in fluorescent colors that drive her crazy.

Sometimes Lenore gets even more invasive: She can shrink herself to 1/16 of an inch and sneak into the unhealed wasp stings on Clara's forehead. These stings are like little tunnels covered with loose scabs that never come off. Then Lenore can trample around in Clara's brain, breaking tiny capillaries here and there. This makes Clara feel rushed and disoriented. Vandalism like this creates the healing tumult Clara needs to wake up and face her problems. At least that's what Lenore hopes for.

5 days left.

Lenore is almost twelve inches tall now when she's outside of Clara's brain. Her legs are unnaturally long; her hairdo is piled up like a stack of pancakes on her head. Her skin is pure lavender. No more casual cowgirl: She means business in black leather pants, black alligator boots, and a black cowgirl shirt swirled with black sequins. She's definitely impatient, and she's scaring Clara to death. Fresh from Vegas or hell, Lenore spends hours in front of the mirror, simpering and primping with Haskell's hair cream. He doesn't know what's with his hair cream disappearing. He just feels a breeze around his head sometimes. He forgets about it.

Lenore gets bored and angry prancing around in the Winnebago by herself, since Clara and Haskell are often outside hiking or lazing by a stream, or going into Elko for supplies, leaving her alone in the hot camper until they return with their sacks of groceries. Her thin skin can't take much sun. She burns painfully to ashy gray, so she's stuck in the camper until dusk. Frustrated, she rolls up her sleeves and takes off her boots to cool down. Her hot skin is sticky and stinky.

Lenore insists on sitting in Clara's lawn chair beside the stream where she and Haskell like to talk in the evenings. Clara has to scrunch to one side of the chair to avoid touching the unpleasant creature. Lenore always sits on the side Haskell can't see.

"Why don't you use the whole chair?" he asks, bemused.

"Don't bother with what's not your business," Clara snaps, cranky in a way that startles both of them. She's got a terrible headache.

"What's wrong? I just asked you a simple question."

"Well, I gave you a simple answer, didn't I?" She draws her legs up and covers herself with her new jacket, though it's not cold in early evening.

"Are you coming down with something?"

"No, I'm not coming down with something." Her tone is querulous, but her eyes dart around nervously. He understands again that whatever is on her mind is something only she can fix. But still he's annoyed.

"OK, I give up." He lights a cigarette. He's back to smoking. They are silent until Clara says she's tired and wants to sleep. They go inside.

What the hell is going on? It's like she's got her period again.

Lenore, along with her growth spurt, has suddenly turned vegetarian. She tears up shrubs around their campsite, stuffing twiggy branches in her mouth, but the twigs are too rough to swallow. She badly tore her gums once. Horrified, Clara saw mangled bloody bark protruding from Lenore's thin purple lips before she spit it out. She tried to get Lenore to gargle with salt water, but she wouldn't do it.

Haskell thinks a mule deer is tearing up things until he

catches a glimpse of a shadowy small creature running away with a mouthful of leaves in its mouth. "What was that?" he exclaims, pointing.

"What did you see?' she asks, suddenly relieved.

"I don't know."

She puts her arm around his waist, cheered by his words. *If he can see Lenore, then I'm not crazy.*

In Lenore's early days, she liked tuna and hamburger. Now Clara tries giving her small salads and canned beets—but she wants no more food from Clara. It's just as well: Her appetite is huge for a creature still smaller than a newborn baby. Sometimes pine needles stick in her throat and give her coughing fits, so Clara has to stick her finger down Lenore's throat and dig out the prickly mass. Then she gets mad because Clara had to help. Lenore acts just like a teenager—except that she forages only at dawn or dusk, not all day long, on account of her sun sensitivity. At this rate, the landscape around them will soon be stripped. She even nibbles the lovely white bark of the quaking aspens, says it makes a good toothbrush. It's true; Lenore never has bad breath.

Clara's in a rough patch all right. No matter how charming Haskell tries to be, she finds something to complain about. The problem is she's scared to death of Lenore's changes, plus she keeps dreaming that Samantha's head is trapped under her kitchen floor and she can't get it out. Her own head feels like it is splitting open these days. Like something is inside her head, gnawing, breaking.

Haskell smokes outside. If the smoke comes Clara's way, she coughs and her eyes water. His clothing and skin smell of smoke, plus his tongue and lips. He knows how she feels about it. Sandra hated his smoking too. "Sorry, Clara, I'll try to stop."

But of course he doesn't stop. He wakes up mornings with a hacking cough, just like Clara used to thirty years ago. At first she gave him deadeye stares. Now she just looks away.

They are quiet this night, a clear tension between them. She's lying on the couch, restless and out of sorts. She closes her eyes, trying to take one of her cat naps. He wanders outside.

Lenore, bored, sneaks outside to annoy him as he sits there smoking. She jumps on the man's head, giving him a throbbing headache. He thinks the headache is because the pasta salad they had for lunch went bad.

Back inside, Lenore does aerial tricks above Clara's head. She floats up and down like a helium balloon, blowing a lungful of Haskell's cigarette smoke right in Clara's face. She coughs, her head hurting so bad she wonders if she needs to go to the hospital. She doesn't know that Lenore is sneaking into her head.

Lenore's got a new refrain and repeats it endlessly:

"Down along the river, dark and deep, stumble all the old folks, blind as sheep."

"Shut up," Clara says from the couch, her mood darkening even more. Haskell, back inside, thinks she's having a dream. Lenore just laughs and repeats the refrain. Clara covers her ears with her hands. Lenore is Miss Universal Expert in Breaking Down Defenses by Being the Worst Brat Ever.

Clara should have made the purple wasp stay in Jackpot the morning she ran off to find Arianna. Now the wasp has turned into this weird twelve-inch thing that stays glued to her like Krazy Glue even if Clara is thirty feet away. It's like Lenore grew out of a hollow space between two of Clara's ribs, a space oddly near her heart. "Damn her purpleness!" Clara murmurs.

Lenore and Clara are engaged in fierce silent warfare about what happened around the time of Samantha's death. Talk or no talk? So far it's a stalemate.

Restless, Clara takes up a new cause. She decides Haskell is undisciplined, so she sets up a schedule for him. If he wants to switch to nature photography, he should *practice* nature photography in different kinds of light. Say from nine thirty to eleven, two to three, and five thirty to six, right? Corralling Haskell will get her mind off Lenore. The schedule doesn't even get off the ground.

"Now see here, Clara. I'll set my own schedule. You can't tell me how to parcel out my days. I've been parceling out my days my whole life, and by God, no one ever told me how to do it."

"But I've watched you. You always shoot at the same time of day. You need shots in all kinds of light."

"Excuse me, but I thought we had a major get-acquainted session going here. I thought things between us were more important than work schedules. Back off, Clara. Either I do this myself or I don't. It's really none of your business."

She studies her fingernails. "Whatever you like," she says blandly. But she knows he's right. Her sudden mood shifts are driving them both nuts. Maybe it's a chemical imbalance. She'll up her vitamin doses. Maybe that'll do the trick.

He's quiet too. Finally, in a fit of irritation, he says, "To hell with it," and goes into the bedroom, slamming the door behind him, to prepare a box of photos for Arianna, accompanied by an explanatory hasty scrawl. He mails it on the sly, without Clara knowing, the next time they drive to Elko for groceries.

Their little idyll is over. She clearly pines for her son. One morning in late June, they drive back to the Rancher's Hotel and hitch Scotty's white Mustang to the back of the Winnebago. Management had watched it for them.

The trip to Jackpot is mostly silent. She wonders what he'll think about the wasps—if they're still there. *He'll think I'm stone-cold nuts and good riddance.*

About five miles outside of Jackpot, she tells him.

"Wasps," he says dully. "You're telling me you have pet wasps."

"All my life." She tries to sound light.

He decides to just focus on the road.

4 days left.

chapter 29

An unexpected sight greets them as the Winnebago lumbers across the vacant lot, hauling the Mustang. Frank, Scotty, and Stella are arranging glass jars around the burned-out house.

"Why are they putting big glass jars around your house?" Haskell asks in wonderment.

"I'll explain later," she says, her heart sinking. *The wasps are gone!*

As the mini-caravan lumbers to a stop, they jump out and Frank grabs her in a bear hug. "I've been trying to call you, Mother! How great! This must be Haskell."

Introductions all around. Clara embraces Stella and then Scotty to much laughter and milling about. She steals dismayed glances at the charred skeleton of her house. Scotty absorbs the scene with the air of a kindly relative who stayed out too late last night.

Frank and Haskell step away from the others to stand side by side and gaze intently at Desert Dan's across the highway. Frank hooks thumbs in his belt; Haskell folds his arms.

"So, Frank," says Haskell. "I hear your mother has unusual pets."

"Don't get me started," Frank says under his breath. He briefly mentions the escaped wasps.

Haskell chuckles. "Well, from what I've seen so far, your mother wouldn't have any ordinary pets."

"You can say that again." Frank smiles. He already likes this Haskell Roberts. Maybe his mother has met her match.

Haskell gestures toward the destroyed house. "So that's where you grew up."

Frank nods. "My dad built it."

"He must have been a great guy. She's told me all about him."

A pale, mournful Darrell flashes into Frank's mind. Unsettled, he runs a hand over his eyes. He's not eager to talk about his father. Neither is Haskell.

Frank and Haskell walk back to join the crowd. Clara walks briskly toward her son and warmly embraces him.

Her voice is hushed. "Do you have a picture of your sculpture? I wish I'd seen the real thing before the buyer carried it off."

He looks intently at her, clearly pleased by her interest. "As a matter of fact, I do have a picture. Another buyer looked at my second piece yesterday and wanted to see a picture of the first one. I'll show you when we go over to Stella's."

"Oh, Frank, you're on your way." She claps her hands together.

"It feels that way," he says, grinning. "Could be just beginner's luck."

Even Lenore is happy with the news. She claps her hands together in the bag, which is really hot in this heat.

Frank, in a happy daze, wanders over to check on Scotty, who's looking tired. Clara and Stella talk excitedly. Stella has resumed her quirky stage pieces at Desert Dan's—now down to two minutes. She adds quietly, "But I'm not drawing customers into my pieces anymore unless I know them." She swallows, her

CLARA at the EDGE

eyes filling. "Clara, none of us knew the girl—Edie. I'm guessing she was furious and humiliated when the bodybuilder made fun of her outfit. Because the very next day she and her boyfriend come to your house and they do a great job of robbing and burning it down. In a very personal way, I might add—all those family pictures on your dresser? I figure it was payback—the older generation can go to hell, as far as they're concerned. Plus they needed money. No surprise there."

Clara studies the ground. "Don't worry about it, Stella. Nobody knew anything would happen." Spontaneously the women hug, relieved something has been said.

Stella draws back, her eyes bright. "OK, girlfriend, give me the lowdown."

Clara goes on about Lamoille Canyon and how Haskell puts up with her moods and is really a good cook. "But to tell the truth, Stella, I'm not counting on anything. He's a worldly man."

Stella, clearly in a buoyant mood, whispers, "Nonsense. I see good things ahead. *Mazel tov!*" She hugs Clara again before rejoining Frank.

Clara digs out the ignition key from her purse and approaches Scotty, who leans happily but tiredly against his long-lost Mustang. *"Voila!"* she says, handing him the key. "I'm sorry, Scotty. I didn't mean to cause trouble. I was frantic to get those pictures."

"No harm done, dear. You're back safe." He kisses her cheek. They lean against the Mustang, talking.

Stella's in deep conversation with Haskell. She discovers he's a commercial photographer. In turn, she tells him her dreams of being on the stage. Both are city people at heart, both performers in their way. Each can arrange a shot, whether of people or products. Frank joins them just as Haskell says, "New York. That's where you belong, young lady. I've lived there all my life. Clara

256

and I are flying to Manhattan very soon. Has she told you? The pictures my niece took of her house are opening at the Metropolitan Museum of Art on July first—next Saturday. "

Stella lets out a shriek. "Omigod! Frank, did you hear that?"

They listen raptly as Haskell explains how the photos will be blown up, colored, or altered in other ways, that "Hidden America: Photography in the New Millennium," will be a stunner, that he and Clara will be at the opening.

Frank stares at the destroyed house. "I can't believe it. The house my father built, and now it's gone. He was the most unpretentious guy on the face of the earth. He'd have been puzzled by a museum show." He looks over at his mother, talking animatedly to Scotty.

Haskell says, "My niece says this particular curator is from Bozeman, Montana, and has a deep feel for the countryside, for handcrafted things."

Frank looks down at his boots. "Well, I'm kind of speechless."

Stella looks inquiringly at Frank. "If you and I could go to the opening, I'd think I'd died and gone to heaven."

Frank nods. "We'll work it out. We won't miss it."

"Wait!" Stella claps her forehead. "July first I'll be in Chicago at my aunt and uncle's fiftieth wedding anniversary. I already have the ticket. Everyone is coming." She looks at Frank. "Can we work this out?"

"Of course. Don't worry. "

They all stand close to one another in the vacant lot, laughing, deep in conversation. In the afternoon sun, the oversized jars look like house jewelry—jewelry made for a house, or in this case, mementos around a tomb.

Lenore is quiet in her bag, as if she's trying to absorb the nature of these people without seeing them right now.

Finally, a natural pause occurs in the conversation. Before Clara has a chance to ask about the baited jars (she knows the answer anyway), Frank says, "Listen up, everyone, I have an announcement. Stella and I are getting married."

Clara exclaims in delight and embraces Stella as the women succumb to joyful tears. Then Clara runs to Frank. Mother and son are in a prolonged hug as she murmurs against his chest, her eyes closed. The others are left to grin and watch.

"Just last night he proposed," Stella says, flushed. "You all are the first to know."

"Good show, man." Scotty shakes Frank's hand. "The last holdout of the class of 1972 finally hits the dust." Clapping, cheers.

Frank collects himself. "OK, let's get practical for a minute. How long are you going to be here, Mother?"

"Well, we thought just one night. I wanted Haskell to meet you all and see the house. We have to be on our way to New York, but I couldn't go without seeing you first, my dear." She chokes up.

Frank gives Stella a meaningful look. "I've got an idea. Maybe we can all drive to Wells tonight and tie the knot. What do you say, Stella?"

"If Scotty will give me the night off." She smiles coquettishly. "I come from a long line of elopers. I always thought I would elope. We can party later." She winks broadly. Everyone chuckles.

Revived, Scotty beams. "No need to go to Wells. I haven't told you yet, Frank, but I became a justice of the peace last year. You're not the only ones who come to Jackpot and decide to get married, you know. It was an easy fit. I've been a short order cook, car mechanic, skating rink manager, bowling alley owner, and real estate developer, not to mention casino owner—so why not justice of the peace?" He gives a little bow.

Frank claps Scotty on the back. "Why, you old son of a gun." He turns to his bride-to-be. "Well, Stella, what do you say? Get married here?"

She takes his arm. "I can't imagine being married to a better man than Frank Breckenridge by a better man than Scotty Horshay on a better day than today."

Everyone whoops.

Lenore dances in the bag. Clara starts dancing too. For once Lenore is giving Clara a minute to enjoy her existing—and growing—family.

"Hold on, boy," Scotty says. "Have you got a ring?"

"Hell yes, I've got a ring. Why do you think I ran off to Twin Falls the other day?"

Clara's heart expands to the sky. Frank has wandered the country and found gold. To see him marry like this—the seemingly right woman for him—is a gift she'd almost despaired of getting, even though the courtship has certainly been fast! Stella's full of spark, a spark that's already affecting him. His eyes are brighter, his walk more vigorous. And his sculpture! She can hardly wait to see it. She imagines his work in a gallery, sees them doing wild theater, rolling around the country, recruiting local actors, eventually landing in New York, doing offbeat shows on off-off-Broadway. By temperament Frank is Stella's straight man. He can build her sets, her theater, their house, can teach her many things—how to round up cattle if need be. She can perform or teach theater; he can get into the construction business or make amazing sculptures for high-end clients. The possibilities are endless.

In the celebratory moment, Haskell lights a cigarette, inhales deeply, and wraps an arm around Clara. The smoke doesn't even bother her now. Joy for her son beats all. Even lost wasps or a demonic Lenore in black leather pants can't bother her right now.

But now Lenore is oddly quiet in Clara's bag. She must have tired herself out, or eaten too many of the potato chips Clara bought in Elko. Lenore's appetite has been flagging lately. Clara's a little worried.

Frank tries to quiet everybody. "We'll do the ceremony at Stella's, then have dinner at Desert Dan's. Sound good?" General hoots. "Give us an hour to get things ready."

Stella opens the door, radiant in a strapless yellow silk dress, her long auburn hair trailing delicate white wildflowers tied with narrow white ribbon. "Give us a hug," she says, throwing her arms wide to Clara and Haskell. Frank stands behind her in a navy-blue suit, white shirt, and a red vintage tie with "Happy New Year" all over it that Stella dug up somewhere. Everyone talks at once, hugging and laughing. Haskell is busy with his camera. He and Clara exclaim in delight at the movie posters—Charlie Chaplin struggling in the giant gears of *Modern Times*, Busby Berkeley's dancers like a giant flower in the overhead shot for *Gold Diggers of 1933*, Gene Kelly dancing around the street lamp in *Singin' in the Rain*.

Before the party really gets going, Frank quietly leads Clara to a small bookcase, takes an 8x10 color photo from a manila envelope, and hands it to her. "Here you go, Mom. This is for you." He has inscribed it on the back.

She catches her breath, dazzled at his sinuous rendering of the languid nude. It looks like the piece might have been done in a few sittings, the lines are so strong and uncluttered. "Oh, Frank, it's stunning."

"Take it. I have other copies."

"Do you mean it?"

"Of course."

Eyes bright, she watches him slip it back into the manila envelope. "You are really on your way, my dear. I'm so very proud of you." They clasp each other, these two lonely family members unable to connect for so long.

Haskell comes for Clara, and they silently waltz to "Shall We Dance?" on Frank's mix. He twirls her round as the others clap and holler. Haskell's a terrific dancer. No one guesses that her tears are anything but tears of joy for the occasion. And of course they are. But her mind's eye is also fixed on the moment just now when her son gave her a photograph she will protect with her life.

Everyone mills about, absorbing the celebratory feeling of this small trailer—the posters, the colorful furniture, the sheer theatrical kitsch of it.

"I could do a photo shoot of your place, Stella," Haskell says in delight. "It would be a hot sell in Manhattan. Seriously: The *New York Times*, Escapes section, 'Homes with Presence.'"

She winks. "I'm holding out for *Architectural Digest*." She plumps the sequined pillows on her purple loveseat.

She's created a *chuppah* using panels of a gauzy Indian fabric that glitters with sequins, embroidery, and tiny pearls. Each panel is a different color: gold, red, lavender, and royal blue. The material radiates out from a central ceiling fan, is tied to a couple of torchieres and cabinet handles. "Like it?" says Stella. "Oh, yes," Clara replies, gazing in wonder. Stella is pleased. The room quiets; everyone listens. "These curtains made a circle around my parents' canopy bed. It was magic. They closed them every night. Their bed was like something from the *Arabian Nights*. I called my mother an hour ago. She was thrilled I'm using the curtains. She and my dad eloped, so she understands how things can develop fast. Frank and I will visit her. I know she and Frank will like each other. I promised her many pictures of tonight. Haskell? Can I count on you?" He's carrying his camera.

"You bet," he says.

"She and my dad will be with us in spirit for the ceremony." In a small voice, she says, "He died in a motorcycle accident when I was seventeen." They all embrace her.

Soon Scotty clears his throat. "Are we ready, ladies and gentlemen, for the main event?"

Stella dashes over to the kitchen counter, where a simple bouquet of long-stemmed grasses are tied together with white ribbon. "Frank got these at Salmon Falls Creek," she says, flushed.

Stella and Frank face each other in the small living room. Eyes brimming, Stella looks at him through the grasses she holds up to her face. Clara's eyes fill too as she stands next to Haskell. Frank, serious, earnest, fumbles in his pocket for the ring. Scotty, a little unsteady on his feet, begins.

"Dearly beloved, we are gathered together here in the presence of these witnesses so that Franklin James Breckenridge and Stella Cheyenne Shapiro may be united in holy matrimony. If anyone objects to this union, please speak now or forever hold your peace." Frank and Stella move even closer. "Please say your vows to each other." Scotty's face is damp. "Do you, Franklin James Breckenridge, take this woman, Stella Cheyenne Shapiro, to be your lawful wedded wife, for better or worse, in sickness and in health, till death do you part?"

"I do," Frank says solemnly.

"And do you, Stella Cheyenne Shapiro, take this man, Franklin James Breckenridge, to be your lawful wedded husband, for better or worse, in sickness and in health, till death do you part?"

"I do," says Stella, radiant. Frank places a simple gold band on her trembling finger.

"I now pronounce you man and wife." The couple kisses with gusto. Cheers, hugs, clapping all around, Haskell clicking away. Scotty sits down heavily.

"We've got champagne from the vast stores at Desert Dan's, thanks to Scotty," Frank announces, opening the first bottle to a noisy pop. A whoop goes up. Stella pours the champagne into her grandmother's cut glass juice glasses.

"I propose a toast," says Clara, gulping back tears of joy.

"Groom's mother, hear, hear," everyone quieting down.

She gropes for words. "To my terrific new daughter-in-law and beloved son, may you find amazement and joy in the most unlikely places." Glasses clink to more cheers.

Then Scotty: "To Stella, the best damn waitress and undiscovered movie star in the business, and to Frank, my best bud since 1969, when we did some things I can't talk about because your mother's in the room."

Laughter, clapping, refills downed. Toasts proliferate until the champagne is gone. Stella's glittering sequin canopy lends an otherworldly air to the proceedings. The fabric sways in a breeze coming in from the desert. Stella has left the door partly ajar for ventilation. Frank steals over to the CD player and puts on a remastered collection of ballads—Diana Krall, Harry Connick, Sarah Vaughan, Ella Fitzgerald, Billy Eckstine, Frank Sinatra. The group quiets, watching the newlyweds dance to "Tenderly" by Sarah Vaughan. Whispering, the couple wraps themselves together. He twirls her slowly, bends her back, building toward a performance number, like they do in private, oblivious of the others.

Haskell and Clara, dancing now too, see Scotty on the couch looking on with tears in his eyes, smiling and looking pale. The music shifts to "Autumn in New York" by Ella Fitzgerald. Haskell whispers something to Clara, who nods, goes over to Scotty, and sits on the couch with him.

"You brought us all together, Scotty. Without you, Frank and Stella would never have met, and I'd have never met Haskell."

A slow grin lights Scotty's face. "I never thought of that." He studies her. "Now look, Clara, if you ever get tired of New York, you've always got a job as crowd handler at Desert Dan's."

Her mood abruptly darkens. "Who says I won't be back? Of course I'll be back." She pauses. "You think I'm *moving?*"

At a sudden disturbance in the air, she looks at the open door. Lenore just barged in, her black cowgirl outfit now blood red. Lenore has escaped from her bag! Hurriedly

Clara stands up as the creature makes a beeline for her and stamps on her foot. She recoils in surprise as Lenore scampers out the door.

Blinking, Clara tries to focus again on Scotty, but Lenore's attack leaves her deeply unsettled. The creature interrupted the wedding of her only surviving child. She's getting reckless, disrespectful. Clara is afraid. Wordlessly, she returns to Haskell. They dance, but her head is whirling. *Time is running out. I've got to deal with Samantha.*

As Haskell holds her close, she has a sudden vision of an adult Samantha in her wedding dress, a sight she will never see. Swallowing tears, she recalls the cascade of years when Frank, withdrawn and alone as an adult, would visit her once a year and they would sit stiffly in the living room together, discussing the headlines and the weather. Now she watches his radiant face as he embraces his bride.

❖

A few dances later, Frank whispers to Scotty, who nods and announces to everyone, "I've got a great idea, folks. How about dinner?"

Cheers go up. Everyone files out as Clara takes a last look at the magical space Stella has created. She blows the room a kiss before she peers into the darkening night. Scotty has collected himself, but he's still sweating and pale. He looks quite ill, and she can't bear to think about it. On the way to the casino, Frank whispers to Clara that Scotty is getting more open to seeing a doctor. She thanks him for this update, knowing the news will be bad. Nevertheless, they all link arms, a brigade of five, laughing, carrying on, making their way to the casino.

Dinner is a lavish affair. Scotty has ordered a full-court press for their little group: lobster, chicken, steak, wine, side dishes—wedding cake baked on very short notice, brought out by the head waiter to much applause throughout the restaurant. The newlyweds eat and drink sparingly, causing much ribbing. Scotty picks at his food, announces that everyone in the restaurant can take away as much wedding cake as they want. The celebration concludes on a wave of good will and gentleness.

Clara's spirits briefly restored, it's time to say goodbye. She and Haskell have to leave in the morning. She stands in a quiet corner of the parking lot and gently takes her son's face in her hands. Haskell stands aside. Eyes brimming, she says, "I wish you every happiness, my dear son. Stella's a wonderful woman. And your career has started! You're both so talented. It's amazing, all of it."

He embraces her. "Haskell seems like a great guy, Mom. You've been alone so long. I want you to be happy too." His words tumble out. "Imagine what Dad would have thought—pictures of our house at a famous museum!" He kisses her cheek and turns to his bride, who embraces Clara. The women laugh and whisper. The men shake hands.

"I'll check on plane reservations tomorrow, Mother. It seems like a dream. Hang tough, you hear? We're taking on the Big Apple!"

"I can't believe it!" cries Stella.

"Be well," Clara calls after them.

Frank stops, looks back at her. "I love you, Mom."

She had despaired of ever hearing these words. "And I love you, my son." Her voice trembles. They stand looking at each other.

She's afraid if she says anything more, Frank will take back these words she has longed to hear her whole life.

chapter 25

*C*lara and Haskell disappear into the darkness. Silently they crunch across the vacant lot to the destroyed house still clamped to the flatbed. A lone car whooshes down the highway. The sky is awash with stars. Sagebrush—aromatic, astringent—fills their nostrils.

She's forgotten all about the Winnebago. It doesn't even exist for her now. Only this charcoal skeleton of her house exists, crammed with life history she can't forget or purge, despite her efforts to gain oblivion. Haskell regards its shadowy outlines with awe, having heard about its every nook and cranny. It looks hijacked, a blackened mausoleum dropped there by aliens. They are stunned by the untouched kitchen table and the three upright chairs, but especially the toppled chair, still where it landed after her forceful escape. She runs her fingers over this ancient table where she drank coffee and contemplated her life for almost forty years, the table now dusty from Frank's sculpting.

Out of the night comes a buzzing sound—not a swarm, but a single loud buzzing. "What's that?" he asks. Before she can answer, she gets stung—twice—on her arm and the back of her neck. She shrieks in pain, dropping her purse and bag. A sting virgin all her life until a few weeks ago, now she has four! The unhealed stings above her eyebrows vibrate in sympathetic pain. The angry buzz gets louder.

"Get away!" she shouts. She and Haskell try to beat away the flying attacker. Its buzz is deep, more like a big yellow jacket or bumble bee. But bees don't fly at night. They have to sleep just like everyone else. Haskell and Clara know this. The throaty buzz fades into the night sky. Whatever it was, it was a one-time guerilla attack.

She shudders. It's as if the yellow jacket tried to stop her from entering the house. But there's no house anymore–just ash and litter. Hastily she picks up her purse and Lenore's bag, shooing Haskell up onto the flatbed before her.

Lenore whimpered when the yellow jacket attacked, but now she's quiet in her bag. Clara doesn't want to look at her. She's still angry about the wedding invasion. She sits down heavily at the kitchen table. Haskell plops down across from her. They sit in darkness.

"What was all that about?"

"I don't know. I better look after these bites." Except she can't. Someone has carted off the refrigerator where she kept the baking soda. The stove is gone too. She gets a flashlight and a couple of aspirin from her purse, mashes them in a bottle cap, adds bottled water, and smears this paste on her arm and neck. The pain eases.

"I'd like to take a look around." He gingerly steps into the living room, outlined by scorched timbers.

Clara sits alone at the kitchen table with her flashlight on. She just saw six wasps perched on the remaining kitchen counter. Not twelve, but six. And all purple.

At her squeal of delight, they assume the air and land on her head. The first one seeks her bare scalp where a cowlick creates a whorl. She fears the wasp will sting her, but it just tickles. The writhing insects form a little waspian tower, swaying back and forth on her head. Amazed, she watches them with the flashlight and a mirror from her purse.

"Look!" Delighted, she points to her head as Haskell finishes his inspection. He steps closer in surprise. The wasps are flipping end over end in a group cartwheel. They both see this. Her face is alight. "They're doing a Slinky number, Haskell. Remember that old children's toy? You'd flip a Slinky over at the top of the stairs and it would come flipping down the stairs on its own." She does an impromptu dance step and puts her arms out to dance with him. "They're performing for us, Haskell. They're saying hello."

He recoils. He does not want to dance with a woman who has wasps on her head.

This situation is stranger than anything he could have anticipated. "These aren't normal wasps, Clara. Where did they come from?"

"Eugene. Sixteen of them. They nested in my eaves. But they've changed. In Eugene they were normal. Only one was purple. Now they're all purple, and it looks like we're down to six."

"Purple! They aren't purple. They're just wasps—dark, with stripes."

"Maybe you're color blind. Maybe you'll see them in daylight. They're purple."

"I'm not going to argue about what color they are, Clara. None of this makes any sense. Cartwheeling wasps that may or may not be purple? What's going on here?" He flops heavily onto a chair, sending up a plume of dust that makes him cough. He jumps up and swats off his behind.

Still dancing around the kitchen with the wasps on her head, she ignores him. "I *knew* they'd come back. This is their home."

He frowns. Does she really think wasps are *loyal*? On par with *dogs* maybe? To him, it's as natural as day that the creatures flew away from the fire. It is unnatural these few have returned. And this is their *home*? *Now*? What's she talking about?

He wonders if she's actually batty. Maybe the woman he's given his heart to has slid down the chute of no return. Maybe she's like one of those snake handlers they have in the South who handle poisonous snakes and don't get bitten. He considers this. But those snake handlers get in a trance and say the snakes get them closer to the Holy Spirit. Clara's not in any trance. She's never talked about any Holy Spirit. She's just dancing, looking happy to have her pets back. And the wasps, doing cartwheels there on her head, look happy too.

Fearful now for his *own* sanity, he squelches any thoughts of snake handlers. He draws a line on the dusty table. Maybe he should have paid closer attention to her strange behavior the past few weeks—jiggling her canvas bag when nothing was in it (and what was that shadowy thing?), not telling him why holes were cut in the bag, making loud comments to an empty room, scrunching to one side of the lawn chair when she was the only one in it.

They were so close in Lamoille Canyon. He was almost ready to sign on the dotted line. He never dreamed anything like *this* would come between them. Grimacing, he watches her dance with the wasps. Maybe he'll be next, do still weirder things—attract not-yet-imagined creatures to his bidding. Maybe this is a preview of the precipitous decline that awaits us all. Maybe Stella put something in that champagne they had tonight. He shakes his head as if to drive out a nest of insects lurking in his own cranium.

"Shall we retire to the Winnebago? I'm bushed," he says.

"What?" she says, still prancing around the kitchen.

"I don't want to sleep with a bunch of wasps, Clara, if that's what you're thinking. I don't want them in my vehicle." He speaks like a man who's had his fill of nonsense. His voice is low, definite.

Steadily she looks at him. "I never said you had to."

Never show weakness. She'd learned that lesson well–her mother always cowered right before her father started to beat on her. And then he'd beat her more. So when he came after Clara in the barn, her steely child's glance and the powerful wasps that churned the air around her drove her father away. She gives that same hard glance to Haskell, who only looks away.

She says, "They're not going to sting us. They know you're with me." The wasps have stopped gyrating and crawl willy-nilly over her hair. She looks deep in thought. "What would you do if they stung you or landed on you? Would you try to kill them?"

He's momentarily flustered. "Well, for God's sake, I haven't had time to think of what I'd do. Come on, Clara, this is silly." He's angry now. "Do you really need to have these insects around? Does being with you mean I have to live with these creatures?" He's pacing around the kitchen. "Let's be reasonable here. We've got a chance at a new life together. You know we do. And I thought we both wanted a fairly peaceful life. I don't want to live with wasps. I mean not really. Not like this." He points to her hair, still full of insects. He rolls his eyes. "What next? Are you going to replace the ones you *lost?* Take them to New York?"

Something deep flares in her. He has no way of knowing the wasps are wordless sentries that have protected her very life and sanity over the years. His sensible comments make her crazy. *His* own life and sanity have probably never been threatened. She covers her eyes to block the image that rises despite her furious policing—her daughter's lithe form cooling on the street.

A sudden fear makes her stomach clutch. Of course! Lenore is tearing down her Brain Rooms! That's why things are getting so bad. The purple wasp became a hybrid freak so she could expose everything about Clara's past. Clara has allowed a stick of dynamite into her life.

She lashes out. "That's just fine then. I *know* the wasps won't hurt you. I thought you trusted me. Living things can sense the needs of other living things. Trees know when nearby trees are sick. They've done studies. But you only see what's right in front of you—physical things—and you think that's all there is. Don't you know that the things you *can't* see—atoms, quarks, trust, love—are the backbone of everything?"

Deeply tired, she gestures broadly. "We have too many differences, Haskell." She gropes for an example. "You have granite countertops in your RV, for God's sake. How sensible is that? *My* countertop"—she fist-thumps the tired linoleum counter on the one remaining wall—"is—was—just something to put food on." She pauses. "I lay my cards with simple things and the invisible world, Haskell. Always have, always will. And yes, I might be talking nonsense. But I don't think so."

Head throbbing, she rubs her eyes in despair, a gesture he mistakes for tears. He moves toward her, and she backs away. She can't tolerate any paternal approach just now. Something's ready to snap in her, and she's not sure what or why. Finally she speaks in a dull, sober voice. "I've been thinking about this, Haskell. We've been going way too fast. All these changes for me after thirty years? I just can't take it. We've got to slow things down. It scares me, if you want to know the truth." He stares at her, not comprehending. After a moment, she looks at him. "I really need some time alone. I think it's best that I go to New York by myself."

He's dumbstruck. "You can't mean that, Clara. Of *course* you're going to New York with me. We're both completely exhausted right now. We're overtired from the drive and the wedding. This has been quite a day! Let's talk in the morning when our heads are clear. We need peace and happiness, not all this wrangling."

Braced against the counter, she speaks quietly. "Peace and happiness are the *last* things I've been able to get since half my family died. Peace and happiness aren't possible anyway in this fallen world except in minutes here and there. And if peace and happiness means everything can be settled with a good dinner and a round of sex, why I just won't have it, Haskell. Food and sex, food and sex. Really? Then we die? That's a Band-Aid approach. Life has too much mystery and suffering for that to be all. Half the time it's like I'm pinned underwater, struggling to the surface where very few can hear me anyway. So I play a simple woman because it makes things easier. I get through my days that way. Or did," she mutters, looking down.

Hearing these revealing words, Lenore leaps ecstatically from behind the dried bean canister to straddle Clara's neck and accidentally jabs her boot heels into Clara's breasts. This really hurts. She hurls the creature to the floor. Blood spurts from a gash on Lenore's forehead. *She has blood like the rest of us!* The creature jumps down from the flatbed and disappears into the night.

For his part, Haskell feels a disturbance in the air and steps backward, wondering how a sudden breeze came up on a calm night. Collecting himself, his voice is quiet.

"It's not about having fancy or simple things. We're arguing about whether I could have wasps in my house, and the answer is no. For Christ's sake, Clara, objects don't define who I am. You don't understand that, do you?" He takes a step toward her. "I think you're upset about something else, not just the wasps. I've thought that for a long time. And it's making you overreact to other things." He searches her eyes for confirmation. She backs away.

"I'm right, aren't I?"

She keeps backing.

"I'm right." He jumps off the flatbed and holds out his hand. "Come on, let's go to the RV. I'll make your favorite omelet in the morning, and we'll talk."

A long pause before she says, "Give me a while."

"Sure thing." He walks over to the RV, parked in the vacant lot, and goes inside.

It's *not* just the wasps. Shining her flashlight, alone in her skeletal house, she opens the dishtowel drawer where the broken porcelain ballerina lies covered in dishtowels. The dancer's blank eyes stare back at her. Quietly, she closes the drawer. She doesn't want the statue anymore. It doesn't help.

Gingerly she walks through the shattered house, the walls wispy or gone, dust everywhere, the spaces that used to be rooms now littered with shreds of unidentifiable things that were once a baggy couch, a bare oak rocker, a nicked coffee table, shabby bookcases, a twelve-inch TV, a Singer sewing machine, a broken window, a narrow bed, a double bed and the quilt she made for it, a dresser swamped with family pictures, Lillian's painting facing her when she would lie in bed. Passing the bathroom, she remembers the faint smell of urine from the camp toilet that marked her last days here.

The house is broken, but she isn't. She thought she needed

refuge with Haskell, but now she's not so sure. She doesn't need a dad, but she does need a place to sleep tonight. Quietly she lets herself into his RV.

Lenore is still outside, curled under the RV. Haskell is already asleep in the bedroom. She hears his deep breathing. Wide awake, she takes off her shoes and lies down on the couch. This first real fight came on like a sudden summer thunderstorm. The beautiful day, the unexpected wedding, her words with Frank, seeing everyone—she'd felt a sense of closure. Peace and happiness *were* hers for a few hours. Until Lenore barged in, until the huge bee stung her, until this fight with Haskell erupted like a delayed reckoning of some kind. *Is this thing with Haskell going to last?*

It's the wasps, she decides. She can't imagine life without them. But then no one will want to live with her. It's as simple as that. Does she care? She lies back down, trying to turn her thoughts off.

She's almost dozing off when the bright colors in Lillian's painting surge from her memory like an oncoming train. One day, when they were eighteen and free, she and Lillian simply took the Greyhound from Fargo to Eugene and never came back. It was so easy. Carsick and giggly, they seemed to fly across the country, avoiding beady-eyed men who stared and smiled at them while the girls stuffed packets of saltines into their purses at meal stops in case they had to run from those creeps and hide somewhere.

It was raining hard in Eugene when they got there. Loretta was waiting in her pickup and took them to her house and fed them fried chicken and applesauce, and the girls thought they were in heaven. Their parents never looked for them. Not a word. Clara cried a few times in private. Then she decided it was all right. And this is her life now.

Her watch says it's one thirty. Something is making her unbalanced these days. A devouring white light laps at her heels—when Lenore tries her beyond reason, as she did at the wedding, and just now, jumping on Clara's shoulders and piercing her breasts. She holds her temples. These headaches. And this chest pain that comes and goes, confusing her. She should check with a doctor. Why aren't those stings on her forehead healing? She turns onto her stomach and sneezes into the leather couch.

She's buffaloed. She can't deal with Haskell and the wasps at the same time. The issues are too big to be settled quickly. She can only work through one thing at a time. It's always been like that for her. The truth is, she doesn't *want* Haskell's spicy omelet in the morning—or his excellent coffee. She wants to choose her own food.

She knows the actual family photos are gone. So are the real lilacs. But the celluloid lilacs that stippled the lousy paint jobs still call her in a siren song. As do the family photos. She must see the house as it once was before she can move ahead. Now that her son is married, nothing for now interests her more than these photos. The only way forward is to feel her own thoughts alone, be in her own airspace alone, go to New York alone. With that realization, she finally sleeps.

3 days left.

chapter 26

She wakes early. Haskell is still asleep. The sky is silver gray, the time of day she loves, when the new day has barely arrived and everything seems full of promise. She packs a small bag, aware of leaving behind many things in Haskell's RV. She will call Frank later. He has a honeymoon to attend to.

She leaves a note for Haskell, creeps as quietly as she can out the door, stows a disgruntled Lenore in her bag, and walks over to Desert Dan's. In the restaurant, she orders ham and eggs with orange juice and coffee, eats heartily. Lenore, sullen after her uncomfortable night outside, has a nasty bruise on her forehead. She picks at her toast, mopes on her side of the booth, doesn't talk. That's fine. Clara doesn't want to talk to her either. But Lenore's head is swollen. Clara's eyes unexpectedly fill with tears.

The Greyhound pulls in at 6:30 sharp. She buys a ticket and sets her checked bag on the cement with the others for loading into the belly of the bus. She finds an aisle seat in the middle section, settles in, and looks around. The bus is more crowded than she'd have predicted for the barrens of Nevada.

Her thoughts circle back to Haskell. He's right here. He listens and enjoys and learns new things—nature photography, for instance. He likes thunderstorms and meteor showers and is an inventive lover, though something still holds her back. Way back. He's patient, worldly, a great cook. She's got his cell phone number.

Her misery grows as the bus gets more crowded. She should get off right now. What's she doing here? She knows this man's sorrow, his sensuality, his possible sterility, his desire to make beauty, his fierce love for his family. He flings himself into the glorious mess of life. All this strikes her as very sexy, very human.

Maybe that's what's holding her back. He's a lover. Lovers are at home in the world. She's not. She's a seeker more than a lover. Seekers search more than they find. She has the habit of holding back, of ruling out rather than ruling in. To a fault.

Can they fit? Does she want to? Need to?

Give it a break, she tells herself, already exhausted. Lenore has fallen asleep in her bag. Carefully she sets the bag under the seat in front of her.

The bus is full. Single mothers with straggly hair and multiple kids, old tired-looking cowboys, young people barely past high school with pasty faces and pierced noses. Seeing the desert go by, she's vaguely carsick as the bus lumbers north to Twin Falls. A cranky baby cries across the aisle. The mother gets no help from her angry-looking husband, who just sits with his arms folded across his chest. The baby is maybe six months old. The mother jostles the baby, who still fusses. The bus is already warm. The driver apologizes for the faulty air conditioning; it will get fixed in Twin Falls. The baby is dressed too warmly in a long-sleeved terry sleeper. Droplets of sweat line its forehead. The mother offers her forefinger for the baby to suck. Did she not bring water? Clara is horrified. The baby's huge brown eyes startle wide, no doubt from the taste of the salty finger.

Clara leans back, trying to clear her mind for sleep. Drowsily she recalls another desert, the one in New Mexico that she and Darrell visited in 1951, the year before Samantha was born. Outside Santa Fe, they went to Bandelier National Monument, full of Anasazi cave dwellings and inscriptions. Darrell immediately clambered up the ladders to the cliffside dwellings while she explored the ground area.

Off to one side was a tomb, a dug-out rectangle with an incomplete human skeleton still in it. She was amazed any of it was left, but this was Native American ground, protected by law. She bent down to stare at the bleached crumbling bones, the cracked skull, vacant eye sockets, the strong jaw clamping the crooked yellow teeth together in their terrible death grin.

It was the empty skull that interested her—its contents eaten long ago by worms that feast on jelly eyes, harp-like ear bones, chewy nose cartilage. A carpet of skin had covered the skull and sausage-like brain, its two hemispheres wired to a jangle of memories and sensations that answer the question, "Who am I?" Without the jiggly stuff, the bones meant nothing to her. The bones could better be used as drum sticks to beat on stretched hides, calling the gods of death to have pity on us—to pass us by, let us live forever or take us now.

She climbed down a rough ladder into an underground kiva, a circular prayer room used for spiritual purification, and sat cross-legged on the ground. The sounds above her were muffled, the space shadowed and cool. In the kiva, she felt peace and simplicity, the way she wanted life to be with Darrell.

Above ground again, she stared at the bones of a small dead bird lying nearby. A few frazzled feathers lay near it. The skull was severed from its spine by its predator and then abandoned. Its beak was open, as if yawning in death; its wilted claws clutched the air. Furtively she picked up the bird's skull, wrapped it in a Kleenex, and put it in her purse. She couldn't explain why she did this. She felt sorry for it, even as she left its body headless in the desert.

One time not long before he died, Darrell opened her small ivory jewelry box on the dresser, looking for a misplaced tie clasp as she changed the sheets. The fake ivory jewelry box was her only keepsake from her mother, given when Clara was sixteen.

"What are you doing with this bird skull?" he said. His tone was mild, bemused, his eyes alert as he turned from the dresser to watch her changing the sheets. The sheets were white and fragrant and fluttered the air as she shook them out before fitting them to the mattress.

"I don't think I could tell you why," she said. "I got it that time we went to New Mexico. Remember?"

"It was a wonderful trip." He sat down beside her on the freshly made bed. He brought the ivory box with him. They peered in it together.

"See how its beak gapes so horribly open, like it still begs for food, like it's still hungry?" she asked softly. He nodded. "That's how I feel. Nothing is ever enough. I'm ravenous every day for you and the kids. I love our life so much that I can't bear to think it will end someday. I can't believe I even have this life."

He laughed softly, setting the box on the bedside table. "But we've got a long life together. It's not ending anytime soon. I'm ravenous too." He buried his face in her neck, falling back onto the bed with her, both of them laughing. He could always get her to laugh.

In due time, she spread her arms on the bed, grasping the blankets, sighing deeply as he entered her, and she came quickly. Then, after much silly murmuring and more laughter, the second time around she rode him as he watched her face clenched in ecstasy. She opened her eyes just before she cried out, locking her eyes with his in blank absorption. She shrieked. He roared.

As the bus approaches the irrigated farmland outside Twin Falls, so green after all the gray desert, she blows her nose and tries to compose herself as they pull into the Greyhound depot, basically a countertop in a strip mall. She walks around to stretch her legs before claiming her bag that sits warmly on the concrete. Inside, she asks about getting a cab to the local airport with the grand-sounding name, Magic Valley Regional Airport. The bored ticket fellow says, "Phone's on the wall, ma'am. Phone book on the chain." As if swimming underwater, he returns to his Game Boy before the next person shuffles up.

She catches a plane to Boise, then Chicago and New York. The trip is a blur of bad food, bland seatmates, a bad movie, and layovers that leave her headachy and exhausted. Lenore, unusually docile the whole way, stays in her bag. Finally at nine p.m., Eastern time, the plane lands at JFK. Surprisingly, Lenore gets through security the whole way with no problem.

Her cab driver into Manhattan (she's splurging, to feel safe) is surly with a pronounced accent and a bristling beard. The cab smells of hair grease. He courteously loads her bag into the trunk, but after she's settled in the back seat, he looks once in the rearview mirror, then looks away as if no one is there. She looks out the window as his tape deck blares mournful Middle Eastern music. The ride in from JFK is bewildering and scary to her: all the big, dirty buildings and bridges, the jammed traffic, all the people still on the streets, everything dark and everyone impatient, honking or swearing or dashing in front of the cab, her cabdriver leaning out the window and cursing at them in heavily accented English, making precipitous lane changes, escaping collision by a hairsbreadth. This new environment–light years away from Eugene, with its rampant greenery, and from Jackpot, with its open skies and sagebrush clumps light as kites in a windstorm–clears her mind in a hurry and makes her watchful for her very life. She frowns at the cab driver. *I'm here, I exist. Don't look in your rearview mirror as if no one is in your back seat. Do you hear me?* She's had enough tiring encounters for one day, thank you very much.

She's frightened but doesn't want to show it. Primly but assertively, as if she's in the classroom, she says, "Young man, I need to be as close as I can to the Metropolitan Museum. But I can only pay eighty dollars a night. Do you know a suitable place?"

Silently, he looks at her through the rearview mirror. She waits. Wonders if he does not understand English. Patiently, she repeats her request.

He seems amused, impatient. "Yes, I am thinking, madam. I will take to Bridgeport Hotel. Hotels close to Metropolitan very expensive. This one further away, but nice. They know me there. They give nice discount."

She is taken aback by his kindness and looks at his name posted on the protective screen by his head. "Thank you very much, Mr. Mahmoud Hashin." She says his name deliberately, as if committing it to memory. He nods stiffly at her in the rearview mirror. His eyes, like hers, are large brown pools.

The rest of the ride is silent. Suddenly the city seems friendlier. Her spirits rise, thinking of what might happen in the next few days. She can go to the opening with Arianna and Frank. Stella will come later, after visiting her relatives in Chicago. Will Haskell come? Abruptly, she realizes Frank and Haskell will be worrying. She'll call them tonight. What was she thinking, doing this?

Things are happening way too fast. She's scared. Lenore has seized control of her entire brain. She can't control anything anymore.

Mahmoud Hashin pulls up to the Bridgeport Hotel—downtown, in the 20s, a dingy building, but in New York. That's all she cares about at this point. Mr. Hashin takes her bag into the lobby, leans across the counter, and speaks confidentially in a foreign language to the muscular dark-haired man who has his feet up on the desk. The man nods and sleepily shoves a piece of paper toward her to fill out, then gives her a room key, his face a mask.

Mr. Hashin says, "I take bag to room." She protests, saying she can carry it. He looks at her. "Please. I take care. You remind me of mother."

They take the creaky elevator to the third floor, avoiding each other's eyes now. Carrying her bag, he walks to the room near the elevator. She hands him the key, and he unlocks the door, steps inside, and turns on the light as if he's done this kind of thing a million times. She's momentarily terrified that she let him into the room.

She looks around, her heart beating hard. The room smells musty, unused. A thin double bed covered with a schoolroom green bedspread patterned with pineapples nearly fills the room. A bruised tan dresser, small bathroom, old corroded fixtures, dripping faucet. A lone picture on the wall of a palm tree on a desert island. Mahmoud Hashin stands rigid near the open door.

She turns to tip him, rifling through her purse.

"Please. No tip. Not necessary. Have nice sleep. You are safe here." Mahmoud Hashin gives a slight bow.

Clara finds herself returning his bow. He walks toward the door and turns around to look at her. Slightly inclining his head, he brings his right hand to his heart in a gesture that seems very kind. Moved, she returns the gesture.

"Thank you, Mr. Hashin."

He smiles ever so slightly, bows again, turns with great dignity, and walks down the hall. For a moment she watches him, then steps back, locks and bolts the door. She leans against it, only then letting out a breath she must have been holding ever since she boarded the bus in Jackpot.

Once more, she wonders what she's done. She's running all over the country, with barely a moment's notice each time, as if some foreign force has invaded her body and commandeered her brain. This after staying planted for years in Eugene like a tree. "I'm causing damage, raking over people I love, all for a pile of photographs." She stands beside the door, massaging her forehead. "I'm losing the good sense God gave me. If I'd stayed in Jackpot, I wouldn't need any photographs of lilac stains. The house would be right in front of me." In her exhaustion, she forgets the lilac stains are all burned up.

She walks into the bathroom and looks at herself in the wavy mirror. Her face is distorted, as in a semi-funhouse mirror. Pronounced bags under her eyes, brought on by this extraordinary day, make her look a decade older than she is. The wrinkles on her face have deepened. Her sprightly gray hair looks dry and strawlike.

In slow but mounting panic, she sees her cell phone is still turned off. She turns it on, sees all the messages. She calls Frank, then Haskell. She tells them the name of the hotel, how she got here. Both men are flabbergasted, then alarmed.

"Mother, how could you do this? At least you're safe. What

were you thinking? Taking off again with no warning. We've all been frantic. You're beginning to make this a habit, for God's sake." Clara begins to cry. "Frank, don't be mad. I don't think I can stand it. Haskell and I had a big fight last night after the wedding. I guess he hasn't told you. I didn't want to see him for a while, so I just took off. I didn't want to disturb your honeymoon. And I don't want any of us to miss the exhibition. Of course I know we won't, but well, I thought I'd have a lark, and it's been a nightmare. But I had the nicest cab driver. He found this hotel for me, even though it's a dump, but I'm pretty sure he got a price reduction. The bedspread has pineapples on it. The faucet is leaking. I hope I can sleep. The walls are thin. So far it's quiet." She feels disoriented.

Stella takes the phone. "Clara, thank God. We were so worried." Clara apologizes for interrupting their honeymoon.

"Don't worry, hon," Stella says. "We're fine, now we know where you are. You'll see Frank the day after tomorrow. I'll join you the day after that, from Chicago. It will all work out. We're juggling red-eyes into Kennedy."

"Good plan."

Frank again. "I don't like the sound of that hotel you're in, Mother. I'd feel a whole lot better if you'd call that photographer, Arianna what's-her-name. I have her card somewhere. Maybe you can stay with her. And then we'll *really* feel all right. Do you have her number?"

"I do."

She calls Haskell.

"Clara! My God! I never dreamed you'd get on a plane before we talked!" He sounds a bit frantic. "I'll drop off the RV somewhere, catch a flight. I'll see you as soon as I can. The fight was just silly. We can work things out."

Her eyes are closed. "I don't know why I did this, Haskell."
Her voice drops to a whisper, as if someone is listening behind
the wall. "I think I'm losing my mind. I'm doing these crazy
things."

"Nonsense. You're fine. It's just been very intense lately, with
your son getting married, and you and I meeting unexpectedly,
things developing so fast." Now he sounds far calmer than she.
They say goodbye.

She sits on the bed, hunched over her thighs to contain the
shock of the day. In Lamoille Canyon, she thought she loved
him. Since then, she's tried to tear down this idea any way she
can. He's too urban, too rich, treats her like a child. She's not
used to anybody being protective of her. He wouldn't stay with
a no-frills person like her anyway when he's got a gazillion beautiful women—blah, blah, blah.

Why does she even *need* a man at her age?

Why *not?* She wants to extract every drop of life—if she's still
sane, still able, if there's still time. Well, he could be a friend.
She's sure of that. A good friend.

She looks at her hands. Will she ever find that quiet place in
her head beyond the throbbing veins, the kiva she internalized
from Bandolier?

She's a failed aspirant.

Or a hard sell.

She looks around the hotel room. All the upset started when
the house burned down and she had to get the pictures. Then
in Scotty's car, the purple wasp became Lenore, strong enough
to bring Clara to her knees about Samantha's death. This antic
entertainer—pushy, hypnotic, strange—took hold of her soul at
hello and is taking her on a rampage. Almost made her crash
Scotty's car in the desert! Stamped on her foot! Hurt her breasts!

Won't let her wasp/bee stings heal! But where *is* the pest? Frantically she looks around the barren room. Trapped in her suitcase? She unzips it. Nothing. Ah! There she is, hiding in the crease where the bedspread rises to cover the pillows. Clara sighs in disappointment. The creature's not done with her.

No sounds from other rooms, only the constant dull roar of traffic and sirens. She must be the only one on this floor. Her pulse quickens. Desperate people will invade her room, carry her off to an unmarked grave in some deserted place. She rifles her hair to clear her brain. For once, she decides to heed Frank's suggestion. Despite the cabbie's help, in this huge city she'll feel better staying with someone she knows.

She calls Arianna, even though it's almost eleven. Arianna's response brooks no nonsense. "Clara! I'll be right over. You're not with Haskell? Nevermind, you're going to stay with me. No sense in paying a hotel bill. Besides, that hotel is not in a good area. I'm catching a cab right now. Give me Frank's number. I'll call him on the way over."

Feeling small, Clara holds herself very still on the edge of the bed and clasps her knees. She's turning herself and everyone else inside out. Taking her bags, she goes downstairs to settle the bill.

In Arianna's building, the large industrial elevator groans and stops at a fifth floor loft. A dark, miniscule kitchen has forties' plumbing, tiny old appliances, and a bathtub next to the refrigerator. She's never seen a bathtub in a kitchen before. A ten-foot-high window offers a modesty drape of bright Indian fabric to prevent complete disclosure. The ceiling—at least twelve feet high—dwarfs her. Arianna leads her down the short hall past a small living room with a Murphy bed, past a half bath with a toilet and washbowl. So one *does* bathe in the kitchen!

Arianna's studio is the largest room by far, photographs wall to wall, mostly black and white. Work tables, chemical baths, blackout drapes, clotheslines hung with photos crisscrossing the room in an orderly tangle, a single bed hugging a wall.

"I'd like you to sleep in the studio, Clara. It's closer to the bathroom. I'll take the Murphy." Arianna, in a stained shirt and jeans, pushes up her drifting glasses, anchors unruly hair behind her ears, studies her unexpected guest as if looking for signs of derangement. Her voice softens. "Would you like some hot chocolate after this amazing day you've had?"

She's grateful for the offer but declines. "Maybe tomorrow. Right now I think I need to fall right onto that bed."

"Right-oh. Let me know if you need anything. Towels in the bathroom, hang your clothes over there." She points to a portable garment rack hung with her own clothes. She wants to reassure Clara she's not offended by the late-night change of lodgings, though secretly she is. Her work has hit a glitch, and she's irritable. Even so, an older woman running off to New York for the first time—alone—catches one's attention. She gives Clara a hug. "What a dear, brave woman you are."

Clara looks intently at her. "More like crazy."

"Not at all," Arianna replies briskly. "*Adventurous* is the word. See you in the morning."

Clara unzips her small wheeled luggage bag, hangs up some clothes, and makes her way to the bathroom. Even the *bathroom* has a high ceiling. The sound of running water in the washbowl makes a hollow echo as she washes her face. It's like she's in a dream or on a movie set. At least *this* bathroom won't go wandering down the highway like her other bathrooms have for the past two months, starting with her own house.

Brushing her teeth, she stares into the mirror. "So where do you live, lady?"

At the Bridgeport Hotel, she listed her address as Desert Dan's, Jackpot, Nevada. She has no street address. She smiles, her throat tightening. She's unwittingly made herself homeless—in the few weeks with Haskell, doubly so. No letters could reach her in Lamoille Canyon. Nobody knew she was there, not even Frank. Meaningful mail, though, is a dead issue for her. All her important friends are either dead or she's lost track of them because they moved closer to their kids. She rinses her mouth. She's homesick. Let us count the ways. Her belly aches with it.

The only place she can call home right now is her teeming, unreliable brain, its networks housed in fragile bone, easily cracked open and reduced to smithereens. She looks at her hollowed-out face in the mirror. Strains of Mahmoud's mournful Middle Eastern music echo in her head. She tries to hum the tune, not succeeding. She had recognized the instrument—an oud—and two singers in some kind of dialogue. The sad sound had brought tears to her eyes as his cab careened down Manhattan streets. She had wondered then if Mahmoud was homesick too.

Needing comfort in her new predicament, she thinks of the small glasses of sugared tea offered to strangers and friends in Middle Eastern countries. She's seen these scenes on CNN and the Discovery Channel. She's always wanted to travel there. She's heard about the code of desert hospitality, where it's a point of family and tribal honor to care for the stranger. Right now, this very instant, thank you, she would like some hot sugared tea and some little cakes please, offered by unknown but kindly hands.

She shakes her head. She's got to sleep.

2 days left.

chapter 27

I t's strange to wake in a workplace and not strictly a sleep place. No rugs soften the scarred floor, no dresser or family photos: This is a room for work. From the Spartan bed, she gazes at the welter of photos clipped to clotheslines crisscrossing the room—images of rushing water, decaying streets, bodies not wholly in the frame, architectural details, dead bodies beside the road, their arms flung over each other. Walls are covered with abstract compositions of light and dark—blurred bodies kneeling near walls of flame, hands clasped or raised high; elaborate clusters of burning candles; rough incisions in ancient stone walls—the photos mysterious and pure. She stares, thinks of kneeling, praying, doesn't.

Arianna rattles things in the kitchen. She bought fresh bagels and is making strong coffee, by the smell of it. Clara puts on her green robe and slippers, washes up, and greets her. "This is terrific—someone making my breakfast. I don't often have the pleasure." Except that Haskell did it all the time in Lamoille. She winces. But still, her spirits are higher this morning.

"I checked on you before I went out. You were sleeping like a baby. You didn't even wake up when Haskell called a half hour ago. He drove to Boise last night. His flight arrives at five. He'll take a cab here."

She's grateful Arianna didn't ask why she came to New York alone. "This is all wonderful," she says, gesturing at the bare bone rooms.

The bagels, with fresh cream cheese and fresh orange juice, taste scrumptious. The coffee, fragrant and strong, could raise the dead. They eat, chat, and read the *New York Times*. The rickety kitchen table for two is around the corner in the living room. She's grateful to be at Arianna's. The idea of eating breakfast alone in some café near the Bridgeport Hotel is not pleasant, when she would've been in full shock over her rash journey. After they straighten the kitchen, Arianna works in the studio while Clara bathes in the kitchen bathtub. And it's not so strange to bathe in the kitchen, except that it *is* strange, just like everything else here.

Lenore sits tiredly on the lowered soap dish, stretches to kick her red boots in the water. She splashes Clara, indicates she wants to take a bath too. Clara towels off, drains the tub, and refills it as she dresses. Lenore pushes aside the Indian fabric on the lower window. No modesty for her, apparently.

As Lenore undresses, Clara surreptitiously looks at her ashy purple skin, naked in the window light. She's never seen her naked before.

She's got some kind of sores all over her—a rash festering with pus. And the slit in her arm is inflamed. The tattered lavender wing still protrudes but looks wilted now. She looks like an old woman with a bad skin problem. Her head is more swollen than ever, inexplicably causing Clara's head to hurt too. She's shocked.

"Lenore, what on earth is the matter with you? What's that rash? You should've told me. Here, let me put some baking soda in your bath water. Give yourself a good soak." She looks for baking soda in the cupboard, finds none, opens the refrigerator, finds a box of it. She pours some into the bath water, trying to act calm.

Lenore meekly accepts her fussing for a change. Maybe she's just got jet lag.

Their relationship is so fraught that Clara won't even consider that Lenore might be dying. She hardly moves this morning. Sitting listlessly in the water, she refuses a piece of bagel, waves away a teaspoon of orange juice. Even so, Clara is afraid to talk with her. In the dead of night, she calls herself a coward. She would take Lenore to the doctor, but there is no doctor on earth for a creature like Lenore.

The creature controls something in Clara, something she fears and recognizes. A reckoning of some sort. All this time, Lenore has been trying to force open Clara's rustiest Brain Room, the one crammed with Samantha's last days—the day she died and the day before. Before Lenore dies, she wants Clara to just say it, splay it, roll in it—all of it—to gain the peace that comes from full disclosure. To make amends.

But Clara would still rather die than open that rotting dungeon in her brain.

She and Arianna decide to go to Central Park. Clara needs an easy day, but she's worried about Lenore. She's not eating. Maybe fresh air will help. She takes her along in her ventilated bag. They walk to the Fourteenth Street subway entrance. At the end of the platform in the muggy heat, a homeless man has passed out, lying face down. One filthy tennis shoe is off. A ring of grime circles his ankle where the shoe ended. A rank smell of urine, filth, and sweat curdles the air around him. His hair is matted, his unshaven face blurred with sweat, his clothes wilted into blurred colors.

Clara has no defenses this morning after seeing Lenore's suffering. Raw to the pain of the world, she steps toward the man and rummages in her purse. Normally she would never do this. The other people studiously avoid looking at him or Clara, who now kneels beside him.

Arianna gently touches Clara's shoulder, whispers, "That just encourages them in public places."

Clara's tone is brusque. "We all have to eat." She deposits a five-dollar bill in the man's limp hand and returns stone-faced to Arianna, who has moved down the platform.

"He won't use it to eat. You know that. The city's tried to clean up stuff like this. It's sad, of course, but this is life in the big city."

"We have homeless people in Eugene too. It's not like I've never seen one. It always bothers me, you know, to see someone like this. I don't care if he won't use it to eat. He needs a gesture. Everyone needs a gesture."

Arianna's face is tight. "Well, you get mugged once or twice, and you forget about gestures. You want sterner measures. You just want to be safe and live in peace."

"You've been mugged?"

Just then, a tall man with baggy pants and a red Afro darts from the crowd. He snatches the five-dollar bill from the drunk's hand and runs up the stairs.

Incensed, Clara takes out running after him. "Just a minute, young man," she shouts. "This man can't defend himself right now. You can't take his money."

The small crowd turns to look, their faces blank with disbelief. Arianna runs after her, grabs her arm. "Clara, stop! He's already up the stairs. You'll never catch him. Chalk it up—five bucks down the drain."

"I will do no such thing." Clara angrily rummages in her purse again, this time pulls out a ten. Panting, she's beyond reason now. "The world's going to collapse one day. So will we just beat each other over the head with clubs?"

Arianna looks blankly at Clara. "I would say so. Yes. Definitely."

Crouching on her haunches, Clara stuffs the bill into the man's front pants pocket—hard to reach since he's lying on his stomach. To do so, she has to get closer to his private parts than she would like. The man stirs, groans. She murmurs, "I'm not going to hurt you, young man. Just look in your pocket when you sober up. Surprise yourself by doing something good for yourself. You don't have to be this way forever."

Appalled, Arianna hears this and shakes her head.

Clara stands as the train rumbles into the station. Head throbbing, she knows very well this man will use the ten for drugs. She's acting stupid. It's Lenore. The creature will push her until she breaks. Lenore squirms in her bag just then. Clara puts a protective hand over her. The creature quiets.

The packed train drones and sways to the transfer point. The two women disembark and walk down a long, dirty-tiled hallway to another train, get off at the Central Park exit, and hurry into the park. Willing her strong morning emotions to pass, Clara is relieved to be amidst greenery again, though she soon starts sneezing. Lenore is limp in her bag.

Mothers and nannies stroll by, chatting amiably, their well-dressed babies in buggies bristling with levers and hinges. Tough-looking teenagers swagger four and five abreast, parading their baggy clothes, tattoos, and body piercings with a syncopated walk that features a recurring hitch. Speedo-clad cyclists crouch over their water bottles; glassy-eyed joggers are wired to arm radios with earphones. Business people with brown bag or takeout food lounge on benches; sirens roar in the distance. Everything interests her, despite whatever is making her nose run. They amble toward the pond, where they sit and quietly watch the ducks gliding through the water.

Relieved that Clara's enjoying the scene, Arianna says, "I should do this more often. Outside the city, I'm in countryside all the time. Here, my world shrinks to concrete and work. I never see the sun." She rubs her temples, takes off her glasses. "I've got a glitch with my Santa Monica show. Some photos haven't shown up, some of my best shots, and the show has already opened. I've got a tracer on them. In the meantime, yesterday I did reprints and FedExed them. The gallery owner is having a cow. He's a real *diva*. It's good you came, Clara. With you and Haskell here, I'll be distracted and we'll just enjoy the Met opening. But I'm a perfectionist, so let me apologize in advance if I get irritable. Frankly, I'm not sure the reprints are as good as the originals." She pushes her glasses up.

Clara says, "Sometimes I wish Haskell was more of a perfectionist."

"But he *is*. He's a very successful commercial photographer. He spends hours lining up a shot. He has loyal clients, is always booked. He drives himself crazy. Why do you say that?"

"Oh, it's just that he got some great nature shots from his trip. I think he has a real talent for this type of photography. But he's so casual about it. He doesn't think it could lead anywhere. I think it could, if he'd just work at it."

Arianna winks. "Give him some rope. He'll work it out."

Clara sighs. "So tell me about your favorite uncle."

"He's a great guy." She smiles. "Used to take me to Broadway shows after he started making it—*Threepenny Opera, The Fantasticks, Cats, The Wiz,* a lot of foreign movies—Truffaut, Fellini, Renoir—especially after Sandra left him. My father left the family when I was ten; my mother died three years ago. I'm the only child. So it was rough, but Haskell's always been around, ready to whip up killer lasagna or a batch of sushi."

Clara looks at her with vague foreboding. "You think he's wedded to the city?"

She's thinking of Frank and Stella—Frank wouldn't live here.

"I hope so, for my sake. He's certainly a true New Yorker, knows it like the back of his hand." She claps her hand on Clara's knee. "I can just see you zipping around Manhattan, taking it by storm, doing wonderful and outrageous things."

"The noise, the crowds. I'm not sure the climate agrees with me." She sneezes, as if for emphasis.

"I don't believe a word of it. Manhattan thrives on people like you."

They walk out of the park onto Fifth Avenue. Soon her mood lifts, buoyed by Arianna's brisk dismissal of her misgivings. She's getting energized by the crowds as they walk down Fifth toward Bergdorf's. The sidewalks are crammed with stylish people hurrying, talking, laughing, arguing. Horns blare, drivers shout, sirens wail in the background roar of a city furiously awake and on the move. A man in a well-cut suit winks at her. A young woman gives her a thumbs-up. She marvels. Strangers on the street—so nice! She and Arianna walk past Tiffany's, the Plaza, other names she's only read about or seen in the movies. The romance and energy of the place entrances her. She's like a schoolgirl seeing something wonderful for the first time. "This is fabulous!" she exclaims. "I can't believe it."

Arianna squeezes her hand. "I knew you'd like it."

Back at the loft, she falls into a deep sleep as if drugged. She doesn't wake until the commotion of Haskell's arrival makes her think she's in a bus station. She sits on the edge of the bed rubbing her temples. He comes into the studio. Wordlessly they embrace. Arianna discretely steps into the kitchen, rattles pans.

He closes the door. "How's my girl?" he murmurs, burying his face in her hair. His clothes are rumpled, his hair mussed.

"How many days do you have to listen?" she says lightly.

"Try me." He strokes her hair. "Let's blow this joint."

"My thoughts precisely."

They thank Arianna profusely for her help, gather their bags, and take a cab to his loft near Sixteenth and Madison. He buzzes them inside a blue door. The elevator opens onto a large, sparsely furnished living/dining/kitchen area with enormous floor to ceiling windows and natural maple cabinets. Down a hallway, a huge photography studio, big master bedroom, small study, second bedroom, large bathroom, more high ceilings. He has the whole third floor. She's never been in a living space this large.

"It's beautiful," she says simply.

He shrugs. "I've dumped a lot of stuff. I never needed anything this big."

They need to talk, but this is not a night for talking. He's exhausted; she's unmoored. Against her will, the dungeons in her brain are bulging with events from long ago. Lenore stays in the cloth bag, mired in her own deterioration. She nibbles the corner of a Saltine and barely moves. Clara can hardly look at her.

Haskell orders up a lovely pistou soup, a ravioli salad, and a white bordeaux. They are in bed by nine. With a strong headache returning, she lies close to him.

"Hello," she says, lightly nuzzling him.

"Hi, you."

In the night, she wakes with a start. She was trapped in a stuffy closet, the air running out.

"Bad dream?"

"Yes."

"You're OK?"

"Yes." She is awake the rest of the night, waiting for her son.

1 day left.

The cab double-parks in front of the Met, horns blaring as Haskell pays the driver. She couldn't rouse Lenore this morning, so she brought her along in her cloth bag. She seems much lighter than before, more shrunken. Clara's hands sweat as she sees the big banner hung across the entrance: "Hidden America: Photography in the New Millennium. July 1–August 10." She nervously grips Haskell's arm to steady herself. Where's Frank? He was supposed to meet them here on the steps. The stately museum with its grand entry steps looks like a European capital building to her. They take in the crowded scene. On the sidewalk, a saxophonist is playing "Summertime," one of their favorite songs. The notes echo in the communal outdoor space. Lenore briefly stirs; Clara's heart flutters.

Her cell phone rings. It's Frank. "I'm about six blocks away. The red-eye was late. I'll meet you inside the exhibition."

"Yes," she says. "Good." Her heartbeat quickens.

A motley crowd lounges on the steps, sunning themselves– camera-toting tourists in Bermuda shorts and T-shirts; a couple of nursing mothers, their babies wrapped like burritos; people in business suits talking fast on cell phones; people buying pretzels and hot dogs from sidewalk venders. Women of a certain age saunter up the steps with their impeccable hairdos, tasteful jackets, and elegant dresses. Clara looks down at her red Keds, cornflower-blue blouse, and old Levi's. She feels like a hick, but only for a moment. She and Haskell deliberately wore their Nevada duds in the spirit of her entry. He's in Levi's, a denim shirt, and old cowboy boots. He refers to the exhibition as "your show" and "your opening." She smiles at his gallantry. Her head still throbs. A few people murmur discretely to each other as they come back down the steps, possibly having already seen the show. A corridor of quiet expands on either side of her. They study Clara silently, as if they recognize her. The outsider from Eugene gradually notices this. Her nervousness grows.

Arianna stands on the top step, grinning down at them, glasses sliding down her nose. They reach the top, hug, and stand there a minute, taking in the thick crowds. The air is still. "Are you ready, Clara?"

"Ready as I'll ever be." Her hands are like ice.

Arianna leads the way. They pass through the vast lobby thronged with people, a hubbub of voices echoing in the large chamber, and make their way to the room where Arianna's photos hang.

Her pictures cover one long wall and the adjacent shorter wall. Set in seven framed sections, separate video screens fill most of each wall. Each section has a speaker above it with its own soundtrack. In the first section, pine and broadleaf forests sweep past the viewer. The sound of a husky motor drones in the background, as if someone is driving through these forests. The trees are life-size, in many shades of green, some still wet with dew.

Clara's chest thumps as if someone has struck her. "Haskell— she used some of your photos!"

He exclaims to Arianna, "My God, they're huge. And you've made them into videos!"

Arianna smiles coyly. "This is my surprise. Let's keep looking."

In the second frame, the forests gradually turn sepia, then gray, as if some bleaching process has set in. An occasional green tree survives among the dying ones. Then we come alongside a grim Clara hunched inside a dusty U-Haul that trails behind a twelve-axle flatbed truck with a small white house anchored to it. Inside the black trailer cab is Frank, looking exhausted. A close-up of Clara shows her jawline clenched and firm as her pinioned house lumbers ahead on the flatbed.

Amazed, she turns to Arianna. "How did you do it?"

"I talked to Frank. He told me all about your trip down from Oregon." Seeing Clara's puzzled look, she adds, "Don't worry about how we did it–tinting, inserted images, lots of tricks even up to last night. Frank showed me the pictures you and he took when you stopped by the side of the road and people would wave." She checks her watch. "How about if I talk to you two tomorrow? I've got a meeting with the curator just now. Enjoy!" She hugs them both and slips away.

At that moment, Frank rushes into the room, embraces his mother, and shakes Haskell's hand. "Let me catch up with you." Clara and Haskell stand to the side and watch as Frank examines the first two sections with a smile on his face. "Whew!" he says. "Arianna listened well."

In the third section, people in pickups and cars and SUVs wave and honk at Clara and Frank as they pass them. Sun-burned men and women give them thumbs up and V-for-victory signs from their own ancient vehicles, as if the Breckenridge car-avan has made them remember simple and wonderful things from their own past and they're grateful to Clara and Frank for awakening these memories. These people hang from car windows, stare raptly at the unlikely mother-son caravan until their vehicles disappear from the frame. The cars are mostly weather-beaten and filled with kids. Grinning, murmuring, Clara and Frank walk slowly together—arms loosely around each other's waists now—exclaiming about these travelers, how they both loved their startled good cheer.

In the fourth frame, shots of clear-cut forests in earnest now. Oil derricks pumping on denuded slopes, a close-up of her house shuddering past dead and fallen trees, their trunks and branches strangled by a strange orange fungus. The three of them are silent, unsmiling. Haskell falls back some, to give Clara and Frank more privacy. He senses the crucial mother-son meeting unfolding before him.

Next is a group of 10x12 interior shots of Clara's house, as personal to her as her own naked body. Outraged, she sees these in a blur—the green Formica table and chairs, the sagging navy couch, the old Singer sewing machine, Frank's narrow bed, her own worn bed and faded quilt—all the particulars of the plain house that Arianna was so taken with. To see her private house in these public photos hits Clara like a punch in the gut.

Frank murmurs, "What's so special about the furniture anyway?"

She shrugs, trying to hide her anger. "Part of the story, I guess. The hidden part."

The sixth panel features Clara herself in an oversized black-and-white portrait taken in harsh desert light. She stares directly at the viewer, eyes hostile, as if protecting her house from invaders. She frowns with pursed lips, arms folded across her breasts, all her wrinkles emphasized in the unforgiving shot. Viewers gather silently around it. To some she might be an avenging angel, judging everyone's material folly. But to Clara, the portrait shows the angry fear of someone teetering over a precipice—about to obey a creature that can't possibly exist, that will make her reveal secrets that will destroy her.

Frank stares at this portrait. "You look powerful. Did you know that, Mother?" She looks at him, saying nothing. He's never said anything like that before.

Last we see a close-up video of Clara crouching beside the two beef jerky jars in her closet. The imprisoned wasps are swarming—dense, furious, wild with life, the original sixteen wasps she brought from Eugene. Her hand lies protectively on the glass. The wasps grow calm under her touch. Side battles erupt among those that can't get close.

Now a misfit appears among the crew, a healthy wasp with lavender wings, lavender stripes, and an enlarged purple head. Other wasps, yellow and black, gather round this alpha wasp, nosing its thorax, stroking its wings. At first its color seems to be a freak of light—the glass jar glints in pale sunlight. But the color stays, no matter the angle. A close-up of the purple wasp shows its mouth opening and closing, as if it's trying to speak to us in urgent monotone, incomprehensible to humans. Viewers stand entranced. Haskell and Frank stand closer to Clara, knowing how private she is about the wasps.

Furiously she whispers, "I never wanted the wasps made public. I must have signed my rights away! Your niece will do anything for publicity, Haskell."

"Don't worry, we'll check. But by God, Clara, the wasp is purple, I can see it." *Unless Arianna tinted it*, he thinks, desperately trying to hold onto reason. Yes, that's it—that must be what she did. But he sees no evidence of tinting. The wasp is an overripe purple, a freak of nature.

Clara folds her arms. "So I'm not totally nuts."

"As far as I can see, no."

"I can see it too," says Frank. "The wasp is purple. Like grape juice. This is nuts, Mom."

She smiles, then suddenly holds her breath. Finally on the entire adjacent wall, we see the whole house from the rear, untouched by fire—and to Clara's great astonishment, the sight she came across the entire country to see.

The lower half of the siding is clotted with paint stuck with powdery dead lilac petals turned beige, rust, sepia, and gray. These wispy petals look torn from thin stems, scattered and smeared among imprints of whole lilac branches, their stems incised in the pale yellow paint. Old careless paint jobs mar the siding everywhere until dingy white dominates the higher you look. The shredded lilacs swirl more wildly before the eye, as if the ghostly blooms are about to revive and sway again in the wind. Gradually, through the photographer's art, the lilac petals *do* enlarge and separate from the house—until they take on a life of their own, transformed now into huge living lilac sprays that fling themselves about in the wind, ungoverned and hallucinatory and rapturous. She grasps Frank's hand for a moment, and they find a bench to sit on.

It all comes back to her. Haskell listens quietly. Frank and Clara trade details. They lean toward each other, looking dazed.

Lying on quilts in the dappled summer light, the four of them would watch the swaying lilac canopy over their heads as if they were hypnotized. In these backyard picnics, they drank Clara's homemade lemonade from thick, sweaty glasses and gorged on her fried chicken, Darrell's potato salad, and sliced tomatoes laid out on thrift-store china plates. Then Darrell would plop onto his back, spread his arms wide for Samantha and Frank to array themselves on either side of him, everyone blinking and sleepy in the muted light, hidden from the hot summer sun by the lilacs, the wasps circling lazily above them. After she cleared the food away, they would all doze off together, arms and bodies entwined, each parent nuzzling a child. As the sun faded, they woke and munched on slabs of cantaloupe and homemade spice cake with powdered sugar frosting or homemade brownies with strawberries and blueberries they had all picked together at farms just outside of Eugene that same morning. In the mottled shade, they laughed at their blue-stained tongues and teeth, and they rubbed their cheeks with strawberry juice. Then the four of them would bunch together in the lawn swing to watch the falling sun sink below the horizon, one child on each parent's lap. Clara would nuzzle her children's hair, closing her eyes to imprint the smell of Johnson's Baby Shampoo when they were small; later Frank's Palmolive, like his father's, and Samantha's Prell, like hers. When the kids were little, each parent carried a child to bed. Then Clara and Darrell returned to the lawn swing and sat wrapped together, talking, not talking, inhaling the luscious lilac stink. Sometimes Frank and Samantha got out of bed and spied on their parents. Sometimes their parents went back inside, turned the record player on low, and danced to Glenn Miller. It all seemed to happen a day ago.

She and Frank share these jumbled stories. They try to be quiet in the museum, but they get noisy with memories and must move to the hall and then outside. Haskell is silent in their torrent of words. His eyes betray a longing hurt—for times like these he never had? In confusion, she wonders if he's getting too much information. She sees his discomfort and feels new again to the skills of relationship after years of nunlike isolation. Even so, joy at seeing Frank makes her remember crazy details, like the time they went overboard with the strawberries and smeared strawberry juice on each other and ruined their clothes. Clara ran inside to get the camera for a fast picture. That picture was burned up too, along with everything else.

With sudden foreboding, she peers into the fabric bag that hangs from her shoulder. Lenore, desiccated and naked, barely stirs. She is down from about ten to four inches. Only a smidgeon of lavender skin remains on top of her swollen bald head. The rest of her body is gray. Frightened, Clara looks around and quickly closes the bag, as if she's guilty of a crime. She takes a deep breath.

Seeing the amazing video work makes her feel like a whole person again—as if her living family, the lilacs, and the guardian wasps still surround her under the drowsy sun. The joy of it makes her feel hot and sleepy. Then her decades of silence and stiffness around Frank, with no explanation as to why, come crashing around her with a cold chill. How could she have mistreated him so much without even realizing it? She's got to explain things to him before it's too late.

Her heart thumps. "You loved those picnics, didn't you, Frank?"

"I remember everything about them."

Clara and Frank have left the museum and are sitting in a quiet area of the steps. Haskell strolls over to a snack cart, gets a lemonade, and stands there sipping it. Clara and Frank signal they don't want any.

She is saying, "When you and I were the only ones left of our family, I didn't know what to do or how to act, and neither did you. All those years, you must have wondered why I was so distant after Dad and Samantha died."

He's silent for an eternity, looking down at his shoes on the steps. She holds her forehead in distress, dreading what he might say. He speaks slowly, his voice grave and measured. "I did wonder, Mom. It was strange. I didn't know what to think. I really didn't. I thought I had done something wrong."

She laughs in bitter surprise. "But *I* was the one who did something wrong."

Haskell returns and asks if they want something to eat. They look at him, distracted, noncommittal. He is insistent. "It's two o'clock. We've got to eat. I know of a good restaurant on the corner of Eighty-fourth and Madison," he says, sounding cheerful, perhaps overly so. They decide to do it, walk there and have some food. The three of them have little to say, but the physical exercise lifts everyone's spirits after such an intense show and the needed conversation beginning to unfold between Clara and her son. Haskell intuits that something grave and important is unfolding between them. The restaurant is quiet, the service attentive—it's the perfect choice. They sit at a table near the front. Other customers are tucked away in dim corners. The two men tackle paninis. She picks at a salmon pasta.

Back at his place, Haskell makes tea for them, says he's got errands to run and they should make themselves at home. They thank him, and he goes downstairs on the big elevator. Frank and his mother sit on the couch and look out the window.

The swollen unhealed stings on her forehead are near to breaking. Whatever is inside her head is gnawing, stamping, pounding on the bones of her head. And it won't stop. It won't stop. She begins.

"I had a lot of difficulty with your father's death, Frank."

"I could see that. You just sat at the table or in your rocker all the time—when you weren't cleaning house like a maniac. You became a zombie workaholic, Mom."

She smiles. "It was that bad?"

"You wouldn't talk to me, but the house always smelled like Clorox or lemon oil."

"I wanted to take care of you—protect you, Frank."

He cocks his head at her, smiles. "With Clorox and lemon oil?"

She flinches. "Actually, Frank, I think it was guilt."

"Guilt? But you didn't cause Dad's death."

"No, but I was crushed and lonely. So what happened was I got involved in an affair shortly after he died."

"Really? You, Mom?" He takes a deep breath. "I don't know what to say."

"Neither do I."

"Do you want to tell me just a little bit about it? Not too much now."

She looks at her son, so surprised and trusting, as Samantha's Brain Room splits open in her head. In the afternoon light, flashes of that hellish day roll before her eyes, as if for years she has looked through cloudy plastic. The collar of Martin's shirt—her lover's shirt, the collar frayed at the points, his shirt the color of veins on the back of an old white person's hands. A purple shirt that a dealer in Vegas would wear. A shaving nick on his chin, a blackhead on his nose, the suffocating smell of his shaving lotion. She was standing at the intersection with Martin, and she wanted to run. She looked hard at his shirt because she didn't want to look down.

Little Myra, the patrol captain that week, had come pounding on Clara's office door. She and Martin hastily composed

307

themselves. "An accident, there's been a terrible accident," Myra said in her high, sweet voice. She smelled of urine. Her shoes were sloshing with urine. Myra was Samantha's best friend, and she had wet her pants as she came running into the school. The three of them ran out to the four-corner intersection and stood there. Clara refused to look. She could smell Myra's urine and Martin's shaving lotion. She didn't want to look down at the pavement. And she didn't want to stand that close to Martin. She had left her light blue panties in his car last night. She wanted to run from him. But she looked down. She couldn't avoid looking down at the pavement. She screamed. She must have screamed. She doesn't remember.

On the pavement, Samantha's cooling form, her daughter's open, parched mouth, her eyes permanently open, her body unnaturally twisted. She never saw Martin again. He moved somewhere else. So did Myra. The truck driver was charged.

She looks at Frank now. "There was this teacher," she says softly, then looks away. "I taught with him a number of years before I became principal. He was moody, charismatic, rotten marriage, wife an alcoholic. All the women were in love with him. The kids were fascinated. His standards were very high. He was the student patrol advisor. Everyone wanted to be on patrol."

"OK, OK, that's enough, Mom. I wish I had known about this. I would have knocked his block off."

She is touched. "Oh, Frank, you are very sweet. Thank you."

He is quite ruffled. He sets his tea down to pace around the living room, staring at the floor, pursing his lips. "He took advantage of you, Mom! What a jerk! You didn't talk to me because you were involved with a jerk! Look, Mom"—he gathers his breath—"I can understand you having an affair. You just lost your husband. You were very vulnerable." He pauses, looking at her. "You haven't been carrying this for all these years, have you? Thirty-eight years?"

"The affair is the least of my worries." She looks at him. "Do you want to hear more, Frank? There's more."

"OK," he says. "So what is it?"

"Do you remember Samantha and I had a big fight the morning of the accident?"

"Not really. I could see you both were unhappy about something."

"She wanted to work on her Alexandria report in my office after school. Then she could ride home with me. So I lied. I was going to meet Martin, but I told her I had a committee meeting in my office, so she had to study in the library after school. She threw a tantrum. She said she wanted to work in my office because it was quiet and she could ask me questions and consult the encyclopedias I had there. We got into a big fight. I said it would be too noisy in my office because of the meeting."

She covers her face with her hands. Her head is almost bursting with Lenore's continued stomping. The creature has gathered her last strength to shrink herself and crawl inside Clara's brain and make her speak. She has trouble catching her breath.

"And another thing. For about a week, Martin and I had started meeting at night. The day before the accident, we were out till almost midnight. Think, Frank. On a school night. When Samantha was eleven and you were nine. With no father there, no babysitter. I thought you'd still be sleeping." She shakes her head. "You kids were still up when I got home. You were scared and crying, running around the house. I had never done such a thing before, staying out late with no babysitter for you.

Anything could have happened. Anything. It's unforgivable. Do you remember it, Frank?"

"I do. It was kind of scary. We wondered if you got kidnapped or in an accident."

"I was so stupid. I'm so sorry." Eyes brimming, she tries to catch her breath.

"So the next morning, on the last day of her life, Samantha asks me why I don't want to be around you and her anymore since Dad died. '*Maybe you'd like it better if we died too!*' she shouted. I was stunned, couldn't speak. She stormed out of the kitchen, was silent on the way to school. I had already put her bike in the trunk. You were silent too in the back seat beside her. Before you both got out of the car, I told Samantha she couldn't always have her way. Adults had things they needed to do too. I got her bike out of the trunk for her. She didn't say a word, and she didn't go to the library. She was apparently going straight home.

"If only she'd gone to the library! Or my office! If only I had cancelled my date with Martin, the accident wouldn't have happened, and Samantha would have been safe. I left my parents' home to be safe, came clear across the country to be safe. And I failed to keep my own kids safe. Instead, I pushed you into danger!" She covers her ears with her hands. "So it comes down to this: On the day of the accident, I ignored your sister when she needed me. If I had done what she wanted, the accident wouldn't have happened. She would have been in my office. I would be answering her questions. We could go home together and have milk and cookies. Live the dream. The perfect mother. The perfect daughter." She holds her forehead again. "Oh, Frank, I'm so sorry. I just didn't know how to deal with this affair and your father's death and you kids all at once."

Frank is silent. Finally he says, "So you've kept all this inside you all these years."

"It's been torture. I couldn't forgive myself. Or speak of it. I became like a nun so nothing else bad would happen to us. Imagine. A nun. For all these years." She swallows. "And now I'm telling you this on your *honeymoon*, Frank!" She laughs. "I never did have good timing, did I?" He doesn't laugh or say anything, and she panics. "We could have talked all this out a long time ago if I'd been able to tell you. Can you ever forgive me?"

"Mom. Of course." And then, "Thank you." They fall silent. The afternoon sun is starting to fade. A fire engine shrieks by, jackhammers sound in the distance, dogs yip back and forth on the sidewalk.

Tiredly he looks at her. "So you connect the sex with the accident?"

Her voice is toneless. "I was with my lover in my office when a big truck swung around the corner and knocked my daughter down and killed her at the four-corner intersection. End of story."

"But Mom . . ."

"Look, I'm not asking for absolution here. I started adult patrols afterward, but it was too late for me and Samantha. I've been trying my whole life to make up for it, fix any damaged soul I can find." Her voice ends in a whisper. "There are a lot of damaged souls. The kids who burned down my house, for instance. "

He takes her hand, says softly, "Mom, listen. Having sex that day has no connection to Samantha's death. They were two separate events. It was just an unfortunate coincidence. A roll of the dice."

"You don't understand. I could have been *out* there. *Martin* could have been out there. He was the patrol advisor."

"Were you or Martin *supposed* to be out there?"

"No. But at least once a week he would go out to the intersection and chitchat with the kids. They loved it. He told Myra he would be out there that day. And he wasn't." She bows her head, says nothing for a while. "All those years." She absently strokes a pillow.

"Mom. You've been too hard on yourself. You're a human being; you did a human thing. Even if Martin *had* gone out there, he might not have been there at the exact moment the accident was lining up to happen. So it might have happened anyway. You've got to forgive yourself."

She looks at him. "I don't think it's possible."

He persists. "It was over thirty years ago. You've got to move on. It's done. You've got time left to live—still."

She looks at him. Where did this son of hers get all this wisdom?

Haskell is back from his errands and calmly sorts the mail. After the three of them have a light dinner of deli food, Frank goes straight to bed, exhausted from the red-eye, the exhibit, and their talk. Tomorrow is a special day for Frank: Stella will arrive from Chicago to see the exhibition with him. The plane ticket is an unexpected gift from her aunt and uncle. The newlyweds are delighted. And Frank has lots to tell his bride.

Clara is wrought up and exhausted. She was awake the whole night. She wanders around the loft, examines every room, object, and surface, stares out into the darkening night. Haskell is barely awake with the newspaper. She obsessively checks on Lenore, who still throbs lightly in her bag on top of the dresser. She tries to feed Lenore a few crumbs of graham cracker, but the creature pushes the crumbs away with her tiny feet and arms.

Clara bends over the doomed creature in her bag and whispers, "Thank you, my darling. Stay a little longer."

0 days left.

Haskell wakes to see Clara staring out the window. "What is it?" he asks.

"Your niece," she says. "Arianna tried to make me out a saint in that show, a crusader against excess." Pained, she looks at him. "Nothing could be further from the truth. I can't save the world. I can't even save myself." She runs her hand over her eyes. "I've been awake for hours. Frank already left to pick up Stella at the airport."

She looks over at Haskell, calmly sitting on the couch, looking at her. A wave of longing comes over her. More than ever, she needs a friend right now, a good friend. Someone she could talk to, someone who would talk to her. She wonders how Haskell would react to her story. She looks up. He's studying her.

"How are you?" he asks quietly. "Are you all right?"

She doesn't yet know how to answer that question. She says, "Do you want to hear a story?"

"I always like to hear stories."

She decides then to tell him the whole story, her affair, all of it, the same as she told Frank—the late night dates, lying about a meeting, the fight, the accident.

"So that's what's been bothering you. I've known for a long time something was bothering you. Maybe now you'll begin to forgive yourself."

"Forgive? That's a funny word. I don't know anything about it." She shifts her attention to Lenore, who throbs faintly in her bag on the dresser. Before she eats her own breakfast, Clara again tries to feed the creature–this time a crushed Cheerio, but Lenore won't eat. So she folds a cloth napkin to make a little mattress for Lenore in her bag, but the creature twitches and tries to slide off it, as if the fabric hurts her.

There is nothing Clara can do for her.

After they get dressed, Clara and Haskell sit on the couch together.

Haskell, wanting to distract her, talks about selling the loft. He wants to get out of the city. "This trip has showed me another way to live. I'll always love Manhattan, but I'd like to go out West. I've had enough crowding for a while. I'm going to call my sister. My niece is coming here in winter quarter for school, and Pam has often said she'd like to buy my loft. They've got money coming out the wazoo."

Clara considers this, muses. "I want to be where Frank is. That's what I know. I'm not going to blow this. And I like Stella. Very much."

He nods. "Frank calls it straight. And Stella is dynamite."

"I have to agree. They rushed it, though."

He laughs. "They did."

They are quiet, sitting on the couch. She is talking again about her failure to keep her kids safe. Haskell has an arm around her. Finally he says, "Listen to me, Clara. Things happen, chance things–things we could not possibly anticipate, would never ever want in a million years. You had no idea there would be an accident. Neither did your daughter. For God's sake, Clara, don't be so hard on yourself. You're a good person. Your son is right."

She murmurs, "I'm just so exhausted. I could sleep for days. Really days. I've been trying to sleep all these years. I can never get enough sleep. I go to bed and lay there all night,

night after night. It's like I always have a searchlight on in my brain. I thought Frank would run out on me if he knew how I'd neglected both of them, so I've slept even less these last weeks, knowing I had to finally talk about it. I get so tired. I can't even talk straight when I get this way."

"Why don't you go and lie down? I have things to do around here, another errand. I'll try to be quiet." He kisses her lightly. "We'll get through this, Clara."

She barely responds.

With sudden intuition, she dashes over to Lenore's bag in the bedroom and carefully opens it. "Quick, Haskell, come here. Oh, God."

Spellbound, they peer into the bag together. Lenore is gray and naked. She has shrunk from four inches to two inches and is still shrinking. Her tiny face is contorted in agony, as if she's giving birth. Translucent wing buds are coming out right now from her shoulder blades. Her arms and legs are shrinking to the toothpick limbs of wasps. Her face is re-forming to oblong with big eyes and proboscis snout. Her head is no longer swollen. The painful reverse transformation is happening right before their eyes.

Clara speaks quietly to her. "Let me help. What can I do?"

In the smallest of voices, Lenore says, "You can begin to heal. My work is done; I can die as I came. This is how much I loved you."

Haskell whispers, "This is nuts, Clara. I can hear her and see her. I used to hear static and breezes, and that was bad enough. I don't understand this."

"Neither do I. You're beginning to see around the edges of things."

"I'm going nuts."

Lenore's body is finally still, once more shaped like a wasp, but gray. Clara bends over the open bag, her eyes wet. Carefully she lifts the weightless form out of the bag and rests it on a folded Kleenex. She places Lenore's remains inside a Chlor-Trimeton box after stowing the last sheet of pills separately in her purse. She sets the box on Haskell's dresser.

He gives a low whistle in response to all this and asks Clara if she's all right. "I don't need to go out. There's more food."

"I'm OK," she says. "I'm just really tired. Go ahead. I'll just rest awhile."

She flings herself across the bed and stares at the ceiling, trying to sleep. But she's wide awake. Finally she dozes off for maybe half an hour. When she wakes, the loft is silent. Haskell must have gone out for something after all. He has put a light blanket over her. Her brain is addled from lack of sleep, from everything that has happened. She doesn't know what day it is, what month. She needs some air. She finds a note. He had to go to the post office. Quietly she lets herself out the weathered blue door. She will just walk awhile to clear her mind. Maybe then she can sleep.

chapter 28

She's been walking for some time, not noticing street signs or people, only the smell of diesel and ripe garbage. After a while, she starts noticing people. They are all talking on their cell phones, eyes glazed, not registering what's in front of them. They are floating, just like she is, but she has no cell phone. She left it at Haskell's.

It is late afternoon and she is hungry again, tired again, always these things follow her around. She pulls out three one-dollar bills and some change from her Levi's pocket and stops to buy a sausage from a street vender. It squirts when she bites it, staining her blouse, but it tastes good. She has a dollar and some change left.

A heavy homeless woman sitting cross-legged on the sidewalk panhandles her. She gives the woman a quarter. Frowning, the woman pockets it. Lying next to the woman is a panting brown dog with open bloody sores on its side. Clara sits down beside the woman. Night will come, and she doesn't want to be alone just now. The dog sniffs her hand. Its nose is dry. She pets it on the head.

The woman exclaims in fright. "What do you want? I don't have anything." A strong unwashed smell comes from her.

"I don't want anything. I just want to pet your dog." Clara holds her breath to avoid retching at the smell.

"I can't help you, lady. You should move on. The streets don't stay friendly after dark."

"How long have you been out here?"

The woman looks at Clara as if she's crazy. "Few months. Me and my dog."

"What's your dog's name?"

"Oscar. His name's Oscar." She looks at Clara. "You some reporter?"

"No. No. Just resting a minute." Clara looks around. She's loose now. Everything is ruled in. She might just float away. Fancy that. She told everything and nothing happened. After all those years of nailing herself down. She feels a sharp stab of grief for Lenore, her faithful and overpowering companion these last weeks. It seems longer, as if Lenore has been her companion her whole life. She feels dizzy and light-headed. She laughs. The woman looks at Clara in alarm, but calms down when Clara continues to sit peacefully on the sidewalk.

The woman's complexion is florid, her hair an oily dark clump at the back of her neck, her dark clothes stretched out and filthy. Clara edges a little farther away from her. The woman brings out a forty-ounce can of Old English 800 malt liquor from a welter of plastic bags. She offers it to Clara, who hesitates, then takes it. It might help her sleep a little. She wants to be sure to sleep now. A nap will clear her mind. She drinks maybe a cup of the liquor. It's a very tall can. She can't drink any more, but she's still hungry after the sausage. She passes the can back to the woman. "Thanks," Clara says.

There is a lot left for the woman. The woman sets the can on the sidewalk. Clara leans against the building as she sits on the sidewalk. She will get up and leave in just a minute. The sun is fading.

Sleep comes on her like a sudden plunge off a cliff. At some point she feels someone roughly searching her pockets, but she's too tired to rouse herself. When she wakes, the homeless woman and her dog are gone. She wonders what time it is. It's late. She's hungry. She checks her watch, but the watch is gone, a white circle on her wrist where her watch usually is. People passing by stare at her. Her blouse is dirty. Her money is gone.

She begins walking and goes into a coffee shop to relieve herself. *I better start paying attention to street signs,* she thinks, but it seems impossible that she would get lost in this city where buildings are warm to the touch and packed with thousands—millions—of people. But she doesn't know where she is.

She is walking south on First Avenue, the same direction she'd been walking last night. Sirens, smoke, haze—there's a fire somewhere to the north. Her eyes are stinging, she has a thumping headache, her stomach is upset. People walk past her in either direction, always hurrying.

A clock in a store window says eight thirty. So it's not that late. Not completely dark yet. Being overtired means she wakes up at the slightest bother. How can she sleep at all when she's on the street and not in a bed? How can she even *be* on the street? Never in her life. People passing by her look worried about something. Maybe they're worried about the sirens. Maybe they're going to see the fire for themselves. People are always fascinated by fires. She might go to the fire too, but she doesn't have the strength. Not today. Let other people go to the fire. The haze and smoke remind her of her own house burning. Bubbles and muck, the smell of gas, Dawson tying her up and putting his arms around her after he threw gas on her. She had slapped him. He got tears in his eyes. What a mess.

Well, no one is putting their arms around her now. She's lost and scared. She's got to get back! She turns north onto St. Marks Place and comes to Second Avenue. She keeps going north. It's the opposite direction she came from last night, so it has to be the right way. The fire is to the west now, not even that close to her. More police, more yowling sirens, people walking like they don't even notice it or care. She pulls up her blouse collar to cover her mouth and nose from the smoke, but the smoke isn't really that bad. She lets the collar go.

Nothing looks familiar. She is lost. She gets to Fifth and keeps going north. Out of breath and coughing, she leans against a building in the teens to rest a minute before she starts walking again.

She walks past a doorway in the haze. She is lost or maybe just confused and tired, unable to think. She slides to the sidewalk along the side of the building with the doorway and hugs her knees. She's so hungry. She lowers her head onto her knees and dozes off.

She wakens to a woman wrapping Clara's hand around a ten-dollar bill. The woman seems to be about the same age as Clara. She is wearing a white silk shirt and black linen pants, so different from Clara's old blouse and Levi's. "Find shelter, my dear," says the woman. "You don't want to be out on the streets like this. Do you have a place to go?" She seems to be in a hurry, backs away from Clara sitting on the sidewalk and quickly walks away.

Clara shoves the ten-dollar bill into her Levi's pocket. After a while, she manages to stand, readying herself to move on to find some safe place.

Suddenly an enormous moving cloud darkens the sky above her. Terrified, she looks up as the low hum grows deafening around her ears. Blurry minions escape from the cloud and land on her head and shoulders one by one. She's about to scream in her exhaustion until she realizes the cloud is a swarm of wasps. A part of her brain lights up. Frank had told her about Scotty's Internet research after the wasps escaped. Now she wonders if her own lost wasps have come east, after attracting hundreds, maybe thousands of wasps, all along the way, to say goodbye and to absorb her smells one last time before plunging into the Atlantic to die.

Descending from the dark cloud, a small number of wasps are poking around her hair and arms and neck, dragging their wings on her skin to absorb the lifelong smells of Prell shampoo, Jergens lotion, Ivory soap, and Secret deodorant embedded in her skin. Briefly these few wasps linger, then rise for the last time and head for the Atlantic, joining the alto swarm they had recruited from all across the country.

She watches them in wonder, their chaotic low dazzling hum filling the sky in contrast to the brassy sirens on the streets of New York City. In total exhaustion, she leans her head and hands against the blue door, accidentally pushing the buzzer. Almost immediately, he buzzes her in.

postscript

Clara is needed in Jackpot: Scotty is dying of lung cancer. Refusing all treatment, he is in hospice at his home. He has sold Desert Dan's to a buyer from Seattle. Frank is with Scotty most of the day, Stella joins him off-shifts, Clara pinch hits to give them both a break, a nurse comes daily. Clara flew home the same day Frank told her about it, followed by Frank and Stella. Nine days later, Scotty died. They scatter his ashes in the desert, on a gentle rise with a wide view of the everlasting desert, the same spot Frank and Scotty drove to on the day Scotty got his diagnosis. Frank had brought a bottle of Jack Daniels and two shot glasses. The two old friends enjoyed themselves as much as they could that day. Clara has rented a small apartment suitable for hosting Frank and Stella for dinner and "good rum drinks," as she always says. She has allowed her destroyed house to be cleared away.

During this chaotic time, Clara and Frank go for long walks in the desert. They spend a lot of time at Salmon Falls Creek. He tells her about escapades he had wandering the country. She tells him just a little about her parents, and he feels he has gained some new understanding of his mother. Talking to him, feeling the thick ties of mother and son, helps her more than anything else to feel she has finally joined life again. They share Samantha and Darrell stories—they laugh and cry, almost as if the two family members were alive again. The days are precious. Buyers hear about Frank's sculptures through word of mouth. Orders pile up. One day at the creek, when Frank goes to the trailer cab to get his cigarettes, Clara opens her purse, slides open the Chlor-Trimeton box, and scatters Lenore's remains in the tall grasses. She smiles as her eyes fill. "Thank you, Lenore."

Haskell sells his loft to his sister and joins Clara as a friend. He gets commissions for environmental shots around the country, fashion layouts in New York. He travels a good deal. Sometimes Clara goes with him, more often not. In the fall, she will tutor and substitute teach at the Jackpot Middle School and help the after-school kids at the Jackpot library. There is talk of the four of them moving to Ketchum, near Sun Valley, where Frank's sculptures could do well in a gallery. The big excitement is that Stella and Clara want to start a theater company. And Clara is realizing that families grow every which way, regardless of blood.

acknowledgments

I have worked on this novel for twelve years. I couldn't let it go, even though I struggled for several years to find the focus. Finally, I did find the focus—and now I have to let it go.

I am so grateful for the friends, classmates, and colleagues who have offered feedback and encouragement along the way. Stephanie Hammer saw a place where I was stuck and casually mentioned a direction where I could take it. Much later, her suggestion became the turning point of the novel. Laura Taylor Kung read the manuscript as a careful reader would, seeing my novel through her own predispositions and teaching me much. Walter Kirn's encouragement was a lifesaver when I still had not found my direction. Diana Wagman taught me invaluable lessons about pacing and structure, and Aimee Bender had a way to bypass the conscious mind and uncover the richer material that lies in the subconscious. She would say something like this: "Go home and find a book with a green spine in your bookshelves. Pick it up and turn to page 34, second paragraph, sentence 3. This sentence is the first sentence of your new story. Come to class tomorrow with at least five pages."

You can't write ordinary prose with this method. You're going to get an unusual point of view, an unusual character or event—a bump that will let you write exciting prose. That is how the purple wasp came about, that is how I made Clara steal a friend's car, and so on.

Last but not least, I couldn't have written this book without my husband Bernie's help. His unfailing support saw me through this long journey. The final gift is that our two children have become fine adults. We are so grateful that we have them in our lives.

And I thank Brooke Warner for writing to me for the second time, asking if I wanted to consider SWP. Her first invitation got stolen by the computer gremlin. So I said yes, and here we are.

about the author

photo credit: Rick Beltran

Maryl Jo Fox grew up in Idaho and studied music at the University of Idaho before transferring to UC Berkeley for a BA in English. She went on to earn an MA in English at the University of Illinois, Champaign-Urbana. Her short fiction has appeared in *Passages North, Bat City Review,* and other journals. Her writing has also appeared in *LA Weekly* and the *LA Times.* She is a former president of the L.A. Drama Critics Circle. She has taught literature and composition at Pasadena City College, Glendale College, and others, and currently leads a novels discussion group at Vromans bookstore in Pasadena. She discovered her focus in a UCLA Extension Writers' Program class, "Master Sequence in Magic, Surrealism, and the Absurd."

SELECTED TITLES FROM SHE WRITES PRESS

She Writes Press is an independent publishing company founded to serve women writers everywhere. Visit us at **www.shewritespress.com**.

Eden by Jeanne Blasberg. $16.95, 978-1-63152-188-1. As her children and grandchildren assemble for Fourth of July weekend at Eden, the Meister family's grand summer cottage on the Rhode Island shore, Becca decides it's time to introduce the daughter she gave up for adoption fifty years ago.

Tzippy the Thief by Pat Rohner. $16.95, 978-1-63152-153-9. Tzippy has lived her life as a selfish, materialistic woman and mother. Now that she is turning eighty, there is not an infinite amount of time left—and she wonders if she'll be able to repair the damage she's done to her family before it's too late.

A Drop In The Ocean: A Novel by Jenni Ogden. $16.95, 978-1-63152-026-6. When middle-aged Anna Fergusson's research lab is abruptly closed, she flees Boston to an island on Australia's Great Barrier Reef—where, amongst the seabirds, nesting turtles, and eccentric islanders, she finds a family and learns some bittersweet lessons about love.

What is Found, What is Lost by Anne Leigh Parrish. $16.95, 978-1-938314-95-7. After her husband passes away, a series of family crises forces Freddie, a woman raised on religion, to confront long-held questions about her faith.

True Stories at the Smoky View by Jill McCroskey Coupe. $16.95, 978-1-63152-051-8. The lives of a librarian and a ten-year-old boy are changed forever when they become stranded by a blizzard in a Tennessee motel and join forces in a very personal search for justice.

South of Everything by Audrey Taylor Gonzalez. $16.95, 978-1-63152-949-8. A powerful parable about the changing South after World War II, told through the eyes of young white woman whose friendship with her parents' black servant, Old Thomas, initiates her into a world of magic and spiritual richness.